FANG

Volume 2

Edited by Alex Vance

Bad Dog Books

2007

FANG Volume 2
First publication 2005
First revision 2007
Second revision 2010

ISBN: 978-90-79082-14-8

Edited by Alex Vance
baddogbooks@gmail.com

Published by Bad Dog Books
www.baddogbooks.com

Printed by FurPlanet
www . furplanet . com

BAD
DOG
BOOKS

Table of Contents

Preface

This volume has a peculiar history.

After the release of the first volume of FANG, work on the next, focusing on fantasy and erotica, was well underway when there came a clamoring—a damn loud clamoring–for something else. Halloween was coming up, and writers were champing at the bit to submit some horror pieces.

Your humble editor, of course, saw an opportunity, and isn't one to pass those up.

FANG Volume 1 had set the bar, and when it became clear that the first (unsolicited!) stories came rolling off the presses, there was already enough good material for a new, volume even before the fantasy one was ready.

Now, some years later, something curious is apparent: more than half of this book has been written by the Bad Dog Books staff.

Of course, Ben Goodridge wasn't yet in the Bad Dog Band when he penned three of the Arcanum Arcanorum stories. It was, in fact, the talent and attention to deail he displayed in those stories that prompted me to give him a job.

Unintentionally, this volume has become a Big Boys Club, and by that I don't just mean Ben and myself. Kyell Gold. K. M. Hirosaki. Stormcatcher. Whyte Yoté. These aren't newbies. All of them earned their spurs even before they made their debut in FANG Volume 1.

This volume's theme is 'horror' and the authors have taken that theme in all the cardinal directions. Romance. Excitement. Grief. Comedy.

Take a seat.

Dim the light.

Listen to the wind howling outside and those creepy little electrical appliances indoors.

In other words: prepare yourself.

Toys and Trinkets

The monsters under the bed, or in the closet; the slamming windows we are too scared to get up and close; the baleful howls of dreadful creatures outsideÊnone of these inspire such terror as simply being tormented without knowing by whom or why.

The horriblel uncertainty, the near-paralytic paranoia that renders one unable to take even the simplest actionsÊthese are the sad lot of this story's protagonist.

"Plays Well with Others" shows love at its most garish and its most sublime, its jagged limits and the depth of its endurance and forgiveness alike.

Plays Well With Others

Kyell Gold

"I'm getting old," had been Maurice LeClair's first thought at the sharp pain in his leg. He'd been walking along with the two senior City Councilmen, both red foxes like himself, though Mary Anderson at fifty and Chet Martindale at fifty-two belonged to a whole other generation. They'd been discussing the rezoning necessary to bring a new grocery store to the Hilltown downtown area, strolling along one of the parks he'd pushed for in his first year as mayor, and he was walking slower than he was used to, out of courtesy, when pain shot through his right shin, radiating up and down his leg as if he'd smacked it against a rock.

He yelled a curse, stumbled, and clutched his shin, his ears back. The other foxes stopped and looked curiously at him. Across the grass, an otter playing with her kit looked at him disapprovingly, and a scruffy wolf on a bench appeared to be staring at him too. "Stub your toe?" Anderson said, scanning the smooth dirt path for anything he might have hit.

"No," Maurice said through clenched teeth. "Feels like... like I banged my shin into something."

All three of them scanned the path, and then Chet clapped him on the shoulder. "When you hit forty, son, that'll happen more and more often. I get unexplained pains twice a day now."

"Yeah," Maurice said. His leg felt a little better, and when he put it down, the pain didn't get any worse. "Anyway, I was saying... oh, yes. I did mention to Bill that the original plans had also called for—son of a bitch!"

The same jolt of pain ran through his left leg. Cursing, he hopped up and down on his right, clutching his left this time as the other two stared at him in amazement. "Sorry," he said. "Sorry. Just... same thing again." Only it wasn't, quite, and he didn't tell the other two this part because they were already staring at him and their downcurled tails told him that they were starting to be spooked by his behavior.

He was too, and almost more worrisome than the phantom pains in both his legs was the strange feeling moving across the pads of his feet, a pressure applied and released, as though he were jumping up and down on some hard surface. But even as he felt it, he was staring at the leathery black pads on the bottom of his left foot, as he held it in the air some three feet off the ground.

"Maybe we should finish this meeting another time." Mary looked at Chet.

"I'm all right," Maurice said, setting his other leg down. He clenched his teeth and resolved to ignore any other pains he might experience. And for the rest of the afternoon, the only thing he felt was a tugging on his tail, several times. He managed to turn and look without the councilors noticing, but there was nobody there.

"Make me an appointment with Dr. Lyon," he barked when he got back to his office.

The grey fox behind the smaller desk looked up. "How soon?" he said, flipping his cell phone open and picking through the phone book.

"Soon as possible. Christ." Maurice staggered to the larger desk and collapsed behind it. "I'm thirty-four, I'm not supposed to be getting goddamn unexplained pains."

The grey fox dialed and held the phone to his ear. "Hi, Janice, this is Andy Stough from the Mayor's office. Fine, thanks, how about yourself? Great. Listen, can Dr. Lyon squeeze his honor in for a quick appointment?" He covered the mouthpiece and mouthed "why?" to Maurice.

"Unexplained leg pain," Maurice grumbled.

"He's got a pain in his leg," Andy said into the phone. "Which leg?" he asked, ears swiveling towards Maurice.

"Both."

"Both of them, actually. Yes, it sounds like it. Absolutely. Tomorrow morning at ten? No, his honor's not free then. Yes, eight o'clock would work, if Dr. Lyon is willing to come in that early. Sure. Well, thank him for me, and thank you, Janice. We'll see you tomorrow at eight then." He listened, and then laughed. "Well, maybe we'll see you on the way out, then. Okay, you too."

"Eight o'clock?" Maurice said as Andy shut his phone.

"It was either eight o'clock or next Tuesday."

"I've been his patient for ten years, you'd think he could... yes, I know, appearances of impropriety. Sometimes I hate public office."

"Fortunately, those times are few and far between." Andy smiled. "How did the walk go?"

"Apart from this shooting pain in both my shins, it was fine. If Mary or Chet call, tell 'em I'm fine and I'm going to the doctor."

"All right. You got another death threat this morning."

"Put it in the file," Maurice grumbled. "Was it creative?"

"Already filed it," Andy said. "It was okay, just something about feeling the pain of the people."

The natural followup was another question about his legs, but Andy just moved on to the rest of his mail. Maurice loved that he didn't ask anything else. Apart from being jaw-droppingly cute, the grey was also discreet, courteous, and efficient. Maurice doubted he'd have lasted three months in the mayor's office without Andy's help. With all that, you'd have thought he'd be a great lay, too, but he was only starting to get there, with a lot of instruction from Maurice.

Course, it was hard to find the time for that these days, what with the job and his wife and all.

If Amelia LeClair knew about her husband's relationship with the grey fox, she kept that knowledge to herself. He was always careful, and affectionate with her at the right times, and she was happy busying herself with her causes: the possums from the lower west side projects were the latest.

She knew his history, of course; he'd been dating a wolf named Derek when they met. But Derek, though cute and a far better lay than Andy, tended to drink, and anyway, Maurice needed a wife to be a successful politician. He hadn't seen Derek in years, but he knew Amelia suspected that he still had some affairs on the side. She didn't know they were confined to one cute fox, but then again, she didn't need to. As long as they made love a couple times a week, she was happy.

Wednesday night was one of those nights. Maurice had come back from Dr. Lyon the day before, and although the doctor had told him the X-rays were negative, Maurice had persuaded him to write a false report that he had a hairline fracture in one of his shins—nothing dangerous, just enough to account for the pain. At least the councilors wouldn't think he was going crazy.

Despite that, Maurice had been on edge since then, but Tuesday and Wednesday had passed without any more pain. That plus the scotch had helped him relax by the time he and Amelia retired on what she euphemistically called their "date" night.

"Going out to see the possums tomorrow?" he asked from bed, watching her divest her shapely body of her clothing.

"No, I have a society meeting." She stepped behind the screen to put her robe on. "There's only so much misery I can take in a week."

"You should try sitting in on a Council meeting."

"No, thanks." She approached the bed, pink silk robe swirling around her, and smiled. "I'll leave that pain to you. Speaking of which, how is your leg?"

"It's fine when I'm lying down," he said, propping himself up on his elbows. He grinned. "Are you going to wear that robe to bed?"

"No." She leaned over to kiss his nose. "Just to turn off the light."

Her insistence on having the lights off amused him. With the light from the window, he could see her clearly as she slipped the robe from her shoulders, the silvery mounds of her breasts, the flat whiteness of her stomach narrowing to the V between her legs, and the flowing dark length of her tail with the bright white tip at the end.

She came to bed and slid under the covers over to his side immediately. He could smell that she was ready; she usually was when she'd had a couple drinks before bed. She nuzzled up to him and tickled her fingers down his stomach, wasting no time. His paw lingered on her breast, teasing the nipple; she gasped and closed her paw around his sheath.

While she started to stroke him to arousal, he bent his muzzle and played with her nipple, taking it in his teeth and tugging, to her moans of delight. She got him nice and hard quickly, her paw sliding along him with competence, if not passion, and as if they'd been choreographed, he rolled her onto her back and straddled her.

She cupped his hardness in both paws and murmured, "Oh, Maurice."

"Oh, Am—" was all he managed. Sharp pain stabbed through his abdomen and nausea roiled in his stomach. He cried out and rolled to one side, holding his stomach and curling up into a fetal position. The waves of pain grew in intensity, feeling like awful gas, but it had come on so suddenly he thought it couldn't be.

"Maurice?" Amelia had propped herself up and was looking at him, ears askew, eyes gleaming with worry. "What is it, honey?"

"Stomach," he forced out through his clenched teeth. "Oh, God, it hurts... it..." and then he had to stop talking because he felt her press in on his stomach. "Don't touch," he said desperately, feeling his expensive dinner threatening to come back up.

"I didn't," she said. "Do you want some bicarb?"

"Something... urp..." And then he felt, distinctly, a finger sliding down the back of his throat. He clamped his muzzle shut, flailing his head against the pillow, but nothing he did stopped the feeling. It hit the back of his tongue, and he felt the surge of nausea rise in his throat.

Frantically, he rolled over just as the phantom finger pushed down further. He heaved once, and the contents of his stomach splattered over the side of the bed and the floor. Dimly, he heard Amelia cry out behind him, but the pain in his gut wasn't going away, and now the rich, acid smell reached his nose. He gulped, swallowing, feeling the inevitability of the next wave as it built inside him, churning, and then forcing its way up his throat. Another splash of half-digested food hit the floor, and over his horrible retching sounds, he heard Amelia getting up.

She put on her robe, of course, turned on the light, and walked quickly to the door, where Maurice heard her pick up the phone and call the hospital.

He heaved again, or thought he did. He felt the liquid moving up his throat, tasted it in his mouth, but when he coughed over the floor, nothing came out. The sensation was so strong that a moment later, his stomach shuddered again, and this time when he felt it in his muzzle, it splashed to the floor a moment later.

The smell was overwhelming. He didn't want to spread the mess, but he had to get his nose away from the reek of vomit. He rolled off the bed and hunched on the floor on his paws and knees, cradling his stomach, hoping the worst was over.

"The paramedics will be here in a minute." Amelia's voice was high with tension. "Are you okay?"

"Paramedics?" he gagged on the taste in his muzzle and the odor, which he could still smell. "It's just... upset stomach."

"You're really sick, Maurice," Amelia said, hovering a safe distance away from him, clearly afraid she might get something on her robe. "Here, put on your pajama bottoms, at least. You can't be naked when they show up."

He caught the pajamas she tossed, and sat back gingerly on the floor. He wiped his muzzle, trying to get the sour taste out of it, and slowly pushed one leg through the pajamas. When he'd managed that, he looked up at Amelia, still waiting some five feet away, and slowly pulled himself up. The pains in his abdomen still prevented him from standing fully upright, but he was able to stand on one leg and pull the other through the pajama bottoms. He had to lean against the bed to pull the pants up and fasten them, and he gave Amelia a weak smile when he did. "There," he said. "All presentable."

Her ears remained back. "Why don't you lie down again?"

He nodded. "I'd rather sit." He lowered himself to the edge of the bed, leaning forward and trying to breathe evenly. He was starting to feel warm all over, but at least his stomach was settling.

And then the room started to spin.

There was no warning, no time to prepare. Vertigo flooded his brain, and Amelia seemed to tilt at a crazy angle as he grabbed the bedpost, trying to orient himself. He squeezed his eyes shut, but the feeling of spinning just got worse. He felt a lurch in his stomach and thought, please, no, there can't be anything left.

There wasn't for long. He doubled over and fell to his knees, retching onto the carpet. At least he'd gotten close to the first spot, if not entirely in it.

Still dizzy, he sat hunched over and wiped his muzzle again. "Water," he said hoarsely, his throat starting to ache. "Please."

And then, as if someone had thrown a switch inside him, the dizziness and his stomach pains stopped. He supported himself with one paw, breathing through his mouth to avoid the reek of the mess on the floor, but apart from the soreness in his throat and stomach, and the rancid taste in his muzzle, he felt fine.

Amelia said, "Can you walk? I'll pour you a glass."

"I think so." He stood very slowly, bracing himself on the bed again. His legs shook as he took a step, but not seriously. "I feel better."

"Must have been something you ate," Amelia said, but she looked doubtful. "Were you feeling sick all evening?"

He bit back the answer 'no.' There was no need to scare her as much as he was starting to be scared. "A little. I thought I'd be okay when I lay down."

"You should tell me next time." She smiled. "We could've postponed our date night."

He shook his head. "I thought I'd be okay." He took a step towards the bathroom, let go of the bed, and took another. "Can you call the paramedics off?"

"They'll be here in a minute," she said. "You're the mayor."

"I know, but... two doctor visits in a week. That's gonna look bad."

"If there's something wrong, it's better to know," Amelia pointed out, preceding him into the bathroom and pouring a glass of water. "Can't hurt to let them look at you."

Maurice took the water and washed out his muzzle, then drank deeply. His stomach didn't protest, thankfully. "All right," he said, even though he knew his biggest problem was one the paramedics wouldn't be able to help with. He stared at his reflection and tried to quell the fear creeping up within him. The pain in his legs, the sudden nausea and vomiting—itdidn't feel natural, and it didn't feel like any medical condition he knew of. He was afraid they were linked in some mysterious way he couldn't fathom, and what scared him most was that he didn't know what would come next, or when.

On Thursday, he tried to go about his job as he usually would. Andy stayed alert for calls about the mayor's health, but by and large, the press didn't seem to have gotten wind of it. Maurice knew with grim certainty that if he suffered any more episodes, especially in public, that silence wouldn't last.

He wasn't helping his own cause, either. At every twinge he felt, he froze, waiting to see if it would turn into something stronger, painful, or disorienting. Twice during his meetings with citizens groups, he was so distracted that he didn't hear a question asked directly of him. When Andy was with him, he could deflect questions and cover for Maurice, but in closed meetings, the fox had nobody else to look to. At the end of both meetings, people were beginning to look at him strangely; he explained it away by saying that he hadn't slept well the previous night, and apologized. Despite his cover, he heard whispers as he was leaving the meetings, and gritted his teeth. The only thing he could do was hope that his situation didn't get any worse.

"Made it through the day?" Andy said sympathetically as Maurice returned to the office after his last meeting.

The red fox sank down behind his desk. "Barely."

"So, you going to tell me what really happened last night?"

Maurice looked up at the grey fox, whose eyes were sparkling, though his muzzle was serious. "Not yet. Let me get through these papers first."

"All right. I'll be back in an hour and a half." Andy swished his tail as he left, but Maurice barely noticed.

He sat down with the papers and welcomed the chance to focus all his attention on them, shutting out the rest of the world, especially the little pangs and aches he was usually able to ignore. The regularity and precision of the documents, which required all of his attention to be able to process properly, today helped buttress his mind against the worry that had been steadily creeping into it.

When Andy brushed his arm, he jumped. He hadn't even seen the grey fox come in, and it took him a few more seconds to realize that he was wearing only his boxers. "You're really into those documents," Andy said. "Care to get really into something else?"

Maurice grinned. "Something or someone?"

By way of reply, Andy lifted his tail and draped it over Maurice's shoulders. The red fox shivered with the arousal, so different from what he felt with his wife. He reached out and brushed a paw across

Andy's tight, white-furred stomach, and then lower, across the hardness waiting behind the thin cotton boxers. His stomach twitched, and he pulled his fingers back.

Andy looked down at him. "Want me to undress you?"

"No," Maurice said. "Listen, I want to tell you about what happened." His heart was beating fast.

After a moment of silence, Andy said, "Well?"

"I'm not crazy," Maurice said.

The grey fox nodded. "Okay." If he thought it was an odd thing to say, his muzzle didn't betray that. His ears remained cupped forward, his tail draped over Maurice's shoulders.

Maurice brushed it with a paw and remembered the phantom touch on his tail, that Monday that seemed so long ago now. He dropped his paw to his lap. "Remember the thing with my legs on Monday?" Andy nodded. "Something... similar. But different."

He told the story quickly, hesitating over the part about the finger in his throat. He knew now that he'd been convinced then that it was real, but in the waning daylight, talking out loud, it sounded ridiculous. He'd been sick. Couldn't he have imagined it as a way to explain his nausea? His story was crazy enough without it.

Andy listened attentively, and when he was done, just shook his head. "It just went away? Just like that? Well, I don't know. You've... slept with your wife before, right?"

"Of course," Maurice snapped.

"Hey, just asking," Andy said. "I know you like boys more than girls. I wondered if it might be a reaction to sleeping with her. If you're nervous about it. Are you trying to start a family or something?"

"It's not about her."

Andy shrugged, and smiled. "All right. So it's just a weird thing out of nowhere."

"No, the leg thing was a weird thing out of nowhere. This is two weird things out of nowhere. This is a pattern. This means—mmmf."

The grey fox had leaned over suddenly and pressed his muzzle to Maurice's. The kiss was warm and made Maurice tingle all over, but the tongue in his muzzle reminded him uncomfortably of the feel of the finger, and he pulled away from the kiss quicker than he usually would.

Andy grinned, dropping to his knees. "Listen. It's probably nothing. It'll just get worse if you keep worrying about it. Why don't you let me take your mind off it for a while?"

"It's not nothing," Maurice insisted, but he didn't resist as Andy opened his pants, and indeed, for the next fifteen minutes or so, he thought about the matter not at all.

He retired early, leaving Amelia to read her newsgroups on the internet, and opened the door to the bedroom cautiously. The maid had worked for hours, he'd heard, but the first breath of air he took still reeked of vomit. He held his breath and crossed to the window, throwing it open even though the night was cold. With an extra blanket, it would be tolerable.

Indeed, he barely noticed the cold, falling asleep quickly, but his sleep was plagued with dreams, unsettling images: a rat living inside him which chewed on his leg bones and shat in his stomach; living in a glass box where throngs marched past outside and stared at him; a canine shape falling from a cliff, clinging to a rope, which Maurice saw was really his intestine, spilling out through a slash in his abdomen...

He woke to pressure at his side and jumped away, still shuddering from his dreams, though the images faded as soon as he opened his eyes. Amelia's eyes shone back at his, reflecting the moonlight. "I thought we could resume our date night," she said softly. "If you're feeling better."

The memory of the stabbing in his abdomen and the roiling chaos in his stomach were all clearer now. Her scent, warm and female, was doing little to arouse him. He shook his head. "Maybe tomorrow night," he whispered.

Her ears lowered, but she nodded, leaned forward, and kissed him. "Good night," she said, and he scooted away from her attempt to cuddle. She settled for curling her tail over his.

The next day, his worries had retreated somewhat, but he still felt wary. He had a meeting with the City Council, and then appointments with the various city functionaries, and a Friday debriefing with Sharika, the ocelot who served as his chief of staff. He needed to be more alert than he had been with the citizens' groups, so he tried to put the incidents from the previous week out of his mind.

A good night's sleep had helped him relax quite a bit. He was acutely aware when he entered the large chamber, not only of the councilors' stares, but of the eyes of the people sitting in the audience. Anything he did here in this meeting would be sure to be reported widely, so he steeled himself to ignore any small aches or pains—or large ones—that he might feel.

The first half hour passed without incident. Maurice listened while the minutes from the previous meeting were read, followed by the agenda for new business, and the first item, the rezoning he'd discussed with Mary and Chet on Monday. They had heard both positions and Maurice had just begun to speak when he felt someone pulling his tail.

He turned and saw nothing, just his tail hanging behind him as it always did. Cursing himself, he returned to his speech, trying not to let the fear creep back into his words. He got through another sentence before he felt it again, the invisible paw, but not pulling this time. No: stroking. Running along the fur of his tail with a lover's caress.

This time he couldn't help shuddering and stammering over his words. There's nobody there, he told himself. You're imagining it. But his train of thought was broken, the words he'd labored over meaningless scratches on a page sitting in front of him. His ears were folded back; he couldn't help it. Even with his tail curled under him, he still felt those fingers running through the fur of his tail, getting closer and closer to the base.

Then he felt one finger sliding up the underside of his tail.

He squirmed, hurrying through the last remarks as fast as he could. "Thank yoo—oo!" he said, the last word coming out as a squeak as the finger slid warmly between his legs. People stared at him, but he just took his pages as if nothing had happened and went back to his seat.

Andy was trying to catch his eye from one corner of the room. So was Sharika, her spotted muzzle lifting in small jerks designed to draw his attention. He ignored them both, focusing on his papers as if the problem lay in them. The hand had stopped as soon as he'd sat down, but he didn't believe it wouldn't come back. He thought frantically for some excuse to get out of the meeting. If he pled illness, people would find out about his other visits to the doctor. That was a last resort, strictly a last resort.

He felt a light tickling at his side as they moved to a vote on the rezoning. The tickle became a touch, and the touch became another obscene parody of a lover's caress, as if a paw were moving over his side and across his chest. He gritted his teeth, his ears all the way back, but there was nothing he could do except submit to the invisible fingers touching him, stroking him in plain view of everyone.

Except they weren't, of course, in plain view. Nobody but him knew what was going on, nobody else could feel the paws, two of them now, making themselves familiar with his body against his will. They roamed over his chest and stomach, heedless of his clothing, and he squeezed his eyes shut for a moment and prayed don't go lower. Then he had to open them again, force a smile, and endure the meeting. By now fully half the council was clearly aware that something was wrong with him.

He was truly frightened now, because the possibilities had been reduced to two, and neither of them was very appealing. Either this was really happening, some invisible creature was fondling him, or he was having tactile hallucinations. Which meant he was insane, and his career was over.

But for once, his career wasn't the first thing on his mind. He couldn't help squirming, feeling the filthy paws stroke him, and then, despite his prayers, one descended and grasped his sheath.

"No," he whispered aloud, luckily as someone else was talking, but the fingers paid him no mind. They squeezed and stroked, and pumped him up and down, and despite the fact that he was not in the least aroused, he found himself getting hard.

"Please," he whimpered under his breath. "Please, no."

His breath was short, both with fear and with unwilling arousal. The other invisible paw had moved up to his face, where it was tracing fingers over his whiskers and along his lips. He jerked his head to the side reflexively, but the finger would not be shaken. It kept brushing his muzzle while its companion stroked up and down along his shaft. And in his struggle to fight the caresses, he hadn't noticed that everyone in the room was looking at him.

Mary Anderson was at the podium. "I'm so-sorry," he said. "What?"

"You were going to present the city's case for the raising of fees for the extra garbage service."

The paws became more insistent, and his body was responding. He whimpered again. "Yes, I..." he got to his feet and approached the podium, his steps jerky as arousal flooded him. He wouldn't make it through his remarks, he realized. He was going to come right in front of everyone, there at the podium. He'd had nightmares like that, standing naked in public, giving a speech and realizing in the middle of it that his erection was out there for everyone to see. Fleetingly, he wondered if he were dreaming, but the heat of his embarrassment and fear and the prickling of his fur were all too real. He took another jerky step.

Mary looked worried. "Is something wrong, your honor?"

"I have to go to the bathroom!" he blurted out, and ran to the nearest exit, ignoring the snickers that filled the room behind him.

He knew this building well. There were bathrooms nearby, just around the corner. He was getting close now, the paw stroking more quickly as the other caressed his muzzle, and on his right paw, he felt the soft touch of a tongue, licking his sensitive pad. "Please," he gasped, rounding the corner and throwing himself against the bathroom door, bursting inside and staggering to a stall, whining all the while. He fumbled with his pants as the sensations grew stronger, and then he felt the powerful shudder of orgasm, a moment before he got his pants down.

His erection bobbed in front of him, full and hard, but it wasn't until a moment later that he felt another shudder and the pulse of his seed and saw it spurt from his tip, dripping down his length and onto the floor. He leaned against the wall, shaking and half-sobbing as he came, the usual rush of pleasure lost in fear. This was worse than a nightmare. He was a prisoner in his body, helpless to escape.

"If you needed a quickie, you should've told me," Andy said from the doorway. He hurried to Maurice's stall and closed the door, standing outside. "What if someone else walked in?"

"I didn't... do it," Maurice moaned.

"Uh... I can smell it and I saw it," Andy said softly.

"I mean..." Maurice pulled the door open and stuck his paws out, rotating them to show Andy the unsullied black fur.

The grey fox's eyebrows rose. "That's a neat trick. You'll have to show me that one. Later, though. For now, get cleaned up."

One of the invisible paws was still holding his erection, stroking gently. Maurice wanted to seize it, pull it away, but he couldn't touch it; it went with him wherever he moved. "Please," he gasped, not to Andy but to the air, "make it stop!"

"Okay, Mo, you've got to get it together. You need to go out to that meeting and at least finish up. Here, let me." The grey fox sighed and crouched down, taking Maurice's shaft into his muzzle. He cleaned it with a quick suck and lick and then grabbed some toilet paper to dry it off. "At least this way people will think I just blew you. I think that's preferable."

Maurice didn't ask to what, because the answer was clear: preferable to being thought an insane fox who needed to run out of a council meeting to beat off. The touch of Andy's real muzzle had helped calm him, in that he found it much easier to ignore the invisible paws when there was a real muzzle competing for his attention. And now that they weren't really stroking any more, he thought maybe, just maybe, he could make it through the meeting. He couldn't let himself think about what had just happened, or he wouldn't be able to function at all.

"You going to make it?" Andy asked.

He pulled his pants up. "I'll do my best." He followed the grey fox down the hall and back to the council room while the paws kept a grip on his softening member and dug into the fur of his chest.

"Sorry," he said as he re-entered the room, putting on a politician's smile. "I had some of that Indian cuisine last night. I guess I shouldn't do that the day before a meeting." Polite laughter, unconvinced expressions. One of the paws was cupping his balls while the other stroked his ears. He flicked against it, ineffectually, and strode to the podium to deliver his remarks.

He was leaking down the front of his boxers, but he forced himself to say the words. Halfway through his speech, the pressure on his balls increased sharply, as though the paw and suddenly squeezed down there. He gasped, masked it in his speech, and clutched the podium, managing not to double over as the waves of nausea hit.

Somehow, he made it through to the end of his speech, steeled himself against the unnatural groping, and sat rigid in his chair, though he wanted to scream. When he had to approach the podium next, the paws squeezed his sheath and held it, and then, suddenly, let go.

Startled by his sudden freedom, he stumbled over his words again, but quickly recovered. Still avoiding the eyes of his staff, who were now almost waving their arms trying to get his attention, he sat down after speaking and felt well enough to answer some questions. He couldn't shake the feeling that he'd been dropped, as a child might drop a toy it had finished playing with.

For the rest of the meeting, he flinched at a brush of wind on his fur or tail, and it took a great deal of self-control to be able to shake paws as they stood and walked out when it was all over. Several of the councilors asked him if he felt all right; Chet said, "I never could handle that foreign food, myself," and hit him lightly on the shoulder, then folded his ears back when the other fox flinched.

On his way to the limo, a couple reporters ran up to him. He dodged them with practiced ease and slid into the limo. When Andy and Sharika joined him, he tapped on the glass and the car pulled away from the curb and the shouts of reporters.

The grey fox sat beside him while the ocelot sat across from them. "What the hell was that?" she demanded.

"Never mind," Maurice said. "I'm sorry to stick you with the Indian food story, but it's the best I could come up with. I'm just not feeling good, and I don't want to talk about it."

Sharika jotted some notes down. "Anything to do with the hospital visit and the paramedics?"

"I don't want people connecting those, okay?" Maurice sat back against the seat and panted. "God, I thought that meeting would never end."

"It's a lot easier for me to make sure they don't connect them if I know what not to tell them."

He knew she was right, but fear made him snap. "I'm sorry if I'm making your job difficult," he said. "They're not related, end of story."

"Fine," she said, her fur fluffing a little bit. Otherwise, she didn't reveal her irritation. "Let's talk about the meeting. We didn't get the vote we wanted on the housing, but we got everything else, so I think overall it was a success..."

Maurice couldn't devote his whole mind to politics. Part of him was tensely waiting for the next intrusion. Sharika, if she noticed his preoccupied mind, said nothing about it, and he managed to focus at least enough to make sure she had everything she needed from a policy standpoint.

Thankfully, the reporters hadn't made it to City Hall yet. Sharika rode upstairs with them in the elevator and then left to go to her own office while Andy and Maurice walked down the hall to the mayor's.

"Close the door," Maurice said as they walked in.

Even though the mayor's door was supposed to remain open between 9 and 5 each day, Andy shut the large oak door without a word. He watched Maurice walk to his desk and then followed him there, sitting on one of the chairs in front of it. His ears cupped forward, and he waited for the red fox to talk.

Maurice hesitated, but this time, the incident was fresh in his mind. He had to tell someone, and he could trust Andy. But as he started to speak, looking at the grey fox's dark eyes, he was seized with another fear. What if Andy thought he was crazy? He barely believed it himself, and it was happening to him. How could he convince Andy that he was telling the truth?

He couldn't. But Andy had seen him in the restroom, in the grip of whatever it was, and Maurice couldn't think of any other explanation that would sound any better. He had known Andy for three years now, and the grey had always been reliable. As much as he could trust anyone, he had to trust Andy.

"When I got those pains in my leg on Monday," he started, "there was something else I didn't tell you. They came on sharply, like I'd banged my shin, but we were just walking in the park. But after that, a couple times, I thought I felt someone pulling my tail. Hard. I didn't mention it because it was, well, crazy.

"Then Wednesday night, that sickness came on so suddenly, it was freaky. And it left the same way, like someone turning on and off a switch. I didn't know if it was related except that it was just as strange.

"And today..." He stopped to take a breath, his pulse racing at just the memory. "Today it was like someone was feeling me up. And then more. You saw."

Andy nodded, still not saying anything. Maurice exhaled. "That went away quickly too. But I don't know what triggers it. It seems to happen every other day, but is that just coincidence, or a pattern?"

His eyes met Andy's dark ones. He couldn't tell what the grey fox was thinking; his ears had remained steadily in place and his whiskers had only twitched slightly. Andy raised a paw to his muzzle and stroked it.

"So you think someone has a voodoo doll of you somewhere?" he said finally.

"You believe me?" Maurice didn't mean to sound as incredulous as he did.

Andy shrugged. "It's an awful funny thing to make up. If you wanted to sabotage your own career, there are lots better ways to do it. More profitable, too. If you're crazy—don't tell me you haven't thought it—then it's a strange pattern to it. But you don't sound crazy when you're talking about it."

It was hard not to cry with relief. Just having someone else who believed him made him feel miles better. But he had to get at what he wanted to say, because any minute now he would have an appointment knocking on his door. "All right. Here's how I want to handle it. We can try to figure out what's happening later. For the rest of the day, you sit in on all my appointments. If I give you a signal, trip a phone call, tell me it's my wife, and I'll take it somewhere else. And don't mention any of this to anyone."

"Course not," Andy said. "Think this has anything to do with that death threat on Monday?"

"Maybe," Maurice said. "What did it say?"

"That's what I'm trying to remember," Andy said. "I wish I hadn't filed it." He looked at the garbage bin. "Something about... soon you'll feel the pain you've caused."

Maurice sighed. "If another one comes in, hold onto it."

"Yeah. You want me to call my grandmother?"

Maurice stared at him. "Why? You think she might have sent it?"

"She's from voodoo country. She might know something about this."

"Sure, anything." He waved a paw, just as the first knock sounded at his door. "I'm just more worried about getting through the day."

"Yep. I'll get that?" Andy rose when Maurice nodded, and let in the first of his appointments, a burly bear who ran the Sanitation Department.

Maurice focused half his attention on the interviews while the rest of his mind spun around his problem. He wanted to believe this was just a hallucination, but he couldn't deny the proof; his boxers were still sticky from the morning's incident—or attack, if it was indeed someone maliciously manipulating him. Voodoo dolls sounded crazy, but no more crazy than everything that had happened to him in the past week. So it was like a political campaign. Look at where they strike and you'll find out what their real agenda is.

Walking in the park, with city councilors. In bed with his wife. During a city council meeting. The times seemed to have been chosen specifically to cause the most personal and public embarrassment and discomfort. But then, why not when he'd been with Andy? He nodded to the bear and looked at the grey fox again, seated at his desk. Andy was looking back, waiting for a signal to come; when he saw Maurice looking at him, he raised a questioning eyebrow, and Maurice shook his head minutely.

"You don't agree?" the bear said.

"Oh, of course I do. I'm sorry," Maurice said, and went back to thinking, because a terrible thought had just occurred to him. What if it were Andy causing all of this?

The grey fox had certainly not hesitated to believe him. And he just might be jealous of Maurice's wife. Maurice tried to remember whether he'd seen Andy doing anything odd at the council meeting, but of course he could have had another person doing it for him. What could he possibly gain from Maurice losing his job, though?

The answer was easy, and not all that farfetched. Of course, if Maurice lost his job and his wife, Andy would get to spend more time with him, would get the red fox all to himself. Maurice's stomach tightened at the thought. He had been in that situation before; his amateur research online (couldn't see a shrink, because that was professional suicide) told him that many politicians had such a desire to be loved and needed that they tended to fall into possessive relationships.

He'd been sure Andy wasn't like that, but how could he know his own mind, let alone Andy's? The grey fox's calm demeanor seemed sinister now, and the brief sensation of relief he'd felt upon sharing his story was gone.

He began to think with trepidation about the dinner he was supposed to attend the following evening, with Amelia and some of the trustees of the Hilltown Museum. If Andy wanted to continue terrorizing him, that dinner would be the perfect place. Many of the trustees were also active in city government, and had contributed to his campaign. For him to break down at the dinner would be not only embarrassing, but reported even more widely than his city council antics were sure to be.

He hoped Sharika was handling the reporters. He would have to figure out how to handle Andy.

During his third interview, he came up with a plan. "Andy," he said when the room was clear, "can you call the Museum and tell them I won't be attending the dinner tomorrow? I'll make some excuse and send Amelia."

The grey fox's eyes lifted in surprise, but he nodded. "Of course."

"I just don't want to risk anything."

"Smart move, until we know what's going on."

Maurice watched Andy dial, relay the message, and hang up. He turned to Maurice. "So, does that mean we can spend the evening?"

Maurice smiled. "We can have some time in the afternoon, but after that I'd like you to check the Public Library and the university library for anything that might help. See what your grandmother says, and then do a little research. I have a feeling it won't be found online."

"Sure." Andy shrugged. "Anything I can do to help."

You can help by getting out of the way, Maurice thought savagely. He planned to call the museum after Andy had left and tell them he felt well enough to attend, without Andy's knowledge. If the dinner went off without a hitch, he would know for sure that Andy was behind it.

Through the beginning of the dessert course, his plan appeared to have worked. He'd kept Amelia at arm's length during the day, taken a very enjoyable lunch break with Andy during which there were no more attacks, and then sent the grey fox off to the libraries. He and Amelia went to the Museum, and although he felt frayed and tired, he managed to comport himself well through dinner One of his donors even promised him a nice contribution for Amelia's possums. He was still jumpy, but nothing had happened, and anyway, it was scheduled for tomorrow.

As the cake was being served, Maurice was talking to the lion across from Amelia. He heard a distant ringing in his ears and then, without warning, his body was flooded with heat. He stopped talking in mid-sentence and prepared to push back from the table, but before he could, he felt a large, hard shaft slide under his tail and into him and start to pump in and out. Large? No, enormous. Despite himself, he had to reach back and feel under his tail to make sure there was nothing there, and there was nothing he could feel with his paw, but the painful penetration continued, terrifyingly disrespectful of reality.

He pushed back from the table, but the other sensations were starting to catch up with him too, the arousal already in full force surging to his sheath. He became aware, too, of an arm tight around his chest and pressure on his throat. Trying to escape, he thrashed in his chair, oblivious to the stares around him. The pressure on his throat was teeth, a large jaw closing off his windpipe, making him scrabble at his throat and moan. At the same time, he felt a large paw stroking his erection, and, worst of all, the pressure of something bigger behind the erection inside him.

"Are you choking? He's choking!" Amelia said, her voice rising in panic.

Maurice felt arms around him, other arms, and he couldn't distinguish between the real arms and the phantom arms, so he grabbed at both, trying to get them off him. "Settle down," he heard, but the flood of sensations was dizzying, preventing him from processing any of them. He continued to wheeze at the teeth around his throat even though there was nothing there, and then he yelped out loud as he felt the huge knot pressing into and through him, stretching him painfully, and at the same time the paw clenched around his erection. Maurice's own member was as hard as the phantom member being stroked, and once again he felt the powerful shudder of orgasm twice.

This time, the pressure on his throat and around him didn't let up even as his body shook. He was aware of the crowd of people around him, aware that he had been dragged form his chair and was sitting on the floor. Amelia was beside him but not touching him, a lion and wolf were trying to hold his arms as he thrashed—no, he could only see a lion. He looked around wildly, trying to figure out why his lungs were heaving when he could feel his throat being closed off, and the thought ran across his mind that Andy had been angry at his trick and this time had decided to kill him.

But there was no scent or feel of Andy. The teeth on his throat belonged to a large person, the painful knot under his tail belonged to a large person, and mixed with the strong reek in his nostrils of his own musk was that of a wolf.

Other people could smell it too, or at least could smell him, and were backing away, but the lion remained close. "What's wrong?" he was saying.

"I can't breathe," Maurice said. "He's got me... I can't breathe." The wolf behind him, a tangible presence, kept squeezing his chest and throat. Incredibly, although he could feel the air rushing through his throat, dizziness frayed the edge of his vision.

"Just hold on," the lion said, as Amelia said, "Who's got you?"

Paws pulled at his collar, getting his tie off, and he couldn't pull the fingers away this time. There were paws all over him, grabbing his clothes, raking through his fur, and still the bloated fullness under his tail that his sore muscles tried in vain to close around. Someone squeezed his balls again; he kicked out feebly, and his foot encountered only air.

"Hang on," a voice was saying, "we'll get these clothes off." But he didn't want his clothes off, he wanted the paws off him and to be able to breathe again. Panic surged within him and he kept struggling.

The voices rose in the background but blended together as a roaring in his ears. His lungs labored against nothing, the room spun around him, and then blackness swamped him.

The headline in the paper was 'Mayor Collapses At Dinner'. The tone of the article was generally sympathetic; probably due to the presence at the dinner of many people who were heavily invested in seeing his political career succeed. The reporter had not failed to note the health issues earlier than week, though, and though she didn't suggest any connection, the inference was easy for anyone to draw.

Maurice had remained in bed all morning, alone, Amelia having slept somewhere else. He hadn't even seen her since the dinner. He had no idea what her reaction would be, but he assumed that she was mostly interested in his career. At the moment, that was far down on his list of worries.

He was afraid to get out of bed. He didn't know whether he could go to the office on Monday. The escalation of the attacks made him wonder what would be next, and whether there were anything he could do about it. And he was fairly sure there wasn't.

The phone next to his bed rang. He jumped, and reached for it automatically, then hesitated. The caller id said 'Private Number', so it likely wasn't a reporter, but it wasn't Andy either. Maybe his mother, worried because she'd seen the paper. He picked up the phone and said, "Hello?"

"Hi, Mo," a raspy voice said, and then waited.

He didn't recognize the voice. "Who is this?"

There was a dry chuckle. "Don't you know me?"

Dread began to prickle at the roots of his fur. "No."

"And after we had such a nice time last night, too."

His paws felt cold. He urgently wanted to pee. "I didn't think it was nice."

"Oh, I know Perry was a little rough, but I enjoyed myself quite a bit. All the way to the end."

"Who are you?"

"I'm you, Mo."

"I don't understand."

"You never did. But you will."

"What do you want?" He was shaking now, unable to keep the fear out of his voice.

"I want you afraid," the voice said. "I want you to feel what I feel. And I can do that anytime I want."

Suddenly, Maurice felt a constriction in his throat, soreness in his rear and along his tail. "You feel that?" the voice continued. "I could give you a nice little kiss, right now." Maurice felt the touch of a finger on his lips. "Or I could jerk you off. Would you like that?"

He felt a paw on his sheath again. "No," he panted. "Leave me alone."

"I will. Eventually. But I'm going to make you suffer first. You're going to lose everything you care about." The paw left his sheath and closed around his throat.

"Just leave me alone!" he yelled, panicking.

He heard the dry chuckle again, and then the line went dead. The paws stayed on him for another second, then he felt the touch on his lips again. A moment later, all the foreign sensations disappeared.

Amelia came into the room. "What's going on?"

Maurice's fur was still bristled out. He stared at the phone in his paw. "It was... a reporter. I need to talk to Andy. To plan my schedule."

"Oh, he's here," Amelia said. "He's been waiting for half an hour. I thought you were still asleep."

"He has?" Maurice said slowly. "Has he... did he use the phone at all?"

"His phone? I don't know. I was talking to the help. I had them show him to the office. Do you want me to go get him?"

There was a second line in his office, a private line with caller id blocking, as all his lines were. "Yes, please."

The grey fox, wearing a light jacket over his shirt and jeans, hurried to the bedside when he came in. "Why did you go to the dinner?" he said as Amelia closed the door.

"Changed my mind," Maurice said, still suspicious. "Did you find anything?"

"No, but I think I figured something out. Can you get out of bed?"

Maurice nodded, cautiously. He felt weak and shaky, but it was not from any physical ailment.

"The times you were attacked," Andy said as he got up, "were all out in public. The walk with the councilors wasn't publicized, but anyone watching your office could have seen you leave." He offered his arm to the red fox, but Maurice shook his head and followed Andy to the window. "But the attack in your house wasn't public. So either it was lucky timing, or..."

Maurice looked out the window. Beyond the back yard, another row of houses looked over the trees. "One of our neighbors?"

"No, the trees. I walked by there to check, because my grandmother said that the visual connection is important. There are a couple trees you could climb up into and see directly into your bedroom from. And they have enough cover that if you were high enough to see into the bedroom, nobody could see you."

Maurice looked at him. "You were in the trees... just now?"

"No, earlier. Before I got here."

Maurice swallowed. "You know, this guy just called me. He claimed he's doing it... that he has some way of making me feel what he's feeling." He looked up into Andy's dark eyes. "I don't know what he wants, but I'll do whatever I have to, to get him to stop. Whatever he wants."

Andy looked faintly puzzled. "Listen, I know something freaky is going on, but don't give in. This is... hey." He put a finger to the side of his muzzle. "Feel what he feels. So Wednesday night in here, he would've been sick when you were sick?"

"Yeah?" Maurice said slowly.

Andy's ears perked, and he brought his paws up excitedly. "While I was walking around out there, I saw some dried vomit. Someone was sick out there. I remember 'cause I thought it was strange, drunks walking around this neighborhood. But it must've been him."

Maurice blinked slowly. Andy certainly wasn't reacting the way he'd thought he would to the "I'll do whatever he wants" speech. Could it be that the grey fox wasn't the threatening caller, his phantom assailant? He needed to trust someone, and he didn't know who else to turn to. "Could you learn anything from it?"

Andy shrugged. "Doubtful, but I'll go look. You should come along in case you recognize a scent."

"Weren't you an Army Ranger or something?"

Andy laughed. "That doesn't mean I know how to read vomit. Are you okay to take a walk?"

Maurice nodded. "Sure. I'll put some clothes on."

Andy put a paw on his arm. "It's gonna be okay," he said. He leaned in for a kiss. Maurice remembered the touch on his lips and shrank back.

The grey fox tilted his muzzle. "What's the matter?"

"Nothing, he just... when he called, he touched my lips..." Maurice looked out the window. "And he might be watching us now."

Andy looked out the window. "Let's go," he said. "If he's still out there, we'll have a surprise for him." He opened his jacket to show Maurice a leather holster with a handgun.

"Christ! You have a license for that?"

"Of course." His ears folded back. "I wouldn't do anything illegal."

Maurice stared at the gun until Andy closed the jacket over it again.

Amelia was sipping coffee in the kitchen, wearing her robe. As they walked past, Maurice stepped in and tried to smile. "Hi, honey. I'm feeling a little better. I'm just going for a little walk with Andy."

"Oh, I'm not dressed for a walk," she said. "Let me throw on something heavier and I'll go along."

"No, it's okay. Andy just wants to talk business, and I thought it'd be nice to get out."

She nodded. "I'll go straighten up the bedroom, then." She gave him a peck on the cheek and walked back towards the bedroom as Maurice followed Andy outside.

"Are you sure you didn't recognize the voice?" Andy asked. He held open the front gate and walked along at Maurice's side down the sidewalk.

"No. He was trying to disguise it, or..." Maurice rubbed his throat. "Maybe he was recovering. He's been putting himself through hell to do this."

"And he said he hasn't even started," Andy said grimly. "Anyone who wants to hurt you that badly is probably someone you know."

"Who the hell knows, these days?" Maurice said. "It could be any of my exes. It could be anyone I've pissed off politically. This whole scenario is crazy. Why would the reason behind it be any less crazy? If I hadn't felt it, I wouldn't believe it was happening." He sighed. "I still don't understand why you do."

"Not a question of why," Andy said. "Like I said, I don't think you'd make up something this crazy. So either you've gone completely fucking loony, with all due respect, or there's something really bad going down. If you're crazy, I won't make it better by not believing you. If you're not, then you need someone on your side." He looked seriously up at Maurice. "I thought about it a lot last night. My grandmother said there aren't many people who can still do voodoo. I always thought she was crazy when she talked about that, but..."

"Yeah." Maurice sucked on his lip. He'd bitten it hard the night before and now it was sore. "I still wonder if I'm crazy."

"We'll see, won't we?" They rounded the second corner, walking along the wall that separated the back yard from the street. Maurice had always enjoyed walking past the large pines that lined the wall, breathing in their scent and walking on the soft cushion of fallen needles. Now, looking up at the darkness at the heart of each one, they struck him as sinister sentinels, watching his house and waiting for their opportunity to strike.

"Over here." Andy had outpaced him and was pointing at a spot on the ground. "With all the pine, you can't smell it, and it's back against the wall. I wouldn't have seen it if I hadn't been up in the tree."

Maurice crouched down. He could faintly smell the sour tang over the strong pine scent, but he couldn't identify it. With a glance up at Andy, who was still standing, he leaned closer.

The feeling of fur flooded his muzzle. His tongue was trapped against it, his teeth were locked in it. He was biting down on something—or someone. He was hard, again, his body surging with excitement, and as his sheath swelled to match the feelings coursing through him, he felt a phantom paw stroke it and then guide it into something warm and soft.

"Mo?" Andy's voice seemed to be coming from a long way away. Maurice put a paw on the ground to steady himself, panting hard.

His teeth were digging in, he could feel the tension in his jaw muscles. He tasted blood, and then scent filled his nostrils, a scent he knew intimately.

"He's got Amelia," he choked through his mouthful of fur. "He's got Amelia."

Andy took off running, and Maurice forced himself to his feet, following. His shaft was plunging in and out of her now, a stroking that made it hard for him to concentrate on running. He fell twice, the second time getting up and tasting his own blood next to Amelia's. He could feel the liquid dripping over his chin and no longer knew whether it was his or hers.

The front gate was swinging wide open. He ran through it as the pumping on his shaft stopped abruptly and it was withdrawn into the cooler air. He felt his jaw tug on something and then rip free, and cried out.

In his mouth, the phantom tongue was savoring a chunk of flesh and fur. A piece of Amelia.

He fell to his knees and retched on the floor in his hallway, even as he felt the mouth spit out the piece of his wife. He hadn't heard a gunshot yet. Had something happened to Andy? He stumbled to his feet and ran up the stairs, bursting in the bedroom door without thinking.

Andy stood in the far corner by the window, gun drawn but hanging slackly from his right paw. He was staring at the bed, where Amelia lay naked, blood dripping from her torn throat onto the sheets. Her chest was rising and falling, but her eyes were staring blankly.

Standing beside her, his muzzle dripping with blood, was a small, scruffy wolf. He was naked, his member engorged and pulsing, eyes gleaming with a feral shine. One of his paws was resting on Amelia's breast, the other holding what looked like a gold locket on a chain around his neck.

"Hello, Mo," he said in a raspy voice. "Didja miss me?"

Maurice stared at the wolf. "Derek?" he whispered.

"And here I thought you'd forgotten me," Derek rasped. "Just because you didn't call, changed your phone number, set the cops on me... silly me, huh?"

"Jesus," Maurice said. He couldn't stop his eyes from going to the bloody tear in his wife's neck, her blood a bright red contrast to her white and russet fur, but the wolf's manic gaze demanded his attention as well. "Leave her alone," was all he could manage.

"Oh, she'll die soon enough. I just wanted you to taste her blood." He grinned savagely and dropped a paw to his shaft, starting to stroke it. "Did you like the taste, Mo? That bitch you threw me over for, for your career? Did she taste good?" He punctuated each question with a stroke, and Maurice felt each one on his own shaft, now hard as well. He felt his stomach churn again as he saw that the paw that was stroking Derek's was bloody as well, and that what he was feeling on his own member—

He fell to his knees again, heaving, but there was nothing left to come up. Derek laughed mockingly at him.

He lifted his head and his eyes met Andy's. The grey fox's eyes were dark and glistening. "I can't shoot him, Mo," he said softly. "It'd kill you."

"You can imagine my excitement when I found that out," Derek said. "That you'd passed out when I did. It's nice, don't you think? You'll finally get to find out what a broken heart feels like."

His arm moved, and came up with a butcher knife in his paw, the one Maurice had gotten Amelia for their second anniversary, he saw. "You'll get to feel all kinds of pain," Derek said, and traced the point of the knife through his stomach fur, catching it in a couple places. Maurice felt the cold tip, the sharp pricks of pain, and he moaned.

"Why?" he said. "You have to hurt yourself... why?"

"Hurt myself?" Derek laughed again, shrilly. "This doesn't hurt." He drove the knife point into his thigh.

Maurice screamed at the pain. Derek brandished the knife, its point now bloody. "You leaving me, you ripping my heart out... that hurt. But this, this almost makes it better."

Another fiery shaft of pain exploded in Maurice's other leg. Derek withdrew the knife from his own. "And it's better because we're sharing it, isn't it?" he said. "Feeling the same things, for once." Blood ran through his fur. He brought the knife up to his chest, and Maurice felt the point under his ribcage. "Of course," the wolf said in a low snarl, "I thought we did feel the same. I was wrong then. But now—"

The knife dug deeper. Maurice felt tearing inside him and clutched his chest, trying to quench the fire. He cried out again, and Derek laughed. "So sweet," he said. "Do you know how many couples would love to die together? You wanna get back together, Mo? So we can die as a couple?" Maurice wasn't looking at him, but felt the disgusting stroke of his blood-slickened paw along his member and whined against the feeling.

"No? Ah, well." There was a pause. "Looks like your dear wife is almost gone. Then—"

Maurice heard a huge explosion. His ears folded back against his head as at the same instant, he felt a sharp, tearing pain in his neck. He yelped, grabbed his neck, and fell to one side, but by the time he landed on the floor, the pain had vanished.

"Mo!" Andy was at his side immediately. "Mo, are you okay?"

He looked up into the grey fox's eyes. "Yeah," he said. "My God."

"I shot the chain," Andy said, his ears flat as well, his whole face slowly relaxing from frantic anxiety. "I shot the chain. It fell off. I think he's dead. I just... I couldn't let him kill you."

"Amelia," Maurice said, and scrambled to his feet. Andy beat him there, wadding up the sheet and pressing it to her neck.

"Call 911," he said.

The red fox picked up the phone. His paws were still shaking. "Can you do it?" He held out the phone.

Andy reached out, and then pulled his arm back. "The tapes will get out to the media. It'll be better if you do. Be strong, Mo."

Maurice nodded, took a deep breath, and dialed. "I've been attacked," he said when the voice on the other end answered. "My name is Maurice LeClair and my address is 144 Edgecombe Road, in Calique. A wolf broke into my house and attacked my wife, ripped at her throat. She's bleeding, please hurry!"

"They're on their way," he said when he hung up.

"You did good," Andy said.

"Thanks." He walked around and indicated the wadded sheet. "Can I hold that?"

"Sure." Andy waited until Maurice put a paw over his, and then slowly slid his away, letting Maurice hold the sheet against Amelia's neck. "Keep the pressure on."

Maurice shivered, his paw sticky with the blood in the sheet. He hated the blank look in her eyes. "Amelia?" he said, but she didn't respond. "You think she'll..."

"She'll survive," Andy said. "It's harder to tear someone's throat out than you might think."

Maurice winced. "Don't," he said, and Andy rested a paw on the base of his tail.

"Sorry," the grey fox said. "I'm sure she'll be okay. Listen, when the police get here... We were out walking. We heard a scream, rushed back in, and found him attacking her. He got up and I shot him."

"Good," Maurice said. "Simple."

They heard sirens a minute later, and within two more minutes the paramedics had taken over, applying a dressing to Amelia's neck, carrying her onto a stretcher and out to the ambulance. While they were doing that, another set of sirens announced the arrival of the police. They took some pictures of Amelia and then came into the house, moving Maurice and Andy into the hallway while they took pictures of the bedroom. The lead EMT, a short otter, came back inside and told Maurice they were taking Amelia to Maple County Hospital. "You know where that is?"

"Yeah. We'll be there in a bit," Maurice said. "As soon as they finish up with us."

The otter glanced through the bedroom door at the body on the floor, neck lying in the middle of a large red pool, which the paramedics had all ignored up to that point. Maurice still couldn't bring himself to look at it. "Yeah," he said. "We'll do all we can, yer honor."

"Thanks." Maurice shook his paw. "You guys got here really fast. I'll remember that."

The otter gave him a tight smile, then waved and walked down the stairs just as the police lieutenant came back out to take down Andy and Maurice's statements.

Maurice let them close off the bedroom after they'd removed the wolf's body, and went to the office to call the chief. He wouldn't say they were friends, but they had a good working relationship, and after he'd explained to the wolf what happened, Jack actually suggested himself that they keep it as low profile as possible, and promised to help. "You get down there to the hospital," he said.

"I'm on my way, Jack," Maurice said. "Thanks."

Andy took him to the hospital, where they were directed to a waiting room to wait for news of Amelia. She'd made it to the hospital but was waiting for surgery. Dr. Lyon assured Maurice that the surgeon was the hospital's best, and that they'd do all they could.

Maurice took a drink of the water Andy had gotten him, and rested his muzzle in his paws. He felt himself start to shake.

Andy put a paw on his shoulder. "Easy, Mo," he said softly. "It's all over."

"I'm all right," Maurice said, through clenched teeth. "I'm just sorry you killed that bastard, because right now I'd really like to hurt him."

"Mmm." Andy took a drink of water. "Sounds like you already did."

Maurice snarled. "Not like that. I mean..." he sighed. "I want to get him back for what he did. God, Andy, I felt violated! I can't even explain it!"

Andy shook his head. "Don't worry about it. He was crazy, that's for sure."

Something occurred to Maurice. He lifted his head and felt a cold prickling in his fur. "Did the police get the locket? I didn't see them take it, but it wasn't there when they moved the body."

Andy gave him a strange smile and reached a paw into his shirt pocket. His grey-furred fingers drew out a gold chain with a locket on it.

The red fox drew in a sharp breath. "Let me see that." He held out his black paw, and Andy dropped the locket into it.

The front of it bore a photo of him. It looked old. He supposed it was one Derek had had of him somewhere, but he didn't recognize it. Inside the locket, he found a small piece of russet fur. The scent was old and faded, but unmistakably his.

He dumped it out and closed the locket, then looked at the grey fox. "Thanks for keeping this."

Andy held his paw out. Maurice frowned. "Oh, come on," Andy said. "I don't want to hurt you. Though it might be good for some bedtime games... I'm kidding, Mo," he said. "If you want to hold onto it, you can."

Maurice looked for another moment into the fox's eyes, and then dropped the locket into his paw. Andy put it back in his shirt pocket. "I was just thinking," he said softly, "that in the future, if you were to run for governor, say, it would be a terrible thing if your opponent were to have a big fat orgasm in the middle of a debate, or something."

The red fox stared at him, jaw hanging open. "That's... I would never do that."

"Of course not," Andy said. "That's what you have me for."

Maurice smiled and shook his head, then leaned forward to kiss Andy on the cheek. "I love you," he said.

"Of course you do," Andy replied with a smile, one paw resting on the small bulge that sat in his shirt pocket, just over his heart.

Eldritch and Otherwise

In the lonely dark places of the world, dread creatures still lurk, and it is the intrepid explorer who sets all concern for hide and hair aside to seek them out.

One such brave, misguided soul is the hero of this story, a simple mortal with naught but his wit and some typically vulpine characteristics to keep him safe from the things that go, ah, 'bump' in the night.

"The Fox and the Unspeakable Horror" pokes fun where fun is to be had, and pokings to boot. A 'merry romp', one might say, of horrific high jinks.

The Fox and the Unspeakable Horror

K. M. Hirosaki

It is not without fear or trepidation that I bring myself to tell you this story here. What you about to read is true, and I swear I mean that in a manner that is entirely unlike the claims that preface the ribald missives that get featured in burlesque publications. This is a tale that I swear is unlike any other. I feel compelled to warn you now, though, that if you have not the stomach for the grotesque, the bizarre, and the freakish, that you take your attentions away from my story immediately and not think upon it again.

By trade, I am a private eye, and by species, I am a fox; the former, I chose with direct intent to follow in the footsteps of my father, and the latter I didn't choose at all, although again, it comes as a direct result of my father. I should also point out that my story takes place in the 1920s (before our lexicon held such terms as 'bling-bling' and 'hollaback'), and that it is set in the quaint little town of Wolfsborough, Massachusetts.

One peculiar thing about Massachusetts is that it's got a built-in shibboleth that works like an absolute charm. Accents can be faked, some with more ease than others, but one sure-fire test, when it comes to ascertaining whether someone is actually a native Massachusettsian, is to write down the name of three Massachusetts towns at random: only somebody who was truly born and raised in the state would ever be able to pronounce all three of them correctly.

Wolfsborough, of course, does not fit this pattern, as it is admittedly rather easy to pronounce. I assure you, however, that I can flawlessly say aloud the names of Mattapoisett, Sciasconset, and Pettaquamscutt (the last of which is actually located in Rhode Island, but which is far too superb of an example to pass up, and which also serves to prove that I'm knowledgeable of other parts of New England, as well).

Now, Massachusetts, as you may well know, is notable for two things: downright fanatical loyalty to its major sports teams, and an unusual preponderance of shambling eldritch horrors that have brought several generations' worth of untold misery upon the local inhabitants. The funny thing about this word, "shamble," is that I've only ever known three things that actually shamble: the aforementioned eldritch horrors, zombies (however uncommon), and foxes that have been fucked absolutely silly.

Coincidentally enough, all three of these things have a direct relation to the story that I am about to tell.

As I said, the story takes place in Wolfsborough, Massachusetts, where I lived and where I did most of my work. I had been hired by a middle-aged wolf (friendly chap, had a nice, gentle smile) to look into the disappearance of his 'cousin'. I put 'cousin' in quotation marks because, first off, one typically doesn't carry portrait-style photographs of one's cousin in one's wallet, and also, one would have a hard time having a fox for a cousin when one was a wolf. I think you can put the picture together pretty clearly, by now. If you can't, it might help to know that the fox in question's name was Meredeth Rombault du Champarnaud, but that he more commonly known the stage name Merry Romper (recall, of course, that this is the Roaring Twenties, and that, all told, it was a rather fabulous time to be a drag queen).

The initial information I was able to scrounge up on Merry Romper wasn't much, but I was at least able to learn that he was a frequent sight at both The Firkin and Jerkin and at O'Donnough's. Also, by all accounts, he had substantial trust funds and inheritances, and he had little to no problem with things rolling smoothly off of his tongue (the least of which being words like "Narragansett"). Some people might say that O'Donnough's and the Firkin were houses of ill repute, but honestly, their repute was quite good insofar as what they were reputed for. This meant, at the very least, that people had their eyes on Merry Romper, and that as soon as his tail was no longer a constant sight, people would have keened in on it right away.

So, Merry Romper was a rich fox, a pretty fox, and a fox who stood in the spotlight on a very glitzy stage. There were plenty of people who could have benefited from making him disappear, but those people would have to have some big cojones if they wanted to try pulling it off. Rumor had it that Mr. Romper (that is, Mr. Rombault du Champarnaud, Merry's father) had hired a pair of cops to keep permanent watch on his Bohemian son; rumor also had it that those were two very, very lucky cops right there. The long and short of it was that my anonymous wolf's 'cousin's' disappearance was perhaps not entirely unanticipated, but that it was extremely odd that nobody in the circles he scampered through knew who could have pulled the strings.

Throughout documented history, there have been many cases of people who have disappeared without a trace, never to be found. In Merry Romper's case, I was lucky to have at least some leads, and I'd already been forming some suspicions and inclinations, too. Still, with this being Massachusetts and all, I wasn't about to discount the possibility that some of what I'd always heard of as Old Wives' Tales might actually be true. First and foremost, however, I am a professional, and so it behooved me to start by looking at the case from a professional standpoint, following Occam's Razor.

The logical place to check first was, of course, Merry Romper's residence. He lived in a grand little penthouse up on the north side, where the grand little penthouses in Wolfsborough tend to be located. There were no cops outside of his door, on beat, hired, or otherwise, and I confess that I was already getting a chill that wasn't just from anticipation. Yes, I was about to break into the private living quarters of a well-known drag queen, and I'd probably be the first person in there, since the police hadn't been notified, and that probably meant that things were going to be preciously undisturbed, but that wasn't what I was excited about.

Working a little magic with a bobby pin (which I swear is a legitimate trade tool and nothing pertaining to cross-dressing), I unlocked the front door. Once the door was open even a crack, my nose picked up the smell of blood, but I was undaunted, and pushed the door the rest of the way open. In rather spectacular style, Merry had an enormous vanity mirror set up opposite the front entryway, presumably so that the first thing he'd see whenever he came home was himself. I couldn't help but stare at myself in that mirror (and for the record, since I didn't mention, my picture could very well appear next to the dictionary definition for "roguishly handsome," especially when decked out with my gumshoe hat and trench coat); maybe I thought I'd see some insight, faced with the grim specter of the inner self, but instead, all I saw was the same old dick that I always was.

I went to the nearest dresser and started rifling through it at random. To go by his clothing, Merry Romper had had quite the slender and pretty measurements, and I took a moment to try to picture what he must've looked like, and what it would have felt to have had my hands on both of his hips. I noted to myself that this all made it that much more of a shame that I would never get a chance to know Merry Romper, since—near as I could tell—Merry Romper was now little more than a messy red smear on the wall and headboard of the bed. That, by far, was the saddest notion to have crossed my mind all day.

As it would turn out, though, it would be far from the oddest notion I would end up having that day. In case you're wondering—rightly so—what the case of a disappearing drag queen has to do with any sort of unseemly horror, please be advised that I honestly have not lost track of my tale. The dark and mystifying parts of the story become quickly relevant here (or, as is the case with the enormous blood stain, I suppose that the "dark" aspects have already begun).

A cursory investigation of Merry Romper's living space revealed a few interesting clues. The most obvious of these was that, despite there being quite a fair bit of blood all over the walls and the bed, there was no body, nor were there pieces thereof. This was both disturbing and unusual, but it was also an admitted relief, since I quite doubt that I could have coped adequately with either. Not only was there no body, but neither was there any sign of struggle. This fox was definitely someone who looked like he kept his personal affects in meticulous order, and yet nothing looked disturbed: the mirror was unblemished, the bric-a-brac on his nightstands were all still carefully arranged, and not even a single stick of lipstick seemed out of place. Clearly, if something had happened to Merry Romper in this room, it hadn't come to fisticuffs, or even to flailing and slapping.

I pulled out a cigarette and lit it, puffing away as I started to deepen my search. His underwear drawer, while fascinating in its own right, yielded little in the ways of insight or clues; probably, this would be the first place most folks would think to look, so I wasn't surprised, but I still made sure to take my time, just in case. Finding nothing, I continued my search, barreling my way through drawers and cabinets and cases until I came across something that struck me as odd. Granted, compared with what was to come, it wasn't that odd at all, but for what I had to go with, this was my first lead.

What I had found, buried underneath old sweatshirts that looked like hand-me-downs that had been stored in the back of his closet for the sole purpose of being forgotten, was a large cigar box. Not only are cigars entirely unladylike, but by all accounts, while Merry Romper was known to frequently stick things in his mouth, he didn't smoke. Also, this particular cigar box was large and heavy, which probably meant that it held cigars of a size that were more suited for jamming doors open than for smoking.

I tugged the cigar box's lid, and I could feel that it was wedged shut. It wasn't locked, I could see, so I tugged harder, and with a loud fwoop, it flew open. I nearly lost hold of it, and with a rustle and a flutter, a piece of parchment whirled through the air before it came to rest atop Merry Romper's divan. Another trembling sensation went up my arm, spine, and tail as I reached for it, with yet another to follow once my fingers came in contact with the crisp, wrinkled, ancient paper.

Whatever it was, I could tell that it was folded up upon itself. I held it up to the light, and seeing how thick and brittle it was, I decided that I'd rather not fiddle with it there. I stuffed the potential clue in my coat pocket, rifled through the underwear drawer one last time for good measure, and then sauntered back to my office, careful to the leave the fox's room bloody and undisturbed for the cops when they'd eventually be called to the scene.

I couldn't help but think and wonder as to what could possibly have done something like that to little Merry Romper. As awful as kidnapping and possibly torturing a rich urbanite scion in the name of money or jealousy was, it was actually rather terrifying to think that the tales of elder demon beasts were true, and that one of those had so thoroughly destroyed the little fox that neither hide nor hair remained of him. Having never even met him, I felt a twinge of pain and sympathy. Nobody deserved a fate like that. I knew that I needed to get to the bottom of this mystery soon, for his sake, if nothing else.

With the grizzly scene out of my mind, after getting to the office, I felt myself getting more and more preoccupied with finding a way to unfold the parchment as quickly as possible. It was like I was dying and desperate to read it, as if whatever was written on it actively wanted to be read, and it was calling out to me. There was some compulsion to just poke my nose in it, which is different from just the normal vulpine tendency to poke our noses in other people's business in that, whenever I wasn't actively thinking about deciphering the paper's secrets, I would begin to hear menacing voices whispering my name from the shadows, and so focusing on finding a way to unravel this clue quickly became an excellent means of fending off steadily-encroaching terror.

Seeing as microwaves were some decades away from being invented, I wasn't able to try that trick where you stick the paper in along with some water, and besides, that's a trick for removing stamps from envelopes and not for unfolding crisp and decaying paper. At a loss for anything else (and since I was loathe to bring this parchment anyplace else), I decided to just press my luck, and I took dainty hold on the document with my claws, and tried to just work really, really slowly.

The parchment, as it turned out, was not nearly as brittle as I'd assumed, and it folded out—quite nicely, I might add—to reveal its contents. Writing was scrawled all over it, looking like it was penned by the hand of someone who had drunk several servings of coffee whilst on no sleep. Prominently drawn in one corner was the outward face of a building that I immediately recognized, from the cyclopean architecture thereof, as the Wolfsborough Public Library.

The Wolfsborough Public Library, I am told (and I must take the word of others on this, as I have no way to verify it myself), when viewed from above, forms the shape of the ancient Lemurian symbol for "Here." I can only surmise that the symbol in the opposite corner, which appeared to be penned in blood, was the symbol in question. The actual text on the page, though, however illegible, was at the very least readable, and so I focused my attentions on that.

After stumbling over the letters, tripping over some older spellings, and finally figuring out that the silly symbol that looks like a badly-drawn 'f' is actually an 's,' I found myself reading what was clearly a warning. It told of a book that, when read by mere mortals, would slowly and unceasingly drive them mad, well past the brink of sanity, since it was filled with pretentious nonsense terminology and proper names that all seemed to require unnecessary apostrophes and impossible-to-pronounce diphthongs. However, if one could get past the fact that the Great Ancient Ones apparently utilized a great amount of phlegm when naming things, then "ye untolde horrores withine" would be ripe for the plucking.

This book was known as the Gibberstämmer Tome, and its Dewey Decimal call number at the Wolfsborough Public Library was 299.99.91. Massachusetts being the home to anomalous, diabolic, and phantasmagoric terrors that it is, the Wolfsborough Public Library actually has a very large section dedicated specifically to books of this type, although readers very rarely wander into it, as its creaking floorboards sound like the wails of the dead under one's feet, iridescent eyes seem to peer out from the shadows, and the hallway leading up to it is a bit chilly and drafty.

As imposing a prospect as it was, it seemed that my only logical recourse was to go to the library and look for this book myself. I didn't want to, but I knew that I had to. Whatever had happened to Merry Romper had somehow involved this ancient and decrepit text, and at the moment, I was the only person who could find the truth. It could very well come at a terrible cost to my sanity or even my physical well-being, but I was too far along and too invested in it to stop now, so I resolved to delve deeper still.

Having now solved the parchment's mystery, the echoes of menace no longer resonated in my ears, and so I found my way to the library and headed right for the dilapidated section where the book was to be kept. There, nestled neatly on the shelf, in between Hushed Voices from the Blackness and At the Mounting of Madness, was the Gibberstämmer Tome, and there, written neatly on the check-out card tucked in the sleeve inside the front cover, was the signature of one Meredeth Rombault du Champarnaud. His handwriting was a welcome change from the gnarled-looking runes that embossed the heavy book's surface.

The inside of the book was just as foreboding, and despite my having read the parchment's warning, I was unprepared for just how foul and wicked the accursed text was. I can scarcely bring myself to describe it here in full, so please, let it suffice to say that the notion that another living being had dipped a pen in ink scribed out these letters under the full intent that it contained actual meaning is something far too mind-bending to ponder. To this day, any given word that happens to contain a 'G,' an 'X,' and a 'Th' diphthong sends me into recoils of fiendish memory that wrack at my mind. The less said about these details, the better; count yourself lucky that you do not have access to the Wolfsborough Public Library.

I had little trouble figuring out which section of the book had interested Merry Romper the most, however, and as a result, I was spared from having to read the book in its entirety (and if I had, I shan't think that my mind would be in the state where I could tell you this story). The section in question had been dog-eared, and very recent annotations had been made in bright colored pencil. Most prominent among these notes were the words "THIS PASSAGE HERE!", which came complete with an arrow pointing out the passage in question.

I cannot describe how my heart pounded in my nicely-furred chest as I read those words, nor can I give adequate words to explain the non-Euclidean field trip that my brain took as it tried to parse them. My tale is chilling enough without in-depth descriptions of the Corpse City of Hasbaquabog, whose streets were lined with buildings constructed of naught but bones and pelts, and whose inner square was home to a citadel from which echoed the constant wailing of souls who were being tortured eternally beyond the veil of death and oblivion—a citadel in which slept the nigh-indecipherable horror that was Thrynqyr-Slobboloth, the Many-Tentacled Beast of the Beyond.

According to that ancient passage, Thrynqyr-Slobboloth, the Many-Tentacled Beast of the Beyond was a hideous, hideous beast with many tentacles, and he—or it—fed upon the darkness that exists with in men's souls, the fancifulness that exists within women's souls, and the wayward and disturbing anarchistic daydreams of adolescents. Also, he fed upon the flesh of the living and ground the bones of his victims to make his bread, when such was available (that is to say, at times when he roamed the earth as a shambling terror and not when he lay in that darkest of citadels as a sleeping menace beyond the pale). The book also extolled the benefits and glory that came with worshipping His Tentacularness, which included the lucky benefit of being amongst the first to be devoured by his mollusk-like mandibles whenever he arose. Presumably, being devoured was a blissful escape from the fate of having to live someplace like the Corpse City of Hasbaquabog.

The remainder of the text in question told of a way to summon Thrynqyr-Slobboloth from his distant, arcane slumber, and call him forth through space and time to one's own location. This section was underlined in what appeared to be eyebrow pencil. Now, at this point, you're likely wondering the same thing that I was thinking at this point; namely, what possible reason could anyone have for wanting to intentionally summon a many-tentacled monster?

The answer, as it will come to turn out, is actually very straightforward, lacking any real ambiguity.

Actually performing the ceremony to invoke Thrynqyr-Slobboloth didn't involve much more than reciting a chant and sprinkling around some materials that were easily enough acquired at a florist or greengrocer's. The tricky part of the deal was that it needed to be performed on a spot where three ley lines all intersected. Fortuitously enough, the Gibberstämmer Tome contains an appendix on ley lines, complete with lovely hand-drawn maps that were obviously created by someone lucky enough to have a protractor. Then, consulting a series of atlases, I discovered that just such a convergence point of ley lines existed right on the spot where Merry Romper's penthouse was built.

Was I really serious about doing this? I should have been amazed with myself for taking it all at face value that it would work. After all, this was the sort of thing that people told children to frighten them. This was the sort of thing that people wrote and sold as trashy dime novels. This was markedly not the sort of thing that grown men put their faith in while trying to track down someone who was possibly missing and more probably quite dead. Nevertheless, there I was, with the firm decision already made in my mind that I was going to do this, fully expecting it all to be very, very, awfully true.

A few quick pit stops and an hour or so later, I was back in that bloodied bedroom. This time, however, I felt like I could smell more than just the gore on the walls. This time, I felt like I could smell my own fear rising up off of my fur, and in retrospect, I was right to note that. In one hand, I had tucked the Gibberstämmer Tome under my arm, and in the other, I clutched a brown paper bag that carried the ingredients I needed: some larkspur clippings, a piece of sandalwood bark, and some thyme.

Whether it was hallucination or not, I cannot say, but I felt the book vibrating and shaking against my side. Just like when I had been struggling with the parchment, I swore that I could hear my name being muttered from random directions, and as I continued to perceive the book's quivering, I somehow knew that it wanted to be opened up to the page where the summoning spell was written down.

The air inside my lungs felt cold, and it was like the sensation of hands clutching at my chest from the inside, threatening to hold me bodily in place if I attempted to run due to fright. Several long moments passed, each with its own terrified heartbeat resonating in my chest, and I drew a few breaths before I finally willed myself to open the tome to the proper page.

Holding the book open across one palm, I ground the larkspur and thyme together in my hand, and then dropped the bark at my feet. My tail curled up and kept wanting to twitch, and then, I squeezed my eyes shut and steeled my resolve before opening them again in order to read the words written there aloud. Even then, just seeing those words there on the page instilled me with dread. Part of me wanted to stop, but my muzzle started to move, as if on its own accord.

"Mekka-lekka hi, mekka hiney ho!" I called out, and my voice sounded like it echoed from the walls, despite the fact that the acoustics of the room shouldn't have allowed for it.

"Mekka-lekka hi, mekka chonny ho!" I then spoke aloud, finishing the incantation.

Immediately, the room fell silent, and not even the sound of the rattling ventilation duct made its way to my ears. Twilight no longer poured in through the windows, and I could barely see at all as a shape began to take form on the opposite side of the room. Amorphous blackness seemed to congeal, taking its sweet time as it ebbed and clumped and agglutinated, and it gave me quite the case of the heebie-jeebies as the baleful form started to come more and more together.

Finally, the shadow seemed to give way to itself, and I could hear what sounded like something trying to breathe through gelatin. Where was once nothing but darkness was now the ominous form of what I was forced to assume was Thrynqyr-Slobboloth. His countenance was both grim and unnerving: his deformed head was like that of a cuttlefish, and it rested atop wide shoulders and a squat frame resembling that of a frog if stood upright. He also emanated an eerie, almost tangible miasma of putrescence, loathing, and vile mien.

My nostrils stung, and the insides felt like I was breathing in steam directly from a kettle. There was no hit, but there was pungency and tingling, and it sparked a spell of nausea and dizziness. I had to fight to stand upright for the next few moments, and I then forced myself to look back at the creature in front of me, pulling gumption from places that I didn't even know I had.

His tentacles squirmed and wriggled hideously as he first spoke in his venomous voice: "Who dares to desecrate their own presence by summoning me forth by the impious invocation of my name, most profane among those most profane?"

I stood, shaking, from the tips of my ears to the tip of my tail, and I dropped the book from my hand, gibbering and stammering as His Tentacularness addressed me directly, looking me dead in the eye. Had I not just relieved myself on the way over, I would have surely wet my trousers as I stood there, transfixed by terror in its purest form.

One of Thrynqyr-Slobboloth's clammy tentacles whipped out, wrapped around my waist, and squeezed. "Speak, furred mortal," he demanded, "or I shall take it upon myself to assume that you are but a morsel intended for visceral sacrifice to my putrid being."

The thought of being eaten alive by a giant squid-thing snapped me out of my terrible reverie. "Er, yes, Your Contemptible Majesty," I choked out through my dry throat. My brain scrambled for a cover story, and really, I don't know what I had been thinking, summoning up a tentacled beast without having thought about what I'd do once it showed up. "I, ah... seek only to know what we piteous mortals have done to incur your violent displeasure, O Tentacled One, so that we may rectify it, in the name of your hideous glory."

"Displeasure?" came the thing's garbled response, sounding almost confused. To be sure, I thought for sure that I recognized a tilting of the head of that alien form.

"Y-y-yes, mighty Thrynqyr-Slobboloth," I responded. "It seems that your previous, ah, vulpine acolyte was reduced to little more than a thin, bloody paste, and I seek only to ensure that your villainous needs are met appropriately in the future. So, then, if you could tell me what, exactly, this..."

My voice fell silent, as it appeared that Thrynqyr-Slobboloth was still thoroughly dumbfounded by the matter of which I spoke. Once I went quiet, though, the thing's beady eyes narrowed in on me, and more tentacles shot from the shadows and seized me, hoisting me up by all four limbs as if I were nothing more than an orange-furred rag doll. The hammering of my heart competed to drown out the sound of the otherworldly being's breathing, but there seemed to be a mutual dominance between the two as both echoed loudly in my ears.

"You seek to curry my wicked favor, as the other before you?" the monster asked.

"Yes, exactly!" I replied instantly, with a fervent nodding of my head, before I had a split-second's realization. "Wait, I mean, no!"

By then, though, it was too late. Another cold-skinned tentacle had begun to make its way up the leg of my pants, coiling around and trailing up the back until it reached the curve of my buttocks. Yet another wound itself toward me, flicking my hat off of my head before it tore my coat off and shredded my shirt away from my body.

Smaller feelers joined that larger one, and they started to play up and down my bare torso, as if trying to familiarize themselves with the texture of my fur or something like that. My chest felt as heavy as a rock, and each vile caress of those grotesque appendages broke through my attempts to just ignore what was happening. There was no way to kill my focus and just let the terrible treatment happen; the creature had me, and he wanted me to know it.

Now, when you're a fox, there are certain things that you just have to put up with as par for the course. One of the things that's always been something of a pet peeve (or outright frustration) is the sheer futility of trying to convince someone that, just because I happen to be a fox, it does not necessarily follow that I am a submissive little bottom. Historically, it had been difficult enough to convince certain people that my masculine instincts to dominate were quite thankfully intact, and so it seemed that it would be quite impossible to convey such a notion to an incomprehensible alien intelligence from past the veil of our reality.

So it was, then, as my various squeaks, whimpers, and growls of resistance were ignored, and with my trousers then torn away, one of those tentacles began to tease underneath my tail. The smaller feelers wrapped around the base of my fluffy pride and joy and hiked it up obscenely, while the thicker appendage grappled my leg into place, the tip of it rubbing back and forth in slow, squirming circles at my shamefully exposed hole. I didn't even have the presence of mind to wonder how and why this unearthly beast knew to do what it was doing; all I could think of to do was struggle, but the more I thrashed my arms and legs about in vain attempts to wrest myself free, the tighter those fiendish tentacles coiled around me.

Thrynqyr-Slobboloth's tentacles were more dexterous than I had originally given them credit for, and Thrynqyr-Slobboloth himself seemed to know just how to milk fear from my being. The tip of the thick feeler under my tail kept rubbing in the fuzzy run between my rump-cheeks, and if the monster's goal was to force me to squirm uncomfortably, he was succeeding rather admirably. Here and there would come the occasional press at my tight little entrance, as if to test both my reaction and my body's resistance, both of which must have been plainly obvious.

Then, with no further pretense, that tentacle began its slow, uninhibited press underneath my tail. I don't have much else to compare the sensation to, really, but as it happens, the skin of Many-Tentacled Beasts of the Beyond secretes a mucous-like substance with a texture and viscosity not entirely unlike that of petroleum jelly, and so while it certainly wasn't pleasant to have my rear end probed and violated by the creature's appendage, I was at least spared a good deal of chafing. It didn't feel good, of course, but that wasn't exactly the point, I don't think.

I was yanked up even higher and flipped so that my back was parallel to the ground. My legs were then spread apart, giving my tentacled captor an unobstructed view as his smooth tentacle pumped back and forth. My teeth bit into my lower lip, and even though I knew that struggling was past useless, I couldn't just let myself sit by and do nothing. I yapped and snarled as the thing kept sliding in and out underneath my tail, but then a pair of smaller feels bound my muzzle firmly shut, and so all I could do then was whine and growl, and that sounded altogether too pathetic.

Desperate for anything to make the sensations I was feeling go away, I tried to just focus on the rhythm set by the tentacle that had wormed itself beneath my tail. It made for something of a distraction, but it was hard to completely ignore the fact that I was, well, getting fucked by a tentacled demon-beast. Even that minor distraction, though, was short-lived, as another one of those thicker tentacles then began to bump and tap against my sealed-shut lips.

The feelers around the side of my muzzle squeezed inward, forcing my jaw to open bit by unwilling bit, and the rounded tip of that fat tentacle pressed in between my lips in turn. This one lacked the same slick film that the one between my legs had, which I was mildly thankful for, and which left me with just the sensation of taut, smooth, turgid flesh sliding back and forth against my lips and tongue, with the occasional probing foray into the top of my throat.

I also discovered that Thrynqyr-Slobboloth also possessed some peculiar powers of mind control, for even as my body was subjected to such disgusting and unwholesome sexual mistreatment, I found myself getting aroused, slowly but oh-so-surely, starting first with a mere teasing stirring in my sheath, but followed soon by my slick length rapidly emerging thereafter. Imagine, now, the abject horror that I felt as the ghoulish fiend used his psionics to play with my mind, deceiving me into thinking that I was actually deriving gratification from the awful sensations of an overfull muzzle, a tight pressure against my prostate, and a feather-light tickle at the pads of my right paw.

Due to this wicked deception, Thrynqyr-Slobboloth's putrid feelers soon found the bulb of my knot, and began to squeeze and caress it along with the rest of my member, jerking and pumping my completely unwilling erection. I was then flipped backward, so that my head was pointing downward and my face was facing away from the thing that held me. Somehow, though, not being able to see didn't change things much; I was still just as in the dark as I had been, and it didn't stop it from continuing to work its tentacles in and out of my orifices.

The tentacle at my rear slid all the way out of me, and for a moment, I thought that was done with that particular variety of torture, until I felt the blunt end of another, not-as-slick appendage pushing down in its stead. I felt a twinge of humiliation when I felt how little resistance my body put into being violated anew, and as the stalk of the tentacle bulged and throbbed inside of me, it forced the tip of my cock to start leaking down onto the fur of my tummy.

All of this came together to drive my whimpering up several notches, and I couldn't even focus well enough to consider fighting off the compulsion to suck needily on the featureless feeler in my mouth. The tightness around my knot increased as the tinier tentacles squeezed and tugged, and instinct sparked within me, making me moan with even louder sounds of pleasure that betrayed me to this mistreatment. All I could do was whine pitifully out from the thin space between my lips and the monster's flesh before another poke at my throat silenced me.

I felt myself about to pass out from the blood that was rushing to my head, but before I could, I was flipped back a full one hundred eighty degrees, facing upright and forward once more. My face must have looked absolutely ragged and twisted, forced into a strange state between arousal, desperation, and ticklishness. When I tried to look away, my head was yanked back into place, and I could barely even pant through my nostrils as the tension around my knot became so great that I simply couldn't bear it anymore, and I began to empty myself out with spurt after humiliating spurt of pleasure I hadn't ever asked for.

"Oh, dearest me!" Thyrnqyr-Slobboloth sputtered out then, dropping me to the floor in shock as my tender vulpine maleness quivered its last, leaving me to lie there on my back with a lingering trickle of seed down the front of my sheath. "What in all the planes of creation was that?" The most distinct tone in his eerie voice, then, was easily recognizable as shocked embarrassment.

The next part of the conversation, here, I shall not recount. It, by far, is probably the most revolting and horrifying part of my tale, but to sum it all up, after a discussion and a few crude diagrams used to illustrate to Thrynqyr-Slobboloth what happens to the bodies of boy foxes when they reach a certain age, his greenish skin showed a bluish tone that I'm reasonably sure was blushing.

Thrynqyr-Slobboloth, it turned out, was not actually Thrynqyr-Slobbloth—or, rather, up until a few days earlier, his name had been (and I don't know what actual consonant formations and apostrophes go in the native ancient spelling, but from his pronunciation, it sounded like) Carl.

"So, then, what happened to the previous Thrynqyr-Slobboloth?" I asked. "How did you come to, ah... supplant His Great Tentacularness?"

"To my understanding," he burbled, "he has committed truancy."

I blinked. "Truancy?" I asked. I didn't realize that "Many-Tentacled Beast of the Beyond" was a position that could be willingly vacated.

"Indeed," Carl-Slobboloth replied. "By all accounts, he fled the Corpse City of Hasbaquabog, and was last seen in Poughkeepsie, headed towards the Nether Realms of Shombledam with a fuzzy orange creature not unlike yourself in tow."

"So, then, Merry Romper hasn't been brutally slaughtered at the hands of any elder tentacle beasts?" I asked.

The tentacle beast shook its head. "It would seem not," he replied. "I confess that I was confused by your statements to that effect, but once I noticed that you seemed to think you were telling the truth, it made things a lot simpler for me."

"A lot simpler for you in what way?" I asked, cocking my own head.

One of the creature's squirmy appendages waggled dismissively. "Oh, it's nothing," he said, and then he made a throat-clearing sound. "Listen, I really ought to go. The mindless citizenry of the Corpse City has to be kept in line, and all, and... well... you know."

With that, the shambling eldritch horror made its way past me, awkwardly avoiding eye contact, and it squeezed its way out the door, made its way into the hallway, and disappeared around the corner, never to be seen again.

I was then left with nothing else to do but to put on some of Merry Romper's ill-fitting clothing (as mine were in no condition to be worn), and fitting myself into the least ridiculous getup possible, I, too, shambled my way back to my car.

The next morning, I called up the wolf who had hired me to look into Merry Romper's disappearance. I told him the unfortunate news that Merry had left him for an out-of-towner named Theodore something-or-other (inasmuch as a 'cousin' can leave someone, of course). The wolf took it quite well, actually. After all, it was better that he was at least alive and happy, as opposed to being a bloody stain on a wall.

He still offered to pay me for my services, too, but I insisted on only accepting half of what I originally charged him, due to my failure to actually locate the poor boy (I wouldn't have charged him anything, in truth, but the Wolfsborough Public Library had a hefty restocking fee for the Gibberstämmer Tome, which I had left behind at the scene, and which had been confiscated by the police by the time I went back for it).

Also, seeing as the rather gentlemanly wolf was down in the dumps about his cousin's running away, I offered to take him out for a drink and maybe, if he had time, buy him dinner. After all, he seemed like a nice enough guy, at least from what I'd seen. I hope that I seem a friendly fellow, even now, after all that I've seen and experienced—things that mortals were never meant to know (and for reasons which I now understand more fully than I can ever convey).

Besides, since he couldn't pronounce 'Haverhill' right on the first try, I knew that he was an out-of-towner himself, and that meant that he would be none the wiser to the true horror that lurks beneath the surface of the countryside of Massachusetts.

Vengeance

Of the spirits we know to inhabit our world, those malcontents who seek to harm us are the ones that frighten us most.

Not always, however, are they frivolously frightening. Some have tragically good reason to remain, and use the living as tools for their revenge, or whatever other aim they may have.

In "Under the Surface" we see what the will can drive the spirit to do, and how the living can become pawns of the intranquil dead.

Under the Surface

Stormcatcher

Spencer Norton came around the corner of the cubicle that separated the bed area of the school clinic from the sitting area and gave his friend Mackie Thomason the once-over, the tiger blinking at the fennec fox curiously.

"There you are," he rumbled to the vulpine. "What happened to you? Miss Brubaker said that you blacked out," he rumbled, lowering his voice as he stepped nearer so the attractive lapine nurse he'd referred to wouldn't overhear him. Spencer handed Mackie's backpack to him, a wry look on his features.

"Did she flash her bra at you and make you pass out from lust, or did she give you C.P.R. and slip you some tongue? You lucky bastard!" the tiger smirked.

Mackie rolled his eyes and got to his feet, shouldering his pack with a grunt as he shook his head. "You wish. I coulda taken a picture and showed it to you, and made your head explode."

"Oh, twist my arm, why don'tcha," the tiger cracked, smirk growing wider. "Did you? Where is it?"

"Let's go, smartass," Mackie sighed, heading for the door with his friend following him. They made their way through the throngs of kids in the main locker hallway, then headed outside, down the stairs that led to the main parking lot, and out towards their home neighborhood a few blocks away. Spencer waited until all the other kids were out of earshot, then gave Mackie a sideways glance.

"Seriously, though, what happened?" he asked.

Mackie shrugged. "What you said. Miss Brubaker said I started choking while I was getting some water from the fountain, and then I blacked out for a sec. No big deal."

Spencer frowned, brows furrowing. "What made you pass out?"

"I dunno," the fox said. "I musta swallowed the wrong way, or something. Anyway, she said I wasn't out for long, and I feel fine now, so let's drop it."

The tiger paused, immediately sensing something odd. "You sure that's all?" he murmured. He gave the fox a light, playful shove and rumbled, "I know yer a lightweight, but you're not that much of a wuss."

Mackie stumble-stepped sideways from the shove, then shoved back—and although he managed to return the tiger's grin somewhat, it wasn't as joyful. He walked a bit further in silence for a few moments, and he could feel Spencer still looking at him. Finally, he mumbled, "Actually, I didn't quite tell her everything."

The two of them were passing through a small strip mall that was around the corner from their homes two streets over. They passed the decorative fountain that marked the halfway point of the plaza, four ornate marble spigots spouting their streams of water into the catching pool below, then continued on to the far side of the mall. With Halloween so close, many of the stores had appropriately themed decorations on display, and brightly colored jack-o-lanterns, witches, and ghouls of various kinds stared blankly forward as they walked by. The fennec stopped to stare at his reflection in one of the storefront windows, both brows furrowing in unfamiliarity as though he didn't recognize himself.

Spencer watched him, looked at his own reflection, then back at the fox, prodding him with a fingerclaw. "What'd you leave out?" he asked.

"I saw something," Mackie murmured, voice growing quieter. "Just as I started to drink. I felt the water go down the wrong way, but it... it was almost as if it went down the wrong pipe... on it's own, y'know? I didn't swallow wrong." He paused, one handpaw coming up to rub dazedly at his neck, and he shot Spencer a sideways glance that seemed fearful—as though he expected the feline to either laugh at him, or call him crazy.

Spencer looked back humorlessly, shrugging in disinterest. "Sounds like a bad episode of 'The Twilight Zone', to me," he rumbled. "I guess I just don't quite understand why that would've made you go blotto, though. Seems like it would've had to have blocked your windpipe for a couple minutes, and it was just water."

Mackie sighed, then shrugged. "I know, that's what Miss Brubaker said. It doesn't make sense to me, either."

The tiger stared at him thoughtfully, tail flicking idly back and forth behind him as they resumed walking, slowly. Finally, he rumbled, "Well, don't get me wrong—I'm glad you're okay. You gonna tell your folks what happened?"

"Hell, no!" Mackie grunted, giving his friend a sharp look with brows raised and eyes wide. "Are you kidding? Mom would have me down at the E.R. and sign me up for six-months worth of medical tests before I'd get a chance to explain what happened completely. I mean, c'mon, you know what my mom's like."

Mackie laughed out loud, patting the fennec's left shoulder. "Sure I do. She's a typical mother—doting, naggy, and completely high-strung."

"Way," the fox nodded firmly in agreement. "Makes damn good cakes, though."

"Well, c'mon," Spencer grinned to his friend. "Let's find the nearest Preda-Burger. If you can fake that passing out thing again, or maybe throw up when I tell you to, maybe we can sue 'em for big money."

Mackie rolled his eyes and smiled as the pair headed down the street where they both lived. "You are major-league damaged upstairs, stripes," he laughed. "Tempting as it sounds, let's skip it. I got chores to do before my old man comes home, tonight."

The dark blue sedan parked near the corner of the strip mall idled as the driver watched the duo intently, with particular emphasis on the fennec fox. The driver, a decent-sized wolf, drummed a finger-claw restlessly against the steering wheel as he stared at them. He waited until Mackie was out of sight, then the sedan pulled away from the curb slowly, heading down the street in the same direction the tiger had gone a few moments before.

The next morning was sunny, clear, and cool, and Mackie felt the autumn breeze ruffle his whiskers gently as it just barely tousled his headfur.

Spencer greeted him at the intersection where their street joined the main boulevard, as usual, and they began to walk towards the plaza and the school beyond. Once again, Mackie took note of the Halloween decorations in some of the storefront windows, and a thought occurred to him.

"Hey, have you asked anybody to the Halloween dance, yet, Spence?" he murmured to the tiger, turning to him with curiosity on his face.

The tiger's eyes flicked sideways to glance at him, then stared resolutely forward again as the feline rumbled in a bored-sounding voice, "No, I haven't. I'm not real sure I even wanna go, to tell ya the truth. Why should I go to some dumb dance when I could hit a couple of the local walk-through spook-houses, roll a few yards with T.P., scarf candy, and freak out little kids?"

Mackie's ears quirked. "Hey, that's right, I hadn't even considered that angle, with the walk-through spook-houses, and stuff. Would you mind if I tagged along? Now that we're old enough to get in without the 'rents, it might be kinda cool. Although I dunno, I heard that band 'The Rancid Dead' were supposed to play at the school dance—and I heard that they were pretty good. They're supposed to wear real weird Halloween-style costumes and have coffin-shaped speakers, and they spit fake green slime and blood onto the audience while they sing, and stuff like that."

"Wow, that sounds..." Spencer paused, then frowned a bit, chuckling as he shook his head. "Well, I can't really decide how I think it sounds, but I think it's somewhere between weird and lame. Dude, if you want bad makeup and fake monster shit, that's what the spook-houses are for, right? Besides, I hear that they're doing a really killer haunted hayride this year at Maynard's Berry Farm, and would it or would it not be awesome to have Lucia Burke and Megan Stafford all squealy and crawling all over us?" he snickered. "Lucia and I have been making eyes at each other for awhile, now, so this'd be the perfect opportunity for me to—"

Spencer had been so involved in his musing that he'd paced a few steps away from the fox—and by the time he turned back around to face him, the vulpine was gone. The tiger's ears perked sharply, and he blinked.

"Mack?" he rumbled, glancing around in puzzlement. He frowned and stopped in his tracks, looking around himself slowly. It took him a few moments to realize that the fox was directly behind him, and standing so still that he almost seemed like a part of the fountain. The fox had at some point during Spencer's speech removed his own shoes, then stepped into the water in the fountain's basin, his back and fluffy tail to the tiger. His head was lowered, arms by his sides, and his eyes riveted dully on the water, squinting down at it with a rather intense scrutiny.

Spencer called out to him again, but didn't get a response. It was as if his friend had been paralyzed in place.

The tiger stepped over to the edge of the fountain, watching Mackie like a hawk. The fennec didn't even seem to be breathing, and when Spencer reached out to touch him, the fox didn't register it. "Mack?" the tiger said again. "Dammit, what's with you? Why'd you get in there? You're gonna catch a cold!"

The fox's voice was a mumbled whisper, and the tiger barely made it out. "They're in the water..." Mackie murmured.

Spencer lifted a brow, then slowly looked down into the rippling water that Mackie's gaze was so steadfastly staring at. He didn't see anything out of the ordinary, and his eyes slowly panned back up to look at the fox. "What's in the water, Mack?"

"Spots..." Mackie said, his eyes squinting once more as he poked two fingerclaws at the water, as though trying to touch whatever it was he thought he was seeing. "Can't you see 'em? They're everywhere. In the water... on my fur..."

The tiger's sense of unease began to grow, and he swallowed the hackles on the back of his neck raising as he said in a low voice that was as calm as he could muster, "Mack, I dunno what you're talking about. There aren't any spots, at least, none that I can see..." He paused, and then said a bit louder, "Hey, are you feeling alright?"

Mackie paused, then shuddered firmly, closing his eyes for a moment as he touched his fingers to his temples. A moment later, he opened his eyes once more, still staring down at the water intently. He lifted a hand to brush lightly at his ears, and then slowly straightened up, staring straight ahead for a moment.

Parked a few blocks away from the tiger and fox, but still near enough to be within sight, was the same blue sedan and driver that had been near the pair the previous day. The driver's fingerclaw was once more tapping nervously against the steering wheel as he watched the two young males intently, and he was caught quite off-guard when Mackie suddenly turned his head to stare directly at the car. The wolf behind the wheel jumped and fumbled nervously and reflexively with the newspaper lying on the front seat next to him, and he jerked his gaze away from the fox and lifted a cell phone up in front of his face, making a show of pretending to dial it, then listening for a ring tone. He mimed talking to someone, picking up the paper with his other hand and rattling a bit as he carried on a fake conversation, hoping to convince the fennec that nothing was amiss. Mackie's face was frowning, and he narrowed his eyes a bit at the car before slowly turning his attention back to the tiger, and the wolf's fingers shook from anxiety as he tried to keep the phone steady.

"I'm fine, Spence. Sorry, I didn't mean to scare you—I don't know what's wrong with…" Mackie's voice was low but calm as he perked his ears at Spencer in curiosity. The tiger was still standing next to the fountain, eyeing the fennec nervously—and had jumped noticeably when Mackie had faced him, as though startled by something.

"What?" Mackie asked. "What's with you?"

Spencer paused, licking his whiskers nervously as he stared more closely at Mackie's face, angling his head in two directions for a moment as he stared directly at the fox's eyes. Finally, he murmured, "Dang, man, your hallucinations must be contagious. When you turned to face me, just then, I could almost swear that your eyes had changed color. They turned, like, this really intense shade of ice blue. Almost white, even—y'know, like a dead guy's eyes?"

Mackie blinked at him in disbelief. "Are you jerking my tail?" he snorted, smirking at him crookedly as he made his way to the edge of the fountain and stepped out, wiggling his bare feet around one at a time over the sidewalk to try to shake some of the excess water off of them. Then he picked up his shoes and socks, took a seat on one of the benches nearby, and dried his feet off with a handkerchief as best he could before he put his footwear back on again.

Spencer shrugged a bit. "Hey, I'm just telling you what I thought I saw. I dunno, maybe it was the sun shining in my face at the same time, or something, but it sure was creepy."

"Mmm... sounds that way," Mackie said, turning his head sideways again to peer at the blue sedan and the wolf inside of it. The wolf had turned his head sideways to stare at one of the store windows as he continued his fake discussion, but the fennec could tell that the older male was checking him out with his peripheral vision. The wolf frowned a bit, unable to help glancing back more directly at the fox as he laid his hand over the steering wheel, casually.

To his surprise, Mackie smiled at him. More than that, he gave the wolf a wink that was downright flirtatious. The lupine was so surprised that his cell phone slipped from his fingers and clattered to the floorboard of his car, causing him to utter low curse words as he fumbled for it.

Mackie let his grin fade, then he sat up more straight as he tied his shoelaces, turning to the tiger again. "You know what, though? I just realized something, and I can't believe I forgot this, before. I think I'm gonna have to pass on the spook-house thing tomorrow night, Spence. I have some unfinished business to attend to."

"Awww!" Spencer muttered, ears splaying and shoulders drooping a bit at the fennec's announcement. "Whaddya mean, 'unfinished business'? What could be more important then getting some necking in with your girlfriend during a hayride?" he demanded.

"Charity," Mackie winked. "I just realized, there's also gonna be some kind of 'Trick-or-Treat for Tots' at the mall that's gonna benefit the local kid's hospital. You have to chaperone a group of little kids as they go from store to store to get candy, but you get a free dinner and a T-shirt for volunteering..."

"And that beats rolling people's yards and hearing your girlfriend scream at some guy in a costume as she squiggles into your lap?" Spencer demanded. "I need to give you a talk about priorities one of these days, bud."

"You didn't let me finish," Mackie snickered. "It sounds lame, but I was thinking about asking Megan to go with me, 'cause she loves little kids. And when a gal sees how sweet and charity-oriented a nice guy like me can be, and said guy offers to walk her home and maybe watch a movie with her afterwards, since her folks are gonna be gone for the evening..." He smirked widely, not finishing his sentence as he waggled his brows suggestively at his friend.

Spencer took the hint immediately, and he hooted as he snapped his fingers. "Hickey city!" he laughed. "Dude, you're smoother than I give you credit for!"

Mackie stood up and bowed, then chuckled to the tiger as he hefted his bookbag back up onto his shoulder again. "Stick with me, stripes. I'll make a playboy sophisticate outta you, yet."

The tiger fell into step with the fennec as they resumed heading towards the school, and laughed. "I dunno, whaddya say we go more for the 'playboy' angle and just leave it at that?" he grinned.

Mackie nodded at him, then glanced over his shoulder one more time at the wolf in the sedan, who had retrieved his cell phone, but was no longer pretending to talk on it. Once again, the fox made eye contact with him, and winked, even blowing him a kiss with his muzzle. Spencer didn't catch this, but the wolf visibly jumped.

He saw me, the wolf thought, his heart skipping a beat. Shit, I was way too obvious. I shouldn't have parked so close, but he didn't seem to... Damn, am I making a mistake? I don't want things to turn out like last time.

Pangs of guilt rippled through the lupine's brain, and he gnawed at his right lipruff nervously as he drummed the fingerclaws of both hands on the steering wheel. He pondered, then frowned, brows furrowing deliberately.

No, he thought to himself angrily. Things won't go like last time, because I won't let them go down like last time. I'll try to follow him again tonight, see if he makes eye contact again... and if he does, well, then we'll see. But if he does, things will go better. They will. He'll like me, because I'll make him like me.

He nodded decisively, and then he reached down to turn the ignition key, starting the car as he slowly made a U-turn and headed back towards downtown, a wide grin slowly spreading across his features. It was a smile that managed to be beguiling, conniving, handsome, and quietly desperate, all at once.

But mostly, it was full of sharp, slightly off-white teeth.

Mackie and Spencer walked home after school as usual, but when they came to their home street, Mackie paused and bid the tiger goodbye.

"I promised mom I'd go by the store and pick her up three more bags of Halloween candy," he said to Spencer. "She's expecting a pretty heavy volume of cubs to the front door, tonight."

"Ah, okay," Spencer nodded. "Well, in that case—you and Megan have fun with the kiddie-cubs tonight, and don't show them how well you both French kiss!" he chortled, as he waved goodbye and headed for his house.

"Us?" Mackie laughed, calling out after the tiger. "How about you and Lucia? You know they'll throw you off the hayride if you both end up soaking the whole hay cart with drool, right?"

Spencer shook his head and laughed again, playfully flipping his friend off. The fennec grinned back, then turned and passed the end of his street as he walked towards the downtown sector. If he was aware of that same blue sedan following him as it had done the day before and this morning, he didn't show it. His pace was leisurely and relaxed, which meant that the wolf had to keep his driving and parking as unobtrusive as possible, nearly having to let Mackie out of his sight completely before he allowed himself to resume following him again.

Mackie had no real intentions of going to the grocery store, as he'd told Spencer—and he found himself eventually standing next to a video arcade on his right, staring into the tinted windows, the inside of the place alight with flashy neon and noise from the games themselves. A smirk spread over his features, and he turned his head in the opposite direction to look out at the street, scanning his gaze around until he spotted the wolf's blue sedan. The wolf frowned as he saw that he'd been seen yet again, but he didn't bother faking a phone call or anything else, his muzzle partly open in nervousness as his mind stared back at the fennec for any sign of what would come next.

The fennec licked his lips a bit, then gave the wolf the warmest, most open look of invitation he could muster as he nodded his head sideways towards the open doors of the arcade, his hands in his pockets and his thick tail swishing idly behind him. He turned and headed inside, his eyes riveted on the wolf until the last second, his tail giving a playful flick upwards as though beckoning to him.

The wolf's head drooped as he looked down at his lap, and he panted softly, his heartbeat hammering in his chest as his hands gripped the steering wheel tightly. He closed his eyes as guilt began to seep into his mind, and sweat began to congeal on his forehead, which nearly felt feverish.

All right, he told himself. He's seen me. He knows what I'm about, and now he's either just teasing me, or he's looking for some Sugar Daddy action to give him money and buy him pretty things.

Another voice entered his brain during all these musings, and added in the background the warning, That, or the kid's a plant by the feds, and they're finally onto you. Start the car, old man. Get the hell out of here now while you still can. This kid's way too aware, which makes him too much of a risk.

The wolf nodded in agreement, knowing that the voice was right. It was too much of a risk, and the place was way too public. Anyone inside the arcade would be likely to remember an older guy talking with someone the fennec's age, and it'd be obvious from their differing species that they weren't related.

All the same, these worries became glossed over in his mind with the image of Mackie's thick tail swaying to and fro, beckoning to him. And that smile... so dazzling and pure! The fox radiated cuteness and youth, and the wolf knew that if he could cuddle that tail against his face and caress himself with it just once—just once—all past transgressions would be forgiven. He would treat the boy right, and make him happy—and that would be all that mattered.

He became aware of the concrete under his engineer boots only slightly before he felt his body cross into the din of the arcade. He swiped the sweat off his brow with the back of his hand and slid his hands into the pockets of his jeans, looking casually around until he spotted the fennec's lithe form on one of the dancing rhythm games towards the back of the room.

The wolf made his way casually through the crowd towards the fox, his pulse racing but his face smiling and friendly.

Roughly forty-five minutes later, the wolf and fennec came out of the arcade, laughing and talking together as they headed down the sidewalk towards the wolf's sedan.

"I got to tell you, Mackie," the lupine chuckled, shaking his head in disbelief, "You're probably too young to remember that 'Saturday Night Fever' movie, but your moves in there on that game would put the star of that movie's rhythm to shame!"

"Ooh, gawd..." Mackie cringed, even as he chuckled. "That was the whole 'disco' thing, right? Yuck! I'm still trying to figure out why everyone thinks rap is so cool, let alone something that godawful," he teased. "And hey, you didn't do so badly, yourself, if that really was the first time you'd played it, as you claimed."

The wolf got out his car keys and unlocked the driver's side door, then got in and smiled to the fox, closing the door behind him as he rumbled, "Well, I'll probably regret it tomorrow, but watching you made it look so easy, I just kinda figured what the hell, I'll give it a shot."

Mackie nodded, his eyes looking over the wolf's form. The lupine was in decent shape for his age—he was trim but had a bit of muscle to his arms and a subtly-defined chest, implying that he actually did some routine weight training. His navy blue sweater and simple white T-shirt were neat and clean, and there seemed to be a fringe of facial fur that grew all the way around the wolf's muzzle, giving him the appearance of a graying but neatly-clipped beard. The fox leaned against the car door and lifted his hand, placing it onto the wolf's left forearm as he drew his fingers up the lupine's long-sleeved sweater, slowly. "You take good care of yourself, Robert," he noted in a low voice, his eyes focused on the wolf's body before slowly moving up to look at the lupine's face. "It's really nice to see a handsome older guy that takes such pains to look good."

The wolf tensed up visibly at Mackie's touch, but he didn't jerk his arm away. He swallowed hard and his eyes flicked nervously around, watching for anyone that might be keeping tabs on himself and the fox. He coughed softly, then rumbled in a voice that was just as low, "Ahhh... thank you. You're quite an appealing young man, yourself, and you have the most bewitching blue eyes," he murmured, as his gaze fitfully came to rest on the fox's face. He licked his muzzle nervously, his muzzle parted slightly as though he wanted to ask the fox a question, but wasn't sure how well he'd receive it. Finally, he rumbled to him slowly, "Mackie, you... seem to have a bit more of a worldly air around yourself than many guys your age. May I ask why that is?"

Mackie gave the wolf's forearm another few lazy stroking rubs, then shrugged a little as he lifted his hand away to rest his own forearm against the car door. "Boys will be boys... and that's fine, if that's what you're into. But speaking for myself personally, my home life's not the best—and after being stuck around a bunch of juvenile dipshits all day in school, a guy learns to appreciate the maturity of someone older, you know? Someone who he can talk to on his own intellectual level. But don't let my cute looks fool you, Robert," he smirked, winking at him. "I know how to do things that you'll like, and if you're willing to show me some fun sometime, I'll return the favor."

The wolf's heart nearly skipped a beat, upon hearing the fennec's words—and when the fox lifted his hand to massage the closest portion of the wolf's beard, the lupine all but moaned, his eyes sliding shut as he nuzzled his grizzled gray hairs into the fox's palm. "Ohh, I'd... I'd like that," he rumbled softly. "I'd like that very much, and I'm sure that there are a lot of nice things I can buy you, if you'll spend some time with me..." The voices of warning and paranoia in his head screamed at him to stop what he was doing, however, and he reluctantly eased his beard and face away from the fox's fingers, his eyes snapping open and looking all around again as he rumbled lowly, "But not here, and not now. This is far too public for us,"

The fennec nodded, also looking cagily about as he withdrew his hand and leaned against his forearms. "Yeah, you've got a point. Sorry, I just couldn't help myself. And I better get back home before it gets dark, or my parents will freak." He paused, then grinned slowly as he leaned his face in closer to the wolf's.

"You know what, though? I've got an idea," he whispered conspiratorially to the wolf, who perked both big ears and leaned towards him in interest. "I'm supposed to go to this really lame Halloween dance at my school, tomorrow night—or at least, that's where my parents think I'll be. What are the chances that I could talk a certain handsome older guy into picking me up there at 7PM, so we can go off and do things that really matter?"

"I'd say that they're better than average," the wolf rumbled softly, his breath nearly catching in his throat as he looked at the fox with barely-concealed anticipation. "Tomorrow night, seven o'clock. I'll be there."

"You better be, if you don't want to miss the time of your life," Mackie murmured, drawing a fingertip slowly down the bridge of the wolf's nose. "I'd ask you if you knew were the school was, but given that you and I have been eyeing each other for the past day or so, I don't think that's necessary, is it?" he snickered. "I'll see you then, Robert. I'm really glad we met."

And with that, he leaned back and stepped away from the car, tail swishing playfully again as he slid his hands into his jacket pockets and flashed the wolf one more coy grin before turning and heading down the sidewalk towards his home.

Robert's head thumped back against the headrest of his car seat, and a loopy grin of epic proportions slid across his features as his eyes closed again in bliss. He didn't heed the warning voices in his head that told him to get away from the arcade as quickly as possible, because sheer joy overrode them for a few minutes.

Mackie had gone about four blocks on foot, and the sedan was out of his sight as his cold blue eyes were riveted forward, the coy look gone and replaced with seething hatred as his hands clenched spasmodically. He thought about tomorrow night and things to come, and the scowl changed slowly into a baleful smile.

Then his blue eyes faded back into the fox's normal deep chocolate brown color, and the fox blinked, rubbing his head a little as he looked around, confused. It took him a few moments to get his bearings, and although he finally figured out where he was, he found that he didn't remember walking there.

Fear slowly put a freeze around his heart, which began to pump faster to fight the icy tendrils of panic it felt trying to overwhelm it. Fighting to overcome frightened tears, the fox bolted for his home, hoping that his parents wouldn't be there to demand where he'd been and what he'd been doing.

The following night, Robert showed up at Mackie's school as promised, but as 7:30 came and went, the wolf started getting nervous again. He kept his eyes peeled for the fennec, cursing himself inwardly for trusting a teenager to be on time. He began to think that the whole thing was a bad idea, and wondered if it might not very well be a trap, with cops lying in wait to see if the older male would try to take advantage of Mackie. He also considered the possibility that the young fox had just been being a tease--it happened sometimes, and it had happened to the wolf before. The thought made his stomach feel sour, and finally, he couldn't wait in his car any longer. Frowning darkly, he looked at his watch and saw that it was a few minutes past eight. He decided to risk going into the school to see if the tardy fox was hanging out inside, waiting for him. If he was seen and questioned, he could always say that he had dropped off his son or daughter and just needed to use the restroom on his way out. He left his car unlocked as he headed for the gymnasium, where several kids and some older chaperones were headed.

Mackie stepped out of a nearby copse of trees where he'd been waiting all along, making sure that the wolf was out of sight before turning his attention to the wolf's car. He hurriedly but quietly went over to it and opened the driver's side door, crawling into the vehicle as he searched frantically for something. After not finding it in the backseat, floorboards, or glove compartment, he scowled, unsure of what to do next. Then his gaze fell upon the trunk unlocking switch on the driver's side floorboard next to the door. He popped the trunk, got out of the car, and stepped around to look inside. He finally found the object of his search wrapped in a pillowcase and stuffed underneath the thick coils of some jumper cables.

Mackie took the object out of the pillowcase, examined it, and smiled. Turning towards the gym, his eyes flashed blue as he shut the trunk lid.

Robert hadn't seen any sign of Mackie inside the gym, and between the garish Halloween decorations, the jostling of the kids everywhere, and the sheer volume of the band that was hired to play—apparently, not only was 'Rancid' in their name, but it described their sound perfectly—the older wolf had a splitting headache by the time he spilled back out into the cool night air. He rubbed his forehead with both hands, feeling quite agitated—until he thought he caught sight of a familiar-looking figure near the south entrance of the school building.

"Mackie?" he called, squinting at the fox.

The figure turned, and sure enough, it was Mackie—and he appeared to be carrying something in his hand that the wolf couldn't quite see. He beamed brightly at the wolf and beckoned to him, then darted around the corner of the building. The wolf followed at a slower pace, features disapproving. He rounded the corner and looked for the fox, then saw the fennec's bushy tail disappearing into the trees of the woods that bordered the school on the eastern side. Robert blinked, but followed, moving into a loping jog to catch up as he looked hurriedly about to see if there were any kids or teachers that might spot him. A tight frown spread over his face, and try though he did, he couldn't quite tune out the voices in his head that tossed a multitude of echoing warnings into his brain. *Don't follow him,* they said. *He's trouble—forget about him and find another, you'll regret it if you chase him into those woods...*

Robert dismissed those fears as easily as he would a bunch of cobwebs sucked up by a vacuum. *Forget that. He told me he wanted me, and I'm going to have him,* he snarled inwardly. *Besides, I'm a wolf. Forests are my natural element.*

He followed the trail that he found into the woods, his eyes losing sight of the fennec's bushy tail, for a moment. But the trail was easy enough to navigate, and the woods were thick enough to make the notion of leaving the trail undesirable—so he had confidence that he'd be able to find him again easily. He pounded on, the cold night air filling his lungs as his slightly-frozen breath plumed from his nostrils, making him look for a few moments like some sort of pissed-off, fur-covered dragon. He ran up the trail, following it up over a small hill—and as he came down the other side, he saw a bit of a clearing. The trail continued straight through it and out the other side, and there Mackie stood, waiting, that smile firmly plastered on his face—only this time, it seemed more mocking than beguiling.

"Not running too fast for you, am I, 'Robert'?" the fox said to the wolf when the lupine came near enough to overhear him. Robert was panting a little but not winded enough to be exhausted, and he noted the emphasis that Mackie had put around his name, as though accusing him of it being fake. "Geez, as if that's really your name... Ye gods, do you think up the lamest first names you can come up with, then draw one out of a hat whenever you need it?" he snorted.

The fox's words puzzled the wolf, and as he slowed down to catch his breath, he continued to advance on the fox, slowly. "What's the big deal with the chase? You're really starting to ruin what should be a wonderful evening for us both, Mackie," he growled softly, the agitation evident in his voice.

"'Wonderful'?" the fox scoffed, giving the wolf a look of incredulous disbelief. "You actually think that letting your sick ass paw on me all night would be wonderful?" He shook his head in disgust, continuing to edge backwards towards the trail behind him as he said to the wolf, "I'm really glad that this isn't far from being over. You haven't changed a bit. You're every inch the sick, selfish pervert you were the first time I met you."

This made the wolf stop short, a confused look crossing over his features. "First time?" he rumbled. "What do you mean? We've never met, before."

Mackie's eyes were pale blue again, and they almost seemed to glow in the cold autumn moonlight as he replied, "Oh, we most certainly have. I guess I shouldn't be too surprised that you've forgotten me already, but trust me—I'll remind you, soon enough. Besides—you're not going to get a sweet, innocent little foxy get the better of you, are you?" he chided, purposefully taunting the older male with his voice. "Especially when he's got something so very special..." With that, he held up the object he'd found in the trunk of the wolf's car. It was a digital camera, and a fairly expensive-looking one. Robert's shaggy brows shot up in surprise, and his muzzle dropped open in a nearly frightened expression—but he lost his fear quickly, the emotion rapidly turning into rage as he his clenched hands started to stretch in front of himself towards the fox, his neckfur ruffled and teeth bared.

"You stole that!" he snarled, voice accusatory. "Give that back to me right now, you little shit. It's mine!"

"Come and get it, you tired old asswipe!" Mackie laughed, as he turned and raced down the trail once more, waving the camera back at the lupine teasingly.

Robert charged after the fennec with a roar of rage, heedless of the branches of the trees whipping at his jacket and body as he plunged through the forest after his young prey. The buzzing of the voices in his head chided him with every step, making his fury even greater. You should have known this would happen, they said. You know what's on the memory chip, in that camera! When that kid gets it to the authorities, you're busted.

Mackie had been on the trail a few yards in front of him, the fennec's bushy tail whipping behind him as he ran—when suddenly, the fox jumped off the path and tore into the woods, his thin frame ducking overhanging branches and leaping over fallen logs with astoundingly quick reflexes. This slowed the older wolf down a little, his heavier frame crunching down into the piles of dead leaves and sticks as he became forced to lift his heavily-booted feet higher to make his way through. He cursed vehemently, swatting more branches out of his way as he kept his night vision riveted on the fennec.

As the pair ran through the woods, the sound of running water began to reach the wolf's ears. Mackie had pulled ahead significantly, having gained several hundred yards over the wolf but still remaining in sight. The stream where the water sound was coming from quickly came into view, and although it didn't look terribly deep, it was fairly wide and had very few rocks in it to use as stepping stones. The fox had slowed down when he reached the edge of the stream, and he suddenly doubled over, clutching his midsection with both arms as he sank to the ground. A harsh, coughing, hacking sound reached the wolf's ears, the sound almost as loud as the rushing water—and the wolf couldn't help but grin fiendishly as he slowed his own approach, coming up towards the hapless fox as his right hand slipped into his pants and slid a knife handle out of his pocket. He pressed a button, and a trim but sharp-looking blade popped out of it.

"Well, now. Looks like you went and got all choked up on me, didn't you?" he rumbled, the lupine slowly rolling up his sleeves as he came closer still. He couldn't see the fox's face from Mackie's doubled-over angle, but from the way he sounded, the vulpine could have been coughing up a lung. "Maybe that'll teach you not to mess with other people's thi—"

Robert's words were abruptly cut off by a sickly wet, splattering sound. Mackie had hacked something out of his muzzle, but because it was eclipsed by his shadow, what it was wasn't readily apparent. It looked a bit like vomit, at first, but it had mass and volume to it—

and something in the middle of the puddle appeared to be moving. In fact, now that he'd gotten closer, the wolf could see that whatever it was looked to be about the size of a housecat, if not larger—and Robert absently wondered how it could have been possible for Mackie to have been able to cough it up in its entirety.

The fennec, exhausted beyond measure from the chase and the strain of coughing up the creature squirming in front of him, finally succumbed to his fatigue. He fell over sideways and thumped onto the ground, body curled slightly into the fetal position—and the wolf couldn't tell if he was dead or alive. Robert's attention was rapidly diverted from the vulpine, however, when he realized that the thing the fox had vomited out had sat up and was now staring at him with baleful, cold, dead-looking eyes.

The wolf jerked backwards, his eyes not believing what he was seeing as his muzzle dropped open in shock. It was a cat of some kind, all right, its fur as pale and white as milk—and it was starting to grow in size. It closed its eyes for a moment and let out a soft groan of pain as its legs lengthened and thickened, muscles and bones popping into place audibly as its arms did the same. The trunk of its body also thickened and stretched out, along with its tail—and finally, it was able to clamber slowly to its feet and stand on legs that were shaky, but fully-formed. Black rosette markings faded into view all over the feline creature, expect on its chest, face, and inner thighs—and as it rubbed its neck and let out a soft, rueful sigh that sounded ethereal and hollow, the wolf could feel the hackles on the back of his neck prickle, they were standing up so hard. But when the thing finally lifted its face to stare at the wolf, Robert saw that he recognized the face around those hideously dead eyes. He was too frightened and shocked to speak, and some kind of horrible paralysis seemed to have him rooted to the spot as he gaped at the all-too-real apparition.

The snow leopard creature leered at him, his teeth white and his breath frozen in the air, even as the stench of mildew reached the wolf's sensitive nostrils. The thing glanced over towards the stream, ears perking, then looked back at the wolf as it murmured to the wolf in a shadowy voice, "The sound of running water. How appropriate. I remember that sound... it was the last thing I ever heard." The cat took another few steps towards the wolf, who was frantically willing his feet to move and found that they were stubbornly refusing.

The feline cocked its head at Robert, looking inquisitive. "Do you remember that night, now? Is it all coming back to you? It's been three long years, and I bet you were beginning to think that you'd gotten away with it, hadn't you? But here I am."

"Dead," the wolf finally mumbled in a dry, cracked whisper. "You're dead. I saw your body, you died right in my fucking bathroom!" he cried.

"I certainly did, you twisted fuck," the leopard whispered. "A homeless street hustler who needed money, and you knew it. You took me in for the night, and we got cozy… and that's when you said you wanted to try some kinky things. You'd never done it in a bathtub before, and you thought it'd look hot if you took me from behind while I was handcuffed to the bathtub faucet… Hell, I didn't know any better," it shrugged. "I had a nasty little drug habit to feed, and you seemed like a nice enough guy, so I let you do it. You promised me you were going to turn the water off in a minute, but I never counted on your stupid ass falling asleep in front of the television…" it said accusingly, almost spitting the words at the wolf as Robert finally summoned the strength to start moving his quaking limbs backwards.

"It was an accident! I swear it was!" the wolf blurted, his frame continuing to back up as he bumped his posterior up against a tree. He scrabbled to get around it, nearly dropping his knife in the process as he screamed mentally at his legs and tried to run, but his synapses seemed to be firing off orders to his body through a thick wall of syrup that slowed the commands down en route. "I… I just wanted us to fool around, and I was going to pay you—just like I p-promised. I even tried to give you CPR, for heaven's sake!"

The feline shook its head. "Didn't do much good, did it?" it growled, its ears lying flatly and wetly against its skull. That's when the wolf noticed that the corpse's whole body seemed to be drenched, causing the feline to glisten in the bright October moonlight. The pale, spotted fur was matted down all over, and the creature's footsteps were wet and soggy-sounding on the dry ground. Drops of water dripped and leaked from the feline's nose, chin, whiskers, and fingertips, and the very air around him and the wolf seemed to grow colder, by comparison. The frigidity wrapped itself around the lupine's joints and chilled his blood, making him start to shiver considerably. The corpse itself, though, seemed quite at ease as it put itself face to face with the startled wolf, who had backed himself inadvertently up against another tree—but this one was too thick for him to make his way around without taking his eyes off that dead face, and Robert found that he couldn't do so.

The cat leaned in closer. "It's too late for money, now. Now you have to pay me back by showing me how sorry you are," It said, it's hands reaching up to clamp fingerclaws firmly into both sides of the frightened wolf's visage. The gout of water that spurted out of the cat's muzzle and splattered itself against Robert's shirt unnerved the wolf more than the stinging pain of the cat's claws tearing slowly down his face, bloodying it with deep claw grooves. "I want you to kiss me, and make it all better. Kiss me now," it demanded, its voice a soft, dreadful hiss as its muzzle parted and aimed for the wolf's own maw.

Robert screamed, then, thick drops of blood spattering onto his shirt collar from the cat's claw slashes even as he jerked his arm forwards and buried his knife's blade hilt deep into the cat's chest. The leopard didn't even flinch, but its face seemed to get even more wrathful as it jerked the wolf's head down against its mouth, sealing its muzzle with the lupine's. It leaped bodily onto the wolf, entwining its arms and legs with him with a hideous strength, the wolf's terrified mind had just enough time to register the smell of rot and mildew that seeped from the leopard's open mouth, right before it clamped down onto and over his muzzle.

Robert struggled mightily, even as his breath began to fade and the water began to flow.

Halloween night—and for that matter, usually a good chunk of the following early morning—does not always bode well for police officers. If arson cases abound, it's no picnic for firefighters, either.

But a special kind of pall hung over the Centerville police station in Mackie's hometown, tonight. Tempers were short, phone voices were curt and rude—and not even the Halloween decorations, trays full of cookies and donuts, and jars of candy galore could stem the tide of ugliness and general discomfort all over the building, in all departments. The officers had a rather special and extremely unwanted guest, and said guest lay in a body-bag inside the station's pitiful excuse for a forensics room.

Cub murderer.

Those were the words on everyone's mind, and that was why everyone felt so dirty inside.

Police officers could and did tolerate many things out of necessity, but even so, there are some things fell on the 'unforgivable' list. Pedophilia was one of them, and it was unique in that gender didn't seem to matter; any perpetrator with a proven track record of sexually molesting minors could generally count on getting the shit royally beat out of them by the police officers that escorted them to headquarters, and no questions would generally be asked by the commanding officers—especially in smaller towns. Smart molesters learned to take their lumps in stride and keep quiet about it, because those that didn't invariably would end up getting transferred to a state prison—where they would frequently find themselves the victims of gang rapes in the communal showers, often a week or two before they would perish from 'accidental' causes.

Cub murderers, though, were another matter entirely.

Anyone callous and psychotic enough to murder a minor, accidental or not, could pretty much count on not making it out of the local precinct alive. And in this case, the perpetrator had done the investigating officers the favor of being discovered quite dead, already.

But for the busy officers working that night, it didn't matter. Alive or dead, the thing that killed a child was still in their morgue, and still in their presence. And while the powers that be were diligently following through to make sure that all procedures were followed before the case files could be locked away, it still galled all of them to know that the body was still around—and perhaps none more so than homicide detective Mark Halstead. The panther's face was surly and his shirt rumpled, tie loose at the collar as he strode down the stairs to the basement and the combination morgue and forensics unit. A cigarette was stuck firmly into his muzzle, the smoke pluming lazily up to the ceiling as he opened the door to the forensics lab and stepped inside, trench coat flapping a bit as he turned and slammed the door behind him a bit more loudly than was probably necessary. He leaned up against it and all but chewed grumpily on his cigarette, his tongue rolling it back and forth above his jaw as he stared at the body-bag on the examination table in front of him with a look of pure venomous hatred.

Sitting nearby at his workstation, such as it was, was senior forensics analyst and coroner-certified caprine Arthur Lancaster. Given all the room the actual body bank, autopsy tables, and lab equipment took up, his computer and desk were wedged tightly into one of the corners. He was poring over some forensics files on the killer, his dour goat face thin and drawn with wrinkles and his thick spectacles perched firmly over his nose as he tugged restlessly at the bit of chin fuzz on his face. His lab coat, however, was spotless as always, and his burgundy shirt and tan khakis were as unwrinkled and unruffled as he was. Very little rattled Arthur's cage, and although he was just as uncomfortable with having the deceased guest of dishonor in his presence, he still barely flicked an eyelash as the panther came into the room, wincing only at the sound of the door slamming. He stopped moving for a moment, somberly staring at the computer screen in front of him, then took a drink from the coffee mug near his left hand as he gave the cat a moment to calm down.

"Them things'll kill you, you know," Arthur finally murmured, barely looking up at his longtime friend. "And besides, this is a morgue. Put that damn thing out, Mark, you know it's not allowed in here."

The panther turned his glare onto the goat, but he plucked the cigarette from his muzzle and promptly ground it out in a nearby ashtray. "I'm sorry, okay?" he snapped. "I'm having an off night, tonight. Everybody is."

"Yes, they are," Lancaster murmured, adjusting his glasses with his fingers as he looked up from the files. "Jesus, Mark, simmer down. You're even more on edge than everyone else. Can I get you some tea, or maybe some bottled water? Might calm down some of those caffeine jitters."

The panther sighed, inhaling and exhaling slowly as he shook his head. "I better pass—but thanks, Artie. I drink anything else tonight, and it better have alcohol in it."

The goat grinned a bit, for a moment. "I know that feeling," he remarked. Then his smile faded as he looked over at the cat, curiously. "Why the hell is Kerston sticking you with the final write-up, if you don't mind my asking? He got it in for you all of a sudden, or what?"

"Yes," Halstead snarled softly, ears laying flat for a moment as his clenched eyes and furrowed brows regarded the goat angrily. "He knows I want that goddamn promotion, and he knows that Jenkins likes me and that I'm a shoo-in for it—so he's making me suffer a little, in the meantime." The panther rubbed his forehead wearily and muttered, "I haven't slept since 4AM yesterday morning, and I've got enough caffeine in me to kill a herd of buffalo—but I can deal with all that a million times better than knowing that I'll have to lie about this." He looked back at the body bag, still seething quietly. "I hate lying, Artie. I know it comes with the territory, sometimes, but it still drives me fuckin' crazy."

"I know," the goat said, nodding sternly. "That's what makes you so good at what you do. You're obsessed with the truth, and you dig at it till you see it. And if it'll make you feel any better?" The goat took off his glasses and wiped them carefully with a ultra-fine fiber cloth from his lab coat pocket, then held them up to the light to check for any spots he missed as he squinted a little and murmured to the cat, "I've been with this station and in this department for going on eleven years, now—and in all that time, I've never heard of a case that sounded this fucked-up. Never," he frowned, putting his glasses back on to stare morosely at the panther.

Halstead looked mildly surprised. "Seriously? Damn, coming from you, that's saying something, all right," he admitted.

"Well, good God, you read the file, didn't you?" Lancaster demanded, throwing his hands up and out to his sides for a moment in emphasis. "I didn't read the field report, but I read the background info. If I hadn't known any better, I'd say that most of it must've come from a frigging tabloid paper."

"Screw the background file, did you see what was on that camera?" Halstead gaped, a look of pure disgust on his features as he shuddered bodily. "The little girl couldn't have been older than ten, Art.

Ten! If it wasn't for the fact that I've only had caffeine in my stomach for the last twelve hours, I probably would've thrown up, and you know I don't do that easily."

Lancaster smirked a bit, brows furrowing just a little in mean-spirited mirth as he rumbled lowly, "Heard that Kerston did, though."

Halstead actually had to clap a hand over his mouth to keep from cracking up for a moment, nodding wildly and pointing at the goat before he managed to calm himself down enough to respond. "Oh, man, I was right there when he did it, too! It was frigging priceless. That was a distance spew if I ever saw one, not that I blame the guy for doing it for a second. He's got a kid that girl's age, I think, doesn't he?"

"Two of 'em," Lancaster nodded grimly, his face slipping back into stone mode again as he picked up the file folder on his desk and opened it, staring at it critically. "So, what really happened out in the field, are you allowed to tell me?" he asked inquisitively.

The panther inhaled slowly and deeply, then exhaled the same way, sighing a little. "Well... they found the body out in the woods near the high school, after some kid and his girlfriend found the fennec wandering towards the gymnasium, looking like hell. The fox kid kept talking about 'something in the woods,' and he had a death grip on the camera, which was in his hand—so one of the teachers chaperoning their dance checked it out, found the body, and called it in."

"So, the kid's gonna be okay, then," the goat rumbled, rubbing his chin whiskers thoughtfully. "Well, that's good. Was the creep trying to rape him, or something?" he asked, nodding towards the body bag on the table.

The panther shrugged. "Probably. The vulp was pretty disoriented, and he didn't remember much—probably because he's trying to block a lot of it out of his mind, and I don't blame him. He's more than likely gonna need a couple years of therapy, but he wasn't physically hurt." He licked his lips, his muzzle flaps suddenly feeling dry, as he gave his caprine friend a somber look. "But we don't need all of his story to piece the rest together, do we?"

Lancaster's face also looked grim, and he shook his head, flipping the file open to a dossier with a picture of a young snow leopard male on it. He tapped the picture with the tip of his pen and murmured,

"This the kid whose body they found out in that nature preserve, 'bout two and a half years ago?"

Halstead leaned over to look at the picture and the name below it, then nodded. "That's him. Poor kid," he murmured. "Had a pretty troubled past, from the sounds of it, but that's no way for a minor to go. So, you traced this kid's fur to the sample you found stuck just inside the perp's muzzle, eh?"

"Sure as hell did," the goat murmured, shivering a little bit in spite of himself. "Did all the tests m'self. Twice, even. They all came back with the same results—it was this kid's fur, and the DNA wasn't denigrated due to the time factor."

"But Artie, the snow cat's body is buried," the panther insisted, giving the goat a look of frustration. "Doesn't Herran County still have the morgue records? They had the body in their possession for eight months while the investigation was still open, and then they buried him locally."

"That may be true, but let's face it, bud," Arthur said, narrowing his eyes at the panther a little. "We're talking about the body. You can't keep a spirit cooped up in a coffin that easily, especially if it's a vengeful one." The goat fidgeted a bit as he looked over at the body bag uncomfortably, then shifted his gaze back to the feline, lowering his voice. "Face it, Mark. If you died as horribly as this youngster did," he rumbled, tapping the snow leopard's picture again, "... wouldn't you want to come back from the grave somehow and stalk your killer till you got him?"

"You bet your ass I would," the panther readily agreed. The two of them stared at the body bag again, and Halstead shook his head slowly. "I guess I should've known something was up when even the Feds didn't wanna mess with this."

"Yep," the goat sighed, getting to his feet with a low grunt as he pushed on his knees to do it. He rubbed his wrinkled hands, then gave the panther a reluctant look. "Listen, Mark, I don't wanna rush you if you're not ready, but the sooner we get this over with, the sooner we can be rid of the goddamn thing."

The panther nodded, but looked mildly surprised. "You mean to tell me that the follow-up has already been done?" he breathed. "Jesus, that was fast! No known relatives found to notify about his death?"

"The guy's record speaks for itself," Arthur shrugged, looking back at the cat grudgingly. "He was registered as a convicted child molester in two states, and the only relative of his that we were able to verify with by phone was his sister—and she's living under the witness relocation program under a different last name. She and her mother had to move away from their hometown because of the scandal, and her words to me, verbatim, were something along the lines of 'don't even waste taxpayer money on a grave for the bastard.'"

Halstead looked mildly stunned, then shook his head and stepped over next to the table. "In that case, you're right. Let's do this," he murmured, as he opened his copy of the wolf's file and poised his pen above the report form.

Lancaster nodded agreeably, then moved over to stand next to the detective. He unzipped the body bag slowly, and the thick smell of mildew wafted up to greet them both, making their noses wrinkle. The panther fanned the air in front of his nose, coughed once, then stood staring at the corpse in amazement. "Holy shit..." he murmured.

Robert's body jiggled and rolled a bit with any slight movement of the table, because the wolf was bloated nearly beyond recognition. His stomach, legs, lungs, and even his hands were thick and flabby with liquid, and his sightless eyes stared morbidly up at the yellowish service light overhead, the wolf's face frozen in a permanent scream of terror. The wolf's flesh seemed so distended in some places that the fur looked patchy and thin because it was stretched so much.

The panther again shook his head in stark amazement, and the goat opened his morgue file on the wolf, also scribbling some notes on the report form inside as he stared through his thick eyeglasses.

"Time of death?" Halstead asked the goat.

"From the field report, and judging from when the body was found—estimated to be about 09:22," Lancaster said. "Cause of death?"

"Drowning," Halstead muttered, scowling hard as he bore down heavily on his pen, writing. "We believe that the perpetrator chased his potential victim into the woods to rape him, and then fell into the stream in such a manner that his leg got lodged under a rock, causing water to spray up into his face. No one was available to help free him, and he couldn't get his foot free before the water got the better of him." The cat groaned, then pressed a palm against his face, blinking rapidly as he rubbed it slowly down his features. "Shit, that sounds weak even to me—especially considering that the damn body was found more than two hundred feet away from the water."

"You're doing fine," Lancaster encouraged, one brow furrowing as he continued to write. "You're leaving out the incidental, unverified parts, right? Like the fennec kid moaning about spots, and some of that leopard fur found between his own teeth?"

The panther gritted his own teeth behind his flews, and nodded grimly. "The spirit needed a vessel, I guess. And may the kid rest in peace, finally." The two scribbled more notes, and the panther slapped his copy of the file shut with a satisfied snap. "I am now going home to curse my career path, and watch over my kid while he sleeps—because all this shit is gonna make me one clingy dad, for the next couple of weeks."

"Amen to that," the goat nodded. "Have a good one, and be careful on the way home. Oh, and say, could you call Ramos in here on your wa-..."

"Already on it," Halstead murmured. "The way everybody feels about this creep, he's probably the celebrity figure around here, right now. And you got the sister's blessing, so go for it." The panther looked back over his shoulder at the body, then shuddered as he headed out the door. "G'night, Artie."

The goat winked a goodnight to him, then zipped the body bag back up, sat back down at his workstation, and resumed his work on the computer, face expressionless. A few moments later, the door opened again, and a burly hispanic bulldog with thick upper arms and a stocky, rock-solid upper body came into the room, his own face naturally scowling. He peered over at the body bag with disgust, then looked hopefully at the aged goat, one brow perking as he jerked a thumb towards the bag on the table.

"Fries up?" he asked. "The coroner van's ready and waiting."

Lancaster looked at the dog over the rims of his glasses, managing to keep the satisfaction out of his voice as he rumbled lowly, "The fries, my good man... are most definitely up."

The bulldog's face broke into a lethal grin that might have made the devil scream. He clapped his hands together and rubbed his palms fiendishly.

"Solid," he rumbled, as he pulled a gurney into the room, parked it next to the exam table, slid the body bag over onto it with an unceremonious grunt, then pushed the gurney out of the room, muttering to himself, "Gonna go up like Jiffy-Pop, dis one is."

Lancaster grunted, nodding—but he could already feel the pall in the air beginning to lift as the body got wheeled out. Robert's soul had no doubt gotten a warm reception of the most unpleasant kind, and now his body was on its way to do the same.

Redemption

As we shiver, curled up in bed with a candle and a book, we sometimes forget that not only the wicked dead are restless. The none too wicked, who mourn their lives and deaths alike, have equal rights to haunting the living.

"The Thinking Place" paints a sweet, soft picture of tragedy that will not be allowed to remain so painful, but through love, compassion and a stern, firm lesson, sometimes even the most final of past mistakes may be healed.

The Thinking Place

Stormcatcher

It was a shame that Riley felt so desolate, because the surroundings were really quite pleasant. He'd stumbled across the remains of the cabin during a three-hour bike trip earlier in the summer, when he'd veered his bike off the main trail at the nearby Harwell Forest Reserve. The map of the area he'd been using showed a small lake nearby, which sounded like a good spot to break for lunch. What was left of the cabin walls were well back into the woods, jutting up from the ground like a giant skeleton of sorts made out of timber. The trees around the area had been cleared away and the small landing dock that went out over the lake for a few dozen yards or so was overgrown and rickety. It still managed to hold his weight well enough, though, and he'd stood at the end of it and looked out over the quiet, calm water, feeling the heat of the midday sun on his face and staring idly down at the reflection of all the trees that circled the lake in the water, their tops thick with green leaves.

Now it was fall, and most of those leaves were gone. The ones that remained were either just barely hanging on or had already drifted down to float on the water below, but the autumn colors were spectacular to behold. Rich yellows, oranges, and reds surrounded the lake, occasionally getting stirred up by the wind—but it wasn't cold enough yet for things to get uncomfortable. Nevertheless, Riley gathered his red and gold-colored letterman's jacket more closely to his body and shivered, his fingers gripping the hard plastic container in his right front pocket with a vengeance. He stared morosely down into the water and saw that there were so many leaves floating in it that he could no longer see his reflection. Halloween was coming, and soon that orange hue that he saw on so many of the trees around the lake would be coming from a similar glow of jack-o-lanterns as they led the way to the front doors of houses being frequented by trick-or-treaters. He looked slowly around the border of the lake, his big grey ears perked sharply as he listened for the sounds of anyone else out in the woods. But he heard nothing but the rustling of the wind in the leaves and the occasional caw of a crow. He considered sitting on the edge of the dock and dangling his feet off it.

Perhaps it was the fact that his hearing was so sharp (he was a wolf, after all) and the belief that not even his own parents knew where he was at the moment that made the greeting that came from directly behind him such a surprise.

"Heya!" the male voice said.

Riley yelped and whirled around, pale blue eyes wide and staring at the source of the voice. The interloper was a hyena that looked to be about Riley's age, and surprisingly enough, also wearing a letter jacket. The wolf recognized the white and green colors of rival high school Antego High almost immediately, that particular high school having quite a decent football team—and from the looks of this hyena, he was probably one of their fullbacks. Nicely muscled and broad of shoulder, he had a head full of thick black tophair that ruffled idly in the breeze, and his wild, bright grin was every bit worthy of his species.

"Where the hell did you come from?" Riley demanded, his surprise swiftly changing to indignant anger. "I didn't hear you walking up behind me. Have you been following me all this time?" he snarled, his muzzle and nose wrinkling a bit in fury, in spite of himself.

The hyena's ears perked sharply, and he also looked surprised—but his grin faded a bit, and he held both hands up defensively, backing off a step or two.

"Hey, whoa, dude, simmer! Sorry, I didn't mean to scare you. I was just walking through the woods and I thought I saw somebody hanging around out here, so I figured I'd investigate. And hey, a fellow jock, from the looks of things!" he rumbled, his smile easing back onto his features some more as he nodded his nose at Riley's jacket. "Rossdale, right? Man, you guys've given us hell for the champsionship at least three times out of the last five years. Ol' Coach Mathers must really put your team through hell to make you guys so tough, hunh?"

"Uh... yeah, he's... pretty much a hardass," Riley rumbled in reply, nodding just a little as he brushed a hand slowly down the back of his head and tried to get his pulse to relax somewhat. "So, you're on the team, too, then. Halfback? Fullback?" he questioned, one furry brow lifting inquisitively.

"Defensive tackle," the hyena verified, shrugging a bit and smirking modestly. "And second string, even, for what that's worth. But you're a quarterback, aren'tcha?" he grinned, nodding at Riley's form as he slid his hands into the pockets of his own jacket. "I can tell from the physique."

Riley looked mildly stunned, shaking his head slowly. "Wide receiver," he corrected. He tried to keep his voice stern, but he was having trouble doing so. The hyena's grin was contagious, and the wolf found himself warming up to him, slowly—an odd thing, for jocks from different schools. He furrowed his brows at the hyena and cocked his head a bit, looking at him with puzzlement in his face. "I was just about to say, do we know each other? Played against each other at one time, maybe?"

The hyena shook his head. "I doubt it. I'm a senior, and you look just a little bit younger than me, am I right?"

Riley nodded. "Sophomore," he murmured.

Now the hyena's ears perked. "Seriously?" He whistled low, chuckling. "Damn, you're big for your age, guy, but that's a good thing." His tail wagged idly behind himself as he gave Riley the once-over again, then took a half-step forward and offered a burly black hand. "Oh, and I'm Derek, by the way. Derek Barnes."

"Riley Mason," the wolf responded, taking Derek's hand into his own and giving it a firm shake. "Nice to meet you, I guess."

"Likewise," the hyena smiled, his own grip tight and assured. "And whaddya mean 'you guess'? Hell, if anyone should be upset, it should be me. This is my property you're trespassing on, y'know!" he laughed, circling a finger in the air to indicate the whole area in general, and his wink and wide grin let the wolf know that he was only teasing.

Riley gave him a weird look. "Tresspassing? What're you talking about?" he snorted.

"My thinking place!" Derek responded, spreading his arms wide as he looked around the area, then back at Riley, tail wagging faster than ever. "Every guy needs a place to go that he can call his own—a place to kick back and mull things over, and stuff. A thinking place."

"Unh... hunh," Riley muttered, one brow perking higher as he turned sideways towards the lake, but kept his face and eyes trained firmly on the hyena. "Well, if this is your, uhh... 'thinking place', I guess I can leave. Wouldn't want to interrupt those mental gears grinding."

The hyena shook his head a little, tossing his head back and shaking out his dark locks of hair joyfully. "Naaah. That's the good thing about the best thinking places. They're always big enough to share—and check this place out. It's beautiful, hey? Look at those colors on the trees, and smell that air. Don'tcha love that softly rotted smell that you get from the lowest layer of leaves on the ground that've soaked up some wetness?" he asked.

Riley carefully tested the planks of the dock under his feet to see if they would hold his weight if he sat, and they seemed capable enough. He eased himself down onto the dock, sitting Indian-style, as he looked up at Derek with an expression that was slightly puzzled and quietly bemused.

"Yeah, it's a pretty neat smell. It always tells me that autumn is here for certain," the wolf rumbled. He leaned back onto his palms, then again cocked his head a bit at Derek. "Has anyone ever told you that for a jock, you have quite a bit of the romantic in you?"

Derek grinned widely, obviously taking the compliment as it stood as his tail wagged briskly. "Oh, and you don't?" he smirked. "You'd have to be one, yourself, to even have noticed, and that's a good thing—a cool thing," he murmured, as he stepped over to the end of the dock and sat down near the right corner, facing Riley. The two burly young males stared thoughtfully at each other for a moment, then Derek assumed a sitting pose that was almost meditational, closing his eyes as he rested his palms down on his thighs, savoring the cool breeze coming off the lake that ruffled his tophair.

Riley gazed at him placidly, his eyes lidding a bit as he also enjoyed the feel and scent of the wind. He pulled his knees up and rested his forearms on them, and his chin on his arms when Derek stirred a bit, then rumbled to him without opening his eyes, "Maybe we're just special, ya think? We're not like other guys we know."

The hyena opened his eyes slowly, then turned to face Riley with a look that was surprisingly somber. "Maybe that's why you came here, today, hmm? Maybe you came here to think about why you're special, and why you're different."

The wolf looked surprised, but then a bit guarded as his ears lowered a bit, a trace of his initial suspicion edging back onto his features. He shook his head resolutely and murmured to Derek with a frown, "I'm not special. Not at all. I'm no better than anyone else." He gritted his teeth under his muzzle flaps in a way that the hyena couldn't see, and he got up slowly, dusting off the seat of his jeans. "Look, maybe I better let you go. You may be right, I could use a 'thinking place' of my own—but maybe today wouldn't be the best day to share something like that. It was nice meeting you, though." He turned to go, but didn't take three steps before Derek called after him.

"You came here for a reason," he said, his voice sounding bold and clear. "Don't tell me you didn't. This was a good forty-minute ride or so for you on your bike at the least, and you wouldn't have gone through that kind of effort just for the exercise, pal."

Riley's head whipped around to face the other jock, this time not bothering to hide the irritation in his voice. "How the hell would you know that? Maybe I just liked the notion of taking a good, hard bike ride to a scenic place, is that so weird?"

Derek didn't answer, but his own face was starting to look annoyed with the wolf, and his gaze didn't waver from Riley's face.

The wolf turned to face Derek and walked over to him, leaning his face down to get a good look at him. "What the hell's your deal, anyway? You start off by scaring the bejeesus out of me, then you start talking all cryptic. Why are you here, huh?"

"I'll tell you, if you wanna know. I'll tell you exactly, but first—" He licked his chops off slowly, then narrowed his eyes as he growled softly up at Riley's own agitated face and said, "...you gotta tell me what you have in your pocket." He nodded his head and pointed a fingerclaw directly at the pocket of Riley's jacket that held the bottle of pills.

Riley's head jerked back, surprised. The hyena had nailed him, and there was no way that he could possibly have known what the wolf was concealing in his jacket. His expression went from one of anger to one of distinct unease, and he began to back away from Derek steadily, the hackles on the back of his neckruff rising firmly.

"Fuck you," he snarled softly, hoping that the fear in his mind wasn't evident in his voice. "Just... just fuck off, you hear me?" After he'd backed a couple of paces away, he turned and ran towards the remains of the cabin and his bike, his booted feet thumping hard on the dock and the wolf didn't care if he accidentally plunged through any of the weak boards.

Derek was up and after him in a flash, though, and the panicked wolf could hear him tromping up the dock right behind him, catching up almost effortlessly. "I can't, Riley," he snarled, his voice sounding almost desperate as he pursued the wolf haplessly. "You're the one chance I have, and I'm not gonna screw it up!"

Riley tore around the corner of the cabin's remains, trying to make it to his bike before Derek caught up with him—but the thick carpet of leaves on the ground all around the dilapidated shack made a quick getaway harder, and he didn't stand a chance against Derek's experienced football tackling moves. He heard the hyena lunge for him even before he saw his bicycle, and strong fingers jerked down on his thighs with all the hyena's weight as the two males went sprawling onto the ground. Riley struggled fiercely, managing to get back onto his feet, but Derek lowered his right shoulder and slammed him solidly from behind, causing the wolf's back to arch forward and his arms to pinwheel a bit as he smacked full-on into a tree that was a few paces in front of him. Dazed, he nearly fell again, and he tried to dodge around the tree but didn't have time to recover before the hyena's strong arms spun him around and pinned him against the tree, Derek's weight hard against him and his grip like a vise around Riley's forearms.

"Let me go, you bastard!" Riley yelled, his teeth flashing as he tried to bite at Derek's neck. "Leave me alone, damn you!"

Derek pulled his head back and butted his forehead soundly and smartly against Riley's, and the wolf literally saw stars in front of his closed eyes for a split second as his struggles ceased and a groan of pain spat from his lips.

"Owww! Jesus, you fucking psycho, what the hell did you do that, for?" Riley demanded, trying to bring a hand up to rub his sore forehead. Derek wouldn't let him, keeping the wolf's arms fastened firmly by his sides.

"Because I need you to shut up and listen to me, that's why. If you hadn't tried to get away, I wouldn't have had to rough you up, you stooge," Derek snapped. "I need your help, and I think that I just might be able to help you."

"You need my help?" Riley repeated, his eyes opening a crack as he gave the hyena an incredulous look. "You got a mighty suckful way of trying to win folks over to your side, then, I'll tell you tha—" He paused in his words abruptly when he saw Derek's face. "You're bleeding," he rumbled, staring at the other jock's forehead. "That's what you get for headbutting me like that, you jerk."

"What?" Derek said, giving the wolf a look of confusion. Sure enough, the hyena felt a warm trickle of blood running down from just under his hairline, edging around his muzzle and down towards his jaw. He crossed his eyes almost comically, then jerked one of Riley's arms up with his own so he could swipe the back of his hand against his face. A messy smear of red greeted his eyes when he pulled his hand away and looked at the back of it, and he frowned darkly at it. "Shit..." he murmured softly, his brows furrowing together.

Riley blinked at Derek's reaction, then jumped a little when twin trickles of blood began to drip from the hyena's nostrils. "Ick," he grunted, squinching his features up in distaste. "Dude, you must've bashed a few veins open, or something."

"It's not from the headbutt," Derek murmured, his head dropping down a moment as more blood seeped from his forehead and nose. Riley's ears perked sharply as he heard the sound of something crackling softly, and he looked around to see where it was coming from. It took him a moment or two to realize that it seemed to be coming from the back of Derek's head. There was a low splintering sound, then a gout of blood spurted from the back of Derek's skull. Riley couldn't see the hole where the blood came from, but the smell was unmistakable, and Derek's head seemed to be enveloped with the stench of it.

"Holy crap!" Riley cried, his eyes widening in horror as he watched this. "Derek, let my arms go, dammit, we need to call you an ambulance—you're losing blood like crazy!"

Derek shook his head resolutely, spatters of blood shaking in several directions as another thick trickle of crimson started to leak down the other side of his face. "There's no time for that," he insisted, his expression solemn as his blood continued to drench his fur. "Riley, listen to me. You can't save me, it's already too late—but I need you to find someone for me and tell him that I haven't forgotten him."

"Hunh? What are you talking about?" Riley asked, his features getting more and more alarmed as he tried to struggle again. But Derek's strength was greater than the wolf thought, and he didn't stand a chance against the hyena's larger frame. Tiny clumps of Derek's tophair were starting to fall out of his scalp now, and he saw that the hyena's cheekruffs and throat were starting to shrink inwards. Derek's eyes looked larger because the wolf realized that the flesh around them was starting to rot away, but it was as if the spot-shouldered jock was caught in the lens of a camera that filmed in fast forward, because the decomposition was happening at a rate that Riley could visibly see and hear. The wolf could taste the fear welling up in his body in the form of bile in his throat, mingling with the scent of blood and rot in a way that was starting to make his stomach queasy.

Derek also looked terrified, but not because of his bizarre rotting state. He coughed, hacking up a bit of gore in his throat, which he spat from his muzzle after turning his head to the side so it wouldn't land on Riley. At that moment, the wolf saw the hole in the back of Derek's skull where the blood had spurted from earlier, and the wound looked like it had been made violently. The wolf began to quiver in the Derek-thing's grip, Riley realizing all too late that whatever this thing in front of him was, it hadn't been a member of the living for quite some time.

"Wh... what do you want with me?" he whimpered softly, his face pleading for mercy to Derek as his ears splayed helplessly. His legs felt weak, and he felt that if he'd had any water in his system, he might well have voided it out of his bladder and soiled his denims with it. Derek shivered as a piece of skin and fur on the right side of his face came loose, hanging down over one eye as the gleam of his skull got exposed. He tried to wipe the piece of flesh out of his eye by rubbing the side of his face against his forearm, and he only succeeded in smearing a thick blotch of blood and grue against his jacket, the strip of flesh coming off against the material and plopping softly to the ground at his feet. The hyena's clothes were now starting to rot, too, his shirt becoming thinner and developing ragged tears even as it fell away to expose the hyena's emaciated frame beneath. The flesh was shriveling up slowly against Derek's ribcage as his fingers, their tips rupturing wetly against Riley's own jacket, began to scrape their bones against Riley's arms as he continued to be held dreadfully in place.

Derek's eyes rolled jarringly in their sockets as he tried to focus them on Riley, clearing his throat again as the rattle of phlegm and blood in his throat made itself more evident. "Crossgate C—Cemetery," he managed to choke, giving the wolf's arms a firm shaking. "Friday… three o'clock," he hacked. "That's… when he'll be there. Go to him. T-tell him I still luh… love him,"

"What are you t-talking about?" Riley gasped, the wolf shivering in fright as he felt those bony hands clutching his arms, still. Derek's teeth became more pronounced, or seemed to because the flesh around them was rotting away. No one can smile like a hyena, and apparently death was even more proof of that. "God, the smell," Riley gagged, his throat thick with nausea as he tried to turn his face away from the dying horror leering in his face. "Gonna be suh… sick,"

"Promise me," Derek choked again, his face—what was left of it—desperate as the hyena began to have some trouble standing. The ragged strips of denim around his legs hardly constituted jeans anymore, and the thick, strong muscles that had propelled the sturdy jock across the football field in times before were rapidly deteriorating into unsteady, wobbling, bony sticks. "P-please, Riley. I w-wasn't strong enough… too afraid of… being myself, and n-now, my… body's in the lake, gone. I can't r-rest until he knows…"

Riley's face was flushed and sweaty, lolling from side to side and not wanting to make eye contact with the thing that had him pinned to the tree. He might've made it through the incident without getting ill were it not for the sick, telltale splattering of Derek's intestines and other vital parts falling to the ground, bloody and shriveling away fast as they left behind a gaping rib cage and exposed spinal vertebrae.

The wolf turned his head to the side and vomited extravagantly, his breakfast and the energy drink and protein bar he'd consumed during his bike trip rushing up his throat and gushing from his muzzle, then onto the ground, adding yet another myriad of sickening smells to the ones already swimming around his head. Derek's eyes almost looked sympathetic, but Riley barely noticed, for by the time he looked back into the hyena's face, they had shrunk away, leaving two empty eye sockets that still seemed to stare balefully at the hapless wolf.

Riley emptied his stomach until he was dry-heaving, and the act left him so weak that even his fear seemed to diminish a bit, the lupine's head spinning as he prayed for this nightmare to be over. But even as his exhausted eyes opened reluctantly, the corpse's face was still there, hovering in front of his and blasting that awful, awful rotting smell into his nose.

"Guh... you're... a... good guy, Ril...ey," what was left of Derek quavered, just barely holding itself together. The sound was a dry, crackling croak, the hyena's voice box still just barely enough in existence to be able to form the words—and Riley could see the nerves and fleshy cords still connecting it with what was left of Derek's brain, although the corpse was clearly struggling harder with each passing moment to form the words. Oddly enough, the hyena's letter jacket remained intact, albeit caked with blood. "Don't... give in. S-.stay for those that love you. Pro... promise me you'll... t-tell him," it begged, shaking Riley's body rampantly.

The smells, the sensation of those bones clutching his arms, the dizziness in his own brain all worked Riley's fevered mind into a frenzy, and finally, he threw back his head and screamed as loudly as he could, "All right! All right, I'll tell him, whoever the hell 'he' is that you're talking about, just... just let me go!"

And just like that, Derek did. With a final choke, his skeletal remains took a stagger-step backward, nearly falling prone before his knee-bones buckled, and the jock's body seemed to collapse in on itself. Riley's ears expected to hear the clattering of the bones as they fell into a pile, but strangely enough, there was just the sound of the hyena's jacket dropping to the ground, sitting in a heap atop the leaves as the breeze swirled them around the garment.

Riley nearly fell over, himself, his stomach rolling and threatening to make him throw up again. He doubled over and clutched his midsection, his rump pressing back against the tree for support, and he breathed slowly and deeply until he could bring himself to straighten up and look around, cautiously.

The rotting smell and all traces of blood were gone. Only the taint of the wolf's vomit could be detected by his sharp nose, and were it not for the letter jacket of the deceased hyena sitting less than four feet away from him, he might have been able to convince himself that he'd imagined the whole thing.

The wolf stared at the jacket fearfully for what felt like half an hour, but it was actually only about six minutes before he could will his foot to edge forward and nudge at the jacket. It was real enough, bunching up at the touch of his boot, but the corpse of the jock did not suddenly spring back up into horrifying undead reanimation. There were no sounds except for the lapping of the water against the dock, and the occasional cry of birds and geese overhead.

At this point, Riley probably would've given up a winning lottery ticket for the opportunity to leave Derek's letter jacket lying where it was, but the idea of doing so and waking up that night to the corpse of the football player standing at the foot of his bed and pointing at him accusingly killed any such impulses he might have had instantaneously. He picked it up with thumb and forefinger, as gingerly as a cheerleader might pick up a wooden mousetrap with a dead rodent caught in it, and carried towards his bike, grimacing with disgust and wondering how the hell he'd be able to sneak it into his house without his parents noticing. Bloody garments tended to set parental units on edge, and this one was an even bigger exception than normal.

It was only when he'd picked his bike up off the ground and was rolling the jacket up to stick it into his backpack that he realized that there wasn't a spot of blood on it.

By the time that Friday had around, Riley's fears of his parents discovering the letter jacket of a deceased high-schooler hidden in his bedroom had been brushed aside in favor of the fear that whoever the person was that Derek's corpse had referred to would think that he was a pure lunatic for claiming to have spoken with the dead hyena. But at this point, backing out was out of the question, and he was eager to get Derek's jacket out of his possession. He had it in his backpack as he fetched it from his locker, then made a beeline for the cemetery as soon as the last bell at school had rang at the end of the day. He'd made up a lie to his mother about having to stay after school to help the coach move some sporting equipment and walked the eight blocks away from the school to the cemetery, looking warily all around before he slipped inside. Crossgate Cemetery was one of several smaller burial grounds in the area, and although he didn't know who to look for, he figured it had to be someone close to his and Derek's age. He walked down the central walkway that ran between the avenue of trees on both sides, the gravestones sitting in neat rows on either side of him. A small above-ground mausoleum on his left nearly obscured the only other living occupant of the grounds, and if Riley hadn't been careful, he might've breezed right past him.

The rabbit looked a bit less muscled than Riley was prepared for, but he looked to be within the right age range, and as the wolf came nearer, deliberately trying to keep his steps quiet, he could see Derek's name inscribed on the tombstone that the young male was facing. The lapine sat almost without moving, and if he heard Riley approach, he gave no indication of it. The wolf ultimately had to sling his backpack off his back and clear his throat softly to make the rabbit turn his way, and Riley felt his cheeks flush with embarrassment as he tried to get his words to come out in what he hoped was an unobtrusive manner.

"Excuse me," he said lowly. "I, uhh... I know that this is probably not a good time, but I really need to talk with you for a moment, if I could." The rabbit turned his head towards Riley and looked blankly at him, ears lowered and eyes looking a bit puffy, as though he'd been crying. Light brown and shortly-cut tophair lay between his long ears, and his eyes were a rather potent shade of green that seemed unusually sharp and acute, despite his obvious state of mourning. His facial features were as gentle as Riley's were chiseled, and the sheer loneliness radiating from his visage made the wolf feel quite sorry for him, indeed. "I take it, you knew Derek?" he murmured, nodding his head towards the tombstone.

The rabbit nodded once, his voice surprisingly clear and free of quavering or signs of distress. "We went to the same school and both played sports, yeah," he murmured. His face looked both mildly puzzled, and mildly annoyed as he asked, "What's this all about? Who are you?"

"My name's Riley Mason," the wolf offered, taking a step forward. "I, uhh... kind of knew Derek, too, but probably not as well as you did. But he had a message that he wanted me to deliver to you, and I promised him I would."

" 'He' ?" the rabbit asked, his brows furrowing together in consternation. " 'He', who? Listen, no offense, but if this is some kind of goofy joke or something, this really isn't the best time or place to pull it. I was having a moment of mourning, in case you didn't notice."

Riley nodded firmly, sighing in resignation as he lifted his palms up and outward in submission. "I did, and I promise, I won't take but a few moments of your time. Although I freely admit, once I tell you what I need to tell you, you'll probably think that I'm completely out of my gourd."

That caught the rabbit's interest, and although he kept his eyes narrowed a bit, he moved from his kneeling position to an Indian-style sitting position as he nodded to the space near him in indication for Riley to sit. "Not exactly the heartiest endorsement you could make for yourself, but hey—I know what it's like to have a need to get something off your chest, so go ahead and spill it."

The wolf looked grateful and nodded, leaning up against a tree that was next to Derek's grave, right next to the outer cemetery wall. "I'll stand, if you don't mind. I'm feeling awkward enough, as it is. Uhh... would it be too much to ask for your first name?"

The lapine rolled his eyes in annoyance, but it seemed to be intended for himself as he shook his head and rubbed one side of his face, looking tired. "Ahh. Geez, that'd probably help, wouldn't it? Sorry to have been so rude—I'm John, John Newberry," he said. He glanced over at Riley and noted the wolf's letter jacket. "You play ball?" he asked. "You and Derek knew each other from a previous game against each other, maybe."

Riley nodded down at his letter jacket as he slid his backpack off his shoulder and set it down on the ground next to his left foot. "I'm on the football team, yeah, but Derek was a senior, and I'm not. I kinda met him away from school grounds, and the circumstances were..."

The wolf noticed that John's features had shifted back into suspicious mode, only this time, even more keenly than before. The rabbit's green eyes almost glinted accusingly as they narrowed at him, and his ears lay back against his scalp as he said in a low, slow voice of uncertainty, "What do you mean by that?"

Riley facepalmed, then shook his head and held up a hand, palm out at John. "It's not what you think, I promise—although that ties in with what I need to talk to you about. Look, John," he sighed, sinking down onto his knees into a squatting position back against the tree, "Just so you know, anything you and I say to each other right now, I'll keep under my hat. I don't intend on letting anyone know what we talk about, but what I need to tell you ties in with your relationship with Derek. You guys were..." He cleared his throat softly, then looked around uncomfortably to make sure that there was no one else around before looking back into the rabbit's face with a serious expression, easing his head closer and almost whispering the words. "You guys were... 'close', right? As in, dating on the sly?"

John's hands balled up into firm fists by his sides, and even as he saw this, Riley rolled his eyes inwardly and cringed. Great, now he's pissed and on-guard again. I knew that this wasn't gonna be easy, he sighed to himself.

"Who told you that?" John snapped, pointing accusingly at Riley. "And what business is it of yours?" He paused for a moment, his eyes widening for a split-second before going back into an even more venomous glare than before as he said, "One of your bastard teammates put you up to this, didn't they?"

Riley's own features hardened, his brows furrowing together in anger as he began to lose patience with the rabbit. He decided that being subtle wasn't going to do, so he stooped down and unzipped his backpack, took out Derek's letter jacket, and tossed it over towards the lapine. It landed half onto John's lap, and he stared down at it, blinking.

"What the hell is this?" he demanded to the wolf.

"What's it look like?" Riley rumbled back. "Look at the name stitched into the pocket. Smell the material. Tell me whose scent you get."

John continued to look at him suspiciously, for a moment, but finally slowly moved to do as the wolf insisted. Riley heard the breath catch in the rabbit's throat when he saw Derek's name stitched where he said it would be, and when he slowly lifted the jacket to his face to take in the scent, he hesitated after the first whiff, then inhaled deeply again. He sat stock still for a few moments, and then the quivering began. It started with his ears, then spread over his entire frame until Riley could see it all over.

The lapine let out a muffled, choking sob into the jacket, his body beginning to rock back and forth from the waist up. His crying got a bit harder as Riley looked on, and the wolf felt his irritation give way to sympathy. He pondered sitting down next to John and putting an arm around him, but feared that it might be perceived the wrong way—and some things, he reasoned, needed a moment of solitude. He averted his eyes and stared out over the rest of the graveyard, hands in his pockets, as he patiently waited for John to get it out of his system.

It took John several minutes of sobbing before he was able to calm down, and even then, he continued to shiver and rock a little. At last, he lowered the jacket away from his face, then wiped the tears away from his eyes as he kept his head down, sniffling and shuddering as his nose ran. Riley tugged a clean handkerchief from his back pocket and handed it down to the rabbit.

"Here," he offered.

John nodded and took it, then dabbed at his eyes with it before blowing his nose into it to clear his nasal passages. He stared at it, then looked slowly over to Riley, face hesitant.

"Thanks," he said softly. "I, uhh… dunno if you want it back like this."

Riley shook his head absently, still looking away. "Keep it. It's no biggie, I got more at home."

John nodded, his eyes a bit puffy again, but his voice starting to sound a bit stronger. He stared back down at the jacket sadly, stroking it with his hand slowly. "It's his. I'd know his scent anywhere," he verified with a whisper. "Where did you find it?"

The wolf inhaled deeply and slowly, nervousness welling up within him again like an icicle sliding up his spine. "You'll think I'm insane if I tell you John. Seriously."

John closed his eyes and shook his head firmly, once. "At this point, I doubt it. And given that yes, he and I were more or less boyfriends—I think I have a right to know." He turned his face slightly to face Riley, then thumped the ground beside himself. "And for God's sake, sit down. I'm worn out from crying, and watching you stand is making me more tired."

Riley shrugged a shoulder, but nodded and sat down next to the rabbit, positioning his legs so that he was also sitting Indian-style. He licked his flews nervously, then rumbled, "I got that from what I believe was Derek's ghost. We met out in the woods near a lake that I found by accident after I got lost on a biking trip."

The lapine blinked once, and his ears slowly lifted until they were upright again. Riley's own ears splayed, and he waited for the lapine's laughter or scorn to come his way once more—but it didn't. John only nodded, still staring down at the jacket and picking idly at the lint on the collar of it for a few moments. Finally, he whispered, "How did he die?"

"He didn't tell me, exactly," Riley murmured, "but I've got a hunch or two." He shifted on the grass a bit, then rumbled slowly to the rabbit, "John, how long had Derek been missing before the authorities gave up on looking for him? I'm guessing that his folks opened some kind of investigation to find him, didn't they?"

John winced in recollection, and he nodded, staring sadly down at the jacket again as he cradled it in his arms. "About eight months. He and I had been... having some arguments about where our relationship was going, and he was starting to get moody and withdrawn. His folks were beginning to suspect that he was either on drugs, or having some kind of problems with his sexuality, and his father is pretty homophobic. Add to that the fact that a girl at our school claimed that he'd gotten her pregnant, and he was under a hell of a lot of stress."

Riley looked surprised, upon hearing about the possible pregnancy, and his muzzle dropped open a bit, in spite of himself. "Pregnant? Why on earth would she claim something like that?" He paused, then blurted immediately, "It wasn't true, was it?"

"No," John murmured, shaking his head. A trace of anger came into his voice as he scowled at Derek's gravestone. "It was a cop-out. The bitch was looking for someone to support her after high school. Someone she thought was hunky but dumb enough to believe her claims and willing to move in with her or at least get suckered into paying child support. It turned out to be another guy on his football team that was the father, but Derek's parents and I weren't sure, at first. It would've been the perfect cover to convince his asshole of a dad that he was actually straight."

The wolf inhaled sharply through his teeth, and he gave the rabbit a sympathetic look. "Holy shit!" he murmured quietly. "John, I'm sorry. That must have been an awful time for you all."

The rabbit nodded, and he seemed to age beyond his years for a moment from the fatigue and sadness on his face. "It was. Derek wasn't returning any of my phone calls, and he avoided me at school—and I couldn't get too forward in pursuing him without risking having rumors started at school about us that might've caused both our families problems."

"Wow," Riley murmured, shaking his head a little. He uncrossed his ankles and lifted his knees, resting his head forlornly on his hands as he propped his forearms up. "It's all coming together, now." He sighed again, gave John a pained sideways glance, then stared slowly back at Derek's tombstone as he rumbled softly, "John, I think Derek committed suicide."

John jerked bodily, and his face contorted in agony at the wolf's words. Riley winced a bit, as well, believing that the rabbit was about to go into another sobbing fit—but he didn't. He clenched his fists again, then hung his head low over the jacket, only a few solitary tears splashing onto the fake leather arms of it. "Oh, Derek..." he moaned softly. "Why didn't you talk to me?" he lamented.

Riley waited a few minutes to see if John would break down again, and when he didn't, the wolf reached over and rested a hand on the lapine's shoulder, giving it a light squeeze. "Hey, he had a lot on his shoulders. Too much, maybe. He was lonely and scared, and when you're our age, you think you can handle it all." He licked his muzzle again, his mouth feeling dry and his heart feeling a bit sick at the thought of the two males separated due to fear.

"One thing's for certain, though—he loved you very, very much. He told me to tell you that. And he'll never forget you, and..." Riley's own voice caught, and he had to clear it a bit before he could continue, his gaze falling into his lap as he stared uselessly at his hands. "And he's sorry that he left you this way."

"I loved him, too," John whispered softly, his voice breaking just a bit. "But at least now, I know the truth." He turned the jacket so that the name was facing up to him, and he stroked his fingers over the stitching. "I forgive you, Derek. You'll always be my football superstar," he murmured. He kissed Derek's name, then cuddled the jacket against his cheek, rocking it against him as though it were a baby. "Sleep, now."

Riley felt his throat tighten a bit, and he raised a finger to flick a tear out of the corner of his own eye. Take a good, long look, Mason. That could just as easily be you, sitting there feeling that way... Then a haunted look washed over his face as he eyed Derek's grave with a sudden, bone-chilling realization. But it was almost a sealed deal that you would've ended up like poor Derek.

The more Riley thought about it, the more he shivered, and after a few minutes, John's voice broke him out of his reverie.

"I... I don't really know what to do," he whimpered softly, his voice edging upward a little towards the end of the phrase. He looked at Riley as though begging for guidance. "Wh-... what should I tell his parents? You didn't actually see his body, did you? It... it must still be out there, somewhere."

Riley shook his head a bit. "He told me that it was in the lake—but for what it's worth, John, I think his soul is at peace, now. I always heard that ghosts tend to haunt places because they had unfinished business on earth, and his was to tell you that he loved you one last time." He paused, then inhaled slowly, exhaling as he continued to speak. "And his other piece of unfinished business was maybe to stop someone else from making the same mistake he did, by killing himself. He did that, too."

John glanced at him, looking puzzled. "He did?" he murmured. "But you were the last person his spirit talked t…"

Realization sank in suddenly, and John looked thunderstruck. "Oh, my God!" he gasped, reaching out to grasp Riley's arm firmly. "You… you were going to kill yourself, too, weren't you?"

Riley nodded grimly, his face looking both disgruntled and ashamed. "I was sure thinking about it," he admitted. "I'd stolen a bottle of my mother's sleeping pills, and I was gonna overdose on 'em. I thought that that would be the most painless way to go," he muttered, rolling his eyes in disgust at himself. Then he looked at John, his face still grim as he rumbled, "And he knew what I was gonna do. He knew I had the pills in my pocket without even seeing them."

"But… why?" John gaped, cocking his head at the wolf in disbelief. "You seem like such a nice guy! What's wrong?"

The wolf had to chuckle a little, smiling gently at the rabbit as he reached up to scratch at one of his ears self-consciously. "You know, that's exactly what Derek's ghost said? That I was a nice guy," he chuckled. "If it hadn't been for him making me promise to come back and find you, I might've been a dead nice guy."

"You didn't answer my question," John said, his face serious. "What's going on with you that's so bad it'd make you consider offing yourself?"

Riley looked down at his lap again, ashamed. "Because I'm gay, too, and I'm having trouble dealing with it. I'm afraid it's going to shake up my life, and make my family and friends hate me for it."

John looked surprised, but empathetic. He gave Riley's arm a light shake, squeezing it just a bit tighter. "For heaven's sake, Riley, I know how you feel—it's scary, and you feel like no one else will understand—but you can't let it destroy yourself," He licked his own lips, looking actually nervous. "Besides, how will you know unless you find out how they'll react? If it's any comfort, my folks were okay with it, when I came out to them. They weren't exactly thrilled, but they're learning to live with it," he admitted. "And your family and friends will, too, I know they will. And if they don't, I'll be your friend. It's really, really important to have a support network when you first come out, so you'll be around folks that'll…" He paused for a moment, then facepalmed, sighing. "Jeezus, listen to me. I sound like a support group pamphlet."

Riley actually laughed, and he risked reaching his arm around John's shoulder to give him a full-on snug. "That's okay. I get the sentiment that you're trying to convey, and I appreciate it." He shook his head a bit, then looked somber again. "Besides, I can't kill myself, now. I promised Derek that I wouldn't, and I don't want to let his spirit down."

"Damn right," John murmured, nodding firmly and shooting him a stern look. "I'll wait till his ghost is done roughing you up, and then I'll kick your ass around some, myself!" He puffed his chest out a little and tried to make himself look bigger, an act that make Riley laugh again. John's frame was slight, and he wasn't nearly as imposing as his words tried to make him out to be—but the wolf recognized and appreciated the effort.

"Anyway... I feel like a first-class asswipe for even thinking about it, now," Riley muttered, shaking his head ruefully again. "I feel so bad for Derek, you know?" he rumbled, looking back at John again. "I had no idea he was dealing with so much." He glanced down at Derek's jacket, then gave the rabbit an inquisitive look as his ears perked. "It's none of my business, I know—but if you don't mind my asking, how'd you two get together, in the first place?"

John shook his head a bit. "Hey, given what you did for us, if anyone has a right to know, it's you." He gave the jacket a sad but fond smile, stroking it again. "And it wasn't anything major, really. I'm on the track team at school, and my grades have always been pretty decent. Derek and I had seen each other in the hallway a couple times, and he knew that I was good in English and math—so he asked me to tutor him a bit after school." He shrugged a little, then smirked softly as he murmured, "You can probably figure it out, from there. It was just one of those things that shouldn't have happened, and it started off as just innocent experimenting. Jacking off to smut online together, talking to each other about the kind of sexual stuff we wanted to try... and before we knew it, we were doing it. It was awkward as hell, at first, but we didn't want to stop."

Riley smiled at him. "Yeah, I can kind of identify, even though I haven't really had my first full-on guy experience, yet. I'm just seeing the signs, I guess. Can't seem to get it up for my girlfriend, and I think she's losing interest in me, anyway… and I'm enjoying the view in the locker room after game time maybe a bit too much, know what I mean?" he chuckled.

"You think she's losing interest in you?" John gaped. "Is she nuts?"

"No," Riley said, shaking his head and smirking again. "But women are better at figuring out this kind of thing than guys are, and I think she suspects that maybe her guy is a bit too into nuts, of a different variety!" he snickered. "She's a great gal, and as much as it'd suck to see her go, she deserves a guy who'll make her feel good, physically." He sighed, then shrugged a bit as he hoisted himself up onto his feet, grunting softly. "She and I will have 'the talk,' and then I'll have to figure out if I wanna come out to my folks, as you put it, or whatever. But I got a lot to think about, in the next few days."

"Sounds like," John nodded. He looked up at the wolf. "You heading out, already?"

"Yeah," Riley said. "You could probably use a bit more solo time, after having a bomb like the one I laid on you dropped in your lap, and this whole thing has worn me out. I need to go home and crash hard." He patted John's shoulder firmly, and the rabbit surprised him by gripping the wolf's forearm warmly and thankfully.

"Are you going to be all right?" John asked, giving him a worried look as he turned to watch the wolf leave.

Riley looked back at him and nodded. "I'll be fine. Really. I promise I won't do anything drastic."

John nodded again, looking only slightly reassured. He watched the wolf take a few more steps, then called out to him again. "Riley?"

The wolf turned and faced him again. "What?"

"I just wanted to thank you," the rabbit said, wiggling the jacket lightly in his lap. "For everything. It was really kind of you, what you did for Derek and me, and… I was wondering—could we…" He cleared his throat softly, then gave the wolf a hopeful look. "Could we… maybe… hang out, sometime? Maybe shoot some hoops, or grab a pizza, or something?" He paused for a moment, then added, "It would really help me deal with all this better if… if I could talk with someone who knew who Derek really was, you know?"

Riley stared at John thoughtfully for a moment or two, the rabbit's face earnest and almost pleading. There was something in the way the lapine clutched Derek's jacket against himself that made it look like he was holding a security blanket, and the wolf couldn't have turned him down at that moment if he'd wanted to.

He turned to face the rabbit fully, and he nodded. "I'd like that," he rumbled. "I'd like that a lot."

Somewhere from the east, a soft breeze gently ruffled their head-fur, as though in approval.

Satisfaction

Sometimes the dead have neither hatred nor love for the living. Sometimes the pain of their demis is so deeply imprinted on their spirit that they know nothing but that tragedy, and can think of nothing to do but repeat it until the ends of the Earth.

In "From the Sea, the Ghosts" the dead care nothing for the living, one way or the other, and are all the more terrifying for it...

From the Sea, the Ghosts

Alex Vance

Around the campfire sat four foxes. The glow of the fire reddened the foxes' white snouts and the blue of the moon dimmed their red pelts. Three of them were what they called 'friends'; the fourth, named Tom, they mocked to make themselves feel better. Unfair, surely, but when you are too old to be a child but too young to be adult, all life is a game and the rules are what the strong decide and the weak agree to. So the three wore their ragged clothes and played their dreadful music and called each other 'friend', and when they went out as they had tonight they would visit Tom at his house, to lure him away from his parents and his studies with hollow promises of excitement.

The air carried the chafing sound of a limitless ocean and a million years of salt, sea air so thick it is tasted rather than smelled. The smells were of smoke and of pungent alcohol, neither of which made Tom comfortable and this made the other three laugh. In laughing, the three felt a brotherhood they could only feel when they had Tom there to exclude and Tom, for his part, bore it without rancor, because to be brought to a night-time beach-fire and teased was still better than to be left at home and ignored.

"Tonight," announced one of the other foxes, a male whom people called Clip, and he stood up, holding a hand above the crackling flames as if it was by him alone that the glowing embers were wrested from the charred logs and drawn upward. "Tonight the ghosts come out of the sea." His tone was one of authority, and the three foxes in their leather jackets were accustomed to mocking authority and snickered at the sound of it, even Clip as he spoke. Tom, who was accustomed to accepting authority, sat quietly on his side of the fire and looked up at Clip with such attention that he forgot to make himself small, as he usually did.

"Tonight," said one of the other foxes, who wore his sleeves rolled up even in a winter as cold as this and who wore a blue bandana around his head. He stood up as well, shoulder to shoulder with Clip and a match for height, and this fox was called Choke. "Two hundred years ago," said Choke and Tom's eyes locked on this new speaker, "a passenger-ship was sunk on its way around the Cape because the light-house was vandalized. The passengers were only a hundred yards from shore," said Choke gravely and drank from the green glass bottle he held loosely between two fingers, "but there were no lights to guide them ashore and they swam farther out to sea, and not one of them was seen again."

Tom was sitting on his knees, paying no attention to the sand that was creeping into his leather shoes and that was matting his green trousers, which his mother would no doubt berate him for. His triangular ears were pricked forward and his eyes wide and attentive, his breath taken away even by such a simple story, because the mere presence of a campfire lends all stories weight to those who are sensitive to it.

Clip, who was wicked, saw young Tom's rapt attention and like all cruel boys on the cusp of manhood leapt at the weakness. He yelled and clapped his hands and stamped his foot and the sand that flew up over the fire glowed red as if something angry and powerful were coming out of the ground and Tom fell back with a yelp, crawling backward with folded ears and whites around his eyes until he heard the laughter of the three over his panic and crawled back with his eyes on the ground like he always did, and he hoped they would continue the story.

The third fox, who had been silent and to whom Tom had been paying no attention, wore a chain-link necklace tight around his throat that leant a sense of danger to his otherwise slender appearance. He was called Trigger, and when Tom looked at him he saw with some alarm that Trigger now held a rifle. A long wooden box lay in the sand before his boots and he must have been assembling the rifle while Clip and Choke had mesmerized Tom with their story.

Tom whined at the sight of the rifle and drew back as if he could hide his head between his shoulders, but even if they'd been as broad as Clip's that would still have been a folly. Trigger grinned the grin of a fox who could have been in Tom's shoes, the butt of jokes and teasing, without so much as a proper moniker but his given name, but who was fortunate enough that there was a boy in class like Tom, who was smaller still, and more easily frightened.

"Tonight," said Trigger as he loaded a single bullet into the rifle, cocked the mechanism and tossed the heavy weapon to Clip. "We call the dead of the ship Clara Widow!" he yelled and a cheer went u among the three friends that Tom couldn't bring himself to share, feeling a lump in his throat and a coldness in his paws that had nothing to do with the stinging cold of the air or the heat of the fire, but more with Clip, who had put the long rifle's wooden stock to his shoulder and aimed it over Choke's head through the scope. Choke paid no heed to that, if he saw it at all, throwing his head back and drinking more of his rancid beer and howling his approval of this ritual.

"We light the fire," said Clip,

"And douse the light-house," said Choke,

"And call from the sea, the ghosts," said Trigger.

And Choke and Trigger as one man sat heavily down on either side of where Clip stood with his rifle, a cloud of thin sand blowing up beneath them as they plugged their fingers into their ears as Clip pulled the trigger and with the sound of a thunderclap in a rain-barrel the rifle jerked in Clip's arms and spat fire and smoke and light of the light-house, shining in the lonely darkness at the end of the Cape, suddenly turned from bright white to red as it cast its beam toward the beach, and from red to yellow as it turned away again, and finally when the light should have returned there was nothing but a sea of ink and four foxes around a fire.

It was quiet, then, save for the sound of the campfire arguing with the sea over which should be softer. A lone gull shrieked and quickly held its tongue as if it had been chastised by some monstrous librarian. Tom, at last, spoke. "Are they really going to come?" he asked, and Trigger smiled because the softness of Tom's words made his own voice seem more manly by comparison. Tom sat closer to the fire to look at the three foxes on the other side, from one to the other, ears alert and tail fluffed behind him. "The ghosts?"

The three other foxes looked seriously at Tom across the leaping flames, but one by one, their unfeeling laughter seeped through their plain expressions and Tom felt that pain in his stomach that he always felt just before he was belittled. Clip roared with laughter and threw the rifle across the flames and Tom, who was not a strong fox, was knocked backward by the force of it, getting sand in his thick jumper and in the collar of his canvas jacket that tickled his back. Choke howled his laughter as well, putting the bottle to his lips and spitting the beer back out in a spray as if to cause the flames to light the alcoholic mist, but of course, beer does not contain any alcohol and he did nothing but spit his foul beverage all over Tom's clothes. Trigger, who would not stay behind for fear of sharing Tom's lot in life, laughed as hard as he could and kicked sand across the fire as well and covered Tom head to foot.

But Trigger also covered the fire, and the fire had been weakened by neglect and Choke's beer and died when the sand suffocated it as if it were eager for the relief.

Curses that made Tom blush deep red in his ears were flung back and forth and so upset him that he didn't think to be frightened of the sudden darkness. Without the lighthouse and the fire there was no light but the moon, and as if to play a game with the young foxes, the moon quickly hid behind thick clouds that were in no hurry to pass.

The sound of the ocean had won and now that it had no competition it had no need for restraint. As the three mean foxes cursed and Tom tried to sit up the sound of the waves swelled louder as if the sea itself were swelling higher, gathering itself up for a charge onto the mainland.

There was a thundercrack and then lightning, which cased the three to cheer, but Tom, who was a clever fox, grew concerned that the lightning should have come after the thunder. The thunder rolled and glided in all directions, as thunder does, and Tom tried to sit up, fearfully clutching the rifle, and wanted to ask the other three foxes if they could leave now. He knew they would make fun of him and call him cowardly, but that they were afraid also and that they would quickly leave, and take him with them.

He was about to take a breath to speak when his ears, alert and tall as they were pricked, caught the sound of splashing, and the others caught it as well because they ceased their muted chatter at once. Tom spun around to look at the sea but there was no light to see by and the only reason he could tell the dark sea apart from the dark shore was the occasional glint of starlight on a rare, smooth wave.

Another splash caught his ear and now the other three were worried as well. Clip was urging his lighter to produce flame, but the lighter gave no more than sparks and the wood, burned and wetted and sanded and quickly cooled by the merciless frost on the wind would not be so easily convinced to light.

Then the sea went silent. Not merely quiet, but dead still as though the waves had hidden in fear and made no noise lest they be noticed. Clip dropped his lighter, and Choke and Trigger each grabbed one of the sleeves of his leather jacket and the three of them huddled together as they backed away from the fire. Tom couldn't understand why they would do this. Perhaps they were frightened of the rifle he held, he thought – but only a single round had been loaded in it, he had seen that himself, and that had been fired to vandalize the lighthouse. The moon sneaked out of her hiding-place and as she peeked down on the beach below she lit three terrified foxes' faces and slowly Tom turned around to look at what the three friends were seeing.

The ghosts moved with surprising speed. Wispy things they were, creatures of rags and smoke and fleeting glimpses made blue by the curious moon. They surged out from the sea by the dozens, shapeless beings sometimes and horribly recognizable, others, and swept noisily in a dizzying circle around the dead campfire and its four terrified foxes, three of them huddled together in cowardice, one left very alone and afraid.

The ghosts swirled, their speed and trails of blue light forming a wall that was plainly ephemeral, but to none of the foxes did the thought occur that they might simply run through the haze of ghosts. They spun at speed, like leaves in a small whirlwind that can happen on a street near a wall and the foxes drew ever closer, scrabbling on the sand and climbing onto the warm remains of the campfire as the circle of the ghosts grew tighter.

"Satisfaction," said the ghosts as one. Each voice was no more than a whisper, impossible to hear on its own but together they spoke in a tone that invoked dread. "Who was the rifleman?"

Tom heard the words, but they held no meaning to his fear-addled mind. He clutched the rifle like a child clutches its blanket, recognizing the thing not as a weapon but merely an object to be clutched for small comfort. His ears were folded and his eyes showed more whites even than when Clip had frightened him. And his heart beat with the drum that is fear, and the three others for all their bluster were no different.

But Clip, who was wicked even in the face of terror, heard the ghosts' words and with a yell that frightened even his friends he pointed his arm like a weapon across the charred firewood on which they sat, pointed at Tom. "He's the one! He shot the—"

"Liar!" called the ghosts and from the swirling circle a dozen shapes flew up high as if to reach the moon and then swooped down, onto Clip and through him and the circle of ghosts broke for a spell, offering a opening, a doorway to the black, black sea, through which the dozen blue shapes drew Clip. He kicked at his friends as he was taken and screamed for dear life, but the ghosts drew him along at the speed with which they had arrived and in the flash of a heartbeat he was swept to the horizon and disappeared from view. The ghosts closed their circle again.

The three remaining foxes all screamed t that and clutched one another, forgetting that two of them were 'friends' and the other was Tom and simply holding each other, because holding another person helps when you're frightened.

But four foxes remained, sitting on the firewood. Three of them were alive and the fourth was a ghost who looked very much like Clip, but for his clothes and some scars on his muzzle. Unlike the other ghosts he moved at normal speed and the matter that made him was therefore at rest, and easier to see. He wore simple clothes, a simple shirt and simple trousers that were clearly from a time when fashion was not yet a word people used.

"I was the rifleman, I shot the light in the light-house," said this ghost and the three living foxes' jaws gaped as they shook with terror, but before they could think to touch the ghost or ask a question, the others spoke again.

"Satisfaction," said the ghosts. "Who wrought the plan?"

Choke's trembling ceased and his body grew tense and more quickly even than Clip had done, he pointed his arm at Tom even as he clung to the other fox. "He did! It was his idea to come out here—"

"Liar!" called the ghosts and another dozen shapes flew from the circle and into and through the fox called Choke so fiercely that he was ripped from the grasp of Tom and Trigger and he too was swept through the swirling blue circle and out to sea, where his screams died in the forgetfulness and loneliness that only the vast ocean can engender.

But four foxes still sat on the dead campfire. Two of them were alive and terrified, and two were ghosts who did not look at each other. The second wore a blue bandana, as Choke had done, but since his substance was blue in the moonlight it might have been any color when the ghost was still alive. He also wore an ear-ring, which Choke had not done, and he spoke honestly, which Choke had not done either.

"I wrought the plan," said the ghost and hung his head, covering his face with his paws. "I plotted to bring the ship Clara Widow to ruin and profit from her fate."

"Satisfaction," said the ghosts, fewer now in number, as some of them had borne Clip and Choke away to the black sea, but enough remained to surround the campfire. "Who brought the weapon?"

Trigger looked at Tom, and the young foxes looked very much alike. It was true that one of them wore a leather jacket and the other was covered in sand and clutched a rifle, but they were nearly of a size and certainly shared their fear, and were alike in other aspects as well.

"It was me," said Trigger softly, looking at Tom, who was too frightened to understand what the look meant. "I brought..." But then Trigger turned, for a moment, away from Tom and saw the two ghosts looking at him curiously and he, too, was too frightened to understand what the look meant. "No!" he yelled in panic and fear, pushing Tom away from him and the fox ghosts both howled in disappointment. "It was him! He brought the gun, look, he's holding it in—"

"Liar!" called the ghosts and all the shapes circling the campfire swept into and through Trigger and drew the young fox, who did not scream, out to the deathly stillness of the sea.

Four foxes sat by the campfire. Three were what they called 'friends' and one was a living fox called Tom. The third ghost looked more like Tom even than Trigger had, but for the earring that the ghost wore and which Tom nor Trigger had worn.

"But they... they didn't sink the Clara Widow," said Tom, whose fear was such that it no longer clouded his reason. "They were just... they were playing a prank! They didn't kill you – I mean, they didn't kill them," said Tom and pointed to sea as he stood up and tossed the rifle away.

The ghosts simply looked at him.

"You can't take revenge on them, they don't deserve that!" said Tom and tears sprung in his eyes, because although Clip, Choke and Trigger had been the worst of friends, they had still been Tom's only friends. "It isn't fair," he croaked, sinking to his knees as the three ghosts stood up.

"Fair is for the living," said the ghost who looked like Clip. "Satisfaction is for the dead." The ghost who looked like Clip touched Tom on the shoulder and vanished with a sigh of peace.

"Now that those at sea have satisfaction," said the ghost who looked like Choke, "we can have rest." The ghost who looked like Choke nodded to Tom and vanished with a groan of relief.

"In time, there may be others who call the ghosts from the sea," said the ghost who looked like Trigger. "And then your friends may have peace as well." The ghost who looked like Trigger bent and kissed Tom on the cheek and vanished with a look of regret.

And Tom, whose clothes were wet with beer and whose fur was dusted with sand, who had a rifle in his paws and whose body shook with sobs that would neither break into crying nor leave him entirely, was left alone on the beach, left by his 'friends', by the ghosts and by the moon whose entertainment was now over, and he would remain there until the dawn broke to give him warmth and light and strength enough to make the long journey home and perhaps, when he was warmed through and fed and comforted, he would think about what had happened and make some peace with it.

Hunter and Prey

Far too rarely is the intimacy of the hunt exposed in fiction. The depth of passion that can be shared by the hunter and his pray, the height of intimacy.

In "Natural Selection" we see the hunt as it should be and as it is. Shrouded by a harsh clarity, a faint recognition of a thing called guilt like the ringing of a distant school bell.

From the preening of the claws, the selection of a mark, to finally the stalking, and then the toying before that final consumption, this story tells the ale of the consummate hunter, who brings an end to other's lives so that he, himself, may live.

Natural Selection

Whyte Yoté

The two ice cubes floating in my drink make arrogant little clicking sounds as they melt away, chilling the glass and diluting the gin at the same time. I regret not having something with which I can crush the ice, because the only way to have a proper martini is straight up and chilled, without obstructions that can ruin the piney taste of the liquor. I make a mental note to buy something for that, think about plucking the offending cubes from the martini glass, and opt instead to suck them out and crunch the life out of them before finishing the libation, silently bemoaning the downfall of classic drinking as it used to be.

Two more quick swigs send the last ounces of Bombay Sapphire down my throat, adding fire to what already burns in my gut... and in my head. I take the lime wedge from the edge of the glass and bite into it, hating its initial sourness but always enjoying the way it cleanses the palate after a particularly top-shelf drink... the only way I make them. Casting a glance out and up through the twenty-foot windows of my loft apartment, I see a skyline speckled with a large number of lit windows, and an infinitely larger number of stars. The western horizon seems to hang suspended in a kind of lit-from-behind glow, the likes of which will disappear in a matter of minutes.

I cherish this time of twilight. Some of my kind grow to dread its coming; the rest of us sit and wait in lip-licking anticipation, wondering how the hell we made it another month without going insane. Neither is the case for me... usually I use the time to sit and think, letting everything just be during that one time of the month I feel more myself than anytime else. The moon casts a pregnant soft glow through the windows, almost overridden by the combined lights of the city and my apartment. I lift my right hand from the white armrest of the leather sofa, watch its barely perceptible shadow move and know the light is real. The fine hairs on the back of my palm seem to lift from their pores as if drawn upward, one of those little things that only happen 'the night of'.

Sufficiently buzzed and energized, I stand and make my way to the bedroom, deftly setting the martini glass on the counter to await washing. My head feels heavy but extremely loose, akin to a bowling ball suspended by steel bearings. It has no effect on my senses, however; I can feel every strand of carpeting between my bare toes, the nearly nonexistent caress of silk on my skin, and I am acutely aware of my reflection in each doorknob as I pass. My senses are afire, they have been building steadily for two days, and I love it.

As I enter the bedroom I am taken aback momentarily by the assault on my nose. In the thirty minutes I have been drinking in the next room my sensitivity has more than doubled, and—stupid me—I forgot how much my bed still reeks of sex. The collective scents of at least seven different men linger in the air, and the bed itself glows with odor.

When you get close to the big night, scents cease being intangible and become more than abstractions... whether or not my mind is concocting them doesn't change the fact that there are bright pinkish blotches all over the innocently-made bed, remnants of spilled seed slowly blending into everything else. I smile, remembering my tryst two nights ago with a pair of slender college students. They left at sunrise, happily ignorant of how close they came to death. Pity... I wonder if they would have tasted as good as they fucked.

I hyperventilate on purpose as I pad to the bathroom, letting the smells and memories stir my latent arousal and further my intoxication. Lights over the mirror illuminate automatically upon my approach, and I take a look at the man... well, for now... before me. Despite my age, which would be considered too old for the nightclub circuit, I have no trouble fitting in with, or seducing, any number of younger men. For all the burdens put into my life by my curse/blessing, there are a few benefits as well. My face has a self-assured quality, smooth but ruddy skin slightly tanned but not so much as to interfere with my rare natural blond hair. Clear, smoky blue eyes are lined with the beginnings of crow's feet, giving the appearance of wisdom.

Transformation initially demands a lot of the body. If unprepared, it can kill the first time it is summoned. For those who learn to survive, shifting makes a stronger host: increased blood flow and oxygen capacity, flexible muscles and tendons, and (of course) reduced aging. It's like being in the mafia: if you can put up with doing a few despicable things, you are treated well and provided for. Me, I just happen to like paying the price. Call me what you will... no one ever suspects, and no one ever will. No one who wants to keep on living, at least.

The silk robe I wear falls to the floor in a weak, flat heap. I kick it out of the way and it slides along the hardwood, ready for the hamper. Returning to my reflection, I make quick work of polishing up for the night ahead. A quick shot of hairspray with a hand through my scalp and I am sufficiently coiffed. I find that carefully styled or over-gelled hair turns people off. Guys like a man who has clean hair through which they can run their fingers. It's a good get-to-know-you feature, and makes for great foreplay later on. Next comes a light layer of face lotion to moisturize the nagging dry skin on my nose, a little deodorant and cologne (my favorite brand, mesmerize—thank God my mother is an Avon lady), and a healthy dose of mouthwash to kill what the martini didn't.

I stand nude, my entire body shaved bald, for the monthly test run. It's something I find relaxes me on these nights; in some way it enforces the reality that I am truly in control of my body, although at times it would seem the contrary. I raise my right hand until it is in front of my face. The fingers flex, shaking minutely; the beginnings of clamminess appear between the ridges and whorls of skin.

A glance behind me reveals the full moon, now bleached and bright against the night sky. I can feel it, like daggers in my pores, and fight to control the tingling that, if left unchecked, will bypass my own willpower. That cannot happen, not this early, so I focus my mental energy on the hand before my eyes. I look from the palm to the back of the hand, reflected in the mirror. About a second later I feel the tingling drain from my other three limbs and my torso, gathering and building pressure in the forearm. It swells visibly with blood but the skin loses its healthy color, turning to an ashen grey. I hold my breath and let go a short burst of power, like a dam; immediately hundreds upon hundreds of beige-grey hairs sprout from everywhere, covering my arm to the elbow. My fingers shorten, the nails crawling upwards painlessly and curving over into black claws. Bones pop and shift; more little noises signal muscles reforming themselves into a new, more powerful structure.

I make a fist and close my eyes, feeling skin rustle over fur as I pour on the mental blockage again to stop the rest of me from surrendering. When my appendage once more feels normal I look through the slits of my eyelids. What I see satisfies me and I open the rest of the way. From the elbow on down my right arm is completely covered in fur, that same grey-beige color interspersed with lighter cream and also some black. The fingers are truncated and thick, ending in sharp points; I turn my arm and see the soft black pads on the palm and fingertips. I always enjoy looking at this little part of me while I am still human, for my world is usually clouded when I am more... shall I say, 'savage'?

From the hallway comes a soft chiming followed by ten tolls of the hour. I'll be late if I linger further; the best candidates will be just arriving if I time it right. It takes much less time and effort to reverse my transformed arm, and as soon as I am fur-free I walk to the bed, where earlier in the afternoon I carefully chose and laid out my wardrobe. First to go on is a pair of simple black silk boxer shorts... the kind that are especially easy to work a roving hand into and pull off quickly when needed. Next, over my slender but still defined torso I slip on a black mesh tank top, good enough for standing out on the dance floor with a punk quality that applies to a lot of Goth fags.

The rest is simple: a plain white wrinkled shirt left unbuttoned, tight black low-riding Levi's, and black patterned socks shod in shiny slim Allen Edmonds. Next come the watch, ring, wallet/keys/change, and the finishing touch: my brand-new deep burgundy collar. It is my pride and joy, my one link to the other side I can wear in public without bringing questions of bestiality and the like. I tell them a collar isn't as much about animals as it is about power. Tonight it will merely serve as a tertiary identifier and as bait. It's time to go fishing.

An old, creaky cargo elevator, the staple of expensive midtown apartments, lowers me three floors to the parking area underneath my building. My motorcycle, a custom Kawasaki with deep maroon paint, waits in its reserved space, patient and eager to put rubber to asphalt. I straddle the machine and turn the key, breathing life into it, hearing its restrained power and feeling the gentle throb up against my crotch. I don't wear a helmet for fear it will muss both my hair and my chances of a date. The clutch engages with a precise jerk and I weave my way out into the streets of the night.

Traffic is surprisingly light for a Saturday evening. I keep my speed below one hundred, a snail's pace compared with what I usually do. When I hit a jam, I take advantage of my narrow vehicle and pass slowly between lanes, always on the watch for big mirrors. I do not look at the moon... I don't need to look up when my body is practically screaming to be set free. For a fleeting second I fear I won't be able to keep control until time warrants it, but I disregard the thought immediately. Once free of the bottleneck, only seven minutes gets me off the freeway and into downtown, where I park in a secluded garage (I won't be picking the bike up until tomorrow morning).

As I exit the structure a breeze whips around me, carrying with it the odiferous signs of a big city. I mean, where else can you smell baby powder and dead dog in the same whiff? Not that anyone but me has detection of that caliber; not tonight. Instead of trying to ponder some deeper meaning, I begin to whistle a disjointed series of notes, filtering out most of the scents and concentrating on the near future.

I hear my destination well before I see it; even without super-sensitive ears it's hard to miss the thumping beats of techno music from at least five blocks away. Clubs like La Vie aren't meant to be ignored. The hottest night spot in the metro area has that unique kind of power that draws in even the most skittish, with promises of being accepted and, if they're lucky, a partner for the night. These are the people I seek out in my monthly excursions. By the time I get in the door, half my mission has already been accomplished.

Turning a corner, I see it is a relatively light night: a line of fifty people or so extends from the front door down the sidewalk in my direction. Still whistling, I pass by the poor patrons who must wait for their turn to enter. I feel them staring at my back, hating me as I move up the ranks at a leisurely pace. Jimmy, a mammoth man and La Vie's official bouncer, turns from his duties and stares me square in the eyes. His shaved head and construction-worker body, clad in only black pants and a wife-beater, give off a radiant heat despite the temperate and slightly breezy night. He wears a scowl on his face, but we both know it's only to keep up appearances.

"Jimmy." I say evenly, curt but courteous. The bouncer nods, never having been given the benefit of my name. I make it a point not to give it out for obvious reasons. "You look bored."

"You kidding? Broken up two fights tonight already," says Jimmy with abounding neutrality. One would think he despises his job; in fact, he loves it and just doesn't see a need to express it. We've talked thoroughly on this subject. "Slow as hell though. Hey, dipshit!"

Jimmy turns away abruptly to drag an athletic-type back from the door through which he was sneaking. "You see that sign there?" He points to a corner of La Vie's entrance, where sits a sign clearly stating the club's capacity at no more than two hundred eighty-seven persons. After a certain point it is Jimmy's job to regulate capacity as well as maintain a friendly atmosphere. "As soon as someone comes out, you get in. Capisce?" The athletic-type, stuck between retaining his pride and obeying the rules, opts to keep his skin and nods. Jimmy lets him go and mutters something about trying to run a goddamn respectable business here.

A large drag queen, black with a gigantic blue beehive wig atop her head, bursts out of the door with a couple of friends. The three are visibly intoxicated, but all I care about is getting inside.

"May I?" I ask, and get the go-ahead from Jimmy. I can hear groans, curses and complaints from the entire line behind me at the special treatment. The athletic-type steps up and shouts, "Why the hell does he get in?" Uh-oh, stupid question.

Jimmy puffs out his chest in true bouncer fashion and is suddenly a foot taller than everyone else. Poking the athletic-type on his sternum, he says flatly, "Because he's special. End of story. Wait your turn like a good boy." At a loss for words, and knowing he doesn't hold a candle to Jimmy's authority, he backs down.

I am waved through; as I pass I brush my hand over Jimmy's crotch and linger there, squeezing. He stiffens, in more ways than one, and I'm pretty sure he's struggling against a blush as I enter the club. I am the only one Jimmy will let touch him; after all, he's totally straight. He pretty much lets me do whatever I want, most likely because he's the only one who's seen the real me and lived a day beyond. He prefers to keep his life, so he does me favors now and again. We both think of it as a fair deal. He also knows exactly what I am here for tonight, and his blind eye has made my life so much easier and more fun. Still would like to get him in bed, though.

Damn my blasted nose! As I walk in through the heavily tinted door I am nearly pummeled by the color and smell of the place. Yes, it is loud and active and packed full of people, but only one of them has the senses of a completely different species. It takes me off guard: the first thing to hit is the rank bitterness of used cigarette smoke, which burns my sinuses all the way down to the lungs. I pass through the throng of club-goers, not yet paying attention to their faces but instead trying to calm my overwhelmed brain. Alcohol, perspiration, seduction... it's all here, just like every other night. I also sense a fair amount of Ecstasy and meth, along with some other unfamiliar pharmaceuticals. Some people are out to have a good time, while others are out to take advantage. It disgusts me, but I think of my own sanguine task and chide myself for acting like I sit upon a pedestal.

Once given a few minutes to organize the scents, sounds and scenes of La Vie, my respiration regulates and I become one with the atmosphere. Now I can finally see the club as a normal person would... almost, except for the odor-auras which linger no matter how hard I try to filter them out. The club is arranged like a house: up front and center sits a huge circular bar that acts as the main hub for dancers and drinkers. At equidistant tangents of the circular room sit entrances to further rooms: a karaoke lounge, a leather/bear den and the heavy rave room, all of which house their own counters stocked with alcohol. The entire club is bathed in blacklight with sparse neon bars along the walls and ceiling; the only real lights are those above the bartenders... small weak halogens that don't interfere too much with the ambiance of the place.

Bodies pack every available inch of floor space. The unfortunate patrons to have gotten to the front of the drink-ordering line attempt to do so without being crushed. Music flows all around me, a fast and heavy electronic beat that bounces off every available surface and reverberates through what air isn't taken up by dancers. I let the music and crowd move me naturally to the bar, which happens with surprising speed. The jarring bodies are nothing, but so many different flavors of sweat are quickly making my head ache. I order another Sapphire martini, up with two olives, and slap a ten onto the bar. When the drink comes I take it, down it (noting mentally that it can't compare with my own mixing skills) and part company before the bartender can bring change. I don't need it.

The alcohol works within minutes, and the buzz which, up until now, was dying is back to full strength. It's time for me to go to work. I detest, at a basic level, coming here. But unfortunately, not only is it the best place to look for fresh meat, it's nice and crowded so there's little chance of anyone paying enough attention to my shopping trips once a month. There is only Jimmy, but I think he'll stay conveniently ignorant if he wants to keep a price off his head.

My stomach burns from its strong contents; I know my senses have been dulled a bit but it works to my advantage: I am numb enough to perceive reality with a heightened sensitivity but to not be distracted by that selfsame sensitivity. Not just anyone will do to satisfy my picky tastes; it takes a special kind of person to attract me. I need someone who is relatively isolated, sober enough to listen to me, and a bit of a sub. It varies from month to month, but someone usually fits the bill quite well. I've had little trouble since I started this necessary recreation, and I have no intention of having any tonight.

I walk nonchalantly through the building with an air of confidence, something one must do anyway if he or she is to be taken seriously in any respectable gay bar. I pass a few regulars who call out to me as if they know me (they're too intoxicated to care, really), and I indulge them by grinding for a few minutes. Feigning disinterest, I yawn and move quickly to the outer perimeters of the crowd. From room to room I blend in perfectly, all the while smiling to myself knowing none of these people are aware of a true predator in their midst.

The karaoke lounge is filled with punks and Goths and lesbians. After a cursory glance I write the whole depressing lot of them off.

Just looking at all that black sadness leaves a bad aftertaste in my mouth. I give the bear room a chance, even though I've never had any success with the older crowd. My hopes are shattered, however, when I see no one who looks to be under thirty years old in the entire room. That's not a problem in itself... I was hoping tonight to be able to stray from my normal routine, but the club is too segregated to make my life that much more interesting. Fucking gay drama, I think, but then again it's that same gay drama that provides such a crucial backdrop for my little hunting trips.

A sigh escapes my lips; I am visibly bored and a little irritated from that last shitty martini. The feeling doesn't last though, because when I enter the rave room I am faced with a bevy of fine young men. They all seem my type, they're all cute and frail-looking and having fun... but it's up to me who I want to pin down. Now's the time to use those keen senses of mine for their intended purpose.

I make my way onto the dance floor for a better view; there's no way I can shop around from a corner. When my feet hit the flashing tiles I let the beat enter and take over. Dancing comes naturally to me, thankfully, and soon I'm bumping and gyrating with the best of them. For the moment my ultimate goal is put into the back of my mind as I get wholly into the music. So much so, in fact, that I notice those surrounding me starting to back away and form a circle. The last thing I need is undue attention before I have to do my dirty work. I back off drastically and melt back into the crowd, now cognizant that I need to be focusing on more important things than dancing. Once I stop moving, a rain of suspended sweat drips down onto my face, evidencing my exertion. It is transferred to a shirt sleeve.

This time I maintain a close watch on everyone, looking with my eyes at first but slowly letting my other senses in, one by one. First to come back are the odor-auras, but they do no good: everything is coated in varying shades of green, the color of hot humans. Slowly but surely more red creeps into the air as sexual tension escalates. In these terms, I'm looking for someone with very little green and a growing pink glow around them. How many times do you get the chance to go after a guy based on their aura? Yeah, not too often. Suits me just fine.

I sniff the air again, aware on some level that even in here the moon has an effect on me. I can feel tingling around my stomach and groin, just waiting for permission to be released. It will still be a while yet, but I plan to expedite the process as best I can. I know what I need, and the smell is unmistakable. I just have to sift through hundreds of them before hitting paydirt.

Self-confidence here, haughtiness and posing there, a few smatterings of advanced intoxication... then something drifts my way. It caresses my nose just slightly, and I have a fleeting vision of the old cartoons where the character is lured to food by wispy smoke-hands. I close my eyes and let the smell linger, almost flehmening it to determine its origin. Actually, it is coming from directly to my right, so close I wonder how I could have missed such a delicious aroma. Trying to keep the beat, and my incognito status, I angle my body and quickly zero in on what I know will be my target tonight.

A young man sits in the corner; he is of average height and build, with average looks to match. Brown hair, and what are probably brown eyes. Slightly overweight, meaning ten pounds... not enough to matter much but enough for ostracism in this gay bar full of faggoty-ass thin 'bois' who are no more sincere than a manila envelope. His auras confirm what my nose has already told me: a little green all around from just being in the heat of this place, and the barest beginnings of pink hovering over the top of his head and around his groin. There is much sexual reluctance coming from his guarded posture—hands clasped around his drink, foot tapping off the beat, and just the smell of him—that I wonder if he's ever put his equipment to good use. I will be finding out eventually, I suppose.

I make my approach. I watch him as he watches the crowd, and I can almost feel what he is feeling. It sparks a bit of pity in my soul, having been there once myself, but that's another small price to pay. A young man in his early twenties, lonely for any kind of company, goes out to the bar hoping on the outside to dance and have a good time, hoping on the inside that someone will come up to him and start making conversation... suggestions... gestures. I intend to do all three.

The guy sees my movement in his periphery and casts a perfunctory glance my way. I know how good and tempting I look, like I'm seemingly out of his league, and his auras shift uncomfortably over his stationary body. He fears that the wrong move, no matter how small, will somehow scare me off and ruin his chances of anything happening, so much so that he dismisses me outright even before giving me a good once-over. But as I close the last ten feet between us, I crack a genuine smile and two things happen: first, his endorphin levels rise sharply, as do the patches of pink; and second, I get a whiff of his anxiety as it hits the roof. Unfazed, I sit down on the stool next to him, making it seem like I haven't noticed how much of a novice he is. It will be a breeze to seduce him, but first I have to nip his discomfort in the bud.

"Having a good time?" I ask disarmingly, leaning in to be better heard but not making eye contact. He senses no aggression in me, and a good portion of dark orange distrust dissipates. My hands are folded on the table, my back slouched. I'm just one of the guys, you know?

After a length of time, during which my new friend searches for the perfect response, he says, "Good enough." I get to smell his breath for the first time and discover he's been nursing his only drink, now just a sweaty mess in a glass, all night long. Not that it's a problem for me; I prefer not to get a contact buzz when I dine out. Others like to season theirs with alcohol and drugs.

Heathens.

Now that the ice has been broken, albeit with less than ten words, I pretend to pay attention to the dance floor, giving my companion the impression that I was not purely interested in him, but just making polite conversation. He is not expected to respond as if we were engaged in a tête-à-tête, but he feels better now that some attention has been paid to him. As I look everywhere but directly at him, I can still tell what's going on with his body. His muscles have slackened a bit, the nervous twitches and taps gone. He looks less dorky sitting next to me, and his secretive relief is evident. I can smell his sweat, just a light coating of it, an 'unscented' deodorant that is not doing its job and cologne reminiscent of cedar. He smells male, and the combination unnerves even my professional attitude. Now it's my turn to twitch.

Minutes pass while I feel the moon boring into my very being, warming me from the inside out, and it's all I can do to resist taking the young man next to me and ravaging him where he sits.

Trying to maintain a steady voice, I lean over and say loudly, "You come here often?" I make basic comments like this on purpose. I want neither to treat him like a child nor seem haughty, elsewise he might choose to cut off the rapport altogether. When that happens I have no choice but to stalk, and I hate eating without having thoroughly tenderized my meal. Leaves a heaviness in the stomach.

"Actually... no," he replies immediately in a confident tone, indicating I'm doing my job well. He even leans back and makes an effort to be heard. "I don't like to drink, so I don't do this often."

I decide to test the waters. "Why is someone as cute as you sitting alone at a table instead of being out on the floor, grinding against your boyfriend?" A nice double-compliment, assuming his looks and relationship status. My new friend blushes and looks away momentarily.

"I'm single." It doesn't sound dejected or bitter, just rehearsed... like he's used to saying it and resigned to saying it forever. Either he's come off a bad relationship or he's a virgin. I do hope it's the latter.

"Couldn't tell," I say smoothly, and extend my hand. I give him a name, something always contrived on the spot to protect my anonymity should I ever fuck up in any way.

"Devon," he says. No last name, so he doesn't have that much trust in me yet. Par for the course, at least. He relaxes into the table, now making eye contact with me. That's a good sign of either friendliness or flirtiness, but right now there is no telling which. "You probably come here all the time."

"Only when I'm bored... or horny," I admit truthfully, pushing the conversation a little more aggressively in my direction. Devon doesn't respond... not vocally. I smell it rising: the first signs of arousal at my words, the stirring in his pants that, until now, was long forgotten in favor of trying to impress me. Now he realizes two things: not only does he have a shot at getting some tonight, I just semi-advertised my similar intentions. His scent intensifies as fresh, nervous perspiration boils to his body's surface. I practically bathe in it.

As much as it pains me, I must control myself. If I come off desperate, I may not seem dominant to him... it is critical that I am the alpha in this short-lived relationship. "Single or not, why aren't you dancing anyway? Don't know how, or just don't like to?"

"I don't care for trance and stuff. That must sound stupid, me coming here and not liking the music, but it's the only bar where I feel a little comfortable." For the first time I let my guard down and look directly at him, noticing that his eyes are, in fact, deep cobalt blue despite his brown hair. They are intelligent, soft and dilated, a side effect of his arousal. Gods, I must have this man!

"What kinds of music do you like, then?" I ask, thinking to myself You bastard, why are you stringing him along like this? At the same time I pray he won't mention country music. I may have to hurt him if he says he likes country.

Devon smiles genuinely, and I know I've hit some common ground. "Oh, I love to swing. It's practically the only thing I can do well. Just give me a beat and I can swing to it." Now I know one of the main reasons he looked and felt so out-of-place at La Vie: it's hard enough to be gay, but to not like the 'basic' things like trance and clubs? He is stuck in between the worlds of straight and gay, an outcast among outcasts. In this world, it's all about fitting in. Devon is handsome, smart and interesting, but not cliquey enough to be liked by any majority. Suddenly I feel very sorry for him. Then my stomach rumbles and puts me back on track.

"Really? You know, I've been known to cut a rug or two in my time."

"In your time?"

"Let's just say I'm older than you and leave it at that," I wink cryptically,

furthering my seduction just a little. His expression says he doesn't believe me, but I wouldn't be able to give him an honest answer if I tried. The conversation has become more personal and amiable than I'm used to, and I have to hold my higher ground or else Devon might take it into his mind to jump my bones before I do that to him. Given what I've learned thus far, it is a possibility. Time to put on the leash, so to speak.

"Why don't we go out there and you show me what you can do? You look like you've waited long enough," I suggest, gesturing to the dance floor with my head.

Giving me an odd look, Devon replies, "Here? Dance to what?"

"You said any beat, didn't you? As long as there's a time signature you can dance to it, right? Or were you just blowing smoke up my ass?" I rock back and cross my arms and legs, challenging him friendly.

"Oh, I can do it, alright. It'll just look weird doing it here."

"You're among friends, Devon!" I exclaim, opening my arms wide to encompass the whole room. "Who's going to care? I won't, I'll be dancing with you."

"You will?" he looks dumbfounded, not realizing the error of his question.

"Swing dancing takes two, dear," I whisper matter-of-factly, deftly placing a hand on his knee. I feel heat through the denim and less than a second passes before his pulse doubles. We share a moment of solitude in the middle of the din, and I watch, pleased with myself, as his body slowly turns pinker. I am half-erect as it is, and would welcome a distraction. "Come on, Devon," I say, rubbing up his leg a little, so innocently. "Show me what you got."

Devon responds by sliding off his chair (towards me, not away, in order to drag more of his lap under my unmoving hand) and taking me by the hand rather forwardly. I indulge his feelings of superiority and play the part of the follower. There is a hip-hop song blasting through the speakers, its simple meter and repetitive lyrics annoying but predictably easy to dance to when mixed into electronica. Devon looks at the ceiling for a moment and puts his body in sync before looking at me again with an eyebrow raised: you sure you wanna go through with this?

I smile and nod, giving him temporary free reign with me. The shy, introverted young man I greeted not ten minutes ago has turned into a regular dance machine. Seeing this as his one chance to impress the hell out of me and assure some overnight company, he forgets his fears and a cloud of red self-assurance (do I see a hint of arrogance in there?) envelops him, tight to his skin. After a few faltered steps between my feet, he pulls me close and takes my other hand, his lower half moving in a blur as we whip about the floor as one frenzied being.

A few clubgoers stop to watch our non-sequitur moves; some roll their eyes, yet all I can smell is envy... whenever I can manage to smell something other than Devon's mingled confidence and excitement. Taking my role seriously, I match him step for step but quickly realize that my partner is, in fact, more skilled than myself. Best to let him have fun now, because once we get into heavier things he will revert back into his former self... if my suspicions are correct.

I am pulled, turned, dipped, flipped and otherwise hurled around our little dancing space, and reciprocate as much as I am allowed. As we meet mid-turn, our groins touch momentarily and we both wince in pain as our similar arousals are discovered. Devon does it again on purpose, and we hold the pose until it turns into a grind, our concealed flesh rubbing clumsily together. Heat and passion are in his eyes, burning into mine, wanton lust fueled by raging hormones and a lucky break. I must step carefully, as the position of my legs directly affects the pressure on my cock, now rigid and very visible to anyone who cares to venture a glance in that direction.

A sudden blow to my sexual high, the music dies down and voices pick up the loss in noise. Devon brings me in for one final dip. When I come up again I feel a torrent of moisture fall to the floor from my dripping neck. We both breathe hard in the humid, stale atmosphere. I lean my taller frame over his and grip him in a sweaty bear-hug; my left hand moves of its own accord and clutches at the waistbands of his pants and briefs, a desperate move I can't help. I am becoming very hungry.

His soft, round, perfect ear is close to my mouth. "Want to go outside for a smoke?" I ask in a relatively calm manner.

"I don't smoke."

"Neither do I." There is a moment's pause, after which Devon seems completely satisfied with this strange exchange of words; he leads me—like a goddamn puppy, you weakling, I think—out of La Vie. Cold night air hits my upturned face, making me shiver violently and chilling my clothed member into submission once again. It's time to pull the trump card. If he doesn't accept now, I'll have to do something drastic, something sneaky... and the resulting attention is not something I relish dealing with at such a crucial moment.

Devon walks along the wall of the building for a few feet, giddily trailing his hand over its surface. An idiotic smile dominates his face when he leans against it, one leg bent up. How dare he act like this, like my equal, when I was the lone person to spare him a second glance tonight? Give 'em an inch and they'll take a fucking mile, right? It is high time I took his cocksure attitude and squelched it with all the force of stepping on a rotten piece of fruit. My game is nearly at an end, as is my patience.

Still playing the part of the seducer, I fawn over to him, hands in pockets, purposefully making a show of being visibly hesitant. "So, Devon," I purr, standing just enough inside his circle of privacy to make my intentions that much more apparent, "I'm getting bored of this shitty club." Actually, it's a very nice club, but I have a goal to attain. "Wanna do something else?"

"Like what?" His face has been concentrating on the pavement until now, and when he looks up at me his confidence, in mannerisms and in aura, has dwindled markedly. At once I know I've taken this a step beyond what he's accustomed to: the lone kid, who gets all worked up, only to part with the rest of the club-goers at closing time, faced with another night of jerking off to an LCD screen. His bewilderment makes him cute in the way one would find a confused puppy cute, and it instantly takes the edge off my dormant anger. Now that I have the upper hand, again, my job has practically been done for me.

"Oh, I don't know," I resume my low-level seduction by sliding up to him, straddling his legs and leaning oh-so-sluttily into his chest. I can practically smell his erection resurfacing, reminding him of a very basic need whose fulfillment is all but guaranteed at this point. "Why don't we have a nightcap over at your place?" My right hand seeks out the denim covering his thigh and finds its taut surface, vibrating nervously... it could be a shiver from the cold or from my touch, but it most likely is the latter.

Finally I can see his eyes, half-shadowed by the streetlamp above and thirty feet away from us. They dart as if trapped open in R.E.M. sleep. A wolfish (huh, fancy that) grin begins to part my lips; the moon's ivory glow seems to heat my back, trying to draw fur from flesh. I fight to keep my expression even as I quell the natural instinct with force. Damn, it's especially tough tonight! A raw, feral need crawls just under my skin, and it's all I can do to keep from scratching at the phantom feelings.

Subtlety no longer has a place here. In one swift move, I draw my right hand teasingly up his side, successfully diverting his attention while I bend my left arm in front of me. He is so caught up in the light touch on one part of his body that he never notices as I close the gap between us, effectively trapping my palm against his groin. The moment is upon me: my face meets his and travels slightly past it so I can hear the sharp intake of air, the halting gasp, as I cup his balls. As I suspected, the already tumescent flesh rapidly fills under my touch. My new 'friend' has become the luckiest man in the world.

Devon wastes no time grinding up against my hand, and I respond in kind by rolling his penis around between two fingers, knowing his undergarments are helping my stimulation of his body. Finding my mouth conveniently close to an earlobe, I taste it fleetingly with just the very tip of my tongue. Its outer edge is covered in a very light fuzz, but I can feel every single strand. His skin, which reeks of testosterone, is salty to the point of excess. Hopefully it will have lessened by the time I get to my meal.

"Ni... nightcap, yeah, sure, okay," stammers Devon. Interestingly enough, he has not looked around to see if our actions have been spotted. It seems his earlier self-consciousness has almost evaporated away. Good... it means I won't have to worry about seducing him further; I just have to get him home and into bed. Suddenly his face has all the seriousness of a judge as he considers something. His voice is husky, breathless: "My, um, place is a mess. Maybe we should go to yours?" The statement turns to a question with the slight rise of tone.

Now, this is something different. Taking a man home to have casual sex on your own turf is usually something you would prefer. Why does he want to come with me? Is it the thrill of foreign territory? Or is he just too distracted by my ever-present hand? Either way, I can't let him see where I live... in case he were to escape somehow. I smile inwardly at my mind's slow regression into predator-mode.

I pull away from him, still making sure to stand with some part of our bodies touching. Dragging an overdramatic hiss of air through my teeth, I bluff, "Mmm, I would, but I'm fresh outta condoms." There is no reaction from Devon, either way, to this bold and stark statement of intent.

To my luck, he takes the story as truth. There is a moment, however, when he does what nearly every male will when faced with such a decision. I watch it glint behind his eyes: I am so horny right now, I don't think I need a condom... just as long as I get to empty my balls. Of course, there are the pursuing thoughts of hygiene, diseases, and worse, all of which my acute perception catches. Thankfully, he comes to his senses and decides the risk is too great.

"I have some." Considering how many directions we could have gone from that one little predicament, I got off fairly easily. The bit about the condoms is purely for show, of course... they will be little to no help when we finally get down to business.

My hands find his crotch and chest again, rubbing both places in slow, general circles. "Good boy. You have a car?" Devon nods and points, having already gotten used to my attentions. People are too quick to adjust nowadays. Or maybe, Devon just needs a little unexpected twist to his evening.

Managing to pull himself from my pleasurable grasp, Devon takes my hand and leads me (once more) across the street to a quarter-block of gravel that serves as an impromptu parking lot on busy nights here in downtown. He fumbles in his pocket for a few seconds, and we hear a double-beep from four cars down even before we see the corresponding set of keys. I roll my eyes and he smiles at me... this time it is unnerving. I don't like the look of that smile one bit. It's probably just the weak lighting.

As we approach, and enter, his vehicle (a mid-nineties Buick something-or-other, blech!), I try to keep Devon's mind occupied with idle chatter so he doesn't fall off the road and kill us both. Lunar energy swells within me as I ask him stupid questions and he answers. Normally at this point, I would nod and make like I was a compassionate, caring person who really wanted to know more about his personal life. Sometimes I do, honestly, and regret I have to put an end to such people, with their families and friends and nice, comfy jobs. But my needs supersede theirs on nights like these. Tonight... well, I just don't give a shit.

"Do you come here to the bars often?" I ask stalely, purposefully keeping my hands off him as another mild form of a tease. At once I remember that as the first question I asked him, and feel stupid for being redundant. He doesn't seem to mind... either that, or he's hiding himself better than I can see.

"Like I said before, there aren't many times when I feel like going out." We turn onto the downtown expressway and soon are traveling at a healthy sixty-eight miles per hour. I want to open the window and air out my face, but that silly and exposing act is out of the question. Patience for my human body is dwindling. Having nothing better to do at the moment, I continue the conversation. Anything to pass the time.

"What are you into?"

"Oh, books, cars, waterskiing..."

"No, not that. Leather, bears, bondage... animals?" I say this last one with added emphasis, making fun of myself... maybe trying to unnerve him on purpose.

Devon recoils against his side of the car but manages to keep it on a straight course. The city flies by beneath us, the skyline diminishing as we move our way into the suburbs. "Why in the hell would you ask me a question like that?" His tone is resentful, almost hurt. I wonder if he took offense to the whole thing, or just that little bit at the end. At least he didn't kick me out of the car.

"I'm just making conversation. No need to bite my head off," I reply sternly but affectionately, and back up my words by clutching his thigh across the center console. He remains stiff as I squeeze methodically, but eventually returns to the center of his seat.

"Why did you pick me, anyway?" Pick him? Does he still think I just randomly came up to him and chose him to be my partner for the night? Part of that is true, yes, but I'm a finicky eater. He doesn't know the half of why I picked him. He wouldn't believe me if I explained the entire situation with PowerPoint!

"Devon," I murmur, further massaging him into submission, "you have a big self-esteem problem. I walked into the club, looked around, and you immediately caught my eye. I asked myself, 'Why would a handsome man like that be all alone in such a busy place?' I had to find out. You go there and sit, don't you?" I watch his face for an answer, and his deadpan silence affirms what I figured out at minute one by looking at his aura. He knows I know, and he is ashamed for being a sad, lonely, unloved man.

Time to seal the deal. Keeping my hand on his thigh (in fact, I slide it up a few inches for good measure), I put my mouth right next to the curved cartilage of his ear. First nuzzling the earlobe, then curling my lips over my teeth and tugging, I bring him to full erection for the umpteenth time tonight. "You are a very attractive man, Devon. There are dozens of people out there who don't know what they passed up. I know a good time when I see one, and I think we could have a good time... together. I didn't 'pick' you. I like you." It is part seduction and part statement. I mean every word I say.

My friend swallows, making a clicking sound deep within his alcohol-dehydrated throat. "Can't believe it. Can't fucking believe this," he mutters, his eyes never leaving the road.

"Believe it, Devon." My hand between his legs again, grasping his penis through the denim and masturbating him with his own clothes. I feel like a total slut, but I am enjoying this moment... the moment of my triumph over my prey... thoroughly.

The rest of the ride is spent in silence: Devon tries to concentrate on his driving while I find new and pleasurable ways to manipulate his genitals through two layers of fabric, never once making any indication that I want inside. A furtive glance at my watch tells me it is coming on one-thirty, and I have waited way too long for the moon to overtake me. When it comes it will be quick and very uncomfortable. For once, I am not sure I will be able to control myself after that point, but to turn back now, denied, will surely kill me.

Devon pulls into the parking lot of a small but affordable-looking apartment complex. We waste no time in climbing a flight of exterior stairs to a door with 2F painted on its surface. As he searches through his keychain, I enjoy running a line of fingers behind his briefs and through his pubic hair. His whole aura flushes a deep red. We finally make our way into the small apartment, my hand still firmly trapped.

"Well, this is it. Told you it was..." I've had my fill of words and crave only actions now. Using my hand as a grip, I twirl him around and push back, slamming his waist into the edge of a counter. He yelps, and I take advantage of his open mouth by clamping my lips over his in a fierce embrace. I wait two seconds for him to reciprocate, but he just stands there like a dead fish.

Come on, Devon! You can do better than that! my mind screams at him, and I shove my hand deep down into the heat of his essence, the place whose scent threatens to drive me insane. Finally, the exotic feel of flesh surrounding his male bits, squeezing and pulling and teasing with the intent to, ultimately, make him come, encourages his lips to do a little more work. He moans into my mouth; I feel a hand solidly planted in the small of my back, urging me closer. His voice dies, and the only thing I hear is the soft ticking of a clock somewhere in the room... seconds passing before I get to have my fun.

Suddenly, Devon's the most professional kisser in the world. I feel a sense of pride in bringing such an aggressive quality to an otherwise meek person. We match stroke for stroke, tongue for tongue, and I find I must practice the utmost reservation as he actually bites my teeth. This show of bestial bravado impresses me and drives my lust into a higher gear. No longer can I tell whether it is my cock or my mouth that should be fed first; fucking his brains out and eviscerating his throat hold equal places in my mind.

Fortunately, the next thought my upper brain manages to transmit is the realization that I can have both his body and his life, but only in one order. I pull away from Devon's suctioning mouth, producing a comical sound that, because of our collective preoccupation, goes ignored. Hand in pants, I drag him down the hallway to the bedroom (it's the only hallway, so I assume it must lead to a bedroom). My pace increases as the change begins its transformation from the inside, rapidly eating up what mental control I have left. The hand that still clutches Devon's genitals feels thrice its size, throbbing, wanting to reject its current form. Devon doesn't notice, but still the fear remains... and sends more blood to my groin.

Past family pictures that I ignore on purpose, past dark doors and straight through into the black space of Devon's bedroom. I only assume it is dark; with the way my senses are shifting colors and scent-auras the lines between human and lupine have become inexorably mingled. With hardly a sound of warning I toss him bodily onto the mess of sheets that is his bed (its shape and smell, rank with human fluids, is unmistakable). The sound of breaking wood shatters our erotic interlude; apparently I have thrown him a bit harder than intended. My muscles have already started to reform.

Devon curses under his breath, undoubtedly pissed at the rough turn his night has taken. "Jesus, fuck!" The bitter indignation in this short outburst draws up a boiling anger inside me for no apparent reason, but I say nothing as my boiling body is freed in a scattered exodus of cloth. Even the collar must come off, and soon I stand nude in the dark room, and even though Devon can't see me I know he knows what I've done.

He would probably scream bloody murder if he could see me. I'm not a pretty sight when I'm shifting. My body is covered in a sheen of sweat, but it is oily to the touch instead of just plain wet. When I shift back I will be covered in a thick clear jelly that, even to this day, disgusts me. Before I run out of time to keep my secret a surprise, I climb on top of Devon, still stunned and holding his head in one hand. A tentative sniff informs me that I have not yet drawn blood. Good, gives me time to play.

He is impressively strong for his lack of visible muscle, and he resists the weight of my body even though I have, as of yet, given him no reason to fear me. Maybe he's playing. No, the growing scent of fear, that urine-acrid smell, has seeped into the upper layers of his skin. I take a moment to savor; it's almost as intoxicating as other, more viable, fluids.

"Hey... hey! Stop it, okay? Just stop it!" Devon shouts my name du jour and his voice breaks. I grin madly in the room, only dimly lit because of an unfortunate position away from the moon's light. I imagine it is just one of several factors keeping me from losing it immediately.

"Devon, honey," I say as softly as I can manage, simultaneously patronizing and assuring. "Isn't this what you wanted? We've spent the entire evening, invested so much in this moment right now. Can't you feel it? Don't you need it?" The edges of my words are tainted with a husky underhandedness that does nothing to calm the young man's nerves. There's nothing more I can do but try and let it take me over as slowly as possible, until I can find the right moment. I pray that moment comes soon. My stomach starts to curl inward upon itself; pinpricks of light dance across my vision. God, it's so fucking difficult!

The resistance lessens, and I draw back equally right away to give him the impression I mean him no harm. I can see the outlines of his face and body as pale ghosts cast by my goddess outside. Devon's expression is now neutral and smooth, and he truly looks like a kid in a way I can't describe. I instantly feel an insurgence of self-loathing, and a hate I used to have when I first started having to go on my 'hunts'. That was before I started liking them.

I let a little more wolf into my body, squelching the self-incriminating thoughts into oblivion and starting my bones humming. "Aaahh!" The moaning gasp that drops an octave mid-breath is unavoidable. My charade is close to being over.

Devon says that false name again, and it's maddening. "Are you all right? You feel really hot." His concern is genuine, of all things! My hands leave his and I manage to balance above him. I answer his question nonverbally by undoing the buttons which cover his heaving chest. It twitches anticipatorily when he feels the cloth move over his body. I waste no time, going directly from shirt buttons to pants button to fly, spreading each in succession. My hands, no longer as deft or as human, fumble the khaki pants and boxer-briefs down to his knees, where they stop there and stay put.

"Oh, just fine," I puff hotly onto his body. My face is inches from his swollen member, now, as I drop to all fours to catch my breath. I'm aflame; I want to vomit and scream and come all at the same time and with equal desire. This is not at all how I wanted tonight to go. I try to convince myself, sitting there like a mess on top of Devon, that it's all his fault. Something about this man has threatened to undermine me from the get-go. His innocence, his warm charm, and the ever-present childlike demeanor that drives his actions, decisions and speech; it's always so much easier with the others, because they knew what they were doing. Devon's tenderfootedness is disarming to the point of spawning regret. Regret, in a person like me!

Nobody ever trips me up, goddammit. Especially not vanilla pricks like this.

I am so distracted with my mental buildup that I barely hear a minute click near the head of the bed. In the space of a half-second I have just enough time to process what it is, but no time to warn Devon of the danger awaiting him. My arm is raised when I hear a second, identical click, and I am blinded. The simple act of turning on a bedside lamp, out of concern for my well-being, has just very effectively sealed Devon's fate.

When it was dark, I could concentrate. When it was dark, I was still human, with the power to slow the changes invading my body. The silence and shadows were friends helping me remain calm like a hooded hawk. But now... now it's all over. My mask has been lifted; my naked, flexing, melting body exposed in transformation. I watch Devon's eyes as they first adjust to the bright light, then process the thing poised prone above him. His erection begins to deflate immediately.

"Holy G-!" It is infinitely difficult to describe the range of emotions I see on his face. He lets out a yelp, again sounding like a small terrier in the way his voice breaks and belies his age. This is accompanied by him scrambling out from under me; I do not move even though his flailing feet come perilously close to my balls. All I can do is look at him and watch, patiently, power surging up from somewhere within. I never know where it comes from, or where it is stored. It just wells up like some unseen cauldron, painless but overwhelming. It has to be; if it didn't take over my entire consciousness, do you think I would let it happen in the first place?

Devon now cowers, looking even more like a kid dragged into a whole hell of a lot more trouble than he bargained for. I'm sure he's wondering what possessed him to go out in the first place, and I relish the irony of his regret selfishly. My eyes hold his, smiling all the while like I'm insane (sometimes I wonder if that analogy will eventually fulfill itself) as I draw myself into a more stable position. I find it particularly apropos being on all fours; it's the most natural thing in the world right now.

My muscles are afire and twitching against the bone; from the way I convulse and drip onto the bed, which is already damp underneath my hands and knees, you would think I was dying of pneumonia. Instead, it feels like some wonderful drug has been released into my system. Flowing freely now, the changes take effect disturbingly fast. I struggle to form coherent words with the last remaining bits of my human voice. They seem superfluous compared to what Devon is witnessing.

"Watch carefully, Devon," it comes out in a bivocal snarl. "You won't be seeing this again." Of course, my fearful prey is too busy trying to keep control of his bladder to recognize the hidden meaning in my words. I suppose it's all for the best that he not know his ultimate fate. I may be a carnivorous monster, but that doesn't mean I don't have a sense of pity, even in the throes of lycanthropic passion.

Suddenly, my throat closes forcefully upon itself. This has never happened before; then again, I've never let my other side rush in all at once before either. For one terrifying moment I think—this is it—I tried I tried to make it work—I went to the ends of human endurance for this sick fucking disease and I'm still going to die here like a dog—what did I do wrong—but something in the feral heat of my gut pops (it's really the only way to describe it without experiencing it firsthand) and spreads outward to my limbs and head.

It's like a warm breath of supernatural air; as I prepare to put on a show for Devon, it bumps gently into the make-believe obstruction in my throat and powers through it like so much Drano. It's all expelled in a cloud of orange dust that I know can only be seen by my eyes. Mucus drips from flared nostrils as if I had just ingested a spoonful of wasabi; it flows down my philtrum in runnels, over my growing teeth to mingle with the saliva already collecting and overflowing in my lower lip. It all adds to the copious stains on the bedspread.

I've found my voice again, but for now it rests as a constant deep guttural growl where my windpipe was closed off. The room is incredibly, unbearably, hot. I drop my jaw a little more and out pops my tongue, now thin and lolling out the side of my still-human mouth. It must be a sight to Devon, by the look on his face and the way he crushes the sheets in his hands and feet. Yet he doesn't move... or scream... Makes my job that much easier.

What colors I can see in the darkness are dulled and muted before my vision explodes altogether. We are now bathed in varying shades of grey, scent-auras and all, but I can still interpret exactly what they are, even better thanks to my nose, which seems to be pulling away from my face with an abnormal lack of pain.

Of course, as soon as I think about the absence of pain my back chooses that moment to relocate itself. I didn't notice the building pressure there until my reforming muscles pushed the bones past their limits. The snap is a gunshot; Devon screams like a little girl at suddenly seeing my body split at an extremely obtuse angle, and I emit an aggravated snarl while promptly vomiting what little my stomach contains onto the bed. The smell is horribly acrid.

I struggle to remain in a prone position to guard myself in case Devon has a sudden attack of boldness. I have never transformed so quickly, in this position, and with such unbelievable force. Too many things are happening at once for the human side of my brain to process, and I'm sick and tired of being hungry and unsated, so I just let it go. There will be plenty of time to think once I'm a bit more... comfortable.

Hundreds of thousands of tiny hairs make their presences known, emerging from every pore and in between. Normally my skin would simply cease to exist under the fine fuzz that grows to cover my entire body, but in the dark the effect is minimized. My right leg gives out, the tibia and fibula merging and bending into a new, higher, ankle. I fall onto my side, finally unable to keep the threatening posture I had been maintaining to keep Devon in check. Now that he's sufficiently terrified out of his mind, I don't think taking a few moments for comfort will compromise my meal or my safety. The bed's soft pressure on my shifting spine is a welcome relief. There is another, softer pop as my left leg follows the first.

Even though I am now in a rather submissive position, arms and legs flailing at unseen targets in the air as they seek out their new forms, the sounds coming from my mouth—turned muzzle—are no less menacing. I sound like a dog giving birth, the moans and hisses of a soul in turmoil escaping, ever-changing, through a jaw which refuses to stay one length. My teeth and tongue are already done, they just move forward and stretch now along with my face. Oddly enough, there is almost no longer any pain... a little self-satisfaction, even.

There is pain, quite sharp, in my lower back as my spine lengthens and stretches the skin around it, not used to being pinned along the bedclothes underneath me. The semi-tail thrashes like an infant as it evolves and sprouts its own long fur to match the rest of my body, dragging my lower torso to and fro.

At last over the major hurdles of bone- and muscle-shifting, and the itching from my newly-sprouted fur coat nearly gone, I can relax a bit, and do so with a heavy baritone sigh. My limbs go limp, still clutching the air as my fingers shorten, toes elongate, and calluses turn to black pads of flesh. It still amazes me that, as all this change is occurring, I can't feel my skin altering texture or growing into something new, even though by all rights I should. Call it an unsolved mystery of lycanthropy.

A pressure between my legs reminds me of the one thing left unchanged. I manage to bow my head with effort, not worried one bit about Devon (he's made no sound and no movements; I can tell without trying), and cast a glance downward. My crotch is open and exposed to the air, the only area on my body still bare. I get a friendly wave from a tail that now is an extra appendage, regal and fluffy. Yes, now that my mind has regressed (or evolved, take your pick), I want to play.

Surrounded by soft short fuzz, my penis has drawn up to a near-vertical position, the glans staring at my navel. It looks out of place and ridiculously small on my seven-and-a-half foot body. A giggle (and it is quite the sound coming from me at this point) escapes me as I feel my shaft attaching itself as if by zipper to my lower torso. The fuzz follows soon after, sprouting up from underneath the coarse pubic hair and covering every available inch of skin. It makes its way up to the head, surrounding my urethra like a whirlpool, drawing the skin the final few inches over and around to effectively trap my member inside its new furry home. All the while I writhe in pleasure like a puppy as my most sensitive parts are rearranged and enlarged. An odd sensation at the base of my cock signals the formation of a new bone, and my erection is quelled... not that I can tell from the outside; my sheath remains plump and ready.

Finally, after what seems like an eternity but in all reality probably took no more than a minute, my transformation is complete. I am not exhausted though; this time, the combination of tonight's well-played game and the general horniness from being moved into a new body have given me enough energy to remain on keel. I wheel from my back onto paws and knees now, a new being, ready to be consumed by an even larger monster than what I have become—lust.

Though my vision is lacking in color (I can see pale blues and yellows, but little else), I make up for it in sheer sharpness. On Devon's face is a look I've never seen before. Usually my partners/victims are curled up in one corner of the room, mouths agape and blabbering. Some of them take to screaming during the change, and as soon as I am lupine I must take them down immediately... it leaves such a mess, and I end up masturbating over the corpse to an unsatisfying end.

"Christ... fuck... fuck..." Devon swallows again after a few whispered obscenities. I admire his aplomb, considering what he has just seen. His entire body is bathed in sickly green fear (I assume the aura by the scent's massive presence in the room), his eyes are wide and unblinking, but I sense a curiosity in there as well. Intrigued, I crawl forward towards him, my muzzle smiling its wolfy smile, my now-yellow eyes gleaming attractively, meeting his own. I rumble just slightly, assessingly, looking my prey over with a new point of view. But my senses have returned, transformation or no, and I know I still have goals to attain.

Devon has plastered himself to the headboard. His breaths speed up, becoming shallow and forced the closer I get to him. Soon my body covers his, the heat from us both mingling suspended just off the bed. To my surprise his fear evaporates some when he has a good look at my features up close. He must be blocking out the inherent danger of the situation, justifying me as something less, perhaps just an overgrown puppy-dog. It's a common effect of lycanthropic shock.

"You didn't expect this, did you?" I say slowly and evenly so Devon has a chance to get used to my new, deep gravelly voice. He shakes his head just as slowly and evenly. My arousal has again started to make its presence known, this time indicated by pressure around my member as it strains against its fleshy boundaries. I lower my head to his, preparing to give him one hell of a kiss, but he pulls to the side at the last moment, twitching all over, and whimpers. He won't speak a word, so I must try other means of making him talk.

"What's wrong? You're not scared of me, are you?" My tone has switched from menacing to everyday-conversation. I am genuinely concerned about his well-being despite the fact that he has precious little time left on this planet. I want him to enjoy himself without being afraid. Fear tends to sour the taste of the meat.

My companion avoids my eyes still, afraid to talk, to touch, to move. I do it for him. With my right paw I turn his head to face me. When I draw it away the fingerpads are wet; a quick lick confirms the presence of tears. They stain Devon's face in twin trails from eyes back to ears, flowing freely. He doesn't sob... he doesn't sniff or cough... the tears just flow over silently. I honestly cannot tell what's wrong.

I flick my tongue out over his chin, giving a long, warm lick up the sides of his face, cleaning up the tears the way a mother wolf would comfort her pups. I find myself giving into his emotions. This is screwed up... I'm supposed to be the strong one here. There is an air of dominance to be maintained, and I'll be damned if I let myself fall prisoner to such an inane concept as compassion... not this late in the game. I move to speak, but Devon does it for me.

"Not anymore," comes the mumbled, sullen reply. His eyes are everywhere but on my own, as if staring directly at me will bring home the realization that there is a werewolf (I hate that patronizing term with a passion), a creature of myth and horror, hovering over him. "Yeah, scared, surprised, I don't know. This is just so weird." Devon has never been one for words. I don't expect any more from him.

"Understandable, Devon. But don't you think this is much more meaningful than risking some disease-ridden floozy?"

He actually stops and thinks this over; I want to smack him and tell him it obviously is a hell of a lot more interesting than fucking a random guy you just met at a bar, no matter how handsome he is, but once again patience wins over.

"Yes, very much so," Devon agrees with my thoughts. I detect him holding back a giggle but a smile creeps through anyway. A great wave of relief washes over me. Whatever fear he may have had is gone; I am no longer a separate creature to him, but the same man who sauntered into the bar and went about the simple task of seducing him. And now I am covered in fur, tail thrashing happily, still wanting to fuck as much as he does. Devon finally looks at me straight-on, studiously, and I know what he desires. All of my victims want the same thing, no matter who they are: they have access to the taboo, the unreal, and they want a taste.

"Go ahead," I allow. "Touch me. You would like to, wouldn't you?"

Devon doesn't reply, but a hand on the back of my arm says it all. My eyes are closed now, to enhance the touch through my soft, supple fur. There is something to be said about animal sensitivity: when your body is covered in fur, your skin tends to experience a whole lot more than usual. I only get to feel pleasure of this magnitude once a month, and it never fails to blow my mind. I intend to get the most out of it.

Fingertips graze my elbow and drag along my forearm to the bed, where they abruptly change direction and return, against the grain, to the junction of my shoulder. It is merely exploratory, but tinged with just the right amount of daring to make it inherently dangerous to Devon. I open my eyes to see that his are now closed, following my lead. I take the opportunity to move our night along by bringing my rubbery lips to his, and lap at his chin.

His skin is almost too salty, and I normally would shy away from any more taste-testing. But when I feel Devon's body go rigid, his mouth open, I can't stop my tongue from plowing right into him. His plaintive little moan is buried between us, transferred from human to wolf and killed on the spot. I turn my head ever so slightly and open wider to gain better access. Devon puts up no struggle, unless his hands clawing over my arched back are an indication for me to stop anytime soon. His tongue is foreign, thick and wet compared to my own; it neither resists nor encourages me. I couldn't ask for a more willing partner.

If you ask a man whether or not he would ever consider having sex with a werewolf (again, that demeaning term!), despite the fact that we technically 'don't exist', he will refuse and deny it outright. No, that's sick, he will say, never in his life would he consider something so base and immoral. But, once you get him all riled up and in the same room, face-to-muzzle, something changes.

The creature, now that he is so close and the man can see him as a living, breathing, sexual being just like himself, becomes an object of lust and fetish. I am the subject of stories... of urban legends... and the mere proximity of me is enough to change his mind. Any moral thoughts are thrown out the window; here is the once-in-a-lifetime chance to fulfill some latent desire perhaps carried over from every childhood in some form or another, and few are the men who willingly pass up the opportunity. Eat your heart out, Freud.

Without moving my muzzle from Devon's ravenous lips, I draw my body into a scrunched position, something no human could achieve without breaking bones. This spreads my legs to display my sex, resting invitingly upon the man's navel. I know he can feel the heat and weight of my genitals, so different from his own, and that he wants to touch me but can't bring himself to do it. I let the kiss last a few moments longer, pulling away with numerous baby-licks to the underside of his nose. Sitting up, my back goes from convex to concave; supported by my paws on his ribs, I now sit straight, my sheath dangling ponderously just over him.

"Go on, Devon," I purr, lust driving my actions once again. It's definitely good to be caught in this moment, taking my time while wanting a million things to happen all at once. It means there is still some time before I have to consider doing my dirty deed. Right now, it's all about making Devon happy.

The man looks down at my sheathed member, his hands hesitant but making their way nonetheless. This is the breakthrough moment: the hardest decision my lovers must make. They must come to terms with touching a creature of a different species in a sexual manner, for the purpose of gratification. Of course, none of them think of it that way... their minds are too clouded by testosterone at this point to make a justified argument to the contrary. Devon turns out to be no different, and as his hand crosses the last remaining inches I hear myself take in an audible breath and hold it.

Devon grasps my sheath and squeezes.

"Oh, God..."

"Holy shit... oh, wow..."

We both speak simultaneously in the dimly lit room. I lower my head and watch my human friend explore my genitalia as if he were a curious preadolescent inspecting the family pet. I harden quickly in his hand; after all, I've been waiting and working up to this for hours now. The low rumble is back in my chest with a vengeance this time; I grit my teeth and snarl my acquiescence.

Devon squeezes more, runs his hand lightly along the underside of my sheath down to the hidden bulge of my knot, gets more bold and starts pulling the skin back with his strokes. My lupine penis, looking like a veiny hot-dog but swelling and darkening rapidly, is exposed and rehidden as I am slowly masturbated. I am finding it difficult not to hunch forward, but somehow I maintain control.

Balancing with one arm now, I reach behind and search for Devon's cock. It juts stiffly out of his groin, having been pummeled with my tail, and I can only imagine how good it must feel on his bare skin. Devon utters a little gasp and spreads his legs, exploring my groin with both hands. He is enjoying watching the furred skin of my sheath spread and cover, spread and cover my cock as he rolls it around. Then he attacks my balls; his moves are quick and thoughtless, nothing like what a pure lovemaking session would entail, but we are both running on adrenaline and have no time or need for such intimacies.

Eventually my member grows uncomfortable within its home and pleasured rumbles turn to those of mild aggravation. Devon looks up and sees my slightly wrinkled muzzle, knows exactly what it means, and immediately freezes. I can see he wants to say something but is still too afraid to take the risk. Maintaining my stroking, I use my free paw to guide his hand down the length of my shaft, bunching up the sheath as it first hits, then stretches over the knot. We hit the apex and the last two inches pop free with a shared sigh of indulgence and a small stream of preseminal fluid onto Devon's chest. I am now my full nine inches out, gloriously slick and twitching.

The room has taken on the hot, heavy smell of males in rut. My own musk drifts to my nose from between my legs, but since it's my own scent I am already accustomed to it. Devon is a plethora of scents: a little fear, apprehension, self-doubt, and an overriding wantonness in which I revel. This boy wants it no matter who or what I am, that's for sure. I'm going to see if I can give him something special... something I've only ever been able to do once before.

"So, how do you like me now, Devon?" I coo, looking down at him with fondness, my fingerpads becoming slick as they spread pre over his glans.

Devon has this dreamy look in his eyes. He has finally accepted (or allowed himself to accept) the fact that he is about to have rough sex with a walking, talking, stroking wolf. I imagine the gleam in his eyes is matched only by my own. "You're beautiful," he grips me behind the knot and rubs at my left thigh. "I still can't believe this is happening. I've never seen anything like it before." Ah, the vocabulary of foreplay!

"A once-in-a-lifetime experience, my friend," I continue, but Devon still gives no indication he understands the gravity of my words. "I intend to make it unforgettable." With that, I scoot backward a bit, still holding his manhood up, teasing him. Devon has no idea what I am doing until I sit down, hard, and slide three-quarters of his penis under my tail. This is no big deal to me; I've taken much bigger meat than Devon's, so I enjoy the look on his face as he feels my body heat, a full five degrees above his, envelop him. He claws the sheets, staring at the ceiling, lips rounded in an 'O' of blissful surprise.

I bear down again and hilt him on the second thrust. Devon is average, about six inches and a bit narrow, but his cock is very straight and penetrates me with ease. I wriggle my hips back and forth like the raunchy beast I am, making him squirm and screw his eyes shut. There is quite the puddle of wolf-pre on Devon's chest; my balls practically ache from the need for release. I have been saving myself for too long.

My partner bends and raises his knees so they are just behind my arms, to gain better leverage for thrusting up into me. I oblige him by keeping my rear off the majority of his shaft, then letting him close the gap. Grinning, I bring my legs together in a vice around his waist, keeping myself elevated and letting him do all the work. Even though I'm pretty sure mine is the first ass he's ever had, he acts like an experienced fucker, using what he feels to alter his motions for the most possible pleasure. Even though Devon is enjoying himself, he still clutches at my thighs like anchors to keep himself from somehow falling off the bed.

Truth be told, I didn't plan on taking his cock tonight. I just saw his face, the look of pure need for any kind of the physical contact denied him for so long, and decided it couldn't hurt. And it doesn't; Devon goes nice and slow, and I settle to pump myself behind my knot... I feel so good right now, indulging my submissive side, that if I touch my exposed cock it might decide to ejaculate without permission.

Devon pushes in and stays in, bucking my body up against his and igniting my prostate like a button pushed repeatedly. I moan into the night, feeling my torso bending and lowering to Devon's. He has me held prisoner by my tailhole, and I don't even have to keep the grip on my cock to feel the warmth of a climax slowly building. My paws go to his upper chest and just sit there, on either side of my head, as I drool onto his perspiration-moistened skin. It is only now that I realize how long it's been since I was last fucked... since before I became a being of two lives.

I want to give myself up to Devon, content to just lie there and be rammed by his wonderful, wonderful length until my system decides to dump a substantial load onto his chest. My lack of a predatory backbone is too much of a liability at this point, but as I am about to gather the strength to tell Devon to stop, he solves my problem for me. I feel his hand creeping between my fur and his skin, and then a stinging pain as he grips my shaft and strokes it.

"Aaahh! Shit...!" With a feral snarl, I am dragged back into reality. In a purely instinctual reaction I hop to my feet and rise as far as the ceiling will let me. It is difficult to talk myself down from thoughts of breaking his neck, but I overcome my lupine side's attempts to finish the hunt with some good old human logic. Most evident is the fact that I need to come as much as I need to feed. When I can finally see and think clearly, I realize I am standing above him, no longer connected by his member. It sits semi-flaccidly against one leg. But his loss of erection is nowhere near as serious as what my paws did to his chest.

Going to my knees again, I get a good look at the eight parallel bloody furrows I dug in his flesh during my outburst. The irony scent hits me like an old, dear friend inviting me to stay awhile. "I'm sorry," I manage, but I neither regret nor take pride in what I've done. "You... you just can't touch it like that. The salt on your hands is too much." I am quickly becoming mesmerized by the rank odor that blocks out everything else; I swear my vision is turning red even though I have no ability to see the color. My fingertips pat the wounds dearly, becoming wet with his essence.

To my astonishment, Devon is smiling. I have no recollection of him yelling in pain, or any other reaction, but he looks like he actually enjoyed having his flesh ripped apart. "Battle scars," he says proudly. "They'll always remind me of you." Such sickeningly sweet emotion would make my heart break... provided I cared about such things and didn't have the aroma of blood to distract me. Or keep me focused; it can do either one. I bring my fingers to my lips and hesitate, wondering if this will be the thing to set me off. I wait... lick... oh, God, it's so good!

A part screams in relief deep down inside of me. I believe it is my conscience. Now that I have tasted Devon's life-giving fluid, any doubts I may have are swept away like so much dust in the wind. I suppose my conscience, or whatever is left of it, feels it can't compete with such a basic hunger, and that last bit of reservation goes out the window. Mind you, I can still hold back, but there is no longer any argument of whether or not I will be able to go through with my murderous intent. When I feed, it will be a climax in its own right.

My tongue lashes at the stripes of open flesh, making Devon hiss and quiver against me, but I hold him fast. Eventually he settles down when he realizes my cleaning is taking the edge off his pain. Then I feel the bulk of his renewed erection against the underside of my dangling scrotum and realize it's become just another part of the game to him. I am having a field day, digging my taste buds into the tender red meat just inside the parted flesh, fairly drinking him clean and getting an hors d'oeuvre of what the rest of him will taste like. The anticipation builds with every lick. Once the wounds are clean and no longer bleeding, I kiss Devon again, shortly, just long enough to give him a taste of himself. Of course, he finds this unbelievably kinky.

Now fueled with a little liquid appetizer, my body shakes violently, craving more substance. I am down on all fours again, my muzzle snapping at the air involuntarily. Devon rubs his way up my sides to scratch the backs of my perked ears. I collapse halfway, try to remain up and fail, flopping heavily onto the human.

"Puppy likes?" Did he just call me what I think he called me? Puppy? I can see that my befriending Devon has done more than raise his self-esteem. It has brought forth a whole other side, a haughty overconfident bastard who, despite the precarious situation in which he finds himself, sees fit to call me by a pet name.

"Puppy, huh?" Through my weak whimpering, I utter through gritted teeth, "Bad boy. My turn."

My grimace soon turns to a smile as I prepare to take control of this sexual tea-party once and for all. With resistance akin to the Great Wall of China (at least, that's what it feels like), I make swift work of hopping backward and clear of Devon, then bearing forward with my paws on each of his ankles. I grip them and dig in; nothing he can do will be able to overpower my newfound strength. For the first time I see an end in sight, our dragged-out foreplay finally come to a close.

Devon cries out as his legs are lewdly spread and raised. He has to know what's going to happen to him in just a few short moments. Sinews and tendons strain under my paws, yet his legs move nowhere. My smile grows.

"Hey! I'm not ready!" he complains, a tinge of panic creeping into the last word.

"I thought you wanted this. Don't tell me you're entertaining the thought of denying your 'puppy'." The last word is so laced with venom that spittle slews from my mouth in thin streams and lands on Devon's abdomen. He makes tiny airy whines, knowing he's royally offended a creature that could very well rip him apart at any moment. Well, not for a while...

Without compromising my hold on Devon's ankles, I bend down closer to the cleft of his hairless hole, licking stray saliva from my lips. The resistance, so strong before, has abated to the point where Devon feels like a baby waiting to be changed more than a man about to... sniff... be deflowered! I knew it! There is the unmistakable scent of male, tinged with hints of Ivory soap and the ever-present bit of dirtiness that never seems able to be cleaned no matter how hard the area is scrubbed. But there is something in the body's chemistry that changes once an orifice has been filled with cum, and there is no trace of it, nor latex, here. What I have suspected all night has finally played itself true.

I take one long, last sniff and raise my head slowly like a shark surfacing between Devon's outstretched legs. I can only imagine the grin of knowing on my muzzle as I see my human friend's plaintive eyes.

"You're an awful dominant and straightforward person, Devon...

for a virgin," I jibe, and he winces. "That's why you aren't ready, isn't it?" Why didn't you tell me?"

"I... I was afraid you wouldn't want to," he stutters dejectedly. "It's happened before."

I do have to admit that, despite other reasons, I am attracted to Devon physically as well as predatorily. Why anyone would want to pass up a chance with him, the stigma of virginity aside, is beyond me. "You poor thing," my paw travels up to his chin and back, dragging his balls and cock either way. Devon stiffens up again. "Are you going to be okay giving your virginity to a wolf?"

Devon pauses at the obvious, yet strangely-worded question. For him, it's probably still unreal. "No way, man. This is great. I actually... wouldn't want it any other way." He's being quite the good sport.

Huh. Some part of my mind says I should have done this a long time ago if it were going to be this easy, but I must remind myself that tonight's encounter was a complete coincidence. It was, and still is, my most interesting to date, though

"Good." The taste of blood still lingers in my mouth and nose. I urge myself to be patient and enjoy the first half of my satisfaction for the evening. My face disappears again as I prepare to open Devon up, at least a little, for my more-than-ample member. I have no problem with rimming, especially since Devon is so unusually clean (a ritual of hopeful anticipation for people like him), but I intend to expedite our coupling as much as possible.

I make a show of extending my tongue to its full length and running it from his anus to the base of his shaft, taking the excessively salty skin and cleaning it of perspiration, soap and his own scent. His balls are rolled around, examined, lapped at and nibbled, each action gaining a new and more vocal reaction. I would also move my attentions to his cock, giving it a good slathering (and there's really nothing like having your cock in a lupine muzzle... believe me, I have friends), but I don't fancy the taste of my own tailhole that much.

Devon's, however, is proving quite delectable. There was a point in my life when I had a 'never' list. That all changed when I did. One by one, my 'nevers became 'just this one times' and eventually grew into a regular part of my repertoire. Rimming is something I've grown especially fond of, exactly why I can't tell. Maybe because it's a natural part of greeting for wolves, maybe because I just like licking people out. Either way, I like Devon's taste, and he likes me tasting him. I can tell by the way he lifts his butt up to give me better access, of which I take advantage by inserting my tongue ever deeper and in whatever direction I want.

The end of my nose is plastered so deeply into Devon's ballsac that it forces me to breathe through my mouth, around my probing tongue. Even then, his smell is all around me. His thighs tickle my whiskers as he twitches epileptically on the bed.

"Haungh!... Haungh!... Haungh!" Like a fish out of water, I have reduced my human lover to a writhing, panting pile of sweaty skin and bones. The sounds coming out of his slack mouth are irregular and mostly vowels. His hands are on his chest, tweaking his nipples, clutching the bed sheets, clawing at the air, and finally driving my ears, pulling my head so close it hurts. Now I don't even have room to pull my tongue out, so I drive it past his second ring and curl it upwards, brushing against the warm, slightly hard protrusion of his prostate.

I am almost kicked in the shoulder for my efforts. Devon's literal knee-jerk reaction breaks my hold on his right foot and it slices the air just shy of my head. "That's enough of that," I quip after removing my tongue. It is clear by the angry, frustrated grumble I hear that Devon is not in agreement. Nevertheless, my cock has been denied for too long already.

Once I have his ankles firmly secured again, I march my way up to him on my knees, erection swinging lazily this way and that, all the while a string of pre attaching it to the bed, my thighs or Devon's bare skin. His legs slide up and back, gliding along my shoulders until his knees bend and lock him loosely to me. In this position I don't have to worry about him sliding down, and he won't cramp up trying to hold his weight by his legs. My hardness rests directly above his, dwarfing it in size, shape, and leakage.

Both of our faces are masks of concentration. There is a certain amount of sexual edge that disappears once the prospect of intercourse is made a certainty. Some of its eroticism, until now tainted by the unknown, becomes commonplace. It is, however, still easy to keep some spice in sexual play, especially with a virgin like Devon.

He knows what I'm going to do, yet he has no idea how I'm going to do it. I'm glad he won't have the chance to 'get used' to me.

I bring my hips back and guide the head of my cock to Devon's entrance. Looking up, I ask him with my eyes: Are you ready?

"I thought you said you wanted to use a condom," he says meekly.

"Come come now, Devon. Look at me. Personally, I don't think that's a problem now. Do you?"

After short consideration, he agrees with my words of persuasion. He shakes his head, brave but scared shitless just the same. He won't last long, that's for sure. I can only hope I make it worth his while.

I bear forward, and that lovely, hot little tongue-prepped pucker gives way to three inches of wolfhood. Devon inhales at length, then wheezes it all out in short bursts. There is no indication of pain on his face or in his body language, but I stop anyway just to let him become accustomed to having himself filled.

"How do you feel?" I ask

"Wuh-wonderful!" he exclaims in disbelief, as if he expected something completely different from penetration. "I think your tongue really helped." And, just like that, his virginity is bidden a fond farewell.

Without asking, I inch my hips forward, feeling his rings clench around my flesh as it warms to his body heat. I continue to plow past any resistance, and when Devon finally cries, "No more, no more!" I lay on top of him and lap at his neck. He settles down immediately at the distracting pleasure, so much so that he doesn't even notice when I've stopped pushing in.

"Devon?"

"Yeah?"

"I can't go any further."

"You—ooh..." Devon shudders at the realization that he has taken my entire length (sans knot, of course) into his body. Just to prove my point I withdraw almost completely and reinsert myself, smooth as silk. He is powerless to do anything but moan, spread open as he is. Any pain he might be experiencing is undoubtedly overridden by his adrenaline-infused body. It was the same for me, my first time with another lycanthrope. You enjoy yourself immensely, but pay for it dearly afterward.

Devon lowers his legs to wrap them around the small of my furry back, and I make it easier by hunkering down to make full bodily contact with him. Holding his shoulders, my neck encircling his head, I settle into a nice, slow lovemaking rhythm. The room is almost silent, save for Devon's intense, shallow breathing and the occasional grunt from me as I shift to gain a little better angle. This goes on for some time; my lover is being very obedient and quiet, enjoying his initiation with all the sensory gratification a first time should afford. The silence gives me time to think about how I can make his death as painless and pleasurable as possible, simultaneously. There is one way I have rarely used before, and this may be the perfect time to try it.

"Are you enjoying yourself, Devon?" I ask, as an owner would ask a pet.

"M-much... much, sir."

I stop in mid-thrust, lift off and give him a light smack across the cheek. His head recoils, much more than the force I had behind my paw, and he looks horror-stricken up at me. I say, "Never call me 'sir' again. Do you understand?"

"Uh-huh." The human looks about ready to burst into apologetic tears. I digress with as friendly a smile as I can muster.

"Nothing personal. I may be older than you, but I'm not 'sir'. Especially like this. Am I right?" It's not too difficult to talk about nonsexual things while embedded in someone else's ass, if you try.

"Okay." He seems satisfied, and I resume fucking him. This time, I start off at a faster pace with shorter thrusts, and now I can really start to feel the pleasure from Devon's clenching hole. I started off slow more for his pleasure than for mine, to get him used to me and being mounted in general. He took it like a pro; now the haughty bastard I saw before is just a self-assured sexual man, being deflowered in a way few people ever have the chance to experience.

An urgent heat begins to build in my loins, the long-awaited release I have sought for the past month. Normal (human) masturbation cannot satisfy the feral hunger inside of me that screams for more than just a release of semen. I open my eyes long enough to notice that the moon has lowered in the sky; it could either be late evening or early morning. The bright silvery orb has actually snuck into one corner of the window, looking like an overgrown piece of pie. It pulls at my back, then pounds in the reverse direction, seeming to aid my thrusts. Whether I am imagining this whole thing is up for speculation, but I've done odder things under its power.

Now Devon's arms have joined his legs, clasped tightly around my thick neck, effectively rendering him weightless when I raise and lock my arms. With the short distance between us, and Devon dangling as if from a harness, we've got the perfect setup. All I have to do is stay where I am and pound away like a dog, without worrying about things as inconsequential as support and position and cramping. After all, it's things like those that get in the way of a nice powerfuck, and that is quickly becoming the case for me and Devon.

My body trembles with the double effort of sex and increased weight, but my muscles are far from giving in. Since I retain my unfortunate human characteristic of perspiration, I quickly break out in a sweat that lingers below my fur and emits a gentler version of 'wet dog' to mingle with the varied palette already in the room. I can't believe Devon has held on this long; with the pummeling his rear must be taking it's a miracle he hasn't passed out from pure sensation overload. Believe me, I know what my cock can do to people when used effectively.

I dance on my knees and lower my rear a touch, creating an effect akin to a sinking ship: Devon is now forced onto my cock with the help of gravity, no longer just a toy which hangs ready to be played with. He can't help but slide down a little further onto me each time I hunch upwards, my knot forcing him open that much more.

His limbs first quiver, then loosen altogether. He tries to say something, but my gruff treatment of his body is making him hesitant. Feeling him slipping further away from conscious thought, and knowing that is not a good thing at this point, I shrug his arms away and let him fall onto the bed with just his legs clutching me near.

"Getting... ungh... close..." This takes me off guard for two reasons: one, that Devon would have the mental or physical strength to warn me, and two, neither of us has touched his cock as of yet. I admire his youthful vigor and envy his ability to climax without contact, something I have never had the pleasure of accomplishing. Nevertheless, my envy is mixed with pride at being the one to bring him to such a self-satisfying end.

Speeding up approvingly, I growl, "That's what I want to hear, boy. Let it all go." My mind, already shed of its human skin, gradually begins to shut down to its most primitive level. This is the part of lycanthropic mating I fear the most because of its 'Jekyll & Hyde' factor: what's left of my human faculties give way completely to my lupine bloodlust, and after that there is absolutely no control. I fear I will do something truly regrettable and inhuman, mostly because I have done so before. I am not a monster, but that simple fact didn't seem to stop my other, savage side from torturing a young girl for hours before devouring her alive. I am not proud of that. I do not want to repeat it, either. Ever.

"Trying to... to..." blubbers the man beneath me like a young boy. We are both so caught up in our little worlds, both with the same goal, that we seem to forget about the other person and concentrate on the lightning bolts of pleasure radiating from our connected flesh and points beyond. Tail thrashing, raised high in dominance, I go full-bore now, my hips a blur, wondering what Devon will sound like when he climaxes. Words are born and killed in the same breath on his lips, never having formed coherent sentences. His prostate feels like a croaker, gliding over the top of my cock; its hardness and pressure adds a new level of sensation that, if continued, is sure to send me off soon if I don't control myself.

But it is too late for any measure of control. My stomach announces its impatience and I let out a snarling roar to keep its complaints at bay. I lift up to do this, and catch a glimpse of Devon. He is caught up in the ecstasy, his face wrinkled in the intense concentration it takes to push oneself over the brink. I can tell he wants anything to touch his cock, to have me touch it, but I can also tell he wants to shoot unaided even more. Supporting my upper body by my arms once again, I lunge for Devon's neck... I need something to gnaw on until our mating is completed.

Devon emits a startled, elongated raspy breath; the bed vibrates on either side of us underneath his pounding fists. I nibble along his flesh, just hard enough to cause pleasurable pain but not nearly enough to break the skin... yet. I am counting on all my senses to tell me when the moment is right.

Suddenly something breaks loose inside of me, sending my body into a near-panicked state. My orgasm has snuck up on me prematurely! I have quite a bit more time (well, only twenty seconds or so) before I start shooting, but that is not nearly as important as my swelling knot. On an in-thrust, I stop moving completely and dig my footpaws into the sheets. I have to hold Devon down as he starts to wriggle and thrash against my invasive member; the pain he feels must be immense enough to drown out all other sensation. He never tells me to stop.

I smell fresh and copious tears, forced out of eyes closed so tight they look sewn. My jaws clamp down harder, finding good purchase for the final act. Seconds tick by; my balls churn and then spasm, releasing their initial load before I can tie with Devon. His hole, slick with wolf-pre, retains a chokehold on my knot, almost halfway in now. Human fingernails dragged over my shoulders and upper arms do not compare to my paws, now punching little holes above the furrows in his chest. My climax is just around the corner, as is Devon's. Just a little more...

Three long, lazy shots of cum erupt inside Devon's body; I feel it as it is pinched between the walls of his anus and my knot, then sent the rest of the way down my cock. A wail-turned-scream is swiftly interrupted by my muzzle around soft, sweet, healthy flesh. Realizing I have been holding my breath, I exhale; it is enough to send my knot sliding past his sphincter to lock our bodies together.

It all happens as if on cue: physical release finally comes in the form of waves that seem to accelerate my thicker, more potent seed out into Devon. The volleys are long, forceful and tremendously relieving. Instead of relaxing, though, I wait for my lover to come around, which doesn't take too long. Devon starts to sound like he's choking, when in fact he is experiencing an orgasm so complete it takes his entire being prisoner. I detect an abrupt change in body chemistry, almost identical to my own a few moments earlier, and choose that instant to seal his fate.

There is nothing in my world now, except my cock and my jaws. My long lupine climax continues as I apply constantly increasing pressure to Devon's neck, feeling the skin and tendons part before my teeth. Then they sink into the muscle, which gives way without allowing the severing of tendons. An explosion of irony blood, which in all reality is just a superficial trickle, fills my muzzle.

I adjust my angle downward to accommodate my prey's gaping jaw, which is trying to suck in air where none will ever go again. His body gives one lunge upwards, and my left ear and the side of my head are suddenly warm, wet and sticky. It is thin, dripping stuff, soaking into my fur immediately, but it is copious. Through the bestial layers of my current state of mind, I take a little solace in the fact that Devon's last moments on earth are being spent in sexual delight.

The absence of sound from Devon's mouth is a sign I am succeeding. I know there is precious little suffering on his part, but I hump him, rocking back and forth slowly, to make sure he rides the pleasure calmly into death. His hands flail a bit, never trying to push me off, but just searching for something to grab as his vision fades. Eventually even these come to rest on the bed, limp and too weak to move. I feel his pulse through my gums, fading fast until it stops altogether. I wait another minute after that, just to make sure, and then release him. The sacrifice has finally been made.

My mind comes back into some sort of focus, and I see no point in staying tied to a corpse. With some pain, I carefully disconnect myself, still dribbling cum, from Devon's body and set about the gruesome task of filling the other hunger still within me. The heart comes first; it is said, by some of my 'peers', that eating the heart before anything else is the surest way to gain your victim's strength and ensure their soul a place in heaven. I personally think it's a bunch of mythical bullshit, but I'm not about to take my chances. For the next hour I let myself go, rending flesh and bone like a wild animal after bringing down a particularly good kill. There is nothing humane about the way I feed; I view it as something imperative to me if I want to keep on living, nothing more or less.

Oddly enough (or conveniently), I find that most of my conversation with Devon is lost to memory. The more of him I eat, the less I can remember about him... the power of repression at its finest, to be sure.

No part of his body is wasted. Blood soaks deep into the bed (and into my fur) as I work, down to the box spring and, most likely, the floor. By the time I look at the digital alarm clock on the nightstand, seeing the red numbers illuminating 5:00, nothing is left but a pile of loose bones, licked almost clean. Devon's skull lays shattered among them; the skull is usually the most difficult to eat, but the brain is always a wonderful way to wrap up a repast.

The moon has sunk past the horizon, taking with it my ability to hold my lupine form with ease. Little by little I feel it draining from my overstuffed body, and know I must escape before I lose any more darkness. Forcing myself to walk (it's like exercising after Thanksgiving dinner), I go to the kitchen where, after a short search, I find a box of heavy-duty trashcan liners. They always seem to be around when I need them. The bones go into the bag like so many leftovers, as do my clothes, wrapped in their own protective plastic. I now feel out of place, cleaning up my mess with bloody claws.

I take advantage of a quick shower to get the majority of carrion washed from my body. It never disappears fully from the fur, but once I transform back it will no longer matter. Once I am mostly clean and dry, it is time to make my exit into the world again. Full, exhausted, and emotionally drained, I exit Devon's building, bag over my shoulder, draped in a large blanket I also found in the closet. I don't have to worry about locking the door or leaving trace evidence behind; all the police will find is blood, wolf fur and a copious amount of semen, left to their own devices to figure out a scenario involving all three.

At this time, on a Sunday morning, no one who values their life would be out on the streets. This is to my advantage, as I shuffle from shadow to shadow, looking for a dark alleyway in which to become human again. Only three blocks away I spy a dumpster hiding a nice dark spot, make quick work of myself, and try to wipe down without touching that awful clear goo. The transformation back is much less painful and takes no time at all, yet when I emerge into the sickly green glow of the arc-sodium streetlamps my stomach feels almost empty. It constantly amazes me how much energy I burn on my hunt every month. Almost makes it seem like Devon gave his life for nothing, but I remind myself that if he hadn't, I'd be the one dead right now. Survival of the fittest, my ass, I think sarcastically, and I have to chuckle.

Iron languishes in the back of my mouth, heavy and nauseating to my human taste-buds. I need to get home and brush my teeth before I vomit. This is the point where, sometimes, regret would come rushing in to take the place of predatory pleasure, I suppose. It seems I've become a master of my emotions at long last. I am numb, hung over from life. Thank God (I doubt he likes me much by now) my senses are now ignorant and dulled, just like a human's should be. One night a month is enough for me.

After disposing of the bag of bones in another anonymous dumpster ten blocks away from where I reverted, I wander to a main artery and hail a rare early-morning taxi. The driver is quick and direct, honest and not at all intrusive, and I am glad for the bit of normalcy that provides.

I pay dearly for the ride back to my bike, but walking over roughly seven miles of interstate is not an option. Tipping the cabbie, I shuffle over to the bike. Its bright, beautiful paint reminds me of the new dawning day, and last night already seems like a wonderful, horrible sexy nightmare all rolled into one. Its high-strung engine, revved to the redline and back, drowns the thoughts nicely. All I want to do now is sleep.

The ride home is slow and cautious; I've been known to pass out after such busy nights, and I'd rather not do it at eighty miles per hour on a speedbike. I make it all the way to the garage before my vision starts to double and my balance goes to shit. I can barely make it to the cargo elevator, hitting random buttons (that does absolutely nothing, as the only thing that will get me to my loft is a passkey) Finally I collect enough stamina to insert and turn the key, and the elevator rises. My stomach churns on the journey, but I know I must keep my food down or risk my own destruction.

I stumble into my spartanly clean living room. I liked Devon. He was a nice kid. He was cute. He didn't deserve to die.

But he tasted so good...

Entering my blur of a bedroom, I collapse onto my blur of a bed. I am seriously sleep-deprived, and I can't be counted upon to make rash observations. I will sleep away Sunday to face Monday with a renewed spirit and energy, just like every other self-respecting member of the human race. I won't even need to stop by Starbucks to plant a smile on my face. And, come Monday night, rest assured I will be entertaining some anonymous male visitor, this time without the threat or burden of killing him.

By that time, the police will have entered Devon's apartment and cordoned it off.

My cock has erected again, to my annoyance. I feel a strong urge to masturbate to rid myself of residual tension, but there is simply not enough strength to go around. Undressing automatically, I crawl under the sheets, and the soft silk warms and comforts me as I finally let go of consciousness. At this point my sleep will be restful and dreamless, which is exactly what I need to recuperate from my exhausting nocturnal activities.

After all, I have plenty of time for pondering the finer points of my existence. No reason to jump to irrational conclusions now, when it will do nothing but keep my drained mind awake with rambling thoughts. With my eyes closed the world slowly ceases to be, as does the grip of the moon. It's nice to have things back to normal again.

Until next month, that is.

Oh, a Day in the Country...

The English landscape has many charms, and most of those are what it has managed to retain in spite of the crushing march of modernity.

Here we are treated to a glimpse of an England not so far removed from out own, barring a few supernatural creatures that are altogether less familiar to us than they are to the inhabitants of this England.

In a light and fitting prose style, the author takes us on a little trip that has as much to do with the dauntless English spirit as the charms and, it must be said, the lurking horrors of such reliable standbys as manors and libraries and mad lords.

"Arcanum Arcanorum" is our introduction into this marvellous world. Let us pay close attention, and see where it leads...

Arcanum Arcanorum

Ben Goodridge

"Wake up! Wake up! Wake up!"

I can think of many different ways I prefer to wake up. I like to wake up on a warm summer's day with the sun streaming through the open windows and the rich smell of coffee boiling on the stove. I like to wake up to a buttered scone and a neatly folded morning paper, preferably the Times. Having a two hundred pound werewolf jump up and down on me isn't even on the list. It's on a different list, one I don't discuss in polite company.

I grunted, shoved Billy off the bed, and groped for my spectacles. Billy put his huge paw on the edge of the bed and bounced some more, shaking the mattress to the frame."Get up, get up, get up!" His tail was wagging so fast that it fanned the room. I grabbed him by the muzzle and pushed him away, then got out of bed.

"I'm sure you'll explain thoroughly why you chose to roust me like this," I said, stripping off my pajamas. He helped me a little too enthusiastically, and buttons flew around the room.

He crushed a piece of paper into my hand."Telegram arrived this morning. I'll go get us packed." He slapped me heartily on the back, nearly toppling me, and scampered into the other room. I unrumpled the paper and squinted at it.

DISAPPEARANCE AT PALMER MANSION STOP
SUSPECT ARCANUM STOP
PLEASE COME QUICKLY TO ADVISE STOP

I yawned, scratched, and climbed wearily into my morning suit. Billy flashed past, pressing a hot cup of coffee in my hands. I shuffled after him, rubbing my eyes. "Billy?" I said. "Palmer Mansion. Information?"

"The late Lord Palmer was a warlock," said Billy, tossing clothes into a suitcase. "Not a very good one, but he assembled quite a cult. Hunting outfit or summer suit?"

"Summer suit," I said. "Your hunting outfit still has blood all over it."

He looked at the hunting outfit, sniffed derisively, and rolled up the summer suit. "Palmer died about fifty years ago, though. The usual mysterious circumstances that surround the death of all minor Arcana. Personally, I think he fell down the cellar steps and hit his head."

"Who owns the Palmer Mansion now?"

"Chap named Grieves. Heir to a lead fortune, I understand. His father lived in penury until he made quite a phenomenal amount of money in a very short time selling bullets to both sides of the American Civil War. His son came here and bought the Palmer Mansion when it went up for auction after Palmer's heirs died."

"Is he a Warlock? Or a Wizard, at least?"

Billy managed a shrug. "Nothing on him in the more recent books. Chances are he bought Palmer's library with his house and did a little light reading. Probably did himself in with some spell he didn't quite understand."

"I'll go get packed," I said. "Bring whatever books you think we might need."

I knew of a pocketful of investigative services that dabbled in the Arcanum, but only three that specialized. And neither of the other two actually dared to put an Arcanus on staff.

True, Billy is a Lesser Arcanus, the sort that litters the landscape and seasons this mundane Man's world. Vampires, werewolves, some forms of ghosts, poltergeists, boggarts, dumpkins, watersprites... these were the Lesser Arcana. Billy has certain powers that make him tremendously useful.

It's a rare Arcanus that will even show itself to a human, much less ally oneself to one, and to be in the employ of one must have made Billy a pariah to his pack. Of course, poor Billy required some adapting before he fully accepted London life. Getting him to wear clothes was an uphill battle. Twice, the police brought him home after someone fainted watching him snack on squirrels in the park. He preferred to bathe in the Thames instead of a tub. The first few nights he lived in my spare bedroom, I awoke in the middle of the night to find him cuddling me like a stuffed toy. Werewolves, he insisted guiltily, sleep all in a big heap in the middle of the den.

As for the Greater Arcana... well, suffice it to say that I choose to stay out of their way as often as possible. Greater Arcana don't inhabit our domain, our Universe, and those that manage to make the crossing are best forced back where they came from as soon as possible.

Now he was tying a trunk of books to the back of the automobile. "Can I drive?" he said, eagerly.

"No," I said.

"Please?"

"No."

"I promise to be careful."

"No."

"Just a little way?"

"No."

"I've been practicing while you were asleep, you know," he said.

"I doubt that. I'd have heard it."

"With your weak human ears? You'd miss a buffalo stampede."

"Just crank the engine."

He plugged the crank into the engine, muttering to himself in one of the seventeen Arcanum languages that he knew. The engine turned over with a roar and I climbed into the pilot seat. He sat down grumpily next to me, saying, "... maybe I should just go join the Other Side, or something, and when we Arcana take over, you humans will have to turn the crank while we do all the piloting..."

"And when that happens," I said, dropping the automobile into reverse and backing out of the carriage house, "no lamppost in London will be safe."

The automobile was an extravagance, but I preferred to impress our clients, and pulling up in a horseless carriage never failed to satisfy. Many of our visitors believed the locomotion of this strange device to be evidence of our skill in magic arts, though I'm no wizard and Billy is scared of automobiles—at least the ones he's not riding in. Still, though automobiles may grow increasingly common in the years ahead, in this year of 1897, the machine still has the power to turn heads.

The drive to Palmer Mansion took four hours, and Billy read most of the way, scanning his old books for anything that might help us solve a disappearance. His library made him as invaluable as any other traits, for many of his books were in languages I didn't understand and had never heard of.

Though I pay Billy what salary I can afford, it will never be enough if it is doubled a hundred times over. However, werewolves need little to be happy—enough raw meat to fill his belly and a warm place to sleep was all he ever asked, so he amassed a considerable savings and spent much of the balance on finding and reading old books. I'd allocated space above the carriage house and in the stables for them.

The cobblestones of London gave way to farming roads and rutted tracks, and the vast country manors of London's gentry. Palmer Mansion was just one of many of these—a building constructed by people too rich for their own good, a miniature Buckingham Palace with a lawn large enough for a steeplechase. I drove up the road to the front door, and we dismounted the vehicle.

Immediately, Billy's muzzle was in the air, sniffing, probing, waving about as he tried to get some clue as to the nature of this place. "Something in the air," he said. "Musty… can't quite place it."

"Arcanum?"

"Definitely."

We climbed the steps to the front door and tweaked the bell. A moment later, a gaunt servant opened the door a crack.

"Would you tell your master that the investigators are here," I said.

The door closed. A few minutes later, it opened wide. The woman who had answered was young, pretty, and somewhat overdressed for a day in the country. I had motioned for Billy to back off, crouch, tone down his presence, but if I was expecting her to be frightened by him, I was happily disappointed. "Good, good, you're here. Please come in."

Billy followed us into the entrance hall, still sniffing. "What is it, Billy?"

"Stronger in here," he said. "Mustier. Ancient. I don't know for sure."

"Tell us a little about your brother, Ms. Grieves."

"Oh, he met a wizard back in the States," said Ms. Grieves in a pleasant American dialect. "He was terribly impressed by him. Couldn't stop talking about him. I believe that when he made his fortune, he bought this place just because it had been owned by a Warlock."

"Is there a library here?"

"Of course. It's where I last saw my brother."

"Had he uncovered his Arcanum?" said Billy, standing a bit straighter. "I mean, could he... do anything yet?"

"It's difficult to say," said Ms. Grieves. "He did do one thing. Very proud of it. He could light a candle by pointing at it."

Billy glanced at me, and I glanced at him. That was practically the first trick in the Wizard's handbook. One would be hard pressed to find anyone who couldn't do it after a week's practice.

"How long had he been studying?" said Billy.

"Oh... years. Years and years. He met the Wizard ten years ago, when he was only eighteen. Since then, he's been reading everything he can about the Arcana. You should see our garden parties—he invites every vampire, witch, wraith, and werewolf for miles around to join us, just to show his savvy off to the neighbors."

"So he's been practicing for years, but all he's learned is the Illuminatia," said Billy. "And after ten years... "

"...If you haven't gained additional powers, you lose what little you've earned," I finished. "It sounds like his time was up. He may have been getting desperate."

"It sounds like the way he studies, frankly," said Ms. Grieves, a little contemptuously. "He was the same way at Yale. He loved the idea of his work, but not the studying and discipline necessary. He wanted to be a great football player, but never showed up to any practice sessions."

"Hm. I'm getting some conflicting scents here," said Billy. He licked his chops and tried again. "You say he's had Arcana over for garden parties and the like."

"We had one just two weeks ago," said Ms. Grieves.

"I see." Billy bowed slightly. "Ms. Grieves, I hope this isn't too forward, but would you mind terribly if I smelled you for a moment? I want to eliminate some of these conflicting scents."

Reactions to the request often varied from client to client, and Billy had collected his share of hardy slaps in the chops from women unwilling to be sniffed at, but Ms. Grieves took it in stride. "Of course, sir." She even tilted her neck and showed her wrists. Billy put his heavy paws on her shoulders and sniffed at her neck, gently breathing in her whole history from her scents—her health, her diet, some of her personal habits, and even more personal information it does not become a gentleman to mention.

"What can you tell, Mr. Werewolf?" said Ms. Grieves, as Billy licked her wrist, the better to sniff it.

"Hm. Many things." Like a mesmerist performing a parlor trick, he said, "You enjoy a glass of wine before bedtime. You smoke, but not frequently. You had a single Chesterfield two nights ago. You take your tea weak, with sugar. And your cologne is Arabian."

"I'm not wearing cologne," she said, surprised.

"Not now. But no more than eight days ago, you must have been."

I could tell she was counting backward in her mind, and she said, "Well done, Mr. Werewolf. I can see why you are this detective's invaluable companion."

Billy stepped back, holding Ms. Grieves's hands. "I can also tell that you have nothing to do with your brother's library or his interests. The musk of this place is in your clothes and hair as it would be for anyone who lived in this house, but you haven't handled his books or his spells." He released her. "Why are you so afraid of his library?"

She turned away. "I wouldn't offend you, Mr. Werewolf. Not when you've been so… gentlemanly."

"Please. If it will help."

"You'll think me silly, but… I fear the Arcanum. I don't like going into his library even during the day, and at night it's out of the question."

"You have no problems with Billy here," I said.

"Billy has been kind, and gentle. Most of my brother's friends have also been gentlemen. I don't fear the Arcana, just... their powers."

"You're probably correct to be wary, Ms. Grieves," said Billy. "The Arcanum is difficult to wield. Your brother shouldered too great a burden before he was ready."

She sniffed. "You're not going to find my brother alive, are you?" she said.

I answered as honestly as I could. "We won't know until we know what he was working with," I said.

We had arrived at the library at last. The door was broken inwards. "I knew it must have been magic that took him, because the doors were locked from the inside and there were no windows in this place."

The library was not large. Billy wrinkled his nose as he crossed the threshold, but said nothing. His own collection was larger.

"Did your brother add to this library at all?" I said.

"No, he only used the resources that were here."

"Then he would inevitably have been working on whatever Palmer himself was most interested in," said Billy, sniffing along the shelves. He didn't like whatever he smelled, but bore it boldly. "Palmer has a whole shelf here dedicated to Charismatic Empathy."

"That would explain how he amassed a cult," I said, then explained to Ms. Grieves, "A warlock or wizard that wants to tap certain kinds of powers might assemble a... a support system around him, of those who want to see him realize those powers. Of course, to do so takes a lot of charisma. Charisma isn't magic, just good old-fashioned networking." I turned to Billy. "For what kinds of spells is a cult that useful?"

"Oh, all sorts of things. Luck charms, Miracle tokens... if Palmer wanted to imbue an amulet or artifact with his soul, he'd need at least three to lock him into it... "

"How big was Palmer's cult?"

Billy shrugged. "Somewhere around fifteen hundred."

I could feel my jaw drop. Ms. Grieves must have seen the blood drain from my face. Billy must have noticed, too, because he took his muzzle away from the books and glanced at me. "What is it?"

"He must have needed a massive amount of power for a cult that big. Most cults are only five to twenty people. This man had charismatic control of the population of a fairly large village. What do you need that kind of power for?"

Billy slipped three books down from the shelf. "These will tell us," he said. "They have Mr. Grieves's scent all over them. They're the last books he was reading before he disappeared."

As exciting as Arcane investigation seems, you'd be astonished at how much of it is spent in the library hunting down some scrap of information that was deliberately hidden centuries ago by someone who had very good reasons to hide it. Billy sniffed around until he found the chair that he wanted, and slumped down in it. "He was sitting here," he said, "reading."

I sat in another chair and we leafed through the books gingerly. Just opening some Arcane texts can have consequences, and we didn't want to experience any. Every once in a while, he glanced up and looked at the bookcase again, his powerful eyes scanning the spines, then he went back to reading.

Considering the sorts of spells the books could generate, they were desperately boring. Not the slightest bit of care had gone into making them fascinating, or diverting, or even amusing. They were all about tapping higher powers, about focusing your mind on the streams, eddies, and currents that ruled the Arcana, flowing through everything it supported. One of the spells one learns when one is new to the Arcana is a 'gateway' spell, a means of tapping this stream without disturbing it. Even Grieves would have known how to 'gateway', if he could light a candle without a flame.

For someone like Billy, the gate was always open, and the power always poured through. It flowed through Billy now, where he sat, and I imagined I could see it, in my fancy, a stream of swirling light, flowing from—

I looked at Billy, who was looking at the bookcase again. I looked from the bookcase, to Billy, and back to the bookcase. "Get up," I said suddenly.

"Mm?" he said.

"Get up. Let me sit there, just for a minute."

Obligingly, he scrambled to his feet, and I sat down in the chair. The bookcase was perfectly framed in my field of vision now. The books Grieves had been reading were indeed about tapping gateways to the Arcana, but I had assumed he was just looking for a spell that would reify his own connection, which had been on the verge of collapse.

"Stand between me and the bookcase," I said, my heart thumping. Billy shrugged and blocked my view of most of the wall.

"Can you show me your aura?" I said. "Bring your power to the surface."

He looked down, balled his paws into fists, steeling himself. His face screwed up with concentration, and his body seemed to smoke, a swirling mist gathering around him, glowing blue in the library's lamplight. He shone. He was quite beautiful like this, passing his Arcana through the visible spectrum, sparkling like an angel.

And a square of wall glowed behind him, as well, a swirling mist reflecting the light from his body. The room felt cold and crisp, and I could see my breath.

"Well, well," I said softly.

Billy looked at it, touched it with his fingertips. "It's soft," he said.

"Grieves wasn't looking for a spell to tap the power, he was looking for the power itself," I said. "He sat here, let its radiation wash over him for... several hours a day, for several days, I feel sure."

"Probably another reason why he invited Arcana to his garden parties," said Billy. "To charge his own batteries and to see their grasp on the Arcanum."

"And once he had enough power, he..." I shrugged. "Did something. Something he couldn't understand. He tried to open that door, I feel sure."

"A door created by a mad English lord and his fifteen hundred disciples," said Billy. "Are you sure you want to go through there?"

"No."

"Me either. Come on."

He pressed his paws against the wall and forced himself forward. The door wasn't quite open, and he had to push himself through, but the wall swallowed him at last.

I leaned against the wall, wondering if I could penetrate it. I sank into it as if it was mud, strained against it, leaned on it—and then felt a strong grip on my wrist and someone pulled me through.

It was Billy. He held a finger to the tip of his muzzle and took a torch from the wall, then lit it by pointing at it. "He must have come this far."

"You know what's down there, don't you?"

"I can guess."

I wasn't eager to go down and see what Palmer had brought over and Grieves had rousted, and said so, firmly and with conviction.

"Stay if you like, but we must close the Gateway," said Billy. "I don't know why it didn't come through fifty years ago or what woke it up now, but I have a duty as an Arcanus not to let it through."

"No, I'll come with you," I said. "Two heads are better, and all that."

We moved forward down a narrow, slimy stairway that threatened to dump us at any moment. I took a torch as well—light often banished Dark monsters, and it felt like a solid weapon.

After about fifty steps, the passage widened—into a huge, obscene, ugly Cathedral of Hate, a massive vaulted chamber supported by tall black columns, easily as large inside as the Sistine Chapel. Hideous statues grimaced down at us.

And its floor—its floor was covered with some kind of stygian muck, a foul effluvium that whirled and flowed through the chambers and caverns. Billy sank a leg into it, then his other leg. I followed him, trying not to whimper, as the black schlooge soaked into my trousers like crude oil. The slime was waist deep, and had lumpy bits floating in it. The stink was astonishing. I was amazed Billy could breathe.

Billy bent down and picked up something floating in the water. He held it up to the torchlight. It was a long bone, a thighbone, brown and broken at one end. "Hm," he said, and then threw it back into the water.

It had company. Hundreds of bones floated on the surface like logs in a jam, and I pushed them gingerly aside with my fingertips as I moved through them. Objects under the sludge threatened to trip me with every step, and my arm grew tired where it supported the torch.

Billy picked up something in one paw, cradling it to his chest like a rugby ball. "Here, catch," he said, tossing it to me. Yelping, I reached out a hand for it, until I realized what it was. It was a leering skull, its sockets streaming with slime. I caught it in one hand—and crushed it to dust.

Billy picked up another skull and squeezed it. It was as brittle as the other. "These bones are dissolving," he said, curiously.

"Billy," I said, passing my hand over my eyes, "I think I know what all this muck is."

"Nutrient," said Billy, hollowly.

"Which means that the fifteen hundred cult members…"

"Are right here," finished Billy. "We're wading hip-deep in 'em."

"Then we're up against one of the Greater Arcana."

"A doozy, if it took fifteen hundred to slake his appetite." Billy looked around. "If he ate this much, why didn't he break free? All this is still the Gateway, just the place where his reality and ours intersect."

"No way of knowing. Maybe fifteen hundred weren't enough. Maybe it consumed enough to create this door, and then had to go dormant in it."

"And then Grieves stumbles down here, and…"

"Becomes number fifteen hundred and one," I finished. "Which is just enough to wake him up again."

The chamber narrowed up ahead, then widened into an even greater one. We waited, backs against the pillars, and then I slowly turned to take a quick peek at the Greater Arcanus.

It was the size of the manor house. A massive, pulsing, throbbing blob sat heavy in a depression in the ground, surrounded by a tide of black slime. Great rubbery tentacles rolled and writhed over and around it. An eye the size of an automobile blinked redly. It hadn't seen us.

"Wakes up slow, same as you," noted Billy softly.

"Yeah, but all I want is a cup of coffee and the Times," I said. "When this fellow wakes hungry, he's going to eat every living thing on the planet before he's done, and have Mars for afters. How are we going to close the gate?"

"Haven't the faintest," he said, and then a tentacle the thickness of a tree trunk wrapped twice around his chest and dragged him under the surface.

"Billy?" I hissed, then yelled it. "Billy!" He surfaced, twenty yards away, his thick fur slimy with black goo. He yelled, slammed against a pillar, and plunged under the surface again. I saw the water boil and thrash, and then a geyser of blood spouted up from under. Billy surfaced again, still ensnared in tentacle. "It can't see you!" he shouted. "Run!"

"You've got to get out of there!" I cried, obviously.

"It's detecting my Arcana, Boss! That's the only way it can see right now! If it finds you, it'll turn you into this slime!" He disappeared under the surface again, and then reappeared. A second tentacle had wrapped around his arm. Another had hold of his ankle. He looked like a wishbone. He vanished under the surface again. I saw his body dragged, saw the bones separate and swirl in his backwash. He came out again, streaming, his mane obscuring his face. I noticed with horror that his left arm had come off at some point, but it didn't seem to handicap him in the slightest—he still fought like a roped lion, tearing welts into the flesh of the beast. "Go!" he yelled at me, and then the creature rammed him hard into the wall.

He stuck there, a long, thin spear of rock jutting from his chest. His body was bathed in slime and blood. He grabbed hold of the spear, but couldn't drag himself off it. He tried to kick off the wall, but the spear wouldn't shift inside him. And at about that time, I noticed that that huge red eye was looking at me.

That was why the thing had hung Billy on the wall like a picture—I was the appetizer, he was the main course, that squid-thing was saving him for best and last.

They tell me that discretion is the better part of valor. If that's true, then panic must be the better part of discretion. I discreetly made a run for the door, hampered by the black sea, conveniently forgetting that my friend and business partner was pinioned like a butterfly to a board and whether there was anything I could do to rectify it. I had also forgotten where I had left the door, and my first stop was into a dark pillar at full tilt. That it failed to knock some sense into me was evident as I fell backward into the lake.

The stuff tasted as bad as it smelled and worse than it looked, but I wasn't planning on writing a recipe for it. I just no longer wanted to be wallowing in it. Unfortunately, the rather nasty bruise on my forehead prevented me from easily finding a) my feet, b) the door, or c) up, and all I could do was splash around like a child in a wading pool. If it hadn't been a massive demon hell-bent on consuming every living thing on the entire planet, I'm certain the Major Arcanus would have found me hilarious, prior to delicious.

A tentacle the width of an elephant's trunk whipped twice around my waist and dragged me back through the mire. Unfortunately, that's all I feel qualified to relate. Owing in part to a combination of panic, stupidity, concussion, and possession, my narrative of the underground must end here, for no matter how I tried to reassemble the subsequent seconds, the fact remains that my next clear memory is of lying on a sofa in the Palmer library, in an immodest state of undress.

"He's coming around." That was Billy's voice. At least he wasn't bouncing on the bed this time. "Stay there."

I awoke in the library, sprawled across the couch. I was pleased to see that I was unhurt, and that I had been bathed clean, scrubbed as if I'd never touched the slime. I was less pleased to see that I was stark naked.

My body had been painted with swirls and designs, and I recognized Billy's healing sigils. I breathed deep the fresh, clean air of the library and pieced together as much as I could remember, then looked at Billy.

His arm was back on, though whether he'd grown a new one or found the old one and stuck it back into place, I didn't know. Pink flesh ringed his shoulder where it had come loose, and he had a Y-shaped scar on his chest where no hair would grow. Even as I watched, pink faded to white and then darkened to his grayish skin color, and I knew by tomorrow he'd have no sign of a scar. What's more, he was quite naked as well, having discarded the rags of his summer suit in the Gateway temple.

"Gateway," I said, and Billy said, "Don't worry, Boss. It's gone. It's closed." He stood up and knocked on the wall. "I can't even detect a flow anymore."

"How did you close it?" I said rustily, as if I hadn't spoken for a thousand years.

He sat down, his tail twitching nervously. "It was really the only thing I could think of," he said. "If he ate me, he'd have eaten my power as well. He could have easily come through then—the entrance would have shone like a beacon in his mind."

"What did you do?" I insisted.

"Well, I… I bit him."

I sat up a little. "You bit an Elder Nightmare? You bit a Grand Demon?"

"Well, it worked!" he said, sounding hurt. "He was a Greater Arcana. A werewolf is only a lesser Arcana. When I bit him, it must have… demoted him." He shrugged. "He turned into a werewolf, and lacked the power to support the Gateway. It collapsed."

"Good God," I said, running my fingers through my hair. "A Grand Demon bitten by a werewolf. I wish I could have seen it. That's really something to study."

"I'm glad you said so," said Billy, gesturing, and another figure ambled into my field of vision.

He was a lot shorter than Billy, and had the same posture, the same pointed muzzle, the same high ears and brown eyes. His skin, however, was hairless, oily, and black. He shone as if greased. On the insides of his paws, instead of paw pads, he had rubbery suckers. Ridges ran up his arms and legs, and his tail was whiplike and black and reached the floor. His paws and feet were webbed. He opened his mouth, as if to speak, and unrolled two feet of long, red, forked tongue.

He was looking around the room with a naïve, curious interest, wondering at everything he saw. His body language was that of a little boy.

"I've named him Stocky," said Billy, sheepishly.

I sucked all the air from the room. "You brought—" I pointed. "That thing's a Greater Arcana! Billy, there's a Greater Arcana on this side of the—"

"He's a Lesser, Boss, a Lesser. I swear. In fact, I've checked his aura. He's got even less power than me." He wrung his paws before me, pleading. "I've talked to him, Boss. He has a lot to learn about this side. We can teach it all to him, change what he thinks, what he's believed. I know he's a Great Demon dedicated to opening the Gateway and bringing his unholy brethren through to wreak havoc and mayhem on this planet and all worlds, but in the meantime..." He shrugged. "He needs a job."

"A job?" I howled. "You want me to give him a—"

"Sweeter and Lowe would mark their pants if they knew you'd hired him," he said, raising a finger. Stocky took hold of it and sniffed at it. "No one's ever had a plan of action for dealing with Greater Arcana before—just push 'em back through the gates and close them up before they get things on this side too sticky. Now we can not only study one of them on our terms, we can formulate alternatives."

I looked at Stocky. He hadn't said anything yet, and I didn't know if he could talk. He looked harmless enough, and I knew that Billy was enough in tune with the Arcana to go off like a fire bell if Stocky were dangerous. Besides, he was so curious, so childlike. He'd been following a directive, that was all, and now without his powers, he had no directive.

I slumped back down on the sofa. "You won't regret it, Boss," said Billy eagerly. "I swear. I'll teach him everything I know."

I rubbed my eyes wearily. "Well, can he make coffee?" I said.

Tea?

No ritual more English than tea. With biscuits. Neither the incourteous invasion of supernatural creatures, nor unsavory probings of the mind of a formerly dread being, nor any intrafamilial drama or resolution can dilute the symbolic purity of a nice cuppa, as the common folk are wont to say.

"Stocky" is a tale which takes the time simply to talk about people, be they fair-skinned or hairy or with suckers on their fingers, and in reading we may find ourselves forgetting such trifling and old-fashioned matters as dimensions and species.

After all: there's tea.

Stocky

Ben Goodridge

"Relax your mind," said Billy. "Feel the power flow from my paws into your brain. Let me inside."

We were in my London brownstone's copious basement, which had once held quite an eclectic wine cellar. Indeed, I had kept one of the racks after purchasing the place and had collected quite a concatenation of wines such that my means could afford. They weren't all for pleasure, since certain years and vintages made ingredients for powerful potions, but if I had no occasion to make such potions before the wine's age passed its peak spell-casting ability, they often wound up on the dinner table.

The wine that soaked Billy's fur from his ears to his knees was a red at exactly the right age, and had cost me a considerable amount. One reason that it was so expensive was that thus far I had purchased three bottles thus far, only to watch my business partner tip them over his head prior to the casting of this spell. It was my own fault—the wine formed the backbone of an intensely powerful spell of mental protection, the best we could assemble, and the territory Billy trod now was the most dangerous anyone had ever experienced. Each week, he dove into the mind of a Greater Arcana, one of the mammoth squid-like nightmares creeping around the edges of our Universe, looking for any sign of weakness.

The wine plastering his fur was therefore only part of the protective. The potion he had drunk exactly seven minutes prior to placing his paws to Stocky's temples was one of such power that it would be immediate poison to any human. As it was, it was quite a fierce purgative for a werewolf, and his goal was to glean as much information as he could before the toxins roaring through his bloodstream threw him into unconsciousness. He had, at best, two hours for this.

The salt circles, the holy insignia, the patterns scrawled meticulously on the walls and ceiling surrounding the bed we had moved into the cellars, all of them were secondary to the poison burning through Billy's body.

If this all seems like quite a sacrifice, remember that neither Billy nor I had ever encountered anything quite like an Elder Nightmare before. Billy had done something that no werewolf had ever done, which was to transform a Greater Arcana into a Lesser one by biting it and turning it into a werewolf.

Our lives with Stocky were largely unchanged, except that now two werewolves lived in a house where once only one lived. Stocky was easily cared for, blundering through life with an expression of permanent wonder on his shining black face, occasionally trying to eat things that weren't food. He wasn't yet in touch with his wilder instincts, and Billy was of two minds whether to show the creature the wolf within. A more spirited Stocky might be more trouble than it was worth.

At least Billy had something to snuggle with at night now, though I cared not to entertain the image of the two of them bundled together in Billy's quarters. And doing other things, from the sounds that occasionally crept through the registers late at night. Billy's previous celibacy had been involuntary, and I imagined that it was rather pleasantly modern that he refused to let a little thing like gender get in the way of pursuit of carnal delights, though that was as far as I chose to imagine. Still, we approach a new century, and such transitions tend to liberate new ideas.

"Dark," said Billy. "Empty. Sort of... wet."

"You said that last time," I said. There wasn't enough wine in the cellar or all of London to calm my nerves, and I physically restrained myself from reaching for a bottle by gripping the sides of my chair. "And the time before that. Have you discovered nothing?"

By his own testimony, Stocky remembered nothing of his time before his transformation except a long, empty span spent huddled cold and frightened in a dark cavern, a situation that had left him somewhat agoraphobic. Since one who transforms into a werewolf through the bite can only transform if he wishes it, we were trying to discover whether this meant that he had transformed because he was fed up with being an Ancient Nightmare and wanted out of the cave, or because he found it a convenient way to slip into our Universe, hopefully to reclaim his powers at some later date.

Billy had discovered much through his magic, exploring Stocky's vast yet empty mind. His first journey into that wet, swampy mindscape left him convinced that, at least, Stocky believed what he said was true—that he remembered nothing about his former life except his decision to become a werewolf to escape the vast, empty loneliness of his trap. His subsequent journeys, of which this was the third, were to determine the extent of Stocky's powers and whether he'd blocked any part of himself to hide it from us. Billy had found nothing so far, and his journeys were nearly complete. Only one more, he said, would map the farthest reaches of Stocky's mind.

The doorbell rang.

I tried to ignore it. I didn't want to leave Billy alone at this vulnerable stage, though there was nothing I could do if anything went wrong. The second ring was followed by an incessant pounding.

"Aren't you going to get that?" whispered Billy from inside Stocky's mind.

"I didn't want to leave you here."

"Better answer it so it doesn't break my concentration at this point. I'd hate to have to do this a few more times."

I sighed, wishing there was a personal valet or servant willing to accept a position in our household for what we were able to afford. However, those who applied for such position generally found the salary unacceptable for working with a werewolf and a detective with a house full of mysterious glowing things. I climbed the stairs like a weary bear, and approached the trembling door without enthusiasm.

The instant I opened it up, the one outside said, "Let me in, human, or I'll use force."

It wasn't a complete surprise that the creatures waiting outside the door were werewolves. Over the past few weeks, we had accepted delegations from dozens of Arcane organizations, such as magicians unions, Vampire nests, covens, and various orders of wizard and warlock, as each in turn overcame their personal fears and arrived to 'investigate' our new employee. Every other day came some magical whatsit-or-other to cast some kind of diagnostic or revelation spell on Stocky, all of which he sat through with perfect equanimity and the boundless patience of a true idiot. The only thing delaying the werewolf delegation, I felt sure, was the reluctance of a werewolf pack to venture this deep into an urban environment. Billy was something of a rebel in this regard.

"Very well," I said, "since you seem insistent on using violence, I feel I have no choice but to let you invade. However, ask yourself what it means to such a proud and territorial species to enter the lair of an unwilling host. Would you weaken your power over your Pack by weakening your own Law to suit your needs?"

"The Law is all well and good," said the lead werewolf, pushing past, "but these circumstances are extraordinary. One of our Pack has let a Greater Arcana into this world." He was a big one, with shaggy, unkempt gray fur and a long drape of kelp-like mane. His teeth and eyes were the same shade of slightly jaundiced yellow, and a scar split the tip of his nose. He smelled as if he'd crossed several miles of Scottish fen to get here. By a wide margin, he was the meanest of his breed that I had ever seen, and his two companions were practically invisible by comparison—only average for werewolves.

"Ah, then Billy is in your Pack," I said. "Interesting. You must be his Alpha, then. Get out."

The words were a formality only—not only did I not really want the Alpha to leave, I might have been more inviting had an invitation been solicited. However, it was important that I exercise my rights before the werewolves, the better to lodge my complaint in the future. I was far too curious about what the werewolves would do to simply cast them out.

"Where is he?" growled the Alpha, his two lackeys sniffing suspiciously about. One knocked an expensive mantle-clock onto my hearth and looked apologetically at me, until he turned his head away at a glare from his Master.

I heard a familiar double-thud. "Unconscious on the cellar floor, I think," I said. "He has been casting spells on Stocky for weeks, often with some very unpleasant potions bubbling in his belly, and he has found nothing threatening at all."

The Alpha took the door off its hinges with a jerk of his shoulders, and some of the surrounding wood as well. "I wish you hadn't done that," I said. "The cellar door is part of the Enclosure—part of what keeps my workshop magic-safe. Now it will have to be repaired, and according to some very strict specifications."

For a moment, a brief look of regret crossed the Alpha's face, as if all this posturing and threatening was starting to rub against his instinct and his Laws. He overcame it swiftly and leaped down the cellar steps, his two puppets following close. I trailed after them, only to find them hanging back at the sight of Stocky sleeping peacefully on the couch, his black, furless, oily skin almost shiny enough to reflect their amazed faces. Neither seemed to notice the unconscious werewolf laying deadweight at the head of the bed in a puddle of wine and urine.

I knelt next to my business partner, brushed some hair away from his face, and fetched his muzzle a light cuff with the flat of my hand. His eyes flickered and I cuffed him again, and he managed to get them open. "Hey, Boss," he said.

"Hey, yourself," I said, reaching for a conveniently-placed bucket and helping him sit up. "Here you go. Come on, get it all out."

As the magic protecting him finally collapsed, Billy purged a vast amount of his stomach contents into the bucket. He still looked faint, but he forced himself to his feet. "I smell power," he growled, wiping his hair from his eyes and casting them over the Alpha. "I thought I'd see you again."

"They're here without my permission," I said, with a faint hint of satisfaction.

"Ah." Billy approached his Alpha. He looked like an elephant staring down a mouse. "So you flaunt the law when it comes to me, and flout it when it comes to you. You must have known that by forcing your way into this home, you'd lose standing among other Packs. This could cost you your Alpha position."

"They'll forgive my intrusion when they hear of its circumstance," said the Alpha. "We've come to bear witness to this... thing you've created, and to see what threat, if any, it poses to our world."

"You and every other magic user in the country," I said, sitting down comfortably in the chair. "By now, word must have reached even your enormous ears that Stocky poses no threat." Ten minutes ago, I would not have said it so certainly. Now, it seemed necessary.

"By whose proof?"

"By his," I said, pointing to Billy, "and I have faith in it."

The Alpha looked from me to Billy, and then back to me. "You trust this werewolf's casting ability?"

"If I did not, Stocky would not be napping there. I am convinced that Billy has found a way of dealing with Major Arcana who manage to find weaknesses in our world. Werewolves could earn a great deal of status in the Arcane community if it's discovered that they have the power to transform a being like that into a being like this." I waved a hand at Stocky, rather enjoying myself.

Finally, the Alpha seemed to sink a little, embarrassed at his intrusion and probably regretting it. "What is that, then?" he said. "What have you created, Wegnoc?"

"It's Billy now," said my partner.

"So long as I am your Alpha, you are Wegnoc," said the Alpha.

"If you assert your right as my Master, you must also assert my right to exile, which means I am Billy." There was a faint hint of menace in Billy's voice, and I felt the need to put an end to this penis-comparing contest before blood was shed.

"What did you discover this time, Billy?" I said, firmly. My home, my rules, I get to be the boss.

Billy sat down on the floor, cross-legged. "I think he's dying," he said.

It was more comfortable in the parlor, and Billy assured us that Stocky wouldn't wake up for at least four more hours. As high-strung as my guests were, I hoped that the tea would render them less high-strung than coffee, though they took to tea cakes and lady fingers like a school of sharks.

"The magic that holds a werewolf together is also responsible for how difficult it is to kill us," said Billy. "This magic has a lifespan, of course—three, four hundred years, it starts to wear out. Eventually it can't overcome the aging process or some injury is severe enough to outstrip it."

"What does this have to do with Stocky dying?" I said. "He should at least have a couple of centuries in him."

Billy shook his head. "He has fifteen years left to him—perhaps twenty. He only has in him the magic that I gave him—he's cut off from the source he's lived on for millions of years and he has no access to the earth magic of this world. His powers are extremely limited. He'll be as hard to kill as any werewolf, and he may eventually uncover some limited, latent casting ability, but that's all. And if he were ever to attempt to sire another werewolf, the attempt alone would probably kill him. He's not a being of this Universe. The magic holding him together is all that's keeping him alive, and that won't last long."

"Is there anything we can do?" I said.

"Let him die," growled the Alpha. "Let him pass on like all living things and be done with him."

I opened my mouth to protest, but Billy raised a paw. "Actually, Boss, that may well be the best thing for him. One of the things I discovered is that he knew that coming here would be the end of him, and accepted it anyway. He's in rebellion against his kind." He fixed his Master with a cold glare. "I know something of what it is to be a rebel against one's own people. Let's us not make his sacrifice in vain by attempting noble and futile measures to keep him alive."

The Alpha lost the brief battle of wills that followed, one of several battles he was in the process of losing. "He is your sire, therefore your responsibility," he said. "It is the Law."

"If it's a Law you expect me to obey, then I must be a member of a Pack."

The Alpha's eyes turned red. For a moment, I thought he was about to cry. His hubris had already cost him too much, and he was probably wondering whether he'd still be an Alpha in a few days' time. "Very well," he said. "And your orders are that you stay here, with this… this human…" He coughed. "And guide Stocky through his brief span in our world. It will be on you to teach him our ways and laws. And if, given the chance to learn from him what his overlords plan for us—"

"I pledge that you will be privy to that information," said Billy.

"So be it, Weg—Billy," said the Alpha.

I cleared my throat. "You are welcome in my home any time, Lord Alpha."

The Alpha coughed. With one sentence I had swept his slate clean, and no broken Laws threatened his power. He looked as if he wanted to give me a hug. Instead, he bowed, gathered his associates, who thus far had still not said a word, and left the house.

"That was productive," I commented. "They came in here acting as if they wanted to rip both of us apart, and by the time they left, you were not only fully reinstated as a Packmate, but they assigned you to the very job that they had exiled you for." That called for a drink, I felt, so I moved over to the sideboard. Billy, meanwhile, hadn't moved an inch. Since the wine on his body had dried into a sticky red paste, I wondered whether he'd bonded with the chair. "What is it?" I said.

"It's always sad when a werewolf dies," said Billy.

"Not for another couple of decades, at least, we hope," I said, offering him a brandy. He refused.

"That's a short time for a werewolf. He is my sire, and just because it's better this way doesn't mean I must be happy about it."

"What have we discovered from him? That even in his Cathedral of Hate, even before you turned him, even as he waited for centuries for the Gates to open so that he could do with this world as he pleased, he was questioning himself. 'Who am I? Why am I here?' That alone is more than we've learned about the Greater Arcana in thousands of years. That some of them rebel. They even sacrifice. For us. Leave it at that, keep him as your sire, and take care of him in the time he has."

"There is a lot I can teach him," said Billy. "And it isn't as if we couldn't use an extra pair of paws about the place."

"That's the spirit!" I offered the brandy again, and he knocked it back in one gulp, then stood up. "I have to bathe," he said. "I smell like a winery."

He turned and hesitated. Stocky stood in the parlor doorway, his shoulders drooping, long black tail draped onto the ground.

"I've caused trouble again, haven't I, Master," he said, sadly.

"People like you and I, Stocky, we cause no trouble. We are just of the temperament where trouble seeks us out. You and I, we will bring trouble to the door of the Boss's house, and there will be puzzles to solve, boxes to open, and mysteries to unfold. But first, there is a bath to draw and fur to rinse. Stocky, will you do the honors?"

Naughty and Nice

Inundated as we are by sensationalized lore of old and new, the clear-cut distinctions between right and wrong as it exists in the old legends and wisdoms is a welcome comfort in a world where none such certainties are easily to be had.

"Child of the Scroll" reminds us that even in a world where dark creatures poke at every corner of our realm to gain entrance and consume all that lives and thrives, there are darker forces still...

Child of the Scroll

Ben Goodridge

I was sitting in my study on the third floor of my London brownstone one evening, enjoying a pipe and a heavy volume on magic theory that I was reviewing for a local broadsheet. I was prepared to savage the tome in print as I had never attacked such a book before, as I was quite sure that the one who wrote the execrable book had never once seen, performed, or been in any way involved with magic or magic users. Indeed, most of his material seemed to come from three previous volumes, all written about a century prior, all equally discredited in the eyes of any serious warlock or Arcanus.

It was in this ready state, as I was loading my double-barreled typewriter for a shot across its bow, that I heard a werewolf beating on the roof. My study had been a dusty attic prior to my purchasing the home, and apart from some heavy insulation against the winter chill and a couple of wards to keep casual magic use from blowing the roof off, nothing stood between myself and the roof slats. When the werewolf shouted, "Fire!" I rushed to the window in a lather.

I crawled out onto the dormer and, lacking my partner's skill in climbing, braced my feet against the shingles and called up to where he hung onto the chimney. "How now?" I called.

Billy pointed a shaggy paw, directing my gaze to the Thames half a mile distant. A glow suffused the London smog, huddled against the indigent dwellings of London's hardworking yet hard-suffering classes. It was a small glow at first, no more than a window or two, meaning that the home under threat had yet to be consumed. I had only just opened my mouth to speak when I heard the electric telephone jangling unpleasantly in the study I had just vacated. That, I thought, would be Chief Constable Wickett, who always chose inopportune moments to summon my attention, such as when I was clinging to a dormer three floors above a narrow cobbled street.

I felt the simultaneity of the ringing telephone and the growing glow on the waterfront to be no mere coincidence, and directed Billy and his oily sire Stocky into the house at once. Contacting the foremost expert on Arcana and magic use in London just as a blaze broke out on the waterfront could only mean that the fire had magical origins.

Billy clambered into the window opposite and helped Stocky in after him. "What books?" he said.

I seized the telephone. "Ahoy?" I said. "Constable?"

The voice on the other end, which seemed satisfied to reveal only every third word of the conversation, drove home a point I already felt well-made. We were summoned to the site of the emergency. Someone really had to explain the finer points of which end of a telephone to speak into to the poor Constable. One day he would encounter a listener who couldn't decipher his unusual transmission. I thanked the Constable immediately and hung up on him without farewell.

I gestured towards the lower shelves. "Containment, casting, flame enchantments," I said. "You'd better bring the Appendix as well. Stocky, go downstairs at once and open the garage door. We'll be needing the motorcar."

"Your command, my Master," said Stocky, his shining black body disappearing down the stairs in an iridescent swirl. I seized a crate of scrolls from a top shelf and a cloak from the hat rack in the corner, and we vacated the house at speed.

Let me clarify at this point that I am no Warlock. I once had the desire to become an Arcanus and tap into the magic forces that exist all around us, but the dream fled my mind on the day I flooded the second floor of my father's printing shop to a depth of four and a half feet. I was only nine years old at the time. Since a fledgling Warlock loses his ability to cast enchantments after ten years, I chose to let the duration expire gracefully.

I was thus dependent on artifacts should I wish to cast a spell. Artifacts are far safer, being limited only to the spells they contain, requiring a vast and broad depth of Arcane knowledge to release, and wearing out after several uses—some after only one casting. I know of a very pleasant Warlock on Carnaby Street who has served me well, and has been paid lavishly (yet hardly sufficiently for his services, though don't you dare tell him so) to enchant and provide me with enchanted artifacts.

The cloak was one such artifact, imbued with a certain degree of fire resistance. One scroll, when read aloud by one who understood its language, released a simple diagnostic, revealing magic to the reader and explaining the purpose and strength of that magic. Thus, we were well equipped when we approached the fire.

The firefighters were on the scene and had brought with them the engine pumps, which drained water from the Thames and over the surrounding houses. Thus far, the fire had not spread to them, and I was tempted to believe that it was in part due to their diligence. They also played a writhing mass of hoses over the main blaze, without the slightest effect. The water didn't even steam. It just streamed out of the lower floors, providing me with an unpleasant flashback.

The fire itself had consumed the second floor and reached the third by the time we got out of the motorcar, and a goodly crowd had gathered to watch. Those who didn't move back at the sight of the werewolf instead moved back in alarm at the sight of his sire, who seemed nervous by all the commotion and elected a retreat to the car.

Chief Constable Wickett found me before I found him and buttonholed me across the street from the main blaze. "Detective," he said thankfully, seizing my hand and pumping it vigorously. "Bless you for coming down. We're having the devil's own time with this."

"Let me guess," said Billy. "You've emptied the Thames onto it, and it's not going out."

Wickett glanced from me to Billy, as if surprised that the werewolf could speak, though he'd been in Billy's company frequently. "Er, quite," he said. "The firefighters are concentrating their efforts on the homes to either side. Preventing the fire from spreading."

"That's the best place for them," said Billy. "Chances are the charms that protect it are central to the home it's in." He sniffed the air. "I can't tell what it is. My head hurts. Boss?"

I pulled a scroll out of the chest, unrolled it, and read it in a halting lilt. My Elder Megharian has always been rusty as a garden gate, but the flames revealed their purpose to both Billy and myself.

"Officer, are these the men?" The voice was female, and I didn't break concentration as I glanced at the Constable, who stood with a harried young woman, her face covered with ash and streaked with tears. "Can they save my son?"

"Your son?" I cried, and my concentration snapped like a twig. "Officer, is there someone alive in there?"

"Er, yes," said the Constable. "Getting to that, you see..."

"Billy!" I said, tossing him the cloak

"Right, Boss!" He seized the cloak, wrapped it around himself, and dashed into the flames. The woman gave a little shriek.

"Constable, why in the world didn't you tell me that a life was at stake the moment we arrived?"

"Because the thing possessing my son is the cause of all this!" cried the woman.

Her name was Mrs. Holyfield, and she was a widow working as a seamstress while her eight-year-old son Timothy went to school. He was, by all accounts, a diligent student, and had shown proficiency in Arcane studies. Since one of the earliest spells any young Warlock learns is how to create flame from the will, it wasn't a leap of the imagination to conceive that a novice might accidentally burn down one's home, though it was extremely unlikely given the nature of the magic.

This, however, wasn't the issue at hand. Young Timothy had yet to reach the level of ability that would show inborn Arcane talent.

We heard Billy smashing around on the second floor, followed by a string of curse words and a yowl of pain. "Is he all right in there?" said Mrs. Holyfield, nervously.

"He's the least flammable of anyone here," I insisted, though the house was now little more than a box of flame. With a roar, the roof caved in, and the firefighters were having their own hell keeping the embers from setting the surrounding homes alight. We were audience to another long string of curse words. For such an innocent, earthy soul, Billy had an astonishing vocabulary.

"I know my son is possessed," said Mrs. Holyfield. "He's always been a cold, distant child, but just lately…he's seemed so angry, so hateful. He yells at his teachers, at the librarians, even at me. Gutter language, as well. A few weeks ago, a constable brought him home after he threw one of his schoolmates into the river."

"Did he start the fire? Or at least, the thing inside him?"

There was an agonized yell from inside, one that made the crowd shudder and me wince. There followed a crash not unlike a two-hundred-pound werewolf falling through the floor into a sea of flame. "Boss, you owe me big for this one!" he yelled, and came barreling out the door, his whole body ablaze. "Yaaah!"

"Gentlemen! Hoses!" shouted the Constable, thinking quickly for once, and a fire hose swung to bear on Billy, who threw back his head and howled as the icy water doused him. The flames hissed and went out. I could hear the meat of his body still sizzling. He was hideously burned, most of his skin charred and black, his eyes wide like fried eggs, his ears and all his lovely gray fur gone. He sank to his knees in the torrent and laid a little boy on the cobbles.

The house leaned dangerously inward and collapsed in on itself, and suddenly the hoses started hissing where they hit it. Steam rose from the ashes as the firefighters finally got the upper hand on the fire and laboriously started putting it out.

The boy was less than unharmed. Even his pajamas were untouched by fire. He had no ash on his angelic face, no scars on his body. Then he opened glowing red eyes and lashed a forked tongue at me.

"Oh, yeah," said Billy weakly. "He's possessed."

"I had gathered."

Billy sat down on the curb, shivering. Steam still rose from his body. He looked at his seared paws. "I didn't want to touch him because my skin was so hot," he said. "It'd be like pressing a frying pan to him. I thought my own skin would at least slough off onto his, but it hasn't."

"Are you—are you in pain?" said Mrs. Holyfield, as the Constable was violently ill into the river.

"I'll manage," said Billy, obviously in agony. He was right—he had made a sacrifice by fire and I had a debt to settle at some point. Still, he'd already grown ears and eyelids, which was a good start. "I'm guessing you summoned an exorcist for him."

"Father Ronald Wembley," said Mrs. Holyfield. "He came very highly regarded."

"Yeah, by himself and his lackeys," mumbled Billy. Tufts of hair grew from his scalp, and most of his skin was now a rich pink. "Incompetent idiot."

"Did he make it out?" I said.

"Nope. He was still in there. A little pile of ash on the floor next to Billy's bed."

"How horrible," said Mrs. Holyfield. "It was a terrible fire."

"This fire wouldn't have done that," I said, sitting next to Billy and touching his back. He jumped a little, but the pain was apparently subsiding. "Billy might have found a charred body, not a pile of ash. The good Reverend apparently botched a perfectly simple exorcism."

"Your Mom's a maggot," growled little Timmy.

Billy and I looked at each other, then at him. "Yes, and I'm a son of a bitch," said Billy. All of his skin and some of his fur had grown back by now, though he still looked weak and sick. "Come on. Let's see if we can go one better than Father Moron."

If the sound of Billy hollering as a burning house collapsed on him inspired a string of gutter utterances that a stevedore would find embarrassing, it was as nothing compared to little Timothy Holyfield's general attitude and demeanor as we took him home. In quick succession, he had cast various aspersions on the heritage of everyone in the car, bitten Stocky on the leg, torn the upholstery with his teeth, and spent the balance of the ride describing me performing activities with two llamas and a jar of peanut butter that were at the very least medically, if not ethically, impossible.

In short order, Stocky and Billy had moved a bed to the basement, sprinkled salt in a circle around it, and all but flung Timmy onto the mattress, and it was a shame that the impact wasn't more satisfying. Not that that slowed the torrent of abuse—in fact, it more than redoubled, causing the wallpaper to peel around the edges.

Mrs. Holyfield had followed in a taximeter and now stood at the edge of the salt circle wringing her hands. "Are you sure this is safe?"

she said. "He's already burned down one house."

"He's a lot safer here with two werewolves and a well-read detective with a fistful of charms," I said, tossing a handful of small, shining stones in my hand. "And, since I don't see little Timmy's inner demon being easily persuaded, I think the first order of business should be to contact your boy."

"My boy?" said Mrs. Holyfield. "He's still in there?"

"In there and right as rain," said Billy, padding around the circle. "I can smell 'im."

"My partner's muzzle isn't just decorative," I said. "Billy has long since learned to distinguish the various scents of intent. Put very simply, he can smell good and evil." I tossed a stone in one hand, and then stepped into the circle. "Timothy," I said.

Timothy blasted flames at me. They beat at my waistcoat but did it no damage. "Timothy, I'm going to give you this very special sweet. You have to swallow it right down."

More abuse. I took the opportunity while his mouth was open to clap my hand over it. I could feel the stone rattling in his mouth, but he was so surprised that he couldn't help but swallow.

His eyes cleared. His face relaxed. He looked at the foot of the bed.

"Help me," he said pitifully.

Having so rapidly gone from wretch to waif was disconcerting even for me, and I've been present at several such occasions.

"Kid's got power," said Billy. "I'm looking into the deepest bits of him and I can see he's strong. The only reason he isn't fighting harder is because he doesn't know how."

"Help me, please," said Timmy, in that bottom-of-the-well voice. It was a voice to bring tears to the eyes of the strongest of mothers, and though Mrs. Holyfield had surely been through much, she lacked the strength to resist.

"Mommy's brought you to these nice men," she said. "They're going to help you."

I laid the stones across Timmy's chest and belly and sprinkled holy water on his hair. Then I unrolled the scroll. "Mrs. Holyfield, I think you should know that what you're about to see might be very disturbing. You may not want to watch."

"I can bear it," she said.

"The priest tried persuasion, and we can see where that went. We're left only with brute force and blunt trauma. The demon will fight as I cast. In fact, I expect it to. Billy is going to align the magic in his body with the magic in the demon's body and give it a yank. He'll rip the demon right out of him."

"I can bear it," said Mrs. Holyfield. "If it's for Timmy, I can bear anything."

"Very well." I started to read. Billy stepped gingerly into the circle, surely affected by the power swelling at its center. Timmy's eyes faded to red, then black. He lashed out his forked tongue and yelled.

The ground trembled. Plaster sprinkled from the ceiling. Billy reached forward and put his paws on Timmy's shoulders. Timmy's hollering drowned out me, drowned out everything else.

The gas flames leaped up two feet long. A crack appeared in the basement's foundations. Timmy's voice had gone deep, a raging, thundering roar that demanded obedience and swore its everlasting vengeance in an ancient, perverted language. Blood dripped down the walls and pooled on the floor. The room got hotter, and hotter, and hotter, until I thought I was going to explode.

Billy braced his hind legs on the foot of the bed and pulled with every muscle in his body. For a moment, the hideously twisted body of a horrific monster was entwined with the innocent flesh of an unsullied child. Billy tore the monster free from its prisoner, and the moment the bodies separated, the trembling stopped. The yelling stopped. The fire stopped. Everything stopped, and the silence was like a cave.

Stocky huddled under my workbench, whimpering.

Timmy lay on the bed, his face pale and sweating, his breathing even. He looked as if he'd been through Hell, but he was free of it.

At the foot of the bed, Billy had his whole body curled around the demon who had caused all this trouble. It was saying something muffled against Billy's chest, over and over again. Billy grabbed it by its short hair and pulled its head free. We could hear what it was saying.

"Thank you, thank you, thank you, thank you..."

"Be careful," I said, tossing one of the blue stones in my hand.

"Don't let it go."

"Boss," said Billy softly, straightening up, "it isn't dangerous."

Considering everything we'd been through, I wasn't so sure about that, but it was true that a less-offensive demon one could hardly hope to find. Though Billy kept a tight hand on his wings, the demon stood no more than four feet tall and was thin, pale, and trembling so hard that he looked as if he would fall apart. His horns were short, soft nubs, and he had a pair of pince-nez balanced across his long, narrow nose.

"I don't understand," said Mrs. Holyfield.

I knelt in front of the demon. "Billy, what kind of demon is it?"

"It's a Megrahyde," said Billy with surprise. He looked at Timmy, who slept on. "They're powerful magically, but they're a very quiet and peaceable people. Their society is enlightened. How in the world did one get to this world?"

"It was a light," gibbered the Megrahyde. "It was a bright light that swallowed me up, and then, and then, I was a little boy, and I was here. I was here and I was doing all these..." He swallowed. "Terrible things, terrible terrible things..." He started to cry again.

"Is he telling the truth?" I said, looking with horror at Timmy.

"I've met Megrahydes before. They lie really, really badly. He's honest."

"I don't understand!" insisted Mrs. Holyfield. "What's happening? Is my Timmy all right?"

"Mrs. Holyfield," I said quietly, taking her hands and leading her to the work table, "we need to talk."

Timmy glared belligerently at Billy as the werewolf finished his project, humming. It wasn't much to look at—a design painted in a box of sand set at Timmy's feet. Timmy's hands were bound to his knees, and he had a design painted in werewolf blood on one cheek. It glowed with a dull throb, burning away the magic in his body.

"By the Horned One himself, Mrs. Holyfield, I swear I thought I had hold of your son," he said, finishing his work and sitting down. We watched the spell do its work for a moment. "I smelled the good one, I held him, I drew him free. And when I was done, your son was still sitting on the bed. I'm sorry."

"I still don't understand," said Mrs. Holyfield.

"The demon wasn't possessing your son," I said. "Your son was possessing the demon. He was using the Megrahyde's magic to make himself stronger."

"My son is not evil!" said Mrs. Holyfield, slapping the table.

"What is evil?" said Billy, rhetorically. "Timmy is a very angry, very troubled little boy, and he needs a great deal of help, and love, and compassion. He robbed another living being of its identity and its power to make himself feel strong, and people were hurt. You do him no favors by living in denial, nor do you help him by coddling him. His problems may be beyond your powers to heal."

"He's my son," said Mrs. Holyfield. "He's a little boy."

"If you were to give your little boy a gun," I said, "do you imagine he would treat it with respect and responsibility? No, and not because he's good or evil, but because he doesn't understand the power that he wields. My partner is depriving your son of his ability to hurt anyone magically ever again, but what Billy is doing won't heal his anger and pain."

"Still, these are modern times, and we have modern ways of treating your son," said Billy. "There's a whole new science called psychiatry that may help. It studies why people are the way they are, and offers ways to help them heal."

Mrs. Holyfield wasn't crying now. She was red-faced and angry. The mark on her son's cheek had only just stopped glowing when she seized his wrist. "A couple of frauds, you two are," she said hotly. "Timmy and I are going to live with my mother in Manchester for a while, until we get back on our feet. Insisting that my son is evil, indeed! He's just a little boy! What harm could a little boy do?"

"Plenty," said Billy, as Mrs. Holyfield swept out, her son in tow. Timmy wasn't back to his full strength yet, but he had enough to stick out his tongue at Billy as he disappeared up the stairs. A moment later, we heard the door slam.

Billy and I looked at each other. "That cub will be a danger to himself and everyone around him until his mother stops treating him like a baby doll and starts recognizing his anger and pain."

"Wonder what causes something like that," I said, softly. "What in the world could have happened to a seven year old child to make him lash out at everything like that?"

"Boss, I don't even want to guess. We dealt with the possession, we bled away the magic, we sent our demon friend home with a profuse apology and a promise to follow up, and we recommended the best course for a blinded mother to take to help her son. That's everything on the shopping list. We won this one."

"We've won nothing," I said, getting up and reaching for a broom. All I could think of to do now was to clean up.

So that's all I did.

Size Matters

Even a specialist in the intricacies of the supernatural occasionally finds himself, shall we say, stumped. Not all strange and peculiar things come from higher (or lower) astral planes, there is plenty of space in, well, space to produce wonders that are in no way magical or even mystical.

In this fourth story in the Arcanum Arcanorum series, our intrepid heroes find themselves facing a curious monster–but the indomitable British spirit can face any challenge.

Can't it?

The Walking Mountain

Ben Goodridge

It was in the Brigham-on-Chapley region of England that my old flatmate Benchley settled following our graduation from Cambridge. We were thick as thieves in our Denbridge College of Magic days, occasionally exceptional students with troublesome streaks that led us to the sorts of high-spiritedness found only among college students with fine minds and few distractions.

It was, for instance, my idea to change the water in the River Cam to chocolate pudding while the punting team was in practice, but since I was only a theorist and he was the practical wizard, I was the one tasked to research the spell while his job was to engineer it. The spell was only to affect a quarter-mile of the river, to have no deleterious effect on the plant and animal life in it, and to reverse itself within fifteen seconds.

I must here assure the reader that despite the effect that the spell DID have, no permanent or lasting damage was done to either the River Cam or the punting team. I also plead with the reader's indulgence that the shortcomings in the spell were not as a result of any errata on my own researches, as before and after the disaster, I had thoroughly checked every note and page I had studied to design the spell. No, it is with Benchley that the unfortunate debacle must rest.

If one wishes to examine the accounts of that day in September of 1889, one need only regard the pertinent issue of the London Times. Suffice it to say on my part that it resulted in two naked students standing sheepishly before the Dean of Magical Studies, soaked from stem to stern in chocolate pudding while an outraged punting coach, who suffered no such indignity, demanded our immediate and summary expulsion.

On that occasion, if on no other, as we were sternly warned that day, the Dean showed kindness and more than a little good grace and humor in demanding of us only that we paid for the damage done—no small sum, but I for my part could well afford it. Letters were also posted immediately to our parents, which to any Cambridge student caught in the act of hijinks is a fate far worse than death, but which indignity I could also bear, considering what might have been the gruesome outcome.

Benchley was of no such means, and was nearly fainting at the prospect of coming up with such a princely sum. He took out a massive loan at an usurious interest rate from a local savings establishment, and so spent the remainder of his University days swaddled in debts that precluded his ever paying for the beer again and taught him the true meaning of parsimony.

There also circulated a poster for a number of years, created by an enterprising photographer who happened to be on site on that fateful day, photographing the punting team. To date I occasionally see the photograph, which is a fine portrait of Benchley and myself, naked, stricken, and humiliated, both clearly recognizable despite being awash in chocolate pudding, crawling out of the River Cam and the horrific results of our arrogance. I suspected, and history later bore me out, that the College gave quiet and nodding approval to the continued circulation of the photograph, as a warning to later pupils who might find their imagination for pranks outstripping their skills at performing them.

Benchley came into quite a lot of money just before his University career finished, enough to settle his remaining debts and purchase land outside of Northampton, where he maintained a thriving practice in spell analysis and diagnosis when he wasn't spending five months of the year teaching at the very same college where any mention of chocolate pudding gave him the willies. At the time of this narrative, he had surpassed comfort and was becoming quite well-off indeed.

I wouldn't like to say that we fell entirely out of touch following our Cambridge days, as we carried on a lively correspondence that hearkened palmier days as well as described our current status as successful men of business and service. However, I had not seen him for at least five years when the telegram arrived on a sunny summer day.

It was actually my business associate's assistant who signed for the telegram. Billy had made several noble attempts to teach him to write, and Stocky had mastered his name, at least. However, it is through incantation that creatures such as Stocky are conjured, and through writing that the conjurations are recorded. Thus, teaching Stocky had had curious effects upon the household, such as summoning giant yet harmless spiders that draped everything in webs, as if someone planned to paint. A first-form reading primer seemed to go well until we discovered that his repetition of its short and simple lines were etching the same words in a fancy script in the attic beams. Since the wards are stronger on the laboratory in the basement, I suggested to Billy that the lessons continue there, only to have an incantation cleaved from the opening lines of an Oscar Wilde children's book submerge the chamber to a depth of four feet, and unleash a savage, bloodthirsty octopus into the waters, which fought my associate for the better part of two and a half hours.

After that, Billy wisely chose to avoid further education until some means could be derived to prevent the reading of innocent stories from becoming the conjurations of horrible monsters. It wasn't so much the fact that the last one had tried to drown him and eat him, as the fact that each of these events subtracted from the sum total of Stocky's life, which had already promised to be short. Stocky's energy was limited, and each spell, especially the sophisticated ones, cost him some of that energy.

Heeding the warnings, and the very real threat of disaster if he spoke aloud any words from any document longer than a haberdashery sign, Stocky handed the telegram to me, unopened. I thanked him politely and examined the contents.

MUST COME TO BRIGHAM IMMEDIATELY STOP
GREATER ARCANA DESTROYING VILLAGE STOP
YRS, BENCHLEY

I blinked a lot at the telegram, primarily because it made no sense whatsoever. There was not a chance that a Greater Arcana could have arrived the previous night. The day completely lacked signs and portents. The sky was the exact opposite of black and morbid. The ground steadfastly refused to tremble, and were there any rains of goat blood anywhere in the meteorological forecasts, I certainly would have read of them.

What's more, had a Greater Arcana arrived on this world, Billy would have been out the door like a shot, either racing in its direction under its fiendish hypnotic mesmerism to join its hellish army of darkness, or fleeing the country as fast as his shaggy legs could carry him so as not to be caught up in the maelstrom. In this regard, he was in fact an excellent coalmine canary, as any magical wave of that size anywhere in the world would have set him off like an alarm clock.

I decided to put this theory to the test. "Billy?" I called.

He came in from where he was burying something in the garden. I didn't like to think what, since we'd had more than one neighbor over demanding to know what became of his cat, and I was only ninety-five percent certain that my partner wasn't keeping his prowling and hunting skills sharp in this urban environment by utilizing the available prey. His face was a mask of dirt and sweat. He had one of my finer linen tablecloths tied around his waist as a breech-clout. "You bellowed?"

I showed him the telegram. He held it close to his face, and his eyes swept over it. Then he looked down at me. "What's this?"

"Telegram," I said.

"I can see that, Boss," he said, patiently, sitting heavily in a chair. "What do you want me to say about it?"

"Well, is it possible that there's a Greater Arcana marauding about the farm country north of London?"

He stared at me for a moment, obviously gauging whether I was serious. Then he burst out laughing. "Oh, wow, Boss," he said, "you had me going for a moment. I mean, your face. It's so perfectly serious."

"I am perfectly serious. You'll notice I'm not laughing. I don't laugh when I'm being perfectly serious. That very much helps to define how serious I'm perfectly being."

"Come on, Boss. A Greater Arcana in Brigham? And the entire magical community of London NOT in total chaos? Your buddy Benchley's having you on."

"Benchley swore off cheap pranks some time ago," I said, taking the telegram back.

"Oh, right," said Billy. "The pudding." It was inevitable that Billy know about the pudding, given his occasional Cambridge associations. "Then whether there's a Greater Arcana in Brigham or not, your friend Benchley is convinced that there is."

"And that's enough for investigation," I said. "Come, Billy. Let's get to the bottom of this."

The drive to Cambridge was pleasant, along some nice country roads, and every rolling mile served to further convince me that Benchley was delusional. Nothing about the landscape or the day indicated the presence of Greater Arcana.

We had brought Stocky along, because having once been a Greater Arcana himself, he made an even better canary than Billy. We had also tried, prior to departure, to reach Benchley on the telephone, as I was certain that he had one, but no one answered the ring.

We were at the top of a rise when Billy pointed to a distant shadow. "What do you make of that, Boss?"

It was an unusual structure he pointed out. Among other things, it was huge—perhaps five hundred feet tall, perhaps taller. It would have dwarfed the Tower of London. Its sheer size was alarming enough, but for its surreal appearance. It was little more than a large pod-shaped dwelling perched atop three massive iron legs. Some sort of heavy rope, like a boat cable, snaked down from the center and dangled loosely between its metal knees.

Alarming as the sight of the object was, it grew more alarming when it took a step. It rocked back on two of its legs and lifted the third, reaching forwards until it overbalanced on it and dropped heavily onto it. There was a moment for the sound to travel, and then a short, thunderous boom. I imagined the automobile trembling.

"It's metal," I said. "Mechanical, self-locomotive...certainly hydraulic. It's a machine."

"Could that be what your friend mistook for a Greater Arcana?"

"I don't see how, even at this distance," I said. "Still, it travels slowly, and there's little more than farmlands and forests in that direction. We may have time for further investigation before we approach it, unless you'd rather..."

"Erm, given the choice, I choose discretion," said Billy. "Let me join you on your reconnaissance."

"Very well," I said, dropping the automobile back into gear. We continued down the lane, towards the village.

The village, as it happened, didn't look very destroyed.

Brigham is a pleasant little country village with shops, a pub, a cluster of houses surrounding a central square, and miles of farmland in every direction. The soft "boom" of the metal monster's footsteps drifted over the fields every fifteen or twenty minutes, and so long as the beast didn't provide an immediate menace, I chose to head down to the pub and ask if the locals had any intelligence concerning it.

The village square was bustling and active at this time of day as farmers brought their stock in to trade for coin or services. We weren't here on market day, which was a shame, as I suddenly craved a bag of fresh vegetables to take with me back to London. Billy turned few heads, as the sight of a werewolf, even one in a waistcoat and trousers, wasn't entirely unexpected in this community. A young man examined my automobile with envy, and I was pleased to provide him with its particulars and price tag. He indicated that he might well look up its manufacturer.

Stocky was a curious monster in this region, both in the sense that few had seen a werewolf quite like him, and in the sense that he poked his oily black muzzle into all things. When he helped himself to a quail from a brace hanging outdoors of a butcher's shop, thus forcing me to surrender a few quid to the shopkeeper (who was quite understanding about it, all things equal), I felt that I should cease absorbing the local color and hale forth to the pub.

"Innkeeper," I said, taking a seat, "stout for myself and my friends. A pint for me, a pint for Stocky, a gallon for Billy, here."

"Certainly, sir," said the barkeep, filling the draughts and putting them on the table. "One and sixpence."

"Keep the change," I said. "I'm an investigator, working for Mr. Benchley of Hawkling Manor."

"Ah, you must be Lord Bannion. I imagine you'll be wondering about the walking water tower out there."

"Indeed, sir," I said, pleased to find a helpful spirit. "My associate was…less than edifying."

"Scared white, you mean, sir?" The barkeep chuckled. "He was in the pub when it landed. Just about wet his trousers when it reared up over the forests. Couple of his mates took him home after he sent you that message."

"Yet you're not frightened."

"Well, it's not hurting nothin' but the Lordship's trees, really, except it put one hell of a dent in Farmer Morgan's pea patch. Hasn't moved but two miles since it showed up."

"Benchley indicated that it was destroying Brigham."

"With all due respect, your Lordship, Mr. Benchley wasn't thinking terrible clearly when his mates took him out of here. Had some kind of breakdown in the head." He tapped his forehead. "Course, he was a bit in his cups. High spiritedness, you know. Tends to the bottle when he's feeling victorious about summat."

Billy finished his beer in two gulps and let out a belch that rattled the glasses. As if in response, another boom rolled through the pub, and the glasses rattled again. No one noticed. Billy shook down, and the barkeep pulled him another draught. "Machine did step on one of Mr. Benchley's guest houses earlier this morning," he said. "For a moment, it was straddlin' the town like it was just a stream. Took no notice of us, though. Just kept walkin'. I must admit, your Lordship, I was quite in awe of it standin' there."

I finished my stout and reached for another pound for Billy's gallon mug. "On the house, your Lordship," said the barkeep. "Any friend of Benchley's is like to be a friend of the whole village."

"Oh. That's very kind of you. Thank you."

"What you reckon the thing is, though, your Lordship? It don't look like it was made in England. Could it be some French invention?"

"I don't know," I said, as Billy finished his refill. "I do know one thing. It isn't magic. Thanks for your hospitality, sir."

"Any time, your Lordship. Any time."

"So Benchley finishes a spell," I said. "A big spell, one he's been working on for some time. He's in the pub, celebrating..."

"Translation: getting rot-stinking drunk," said Billy. He belched again, more subtly than last time. "Can't blame him. That's some good stout."

"And he gets drunk enough so that when that three-footed monstrosity plummets out of the sky, he associates it with his spell," I said. "Something that big must be an accidentally-conjured Greater Arcana. Benchley holds it together long enough to send off the telegram, or his friends send it for him, and then repairs to his stately manor to...what?"

"Reverse the spell?"

I grimaced. Benchley intoxicated and waving his wand around was more likely to turn him into a cockroach than accomplish anything useful. Benchley intoxicated, insane, and waving his wand around led me to half expect that the manor would be a smoldering crater. Intoxication was a built-in proof against powerful spells, since such things required a clarity of mind that could be found in the bottom of no bottle, but panic has a sobering effect.

The manor, to my relief, was no crater. It was, however, deserted.

It lies at the end of a long dirt road accessible just outside the village of Brigham, with no twists, no turns, and only a single gate held shut by a length of fraying twine. The road was in reasonable shape and the car performed adequately.

Benchley keeps no livestock, nor does he plow the fields, but lets other farmers do as they please with the property so long as they don't approach too close to the house or molest the land, as his isolation serves his business quite well.

I pulled up to the main house. The three of us disembarked from the automobile, and I gave the bell a hearty pull. Nothing answered the ring, which echoed deep within the bowels of the house. Benchley keeps no servants, his most recent butler having resigned after turning himself permanently purple after attempting to "clean" an experiment that Benchley had left percolating in a disused pantry, despite dire warnings of "Keep out" and "Unsafe" all over the door, and Benchley had evidently not yet engaged the services of another. I chose instead to simply push open the door, and we all let ourselves into his home.

"Benchley?" I called. When I heard no response, I turned to Stocky. "Can you smell him?"

"Everywhere," said Stocky. "He is in the house, though. His scent on the stoop is fainter than his scent indoors."

I thought for a moment about where Benchley might be, not wanting to do a room-by-room search. Were I Benchley, convinced that an unimaginable horror was at large in the English countryside, I would want to be somewhere safe, and hidden, and hope the Armies of Darkness wouldn't find me. Failing that, I would want some comfort in my final moments as the world was devoured.

"Wine cellar," I said. Billy grinned widely.

I remembered the location of his wine cellar with cheer. Lighting a lantern, I went to the door and popped the latch, and swung it open. "Benchley?" I called. Though I received no answer, I headed downstairs into darkness.

My own wine cellar has long since been converted for the use of magical experimentation, but for a single rack containing a few common vintages. Benchley, with larger facilities in a more isolated setting, felt safer doing his experiments elsewhere, and his wine cellar was still dedicated to the storage of wine.

Billy sniffed as he reached the bottom of the stairs. "Over here," he said, heading around a corner. Curled up under a table, sound asleep, was Benchley.

If the wine had had any sort of calming effect on him, it hadn't yet registered. He clutched a bottle of Bordeaux as if it were a life buoy and he was lost at sea. He was dirty, trembling, and terrified. He had rent his clothes asunder.

"Benchley, old chap?" I said, crouching down.

"He smells bad," said Stocky. "I think he made water."

"He did indeed," I commented. "Come along, Benchley. Come on out from under there."

Throughout this exchange, Benchley failed to register our presence. I should hope that I never find myself in a situation so terrifying that I am too frightened to drink. Finding him passed out and surrounded by empty bottles might have been better, if not as healthy.

He became conscious of the proximity of his old schoolmate and that schoolmate's werewolf companion, and a silly grin started to wander across his features. It was interrupted in its sojourn by the sight of Stocky, who gave him nothing more than his friendly, vacant smile and childlike optimism. Benchley's pupils contracted to the size of pinpoints, he yelped, and he fainted again.

"Oh dear," I said. "Come on. Let's get him somewhere safe."

We put Benchley on a fainting couch in his parlor. Billy brought up a full cask with him. The two gallons of stout in his belly could in no sense begin to intoxicate him, so he had brought reinforcements.

"I'm going to get started," he said, popping the bung and lifting the cask over his head. He drank at the barrel as if it was no more than a beer mug. Wine gurgled down over his neck and chest. When he stopped to take a breath, he clutched the barrel to his belly. "Is he going to be mad at me for this?"

"I doubt it," I said. "That's a table wine. Last year's. If you'd gotten into the ten-year-old reds, he'd have killed you."

Billy drank again, belly bulging. The sheer quantity of alcohol it took to get him even marginally drunk was shocking. Ordinary beer was like skim milk to him.

"Found these in the kitchen," said Stocky, holding up four bottles of Scotch. Billy put down the half-empty barrel.

"Perfect," he said. "Pour 'em in."

"How do you feel?" I said.

"Not ready yet." Billy helped Stocky pour the fifths into the barrel, then hoisted it again. This time, he closed his eyes tight and drank it as fast as he could. I felt sure the poor dear would explode, especially with his grains mixed like that. Wine washed over him. He spread his legs to stabilize his stance.

With the barrel not holding but a few drops, he let it go. It hit the floor and split. Billy was drenched. He threw his mane out of red, bloodshot eyes. His tongue lolled.

"Let's do it now," he said. "This is as far as I'm gonna get on this guy's cellar."

He licked his chops and knelt next to Benchley, pressing his wet paws against Benchley's cheeks. He opened Benchley's mouth a little, whispering a short chant. Then he inhaled.

Benchley's drunkenness, the degree to which he had poisoned himself, flowed out of his body and into Billy's. This was by no means the first time I'd seen him perform such a spell, but Benchley was profoundly drunk, and I could see that Billy had never experienced such intoxication. As Benchley blinked and rubbed his eyes, Billy sank weakly to the floor, hiccupped, and giggled.

"My goodness," said Benchley. "Bannion. Bannion, you came!" He leaped from the couch, flung his arms around me, and nearly knocked me over. "What's been happening? What horrors are resounding throughout the landscape? Is there news from London?"

I disengaged him gently. "Well, thus far, the only horror on the landscape is my associate, too drunk to stand."

"After the fireball last night," said Benchley. "I remember so little… What has happened? Are the thousand years of darkness begun? Are they over? Have you come to help me rediscover the world?"

He wasn't hysterical, but I was on the verge of slapping him anyway. "Benchley, will you calm yourself for a moment? Billy cast a transference spell to sober you up. That's all. The monstrosity that fell out of the sky is a mostly-harmless tower that's been wandering aimlessly about the forests since it landed. There is no immediate danger. The world continues to spin."

"Does it?" Benchley looked horribly relieved. For a moment, I thought he would faint again. Behind him, on the carpet, Billy belched. "Petit-fours!" he cried out, though for what reason, I didn't know.

"Will he be all right?" said Benchley.

"He'll be fine in half an hour," I said. "At which point, you owe him your gratitude and an apology. He'll be humiliated. He is being the fool you made of yourself."

"Benchley?" said Billy, clutching Benchley's leg. "Benchley? Benchley? Benchley? Benchley?"

"Yes, William, what is it? What do you want to say?"

Billy looked unsteadily up into Benchley's face, and licked his chops. Then he said, "I'm peeing," and flopped back down in hysterical laughter.

"Bloody hell," said Benchley. "The carpet—"

"Let's go into the other room," I said quickly, realizing that Billy's wine-bloated body held some 54 Imperial gallons of table red, rapidly transforming into wastewater. "Stocky, keep your eye on him. Make sure he doesn't hurt himself until he's sober."

"Why did you contact me, and not Cambridge?" I said, pouring Benchley a hot mug of East India tea. "This is a science matter, not a magic one. Even if it were a magic one, Cambridge has those skilled in the arts. I only have Billy's skills to depend on."

"Looking back, I'm not entirely sure that I didn't," said Benchley. "I may have dropped in a call to the Queen while I was about it. However, the Cambridge faculty are not here. You are."

"This is not my field, Bench. You need engineers. I'm a detective."

"And you believe we have no tools for finding out what it is?" He sipped his tea. "What it wants?"

"Well, possibly, but surely there are authorities to handle this. We need to contact the appropriate agency."

"We need," said Benchley, "to contact the machine itself."

"And what makes you so sure someone's piloting it? That it isn't a mindless automaton?"

"Well, for one thing, it destroyed my guest house."

"Yes? And?"

"And that's the ONLY thing it destroyed. It stepped right over the village square, but gave all the buildings a wide berth. It looks like it's even moderated its damage to the fields and is sticking to the forests." He sipped again. "I believe it might be lost."

I sighed. Truth to tell, I had the haunting feeling that I could be of use after all. Billy—sober—knew some cracking translation spells, and we could certainly immobilize it if the cause came to be.

"Boss?"

Billy stood in the doorframe. His body was streaming wet, and wine was no longer the liquid of choice for the occasion. He gazed stupidly at me through a forest of pendulous hair, and when he hung out his tongue, it was black.

"If you plan on expectorating, Billy, I beg you use the barrel," I said. The moderate tone of my voice made him clap his paws to his ears and whimper slightly.

"Billy?" said Benchley. "I want to thank you for shouldering my burden. Your partner has spent most of this hour talking sense into me, and I feel we're on the verge of hatching a plan."

"I had a dream," whispered Billy. "I was drowning…in a water closet…"

I stood up, lifted Billy's chin, and peered into his bloodshot eyes. I could see the blood vessels slowly healing even now, and each time he blinked, his gaze was clearer. I peered over his shoulder and winced. Stocky stood morosely on the fainting couch surrounded by a yellowish sea that spread from wall to wall and reflected the chandelier.

"Benchley, I believe you'd better instruct Stocky on the location of your mop. I will take Billy out to the well house and get him properly bathed. When we are ready, we shall visit this landing site and see what we can glean. Fair?"

I poured a thirtieth bucket of cold water over Billy's head, and he shook down and groaned with pleasure. I sent the bucket back down for another one, though, to be fair, Billy was quite clean at this point. His body shone in the afternoon sun, and his hangover was long since passed. I saw Stocky and Benchley approaching from the house as I pitched another bucket over my business partner and watched him shake it off.

"What's the damage?" I called out.

"Well, we've rolled up the carpet—it was pretty much ruined. The furniture should survive, and Stocky mopped out the floors."

"I'm sorry," said Billy, tying back his mane.

"It's my fault," said Benchley. "It was my intoxication that flooded the room. Are we ready?"

We traveled into the forests as a team, with Billy taking point. He followed the hunting trails for a while, and then veered off towards the river. Every once in a while, he'd bend down to sniff at the base of a tree, or pick up a handful of soil in his paws and press his muzzle to it.

"How now, werewolf?" said Benchley.

Billy looked up. We had walked about a mile into the forests, and the air was close and warm. "The forests are nervous," he said. "There has been disturbance."

"We could have told you that," said Benchley.

Billy tasted the air. His tail twitched, very slightly. "The beasts feel it, Wizard. It's reflected in their trails. You can hear it in the birdsong. Even the trees rustle differently than they usually do. The scars you can see, where the monster left its footprints, will take time to heal. The scars you can't see will take even longer. The forest doesn't smell safe."

"Stocky, how about you? Do you feel anything?"

Stocky shook his head. "No, Master. This thing knows not the ways of magic."

We reached the landing site.

"What, precisely, are we looking for?" said Benchley, as we approached the crater.

The trees here were stripped bare, shattered, scattered like cordwood, even buried. The ground was like a plowed field, fertile and brown, but lifeless as of yet. At the heart of this flatscape was a crater some eighth of a mile across, into which water had flowed freely since the night before, turning it into a sparkling blue pond raised around the outer edges, with a trickle of a stream rushing out the other side and away down the hill.

"Do you still carry a lodestone with you?" I said.

"Certainly," he replied. "I carry one on my wand."

"Let me see your wand."

He handed it over to me, wordlessly, and I stuck it into the soft ground. It was, however, clean when I withdrew it. I examined it with care, but no particles clung to it. "The machine left this crater when it landed. That doesn't sound like a craft under any form of control or with any sort of strategy. Perhaps it's like an automobile with no driver."

"What's the magnet for?"

"To determine whether some element of the craft broke off when it landed. Perhaps if we can determine its composition, we can establish its weakness. This soil may house components or architecture separated from the main structure." I climbed the rim of the crater and looked out over the waters. "Curious," I commented.

"What's that?" said Benchley, joining me on the rim with Stocky.

"Well, notice the ripples in the water, as if a breeze were stirring them up."

"Nothing unusual about that."

"Except there is no breeze. The water ripples towards us, but I feel no wind. The air is still. In fact, what little breeze we feel is coming from another direction."

Billy knelt at the edge of the pond and put his muzzle near the water. "It smells different," he said. "There's something in the smell. Something in the water." He dipped his paw and brought it to his muzzle. He tasted it. "It's pure and clean. There are no poisons, no hazards, no threats. Just something…like it's waiting."

I handed Benchley back his wand, removed my shoes, and waded into the crater, clothes and all. "This water is very warm," I commented. "It's much like a bath."

"That might be an artifact from the crash landing," said Benchley. "Anything moving at that speed would build up a great deal of heat. I'd imagine that the ground was quite hot here last night."

"And solid," I noted. "The ground all around is churned as if a tornado passed over it, but the bowl of the crater is like concrete. At what angle did the craft strike the ground?"

"Ah. Now, that, I have measured," said Benchley. He took a rumpled piece of paper from his pocket and squinted at it. (He never did admit that he was rather farsighted.) Then he indicated a direction into the sky. I visualized a line leading from his hand to the heart of the crater, and waded deeper into the water. It grew quite deep very quickly, and I soon found myself swimming.

"Here," I called. "The deepest part of the crater is here. The water is terribly warm."

"Hold on," said Benchley. "I want to try something."

He drew his wand, but as soon as he held it over the water, the water reached for it. Those are the words I have to describe what I witnessed, which was a talon of water reaching from the surface towards the wand as if to grab it.

He drew his wand away, and the water subsided, but it still seemed interested somehow, drawn towards the wand.

I swam back to the banking and crawled onto the crater lip. "Give me your wand," I said, and Benchley handed it to me as if frightened of it. The water that streamed from my clothes abruptly defied gravity and streamed towards the tip of the wand. Once surrounding the lodestone, the water had nowhere else to go, and simply formed a very large, very heavy sphere at the end of the wand. I needed two hands to hold it up.

"Magnetic water?" said Benchley.

My clothes were completely dry now, but judging from the weight of the wand, they wouldn't stay that way. Billy wrapped his magnificent paw around my fists, helping me hold it up, and even Stocky pitched in, though now the water was only a foot above the surface on the pond, and the pond reached for it again.

Stocky seized me around the waist, and we combined our weight, but I already knew we were fighting a losing battle. The living water poured up onto the wand, yanking all of us down into the water. I felt it drag me across the bottom of the pond, and Billy's claws raked at my suit as he tried to hang on. Still, underwater, all the pressures were equal, and I found that I could let go. I released the wand and broke the surface.

"Are you all right?" called Benchley as we paddled to land once again.

"Yes, but I seem to have lost your wand." I held up my empty hands.

"Bugger the wand," he opined. "I've got a dozen."

We heard the faint "boom" of the metal monster's footstep again. It had been a while since I'd heard one, or at least I'd grown so used to them that I'd learned to ignore them. Billy, however, lifted his streaming head and sniffed the air.

"What is it, Bill?"

Before he could answer, we heard another "boom," closer than the first. "Is it just me," said Benchley, "or are those footsteps a lot closer together?"

"That one was a lot louder, too," said Billy, standing up suddenly. The next one followed right on the heels of his statement, and was thunderous.

"It's coming this way," whispered Benchley.

No sooner had the color drained from his face than we saw it, towering above the surviving trees, felt the rush of wind accompanying its approach. Billy shouted over its roar, "What the hell have you guys been doing?"

"It's the water," I called, raising my voice above the roar of the monster. "It's summoning the tower somehow."

The trees nearest to us exploded in a hail of splinters, and the foot of the creature created a blast of air that knocked us all off our feet and Stocky into the crater. Soaked with mud, Billy scrambled towards us. "Get down!" he shouted. "Get DOWN!"

The monster stepped on him.

The rush of air sent another wave of mud pouring over us, and when I lifted my head, the foot of the beast was no more than ten yards away. It was as large as a small house, at least twelve feet tall, a sloping triangle with a vast rubber shoe on it. It occurred to me that the shoe must serve the same purpose as the tire on my automobile—a soft surface to make the ride easier. This shoe had landed on Billy, crushing him flat and sending a fan of blood spraying for ten feet in every direction. I looked up, and up, and up at the monster, which did not look down at me or regard me any more than I might have regarded an ant on the streets of London. I heard the echoing boom and felt the rush of wind of its other foot landing several yards away, and felt the thud of its third foot trip my heartbeat even further.

So balanced, it started to lift the foot that had flattened my partner. No sooner did it raise the shoe from the indentation than I heard a string of swear words as my immortal associate relieved the outrage he felt at having nearly every bone in his body shattered. He stuck to the shoe of the thing like a beetle, peeling off only when he had reached an altitude of some twenty feet, and plummeted down into the mud again as the foot roared overhead, drowning out his obscenities. The impact of the foot landing on the other side of the crater again knocked me off my feet and sloshed the swirling whirlpool over me, and for a moment I could not surface.

Then the monster stepped on me.

Its other leg, lifting almost as soon as its forward leg landed, roared down and clapped over me. I was flat on my back, sinking slowly into the mud, with perhaps three inches between the surface and the metal sheet pressing into my face. I was definitely sinking deeper, as well, and though water could not pour in over the beast's rubber shoe, it could definitely seep up under it, and I felt the mud oozing up my face.

I don't mind confessing that it was quite a terrifying experience, lying flat on my back in a tiny air pocket—so terrifying that I don't even mind confessing that I made considerable water in my trousers. It was to my fortune that I was already so befouled with mud that no one would notice, but of course for Billy, whose muzzle was better attuned to such changes in atmosphere. I was not eager to die, I did not embrace it, yet I felt powerless as to preventing it. It was not the first time I had been in such a position, and I would later find myself in far more dire straits, yet as keen as I was for survival, I was also curious as to how my companions were faring. Billy was crushed, and somewhere under this vast plain lay Benchley and Stocky, both sinking slowly into the mud under the million-ton weight of the monster.

And then I heard a roar of machinery, and suddenly above me was only blue sky and frightened birds, as the foot swept away like a lid on a dish. It moved so fast that I was caught up in its vacuum, peeled out of the mud, and flung down some twelve to fifteen feet away, which was something of an exhilarating experience. I lifted my head from the slime in time to notice that the vast monster was straddling its own landing site. I saw Billy helping Stocky to stand, and Benchley struggling to free himself from the ground, and felt some light relief. Billy crawled over to me and checked to ensure that I wasn't in some sort of shock or fit, and I assured him that I was made of quite stern stuff and suffered not a bruise from having been stepped on by a walking mountain.

We went to collect Benchley and possibly avoid his eventual fossilization, but he did not extricate easily, and it took some leverage and a long stick to pry him free.

"At least it stopped walking," I said, gazing up at it. The whirlpool still swirled under the body of the machine, and all the water in the vicinity was drawing towards it as fast as it slopped out again. The monster reached its single long tentacle down into the vortex and pulled something free. I only caught a glimpse of it as it rose. It was

Benchley's magic wand.

A sea of water waved after it, and I suddenly found myself in what I can only describe as a reverse rainstorm. Water and mud flew up from the ground and pelted me, and Stocky, and Benchley, and the monster, as the lodestone drew the pond from the crater. The wind drew up into a hurricane.

"How do we get its attention?" shouted Benchley.

"The wand seems to have its interest," I called back. "Maybe if we can use it to cast a spell..."

"How do we get it back?"

Billy nodded. "Leave it to me," he shouted. He scrambled across the mud to the thing's foot and leaped onto its shoe. From there, he clawed his way to its top, and then to the hinge that formed its ankle. I kept a weather-eye on the monster as I watched Billy scrambling up its leg. The next time it swung around to shake the water off the lodestone, Billy leaped out and grabbed it by the tentacle.

He slid down it, upside-down, reaching for the wand. The thing played crack-the-whip again, and Billy's legs swung free. I heard a sound not unlike the chime of the Bells of St. Clemons as his back broke against the leg of the beast, but he did not let go. Finally, he reached his paw down and wrapped it around the wand's head. A huge rock, ripped from the ground by the force of the beast's reverse gravity, smashed the side of his head to a bloody mess, and it started playing crack-the-whip again.

Finally, Billy managed an incantation. I have no idea what one he used, as it absolutely didn't matter, the point being to reveal his presence at the end of the wand. The effect, however, was a delight. The reverse whirlwind ceased. It hailed mud for a few minutes, and a large rock whistled out of the sky and hit the surface of the now-swampy crater with a splash that sent a wave over all of us.

From up on the thing's arm, Billy spat mud and a tooth, his face and back already healed. Then he looked around suddenly, terror across his face. "What's this?" he cried. "What's going on? What's..."

He disappeared.

So far as I know, I never lost consciousness, yet the sensation was similar—one moment I was in one place, the next I was in another, with no explanation forthcoming as to the change of states.

The room was warm, and featureless, and about knee-deep in mud, and it was in this that I was still struggling as if trying to escape its clutches. I wound up scrambling across the floor and supporting myself wearily against the wall, drawing great huge gasps of the rich, dizzying air.

Words floated in, dulcet and androgynous, as if played on a melodion. They tickled me, inside and out, and I found it difficult not to grin. Wherever I was, I was in no immediate danger, and the first thing I heard from my host was an apology, which went a long way towards comforting my jangled nerves.

"I'm so sorry for any discomfort I might have caused," said the dulcet voice. "I was troubled that I might have hurt you, and I'm pleased to see that you are well. Don't be frightened."

Frightened is not a word I would have used to describe my sensations at that moment. I was, of course, apprehensive—it was not lost on me that the walls were made up of the same material as the walking mountain, and I felt that I had achieved my goal of finding a way into its unbreakable hull, though certainly my entrance had been facilitated by the inhabitant.

This small, warm room had a wide open door, and I headed towards it, intent on greeting and perhaps thanking for my life my hosts. Instead, I struck against nothing with a melodious bong and fell splat into the mud again.

A very familiar voice said, "I already tried, Boss. We don't exactly have the run of the place."

I leaned against the flexible nothing that barricaded the door into a wide, round room surrounded by cells very similar to mine. Placing myself at twelve on the clock, I gathered that the entrance to my gilded prison was at six, and Billy was in the cell at three, slimed with mud and leaning gamely against the air. I saw Benchley and Stocky in other cells, also awash in mud, and I wondered what the mud was in aid of.

"Are any of us hurt?" called Benchley. "Are we all right?"

"I'm in one piece," I said.

"I'm still in several, but they're all joining up in the middle," said Billy. "Stocky, say something?"

"Hello, Master."

"That'll do."

"I'm on my way up now," said the host. "Again, I implore you, don't be frightened. I wouldn't have hurt you for anything. I'm going to step into the room now. I only want to talk."

The being that stepped into the room held no horror for one regularly exposed to the presence of demons and other forces of nature, though I did take a moment to marvel at the wonderful shapes that life takes. Our host stood on three legs, much like his machine. He had three arms, each with a long hand ending in three fingers, and three feet with three long toes. He looked around at all of us, with three eyes set into a triangular head with a tuft of yellowish hair at the top. His skin was shiny, scaly, and iridescent, like the skin of a snake. He was a rather handsome being, all things considered, with a long, lithe, flexible body dressed in what looked like silvery long underwear. The object at his side had the rough shape of a pistol, except it had a fat body and no aperture at the front.

What struck me was that our host was even more nervous than he expected us to be. Not that he was terrified of US, per se, just of what our reaction might have been had we not had open minds and curious hearts.

"I am Dodo," he said. "I managed to bring you in here before you were hurt." He looked anxiously around at his captive audience. "You aren't hurt, are you? The furry one took some terrible blows before I could transport him in."

"I'm fine," said Billy. "It takes a lot to damage me permanently."

"I'm Lord Plantagenet Bannion of London," I said. "I'm pleased to make your acquaintance, though I must admit that the circumstances have me confused. This is Billy, my business partner and good friend. We were summoned to investigate this machine of yours. These are Stocky, Billy's assistant, and Benchley, a Wizard."

Dodo looked as sheepish as a creature from another planet could look. "I haven't hurt anyone, have I? Only I think I stepped on a house."

"That would be mine," said Benchley tightly.

Dodo looked sheepish again. I caught Billy trying to get my attention, and looked over at him.

"Hey, Boss," he said. "We're naked."

I looked down. Indeed, the transport had transported us entirely out of our clothes. All I wore was half an inch of black British mud from head to toe.

"I didn't want to transport you up here with any possessions," said Dodo. "That's how I set the filters. I didn't want to take a chance that you'd bring a weapon or something on board. I didn't know what the Tripod's self-defense mechanism might do."

"You didn't know?" I leaned against the air again and tilted my head at my host. "You...you're not quite sure how to drive this machine, are you?"

Dodo bowed his head.

"You managed to transport the mud, though, didn't you?" said Billy, sliming down the fur of his face and chest.

"I did my best," murmured Dodo. "If you want clothes, I can design some for you."

"Thank you," I said. "That would be most satisfactory. Also, if you could do something about...all this mud..."

Dodo's eyes widened with curiosity. "You don't like the mud? I transported it with you because I thought you needed it to survive."

"No," I said, tight-lipped, while Billy tried not to giggle. "I'm not a mudskipper. I function best in dry clothes with a nice cup of tea in one hand."

"I'm sorry, I'm sorry," said Dodo hurriedly. He pulled the pistol from his pocket, adjusted something on it, aimed it at me, and fired.

Something warm flowed from what would have been its muzzle, straight through the solid air, and suddenly it was raining in my chamber. The water was warm, and cleansing, and had a hint of soap in it with a sweet scent, and I found that it made me clean very effectively. The mud swirled away through the drainage system. Across the round room, Billy was also getting a vigorous shower, though with his fur, his took more time.

After the water, the rooms grew hot, and warm air blew in from the doorways. It only took a few seconds to dry, and then the room was full of red, sparkly light. I was clean and dry when what looked like a metal boiler suit appeared hanging on one wall.

I took it down. It was a very soft, very fine fabric, like silk or damask, yet sturdy as iron and sparkling like the surface of a pond. It was a one-piece, and I struggled into it, amazed at how well it fit. The seam closed itself and turned invisible.

"Is that more…comfortable?" said Dodo, and I nodded.

"Much," I said, very pleased. He pressed a button on his pistol, and I felt warm air move past me. The doors were open.

"I feel like an aluminum can," said Benchley, tugging at his sleeves, though there was no way for his costume to be ill-fitting. "Remind me not to wear this in the sunlight if I don't want my associates blinded."

Billy padded over to Dodo and sniffed at him. His tail wagged. "Are you frightened?" he said, showing lots of teeth.

"A little," said Dodo.

"You smell frightened."

Dodo was looking around at us. "Three different species," he said. "But all intelligent, bipedal, binocular, binaural…what a coincidence for this world."

"I'm not sure I understand," I said. "You said you were having trouble guiding this machine? Did you not build it?"

Dodo's eyes widened, apparently a universal expression of surprise. "Oh, no, no! By the stars, no! I…well, I apprehended it. Er… borrowed it."

"You stole it," said Billy, grinning as if he had a mouthful of mints.

"Oh, please," Dodo implored Billy almost desperately. "Please don't take me back. They'll kill me if I go back. There's a war going on, whole worlds devastated…I just had to get away. That's all. So I took one of the Tripods. I doubt they even noticed that it was missing."

"Relax, my friend," I said. "We couldn't send you home even if we wanted to. Nevertheless, it might not be a bad idea if you settled somewhere. It won't be safe for you to blunder about the English countryside in a war machine."

"Perhaps you'll be welcome here on Earth," said Billy. "I wouldn't trust your Tripod in the paws of these…" He gestured in my direction. "…Clumsy warriors, though."

"You'd be an asset at Cambridge," said Benchley. "Or any scientific institute."

"Then we're agreed," I said, though a little tightly. "We shall ask the Parliament to allow Dodo to stay, but we must ask Dodo to return the Tripod from whence it came."

Upon arriving in the chamber that served as the control center for the war machine, I immediately saw what one of Dodo's problems must have been. The place was very large and clearly constructed for a crew of at least three for guidance alone. The controls were arranged on triangular supports, and triangular panels showed images of the view below, moving pictures like those that appear in a Kesselar Mirror or cauldron reflection.

"I think Benchley might have the solution to your piloting problem," said Billy. He held his paws together, then drew them apart. Benchley's wand was between them, and he offered it to the Wizard.

"What's that?" said Dodo.

"My wand," said Benchley. "Think of it as a focusing device. It channels power. And it had a very strange effect on your vehicle."

"Is that the little monster that took over my guidance systems before?" said Dodo. "Let me see it."

Benchley shrugged and handed it over. Dodo examined it stupidly for a moment, like a monkey trying to figure out how to get into a banana. "This is just a nine-unit carbonaceous steel rod with a magnet stuck on the end of it," he said. "I can't think how it jammed my guidance systems."

"Water pooled in the crash site where your vehicle landed," I said. "When the wand touched the water, it summoned the machine."

"It's also," said Billy, snatching the wand away from Dodo, "Benchley's." He handed the wand politely to Benchley. "What do you think?"

"I can give it a try," said Benchley. "Where do you want it?"

Billy folded his arms. "London," he said. "Figure we walk it right up the Thames. That should get the attention of the necessary authorities."

"And then some," I said.

Benchley rolled up his sleeves, lifted his wand, and swept it over the blinking control panels. A deep rumble started up under our feet, and the machine lifted a leg and started to walk.

"How is this possible?" said Dodo, walking all the way around Benchley. "He isn't even touching the equipment!"

"Well, it's just a mechanical device like any mechanical device, really," said Billy. "Benchley doesn't have to know every little thing about how it works in order to make it move."

"This is amazing," said Dodo. "And the ride is so smooth! And swift!"

"You found driving difficult? But you have three paws," said Billy.

"It's not enough for all this equipment. Besides, I lack the expertise of the Master Pilots of my people."

"How much training did you get?"

"Well, licensing and clearance for Tripod command generally takes about eleven hundred and forty hours," said Dodo, his translation device obviously finding our units of time and mathematics no challenge.

"And you're licensed?" I said.

"Er, no," he admitted. "I've only had...four hours' training."

The Tripod stopped so that Benchley could join us in staring at him.

"I'd never even been inside a Tripod before I appropriated this one," said Dodo. "I just watched a few filmstrips. We're moving much more smoothly now."

Billy nudged me. "You're hoping for a Royal audience, aren't you?"

"Why not?" I said. "Our new friend is not a demon, but a visitor from another planet. His case should be put before the proper authorities, and I doubt the Queen of England would listen to us if we just marched straight to Buckingham Palace and said that we were hosting an otherworldly visitor who wanted to talk to an authority figure. No—the Tripod is large, impressive, and, if we can keep from stepping on anything expensive, relatively harmless. Already, in under a minute, an inexperienced pilot has covered a mile."

"And contributed mightily to rural deforestation," said Billy.

"Well, it's all farmland from here to the sea," I said. "Benchley, get a fix on East and travel as much across open space as you can. If we can avoid communities and settlements, we should reach the ocean in a few minutes."

The height of the Tripod was more than a match for the sea. The going was slower in the water, though, and Benchley was growing fatigued. He was sweating quite a lot and his face was growing red. Finally, he lowered the wand and handed it to Billy.

Billy would not last as long as pilot as Benchley did, for two reasons. One, most of Billy's magic went into keeping him alive and holding him together, no matter what, leaving him with much less magic for casting than a skilled Wizard. Two, it wasn't his wand and he lacked an affinity with the magic Benchley had put into it.

His was a clumsy Earth magic, and the going was much rougher. What's more, machinery always aggravated him, and the Tripod was the paragon of machines. The Tripod stumbled forward, plodding nervously along the sea bed, as Billy stood in the center of its console room soaked with sweat and tried not to faint.

Finally, at the mouth of the estuary, he lowered the wand and leaned heavily against a control panel. "I can go no farther," he announced, sitting heavily on the floor. He handed the wand back to Benchley and buried his face in his paws. "Wake me when we get to Picadilly."

"Well done, old chap," I said. Benchley started marching the Tripod up the river, but he'd never quite recovered from his previous turn at the controls, and was sweating in just a few minutes. "Can you get us to London?" I asked.

"Just about," panted Benchley. "Don't expect the express train, though."

"Try not to step on any bridges or boats," I said.

"Cheek."

Dodo watched the whole thing, bemused. "I still don't see how this is possible," he said. "There's no way your primitive people could possibly have concocted a machine this complicated, yet with that metal stick in your hand you guide it like an expert."

"I do have a theory about that," I said. "Your ship was out of control when it crashed, correct?"

"Well, yes."

"Where it landed, it interrupted a stream. Now, water is one of the four magic Life-Elements, the other three being Earth, which was richly disturbed by your impact, Fire, the heat from the hull as you passed through the atmosphere, and Air, which you must have torn open like cloth as you descended. So you damaged the psychic fabric of all four Life-Elements in a single location. Our werewolf Billy detected it before we even reached your crash site. Benchley, your pilot, is highly skilled at manipulating life-forces, and the wand is the instrument he uses to channel them. When that instrument was fully immersed in the initial location of that psychic disturbance, it immediately detected the cause of it. At the same time, there must be some form of equipment on board this ship that recognized the wand as a detector."

"We...we have devices that can tell when we're being scanned by another ship," said Dodo, uncertainly. "Our computers can detect that kind of power source."

I had no idea what a computer was, but I soldiered on. "Then that's it. Your ship felt the wand's psychic call, and responded to it. In essence, this wand became part of the ship's equipment, and the ship wanted to collect it to be complete."

"I see," said Dodo, though he clearly didn't. "And now you can pilot the Tripod just by holding the wand and...wishing?"

"Oh, there's so much more to magic than just wishing, my friend," said Billy, still slumped against the wall.

"Well, as my third father used to say, who cares how it works, as long as it works," said Dodo. "And only Billy and Benchley can do this?"

"Pretty much, yeah," said Billy. He didn't include Stocky, because for Stocky to give a demonstration would have shortened his lifespan by years.

"We're...reaching London, friends," panted Benchley. "I think... we're gonna have...a hell of a reception."

I'd guessed, correctly, that what with our rising from the depths of the Thames and towering over London like a sentinel, we stood a good chance of getting a royal reception. The important thing, I assured Dodo, was that we present an imposing presence without a threatening one.

Of course, bumping into London Bridge and sending the center section crashing into the Thames did not help our image. It was only fortunate that we did no damage to the Tower Bridge.

We watched through the monitors as a crowd gathered on the banks of the Thames to gawk and gape and stare and point, as the water drained out of the cabin and we waited patiently until it was safe to disembark. I elected to go first, on the very sensible grounds that a human being would be less likely to be riddled with bullets than a werewolf or a three-armed space-creature. Given the opportunity, I could possibly explain.

So the transportation beam gathered my atoms from the cabin and sent them down to London Bridge, where the Army had already set up a cordon.

It was night now, and cool, and the clothes I wore offset the chill nicely. Nevertheless, I somehow doubted they were bulletproof, so when every firearm the Army held aimed at my head and made ready to fire, I held up my hands and bravely shouted, "Don't shoot! I'm from Islington!"

That, at least, puzzled them considerably, and there was some consternation concerning whether or not I was still a threat.

"Oy!" called someone in the crowd. "That your machine there?"

I looked up—quite far up—at the Tripod, as if noticing it for the first time. I was awfully tempted in that moment to claim that I had never seen it before in my life, and enquire as to its construction, yet I still had far too many firearms aimed at me for comfort and clarity. "It's a transport," I said. "It's not mine. I'm Lord Plantagenet Bannion. I'm from London. I assure you that this machine is, right now, perfectly safe. None of you are under any threat at all." In direct contradiction of the latter, several feet of London Bridge tumbled into the river and vanished.

I addressed London again. "I need to speak to the Queen."

The Brigadier had had about enough of me. "Look, shiny britches, I don't know where you got that thing or what it's doing in the middle of London, but you get it out of the river right now and bog it off back where it came from."

"I need to speak to the Queen. It's urgent. It's a matter of political asylum. Within that craft is a visitor from another world, washed up on our planet and seeking refuge on our peaceful shores."

A golden glow sparkled about four feet away from the bridge's outer rail. It fully solidified, the glow faded, and Billy plunged out of midair and straight into the river with a yell. The platoon rushed to the edge of the bridge and stared, bemused, at the werewolf floundering about in the water, swearing at the top of his lungs.

"Is...is that him?" said the Brigadier.

"No, sir. That's my business partner. He had the misfortune to be involved in this adventure."

"Lord Bannion?" said the Brigadier, rubbing his mustache. "Seems I've heard your name pop up a few times. You say there's a man from another planet inside that thing?"

"Yes, sir."

"Very well. I think we can assure you a Royal audience. In fact, I don't bloody well see how we can avoid it. If you wouldn't mind waiting here while we arrange things?" He reminded me that he was still holding his pistol and could make things quite uncomfortable for me were I to refuse.

On the riverbank, a half-dozen hale men helped a bedraggled and stinking Billy out of the effluent. When he saw how many rifles surrounded him, he sighed, bowed his head, and raised his paws. Gunfire could do him no permanent damage, but he was in no mood to pick six pounds of lead shot out of his chest cavity.

Benchley was the next person to appear out of nowhere, in a brief rush of displaced air. He panted slightly, looked bewildered at his surroundings, then said, very faintly, "Oh."

"Who is this?"

"Charles Benchley, D-Mag-A, at your service. The occupant apologizes for the delay, but it was felt that sending a human envoy ahead would soothe nerves somewhat. He assures that his intention was only to gain the positive attention of London, not spark an interstellar war. If you are ready, then, gentlemen, Dodo will make his appearance?"

The Army took a step back at the same time as all their rifles came down to aim at us. I looked at Benchley, he looked at me, and we both shrugged. "Ready," said Benchley.

The air glowed golden, and Dodo appeared in the center of the circle of soldiers. He had his head down and all three hands up, and was shouting, "Don't shoot! Don't shoot! Don't shoot!"

Evidently this paranoia was healthy, for despite the Queen's own English spoken mellifluently through the harmless lips of the being, there was a loud rattle of firearms being primed for firing, and I prayed that the British Army had as steady a set of nerves as they claimed, for but one stray bullet would have resulted in an avalanche of gunfire that might have reduced us to butcher's leftovers.

"What is that?" whispered the Brigadier. "Where has it come from?"

"From a world far away. A world at war, Brigadier. He came to us seeking peace, and brings the Tripod as a gift."

"Well, something like that, anyway," said Dodo. "Well, almost something." He grinned mischeviously. "Well, maybe not."

There were so many weapons pointed at my head that I had to turn very, very slowly to look Dodo in the eyes. "What did you say, sport?"

"You surmised much correctly, Earthling," said Dodo. "I am, as I said, a deserter from my ranks. I have no taste for fighting. But glory..." He licked his lips. "Glory is a thing all my people aspire to. I needed a way to win glory without putting myself at risk."

I looked around, gripped with the sinking feeling that I'd been had. "How does this win you glory?" I said, bewildered. "What glory can you win here?"

"Well, as you guessed, the Tripod is fully equipped with devices that detect when it's being scanned. It also comes with a full complement of homing equipment. I crashed on this world deliberately, you see. I had to inflict just enough damage on the Tripod to activate its distress beacons without making it unusable."

The Brigadier lifted his pistol and aimed it very pointedly at the alien. "What is it you're saying, Mr. Dodo?"

"Oh, put that away, Brigadier. Your weapon will do you no good."

The Brigadier fired, but the bullet never struck its target. He fired again, and again, and again, and each time the bullet landed with a harmless clink just outside the perimeter of the Tripod's feet.

"The solid air," I said, horrified. "He's protected by the solid air! The same solid air he used when he brought us aboard!"

As if in response, the Tripod let out a colossal blast. It was muffled where we stood, but it knocked everyone on both sides of the river off their feet and shattered windows all up and down the Thames. Waves thundered out from the center of the Tripod. Several more yards of London Bridge tumbled into the river.

"That was just the warning klaxon, Brigadier. I assure you that were I to unleash the full power of the Tripod's weaponry, I could reduce London to a smouldering crater in seconds." He folded two of his arms. "Trusting, gullible humans," he said, pacing and grinning. "You gave me all I needed to plant our most glorious weapon of conquest in the heart of your greatest city. Now its beacons call its masters. They will be here in hours—the legendary Alaxalarian Parregnum, to find their poor, pitiful, lost wanderer and bring him home—and to seize the planet he has discovered at the outskirts of the Galaxy, with its precious cargo of over one point seven billion slaves, as well as its fuel, its mineral wealth, its habitats, and its water." He grinned lasciviously. "I have effectively become a one-soldier invasion force," he crowed. "There will be glory in abundance—a promotion, a commission, I shall be a pampered officer far from the front lines. And all I had to do was fool a handful of primitives."

I rushed at him, but he pulled the same tool from its holster as he'd used to activate our showers. Held more menacingly, it looked enough like a pistol that I stopped. "Uh uh, human, that's close enough. This bathed you last time. I assure you that on this setting it will strip the skin from your bones."

"Everyone keep back," I said, backing off. "Everyone keep back until I think of something."

"Haven't you done quite enough?" said the Brigadier.

"Yes, I think he's done enough," said Dodo. "More than I could have hoped for, in fact. To be able to pilot the Tripod, and with such skill and precision, why, Benchley and Bannion have proven most able associates in this mission."

"Except you forgot one thing," called Billy from the riverbank. He placed his paws together as if in prayer.

Dodo looked at him curiously, and then his face collapsed. "No," he whispered. "No, that's not fair."

Billy drew his paws apart. He was holding Benchley's wand. He gave it a little flick.

The Tripod lifted its head slightly. The crowd backed away, frightened.

"Sorry about your wand," said Billy.

"Don't worry," said Benchley. "I have hundreds."

Billy flicked Benchley's wand into the Thames.

As soon as the wand touched the surface of the water, the Tripod reached for it with its long, prehensile trunk. The water reached up in response, as the Thames roared from its riverbed, high over London Bridge. The Tripod plunged its trunk into the wave.

"No!" cried Dodo. "No, you mustn't!" He aimed the porcelain pistol again, but the Tripod's shielding had dissipated so that it could reach for the water—the spray in our faces told us that much. A hundred rifles trained on Dodo's head and he dropped the porcelain pistol in a panic. "No, please!" he cried. "I don't belong here! Let me go with it! I promise I shan't return! Please!"

The Tripod must have got hold of the wand, for it abruptly rose from the Thames. Its legs folded under it, and its tentacle, the wand firmly in place, retracted back into its body. A warm glow emanated from under it, and with a single thud that echoed the length and breadth of London, it rose into the air and disappeared into the night sky.

"Where'd you send it?" I said, as Dodo fell gibbering to the ground.

"Mars," called Billy, folding his arms triumphantly. "Then if the Relaxing Parrots come looking for it, they'll find it unmanned on an uninhabited planet. It should bring us no more mischief."

"You're nicked," said the Brigadier, taking the alien by one of its arms.

"I gambled for a billion and lost," said Dodo, looking hopeless and helpless. "My people…my planet…I shall never see them again… what shall I do?"

"Spend the rest of your natural life in the Tower of London," I said, "unless you're prepared to be cooperative. Unfortunately, it is not for us to decide your fate. Only law can do that, and law must decide how to punish you for making war on England."

"Bannion," cried Dodo. "Bannion, you have been my friend. You have been kind. You won't let them hurt me, will you? Bannion? I have seen the error of my ways! I repent! I shall be a good English citizen, I swear!" His voice was fading as the ever-efficient British bobbies swept in and dragged him off. "Bannion, please! I only acted as I did because I was afraid! You understand, don't you? Bannion!"

I nodded. "Yes," I said quietly. "I understand."

Well, that was very much the end of the tale. Once it was determined that Dodo had no further tricks up his sleeves (and the Royal Astronomers assured us that the Tripod was, in fact, on its way to uninhabited and uninhabitable Mars), the poor alien was led off to prison, where, it was hoped, he could eventually be rehabilitated into society. And yes, we were able to meet the Queen.

The waning days of Her Royal Highness and the House of Hanover were upon us, and Queen Victoria was but a small woman, yet as we knelt before her, she remained aware that she was bestowing not merely a national honor, but an historic one.

She stood before Billy, who was fiercely trying to concentrate on a spot of carpet.

"I dub thee," she said, "Sir William, of Wegnoc."

With that stroke of a sword, she wrote history large, for werewolves were not until that moment considered citizens of the British Empire, nor were they eligible for the honors and orders of British citizenship, yet when it was learned that a werewolf had saved not merely London but quite possibly the whole world, the Prime Minister could hardly refuse.

It's my understanding that she was ill the day she conferred the gifts of a grateful Empire, and thus did not stay for the banquet afterwards, where, I'm quite pleased to say, "Sir William" was a perfect gentleman, who ensured that Stocky also minded his manners, much to the astonishment, not to say chagrin, of some of the other assembled nobility.

Afterwards, well-fed and well-rewarded, we repaired to the brownstone, where we pledged to put Benchley up for the night before taking a morning train to Cambridge, where we would be able to recover my automobile.

"You realize," said Billy, examining his medal and enjoying a bottle of wine, "that this puts us in direct service to the Crown."

"I do," I said.

"And the Crown hasn't had a Ministry-level magician since before the Interregnum."

"Is that a fact?" I said.

"It is. The Crown has depended on private services like our own for interaction with magic users. There's a great deal of money to be made by those whose services have attracted the favor of the Crown." He sipped his wine. "Although there is also a great deal more work."

I speculated. "More money?" I said.

"Indeed."

"Give me the bottle."

He handed me the bottle. I handed it back to him nearly empty. Then, I went to bed.

Bollocks

Sometimes the dead come back to life.

Sometimes evil creeps through the border around our realm.

Sometimes you turn a wrong road and end up somewhere unexpected.

And sometimes the living don't take shit from the dead.

The Zombie Curse of Huckleberry Hollow

Alex Vance

A rusty, groaning corpse of a car barreled noisily along a deserted stretch of one-way road flanked by the freezing bleakness of a nighttime desert. Cracked earth stretched hypothetically to the horizon, halved by the tar-black road and the dry brown shrubs that dared to grow by the wayside, subsisting on the dew that settled on the asphalt for a few precious minutes a day. Wasted hope, that: the bushes were all so dry they scarcely rustled when the hulking, foul-orange automobile lumbered past at speed.

"I ain't getting' no reception," said a wolf on the passenger seat. Young and fine-featured, this lad, his blue eyes lively and his expression despite a concerned frown at his uncooperative cellular phone inviting to one and all. Blond hair whipped slightly in the breeze from the window-that-would-not-shut-properly, golden tips dancing on his shoulders, fringe slapping against his Adonical face. Stylish blue shirt, open at the collar, fashionable jeans, all in order.

His companion, a leather-jacketed Dobermann with a few years of age, inches of height and pounds of muscle to his advantage, was staring intently through the windshield as if gripping the steering wheel and tensing the set of his jaw would miraculously dispel the grey fog ahead, which perversely turned the headlights' illumination against their intended purpose, since well-lit mist is even harder to see through than dark. "Mate, who the 'ell you tryin' to reach on that dog?" he said through gritted teeth.

The wolf laid the phone on his lap, closed his eyes and pinched the bridge of his snout between two fingers, taking a deep breath of restrained frustration.

The dog at the wheel utterly failed to contain his smugness and kept glancing sneakily sideways to see if his companion's resigned expression had transformed into the curiosity he'd so hoped for. "It's Cockney rhymin' slang, Owen. You know, dog and—"

"Dog and bone, phone, Malloy, I get it," said the wolf, who was called Owen, and the dog (named Malloy) had to fight to keep his ears up and to prevent a whine of disappointment to escape his lips. Owen picked up the phone again, then had a thought. "Is it even such a good idea, placin' a call on a stolen phone?"

The dog grinned, licking sharp white fangs and straightening his shoulders into the posture of arrogant self-confidence that made his expensive black shirt drape so nicely over his chest. "No worse than placin' a call from a stolen car, I'll wager. And you're the one that wanted to call, not me. Hell, if they traced the call and found us that'd at least give us some clue where we're s'posed to be, cuz we don't 'ave a bloody clue. Unless—"

Owen barked and spun as far as his seatbelt would let him, smacking the giggling dog on the arm. "I told you, I didn't read the map wrong. We shoulda passed two towns on this road already, and that's just a goddamned fact." A deep sigh, then silence, and both young men stared out of their halves of the windshield trying to make something out in the slimy-thick mist other than the bland silhouettes of misshapen trees and the steady swoosh-swoosh of road markings leaping out of the mist's gray void only to be consumed moments later as they passed by.

A slight bump in the road brought some distraction—in particular, the creaking of the suspension and the screech-thud of the rear undercarriage scraping over the road's surface. Two canid heads whipped around at the same time and knocked together, but, this being far from the first time that had happened, both of them simply continued to turn and look out the rear window where red-orange sparks from the undercarriage illuminated the fog. Their curiosity satisfied, they turned their attention forward again, facing the dismal road head and trying not to rub the bumps on their heads for fear of being called a 'pussy'.

"So, Owen..." The dog tried to stay cool as he could, steering with one hand, the other draped casually over the back of his seat. Owen didn't so much as look at him before rolling his eyes. "It's, uh... it's kind of been a while."

Own fixed the dog with a glare, his brow set with determination and ice cold fire burning behind his deep blue eyes. "Only for cash, Malloy. We've been over this a million times."

The dog nodded swiftly. "I know, I know, o'course, and that's a bloody good rule so it is." The words came out like a machine-gun firing blanks: a lot of empty noise in rapid succession. "It's just, ya know, the road's long and—"

"Malloy—"

"I'm good for it, you know as soon as we hit a town I can boost somebody's wallet—"

"Malloy..."

"For shit's sake, Owen, we're friends!"

"Malloy!"

"It won't take long, just a quick—"

Before Owen could answer this time, another bump in the road rocked the car and both its occupants turned their heads again, knocking heads again, this time spending a little more time admiring the spectacle of glowing sparks emitted by the rear undercarriage as it scraped the asphalt. "You gotta wonder what's in the trunk that's so heavy, huh," said Owen and Malloy sighed dramatically, looking at him.

"Don't change the fucking subject, bitch."

Owen couldn't stifle a grin, nor a puckish urge to tease his frustrated friend by 'accidentally' brushing fingers over the dog's thigh. "Maybe there's a dead body in the trunk. Maybe we ripped off a murderer and he's gonna set the cops on us and when they find us we'll be done for murder. You ever been in jail, Malloy? I'm sure I'd be fine. I'd do a few favors and get some protection, but you—eyes on the road!"

Malloy's head whipped around at the sudden shriek, and some well-intentioned instinct in him drove him to stamp his foot on the brake, which is an excellent idea when you're in a car powering toward a person at speed, who's no more than ten feet away. Unfortunately, the whipping of the head and the changing of the topic and more than anything, the distraction of that hand on his thigh caused the dog to miss the brake and instead plunge his boot on the gas pedal, with all the attendant consequences.

A loud thump, a sick crunch, the cacophony of creaking metal and crashing glass, the dull thudding of a body skidding over the roof, bucking dents in the metalwork, screech of tires as the car spins and after the weightlessness of the spin, the sudden jolt of coming to a halt when the trunk smashed against a tree and the car's two occupants are slung sideways in their seatbelts against the door and each other. Blackness and silence. A moment, perhaps two. Two consciousnesses emerged again, both sharp and alert, each having the other as their first thought.

"Owen!"

"Malloy!"

Each was deeply relieved at hearing the other's voice and two pairs of paws instantly began groping, for while neither could see very clearly yet and the world still span somewhat, they could feel that they were lumped together against the door and that there was a scent of blood in the cabin.

"I maybe think I head my hit," said the dog, but in saying it he didn't sound nearly as silly as it may seems when reading the words. Slurred speech, after all, can easily mask strange choice in words. "You all hunky-dory?"

"I'm fine, I'm fine," the younger wolf said urgently, snuffling at the slow-moving dog's face, abandoning civility for the efficacy of age-old canine instincts, using nose and lips and tongue to search for nicks and cuts and bruises on his friend's face. Some quick fumbling undid his seatbelt and allowed Owen's body to slump as far against the driver's seat as it wanted, simultaneously revealing a soreness in his abdomen where the seatbelt had dug into him which the wolf tried his utmost to hide. "Are you okay? I think… I think you hit your head against the door. Can you see okay? Can you wiggle your toes?"

The car lurched forward when Malloy's wriggling toes caused his boot to press the accelerator, the engine promptly died its final death and the car lumbered slowly, quietly back toward the road, riding out this last momentum. "I'm grand, mate. Jesus," the dog said groggily, fumbling with his seat-belt fastening and pawing at the door. "Just let's get outta here, yeah? Windshield's smashed and God knows what else, besides—"

A noise akin to a groan interrupted Malloy, which irked him as most interruptions did, though the sepulchral tone and the unnaturally long sustain caused his teeth to itch. Owen's eyes showed their whites and he gripped Malloy's wrist with great urgency. "Oh, fuck, we hit somebody!" he hissed and pushed against the dog's battered shoulder in order to get out of the passenger side of the car as quickly as possible. "Come on, he sounds hurt!"

The sudden jostling of his already bruised body drew a moan from the dog's lips, which was left utterly insignificant by the deep, throaty wail that echoed through the misty emptiness. "Christ," Malloy muttered, trying vainly to uncouple his seatbelt's bent buckle and settling, in the end, for yanking it loose from its shattered moorings with a grunt and a sense of masculine satisfaction before tumbling out of the driver's side door. "Owen!" he called loudly, for the mist was such that he could scarcely see the road even though it was but a few feet away—and not on account of the darkness, for while there were no street-lights to speak of and the car's headlights were aimed elsewhere, the moon shone lustily through the fog. Twigs cracked under Malloy's boots, and metal. Totaled, thought Malloy, by which he meant that the bits of car he stepped evidenced the car's utter ruin.

"Owen?" the dog called again, trying to convince his body to relax and to ignore the pains and aftershocks that made him want to shorten his breath and rest and limp. The engine's half-hearted rumble died away and an icy silence swept through Malloy's very bones. Zipping up his jacket he quickened his pace, jogging as fast as his uncooperative legs would let him in the direction he thought Owen had gone, almost tripping when he stepped onto the chilly, dew-wet tarmac of the road. He was about to call for the third time, now even bringing his hands to his muzzle to really put some volume behind the call, when a sight appeared from the dim grey fog that turned his call into a childish squeak.

A shape, indistinct but deeply foreboding, seemed to form itself as if it pulled the wisps of light and dark from the still fog toward itself to gain shape. First a blob, the height of a man, then definition to indicate legs and a head. Another moan, louder and shriller and more deeply disturbing set Malloy's teeth a-chatter and caused his ears to flatten, which did not happen often, as the dog had practiced long and hard in his youth to counter that instinct and bolster his standing as a Tough Guy. Nevertheless, his feet slowed, his knees shook slightly and his shoulders tensed to an uncomfortable degree as his body prepared for flight, wishing, it seemed, to be totally ready when the brain issued a decree to flee.

It took all Malloy's art and attitude to appear unfazed and impatient, which was his usual manner, when the shape resolved itself into a limpingly jogging wolf in slightly mussed metrosexual attire and Malloy hoped to high heaven that if indeed his bladder had issued a small sample of its contents into the fabric of his jeans, as he believed it might have during his moment's panic, such a stain would at least be hidden by the dimness. "Uh, Malloy?" said Owen, trotting up to the dog and taking him firmly by the arm, urging him back to the car. "We've, uh, we've maybe got a little problem."

It would be some time before Owen would utter an understatement of greater magnitude.

"Don't look," said Owen as another moan came from behind them and he quickened his pace. Malloy, blessed with longer legs, could easily cope but felt worry return to his experience of the world, and rather than ask redundant questions or protest Owen's taking charge he simply expressed his curiosity by staring at his companion. "It's kinda creepy, but it's pretty slow. Grab your gun."

They'd reached the remains of the car they'd appropriated for the trip. The entire tail end had been snapped off, chunks of metal scattered all around, faintly glinting in the moon's dimmed light. Malloy nodded to Owen's order, for while it was unusual for Owen to issue commands, enough trust existed between the two friends that Malloy decided to act now and question later. "What's slow, Owen?" he asked in a level voice as he trotted toward the passenger door, hopping over chunks of metal and wood, reaching to open the glove compartment.

"The guy we hit. He's up and about again. Hey, your piece is right here," said Owen, kneeling in the wreckage-dappled sand to pick up a half-buried firearm, rising to hand it to Malloy, who turned with a confused expression in his eyes and a gun in his hand, freshly retrieved from the glove compartment. They stared at each other for a time, each holding a weapon indistinguishable from the other in the pale light.

"Bloody 'ell," said Malloy with a chortle, and thrust his gun's muzzle toward Owen's feet to indicate the source of the confusion: there were many guns on the ground. Very, very many guns. "No wonder the car's bum was so 'eavy, she was loaded with 'eat," said Malloy, ever practical, and bent to pick up another of the dozen or so handguns scattered about. What he'd thought to be chunks of fender were revealed to be shotguns of the sawn-off variety and where the broken-off trunk rested against the tree the car had hit, a generous helping of submachine guns spilled from it, all of them bearing a stark resemblance to the weapons so commonly featured in dude flicks.

A brightness stole across Owen's features at this discovery akin to the glow of a child when his parents reveal one more birthday gift, better and bigger than all others put together. "Muchos gracias, Adonai," he giggled, clapping his paws giddily together despite the fact that he was still holding a gun, "and hoo-ray for the NRA. Let's pack this stuff up."

As Owen turned his attention to gathering up the weapons, shaking the sand off and depositing them haphazardly on the back seats, Malloy's attention was caught by a second shape distinguishing itself out in the fog. Having been through the fright of seeing Owen emerge, the dog now had much less trouble controlling his body's fear responses and strode in the figure's direction with great confidence. "Hey, you all right, mate? What the 'ell was ya doin' out on the road in the middle of the night any—"

Three things happened in very rapid succession. Firstly, Malloy saw the figure fully and immediately drew a conclusion, Owen shouted some information to the same effect, and lastly Malloy the zombie in the head.

In the microseconds it took the sound of the gunshot to fade, which was order in an acoustically dead desert, Owen and Malloy on the speed with which they'd concluded that the lumbering body that had issued such unnatural moans and shambled so crookedly toward them was a zombie, and that if indeed zombies didn't exist this shot would very likely and very properly be construed as murder. A great deal of evidence pointed in favor of their mutual conclusion, and quietly the two males stood shoulder to shoulder, inspecting the remains on the ground, satisfying their nagging doubts.

"Dude's head's on back to front," said Owen. "It was like that when he stood up off the ground."

"Mmm," Malloy agreed. "And there's a hatchet in the chest. Looks like a fire-hatchet."

"His eyes are all white, and he doesn't have eyelids or eyebrows. I think the white stuff's his skull."

"Actually, I think it's her skull. Look at those shoes."

"Huh, snakeskin high-heels with a knee-length plaid skirt. Bitch had no taste at all," said Owen with a sigh.

As one man, they turned away from the unmoving body and headed back toward the car, Owen gathering firearms and stuffing them into the back seats, such that they wouldn't slip out through the gaps and also checking the back seats were still anchored securely and wouldn't fall out the hole in the back of the car. Malloy, meanwhile, tossed his jacket into the car and popped its hood, poking at the slightly steaming engine and, if indeed his knockings and shakings didn't actually fix any of the block's stresses and ailments, the force and violence of his interferences at least let the car know the dog meant business. It would think twice before failing to perform and risking the fury of Malloy.

"It's really weird, Malloy," said Owen, carrying an armload of cartridges and clips and magazines—'Guns & Ammo,' naturally—"but I ain't really freaked out."

"Nor I, mate," said Malloy with a certain grimness, giving his paws a quick sand-scrub to get the words of the grease off his fingers. And he was telling the truth, too. The moment he saw the thing's empty, hungry eyes and the way its jaw dangled off its hinges, the weakness in his knees and the hotness of his ears had vanished, replaced by a clear calm. "Weird indeed. You ready to get rollin'?"

Depositing a final armload of Uzis into the rear compartment,

Owen grabbed one of them, two handguns and a short-barreled shotgun and took those with him as he sat in the passenger seat again and slammed the door, loading the clips for the Uzi and the handguns, dropping those into the glove compartment, then slipping some shells into the shotgun. "I ain't never seen a movie about one zombie, dude." Owen laid the shotgun across his lap and checked his phone. "Still no connection, and four hours till dawn."

Malloy turned the key and willed the car back to life, and after a few tuberculotic hacks and whoops the engine settled into a throaty purr that sounded healthier than even before the crash. The dog's lips curled into a satisfied smile and he smacked the steering wheel. "Good job, baby, keep up the good work. How many more d'you think's out there?" he asked, gently easing the car back onto the road, careful not to whip up too much sand and risk getting one of the wheels stuck. "And point that thing th'other way, be a dear."

Owen waggled his eyebrows and stuck out his tongue. "What's wrong, feeling some shaft envy?" the wolf said with a lick of his lips, teasingly jabbing the shotgun's muzzle against the faintly visible and minuscule stain in Malloy's jeans. "I dunno, dude," he continued, laying the gun down so the muzzle pointed door-wise, "I just ain't never seen just one zombie in the movies."

"Well, what 'ave ya seen?" said Malloy, who hadn't been much of a cinema-goer when he was younger. He slowly accelerated the car and within seconds the journey resumed as before: driving into a bleak gray future with dead trees and shrubs whooshing past. Only the coolness of the cabin from the gap in the tail end served as a reminder of their little run-in with an undead.

The wolf smoothed his bangs away from his face and rubbed his eyes, as if touching the smooth, handsome features of his face would soothe his vanity and ease his thinking. "They're slow but persistent. They come out mostly at night, but they walk in the day, too. They can smell living flesh even if it's hidden; they can't talk, not even to each other; only certain way to drop one is to cap 'em in the noggin. And if ya get bit by one, ya get sick, die, and turn into one."

"And who says Hollywood ain't informative? Hey, there's another one," said the dog coolly, pointing out the windshield at the lumbering figure by the roadside and Owen leaned against him to see, as if he were pointing out a point of interest on a sightseeing trip. "You're a regular Steve Irwin for the undead—two more on the right, look—so what else do you know?"

Owen smiled, unable to resist feeling the smugness that he felt whenever Malloy admitted to his media-impaired youth, and licked his lips to impart the wisdom he'd gained by sneaking into the theatres with friends or bribing the homeless to buy them tickets (and later, as Owen discovered his talents, the cinema personnel directly) to scary movies just about every weekend of his teenaged life so far. "Depends on the zombie, really. If they're mutants, like from radiation or some virus or a crashed UFO, they're really just a symptom. They used to be people till they got infected, now they're infecting others. If it's necromancy, Jewish or Voodoo or what have you, there's a shaman or a warlock who's summoned all these. Maybe killing him will undo all of this, or maybe he has to actually un-cast the spell, no way to be sure. Oh, and it could be that the afterlife is full and there's no more room for the dead yet, but those movies were kinda lame and besides, I think Big G's got his shit in order. I don't think he'd slip like that."

"Amen, Pharisee," said the dog with a grin, laying his arm across the backrest of Owen's seat, one-handedly steering the car around the occasional walking or crawling zombie on the road, occasionally 'accidentally' clipping them at the side, sending them spinning off into the ditch moaning eldritch moans and eliciting hearty cackles from the two canids in the car. "Hey, check it!" the dog barked excitedly, nearly poking Owen's eye out as he enthusiastically pointed out the window at the first clue in hours that they were actually going somewhere: a faded and busted-up sign saying 'Welcome to Huckleberry Hollow'.

"Least we're getting somewhere," cheered Owen and pulled the crumpled map out of the glove compartment again to find some bearings while Malloy guided them through ever denser throngs of the unnatural creatures with ever greater disinterest. "Or maybe not. Huckleberry Hollow ain't on the map—and yes, cunt-scum, I did check twice."

Before Malloy could take vengeance for being interrupted, the car stereo, which Owen had given up for dead even after hours of fiddling earlier on, blared to life and a voice that sounded very much like Johnny Cash said "Hey boys! Welcome to Huckleberry Hollow! The natives are friendly and the times are good—stop on over and see for yourself that there ain't nothin' like a real Huck Hollow Hello!"

"The Power of Christ compels you," said Malloy distractedly to the radio, keeping his eyes on the road as he swung the rear-less car through the crowds of slow-moving zombies and occasionally through individual ones as well, passing through hat once must have been a disastrously boring colony of suburbia. "In nomine Patris, et Fillii, et Spiritus—"

"Stop that nonsense, kids, what d'ya think—"

Owen thumped the radio with a fist. "Shema Yisroel, motherfucker, Adonoi elohen—"

Laughter was the radio's response and that fact emphasized the futility of prayer or exorcism, at least to the limited degrees of which the pair were capable. "Oh, you boys, you make my teeth itch. And you know somethin', kids?" asked Johnny Cash, "I sure do got a lot of 'em. But don't you be goin' around all scared or nothin'. I got no designs to hurt yas... wouldn'a bothered with the slow intro, I'da grabbed ya soon as ya turned that third left and gave me the power to, ah, 'redirect' your road. So why don't you just—"

Owen gave Malloy a quizzical look as the Doberman first yanked the clunky old radio out of the dashboard, cracking plastic and snapping wires, and tossed it out the crack of the window. "Nice shot," he remarked with a smile, noting that it hit an otter in a business suit on the one half of his skull that still remained and sent him slumping to the floor, and Malloy grinned his satisfaction, driving more slowly. "Notice 'ow they're all movin' away from town?"

The dog nodded and picked at a tooth with a sharp fingerclaw. "I noticed. But these houses, some of 'em are all busted up. Look at that church, it's black from burnin' but there's no glow of embers or whatever. Whatever happened here happened a while ago but only now the good citizens decided to move on."

"Maybe Johnny Cash is sending 'em out on a mission? Hot crap, did you see that one? Rabbit in the gym tank top? He was mighty fine."

Malloy leaned across the wolf to look at the figure they passed.

"Ooh, yeah," he whistled in appreciation, though of course his attention was caught by very different facets of the young male's body than Owen's was. "Shame about the missing arm. Yeah, maybe it's just lucky timing... or maybe they're leaving because we're arriving. Hey, check that out."

The car was trundling into the town proper, where grocery stores and malls and six-story buildings became more common and white picket fences gave way to plain brick walls. On one of these, a group of decrepit ex-living creatures were tearing chunks off each other and smearing them on a wall to form the phrase 'will you please just listen for one second?' and a block later, on the wall of a basketball court, a group were finishing the last letter of 'I just want to talk. Jeez, guys, rela\'.

Later in life, Malloy would repeat what he did now, which was to suddenly throw the wheel into a spin and the car along with it, sending the vehicle careening off the main road, over the pavement and straight through a glass façade, in this case belonging to the 'Calrton Fifth Shopping Mall'.

Glass shattered, as glass does, in all directions and the flimsy frames of doors designed to withstand no more than the most casual vandalism fell apart like kindling as the Dobie gunned the engine and battered the car into the shopping center.

"I'm having a Blues Brothers flashback," said Owen with a cheer, but the look of barely-hidden embarrassed confusion on Malloy's face caused him to drop that particular subject. "What're we shopping for, man? We got plenty of guns, right?" inquired Owen, who was observant. The car made ever more uncertain noises as Malloy guided it around fountains and across glass-ceilinged plazas, clipping small, exploitatively expensive children's amusement rides with the same casual vengefulness with which he'd 'accidentally' hit some zombies. "Shouldn't we just be getting the hell outta dodge?"

The attractive young wolf's questions were all answered when the car came to a lumbering, groaning, and distressingly final halt in front of McSweeney's Leather Emporium. "Outta petrol," Malloy explained, if such an explanation were necessary, and got out of the car with even less respect for the condition of its doors and Owen felt a well-deserved sense of imminent peril as he followed the confident dog through the shop's glass storefront, easily transformed into a convenient entrance through a few well-placed gunshots.

Emerging, five minutes later, each decked in perfectly-fitting black leather from boots to gloves to high, zipped-up collars, the pair certainly looked like they were ready to go down in style, and while that was something that Owen would occasionally and for some monetary compensation be persuaded to do, neither of them were planning on that any time soon. Each had also strapped to themselves a few leather carrying-bags and it was these and their pockets that the two now began to fill with weapons from the car.

"What's our odds, you think?" asked Owen and he wondered at how calm his voice sounded, considering that the moans from outside were becoming louder and the shuffling of undead footpaws could be heard, though there was nothing yet to be seen in the mall, lit only by the moon shining through the skylight.

Malloy loaded the sawn-off shotgun, cocked it and slung it over his shoulder, unzipping thigh pockets to slip some smaller handguns in there, tucking bigger ones into his belt. "I'd say pretty slim, mate," said Malloy with surprising gentleness, though that quickly broke into his trademark rakish grin and he showed Owen a pocketful of cash he'd pilfered from McSweeney's till. "But if we do survive, I guess I'm getting' the pleasure of yer company after all."

"Now ain't that a sweet sentiment," said Johnny Cash from all around and all of a sudden the lights came on, stinging their eyes. Faint carnival-music came from the merry-go-rounds in different parts of the complex, but none of these cheerful noises could dispel the ever-louder moans of the undead, who just now shambled into view from either direction of the long gallery Owen and Malloy found themselves in. Each reached into the car to get every last gun and clip they could find, and they felt their hearts beating like they'd felt only once before, and they'd been naked that time. "You boys are bein' mighty difficult, and there ain't no need for alla that. I just wanna have a little chat with you boys and see if maybe you can't help an old fella out with a teensy problem he's got, huh? And to show ya I ain't whistling Dixie, I'm gonna have the good citizens of Huckleberry Hollow stand right the fuck back to let ya through."

Malloy and Owen, heavily armed and drop-dead stylish in gleaming leather, strode out into the middle of the gallery. The hordes of zombies were scarcely twenty feet away on either side, and 'horde' was the proper description. Dozens that could be seen, dozens of dozens, with more, likely, around the corner, all brushing shoulders and bumping into things. And they all stopped at once.

The ones that had come from where Malloy had driven the car even took steps back toward the shops, creating a path back toward the exit. "See? Now let's all be civilized."

Malloy looked at Owen and silently asked him a question, as friends who know each other well can do. The question was 'do you know what he's talking about, considering how knowledgeable you are about zombies in Hollywood?' and Owen shrugged, which meant 'I'm absolutely stumped, Malloy, I ain't got a clue what Johnny Cash is talkin' about. Also, you got good taste in jackets, but you really ought to wear the zipper down just enough to expose your Adam's apple. You know, when there's no danger of it being bitten out. Looks better.'

So they turned their backs on the path that had been made for them, opened fire, and charged screaming into the undead in the other direction. To have seen them would have been an absolute treat, two focused men against innumerable unnatural horrors. They were smart about it, realizing that the creatures were terribly slow and that it was therefore prudent to take the time to aim and dispatch them with a headshot—especially Owen, who was new to the shooting game, found this a very useful approach.

Back to back, they spun like slow-motion dervishes as they cut a foul-reeking swath through the throng, having to keep turning because the zombies also threatened to close in behind them and after a few loud minutes of this, minutes filled with gunshots and shouts and the hurried fumbling for a fresh clip or a new weapon altogether, they settled into a solid rhythm that proved immensely successful.

Malloy led the charge, shotgun in hand, but he used it as a club rather than a boom-stick. He walked quickly and with focus and pummeled any grotesque mockery of life in the muzz with the butt of his shotgun, smashing more skulls, literally, in this short time than he'd done figuratively in his youth.

Owen, for his part, cleaned up the scraps. He kept the rear guard, firing into the hordes behind and to the side to keep them from closing up too quickly, keeping pace with Malloy and dispatching whatever bodies still twitched when they hit the ground after meeting with Malloy's variety of shotgun love.

The thing about heroic battles against unfeasible odds that everyone forgets about is how terribly exhausting they are, especially when wrapped ears to toeclaws in thick, tight leather and carrying a small arsenal of firearms. The leather proved more than a decorative extravagance after half an hour's plowing, as the hordes became ever denser and more than once or twice an undead caught hold of one of the two, trying to sink what teeth remained into a well-armored arm or shoulder before the other had a chance to provide assistance.

"I can't keep this up," grunted Malloy, exhaustedly kicking a screeching, skinless child in the stomach, sending it flying back against one of the many pretentious columns that held up the skylight. He half-heartedly bashed the shotgun into the face of what may once have been a clown, considering the garish frilly outfit it wore. "There's too fucking many of them."

"Bullshit!" yelled Owen and threw a nine-millimeter at a soccer mom's eyeless head before drawing another, his second-to-last. He paused form his at-bay-keeping duties and took the time to cross through the small circle of safety they'd kept more or less intact while slashing bloodily through the undead, grabbing Malloy by the shoulder and violently shaking him. "The exit's right there. We're getting out of here, we're getting a car and... Oh, hold on, no, we are gonna die," the wolf said matter-of-factly and slumped against his friend at the sight of yet more throngs of zombies outside.

Malloy wrapped an arm around him and with the other he whipped the shotgun around to hold it properly, firing six loud dragon's-breath bursts of death and flame around them, buying a few more seconds of safety while the shambling hordes approached. "You want me to take care of you, mate?" Malloy asked softly. "It's no sin on you if I do it." He reached into a side pocket, withdrawing a small handgun, ignoring the hungry drooling of the masses. "Course, not that I think Jews go to heaven or anything—"

"Nor hookers," said the blond wolf with a chuckle, and shook his head at the sight of the gun. "Nah, wouldn't be right. I ain't takin' the easy way out."

Malloy's ears pricked up at that last phrase and he clutched Owen a little tighter, backing away from the bloody claws that reached to them from all sides and yelled, "All fucking right! Where d'you wanna meet?"

And just like that, the zombies halted their approach and moved, reluctantly, to the sides of the gallery, pressing against the storefronts of bridal shops and toy stores, and at the sight of what seemed like disappointment and genuine sadness on the faces of these creatures, the tragedy of what had happened in Huckleberry Hollow, whatever its cause, finally caught up with the exhausted canids.

"If Moses won't come to the mountain..." said the creature that approached through the newly created path. He swaggered like a cowboy and was dressed like a pretentious one, too, all in white with rhinestone insets wherever there was room for them. "Real nice dimension you guys have here," said the creature and the words were very loud and very clear, which is what you'd expect from a being whose entire face was mouth. Malloy stifled a heave, but Owen, having seen his share of bad horror, bore it with more dignity. "Took me a while to find a form that wouldn't instantly burn the soul outta whoever saw it, lemme tell ya. I gather I still don't quite look like you folks, but I think I'll learn."

Malloy groaned tiredly and gave Owen a light shove to get him to stand on his own paws again. "Okay, fine, mate, you said you wanted—"

The creature stepped forward, still, expansively gesturing with his arms, though the movements seemed stilted, like a movie being played at double speed. "Seems me bein' here also sorta unstuck Huckleberry Hollow from time, or rather, me comin' here. Most inconvenient. It jumps forward a year or two in a couple weeks, then sticks someplace for a few hours, then moves again... Every time it sticks some of these poor bastards wander out and when they get far enough away from me, well, they just up and die. Course, every time it sticks and the Huck Hollow Highway briefly connects with the real highway there's a chance some poor schmuck'll drive into town... but you guys're the first to manage it. Congrats."

Owen stood wearily on his feet, panting after the effort of plowing through many, many undead. "Look, dude, we really don't care. What do you—"

"Okay, fine! Jesus!" cried the mouth-cowboy, indignantly stamping the ground and the hordes all stepped back, a few of them falling over, fully dead. "I thought you living folks were supposed to be inquisitive! Anyway," it continued, composing itself and adjusting the cowboy necktie under the gaping mouth that was its face. "I don't burn souls outta nobody any more, as you can tell by the fact that you ain't turnin' into one of them, and as soon as I figure out where I can keep all my teeth I can make myself a purdy face like you folks. But I can do that on the road. So, ya know, let's get truckin'."

Malloy and Owen shared a glance that carried a great deal of information, questioning and answers and then nodded, as much to each other as to the creature.

"Awesome. Now let's go."

As they walked, the shambling zombies followed. Out the door and through the streets, past burned schools and shattered homes, a blood-spattered Schul that caused Owen to shiver and what looked to have been a groovy disco, now filled to overflowing with half-consumed skeletons. Through streets and alleys and lanes and avenues, finally emerging in a suburbia not unlike the one through which Malloy and Owen had entered the town, and with every step exhaustion took a greater toll on them. The mouth-creature seemed not to notice, or not to even have any concept of tiredness, though it made the going a little bit easier by causing the street-lights to flicker on wherever it passed.

Until, finally, it came to a house, utterly unremarkable among its totally identical brethren, and the hordes hung back as the mouth-creature walked up the porch and into the door. "Come on, kids, almost there! Just one stop, and we'll be ready to go!" it said cheerfully, and Malloy and Owen nodded to each other again.

They entered the house and found it to be nice, in a quaint way. An open-plan kitchen with avocado-green appliances, psychedelic wallpaper and linoleum on the floors, typical seventies fare. In the living-room were strewn beer-cans, bags of weed and the bodies of young males with long hair in torn, flared jeans, sprawled on their backs, faces burned, around a bizarre pattern marked out in what appeared to be salt. "That's where I came through," said the mouth-creature, as proud as a country boy talking about where he was born.

"That's the book that summoned you?" asked Owen, stepping over the cold, stinking corpses to pick up a leather-bound tome from the middle of the salt-pattern, keeping a thumb between the open pages.

"Hey, how'd you guess that?" asked the mouth-thing with good cheer. "Yeah, you know how it is. Kids find a book in some dusty loft, think it'll be cool to do a ritual, book turns out to be real. I'm just gnawin' on some souls down in the netherworld—I'm a real big shot there, ya know—I see a nice bright opening up in the sky and I fly up and end up here. Now, let's get truckin'. Find ourselves one of those movin' metal things, and let's find me someplace new to live, huh?"

Malloy stepped forward. It took some effort to gather himself, spent as he was from pummeling hundreds of zombies into pulp and oblivion, but the dog managed it. "So who're you runnin' from?" he asked in a deep, low growl, walking right up to the creature's face.

If a mouth could frown, this thing with its millions of teeth did. "What the hell you talkin' about, boy? Come on, quit fuckin' about and let's get rollin'. This town's boring the hell outta me and—"

"I may not know much 'bout magic," said Malloy, walking around the creature and pricking his ears up for that extra bit of height, rolling his shoulders back to make his leather-clad chest all the bolder. "But I know a damn bit about bullies. And you, pretty-boy... you ain't nothin' but a scared fresher who thinks he can convince the preschoolers he's hot shit. I mean, why d'you wanna look like us? Why don't you wanna turn us all into zombies?"

A growl emanated froom the million-toothed maw. "Child, you have no idea of the powers you're-"

"Blah fuckin' blah," said Malloy with a grin and made the duck-quacking gesture with his hand. "You wanna hide, is what you wanna do. You don't mean to take this world over at all, or you wouldn'ta had such a balls-out attitude. No, man, you just wanna disappear. Well, you know what?" asked the dog, grinning ear to ear, that unbearable smugness that could mean anything, and laid a hand on the thing's shoulder. "We don't want you in our little dimension."

The thing spun, then, pulled away from the Doberman's grasp and howled the loudest screech in the world at the sight of Owen, leaning against a picture of Sai Baba and quietly reciting from the leather tome that had summoned the mouth-thing to begin with.

The complex interplay of intuition, blind assumption, irritation and exhaustion that caused both males to draw the same totally specious conclusion at the same time is perhaps too expansive to properly describe, but suffice to say that blue fire sprayed up out of the pattern on the ground, and had Owen or Malloy been as close as the five unfortunate youngsters had been, they'd have had their snouts charred just as horribly.

The mouth-creature was close enough for such a fate, as he'd leapt for Owen. "What are you—" was all it managed to say before, through the flames, an oily tentacle whipped up, wrapped twice around the thing's neck and drew it down into fiery oblivion.

Just like that.

Outside, the horde lost its organization first and the zombies started shambling in different directions, tripping and slowing and then, one by one, falling over, cut off from the unholy energy that kept them animated, finally allowed simply to be dead.

"Not that I ain't glad that worked," said Malloy, sinking back into a plush-upholstered couch. "But it was pretty unlikely that it would. I mean, seriously unlikely."

Owen nodded and shrugged, tossing the slightly smoking book onto the glass coffee-table, dousing it with some whiskey from a half-empty bottle in the liquor cabinet, and set it on fire with a matchbook. "Guess the Big Guy's lookin' out for us. That shit you said about bullies and such made sense, though, I got that vibe from him when he started yappin' over the radio. Guess whoever he was runnin' from found him after all."

"Owen," said Malloy, and laid an arm across his friend's shoulder.

"I know, said the wolf, patting the dog's hand. "We're in a ghost town, battled hundreds of zombies and defeated an evil demon by sending him back to the hell he fled. That's pretty heavy stuff."

"Not that," the dog said with a chuff. "It's just that I got a pocket fulla cash and I could seriously use some lovin' before we hit the road to Maranatha again."

The wolf chuckled slightly, which was as much as he could manage in his state of exhaustion, but he looked up at the tall, strong dog with those blue eyes of his and smiled that smile and Malloy felt a warmth he'd doubted he'd feel again, back in that shopping mall. "Thou dog, Malloy," said the wolf and darted forward to bite the dog's neck as so many of the zombies had tried to do, and amid the corpses and the stink and the horror, the two tired males made some time to play.

AFTERWORD

FANG Volume 3, forthcoming from Bad Dog Books, continues the genre of gay erotica, this time set in the romance and wonder of the fantasy genre. Sweeping vistas, spectacular magic, gleaming armour...

With the challenge of writing for a specific genre, FANG's loyal stable of authors took flight in every imaginable direction. Whyte Yoté returns with a tale of lupine primitives, and the voyage of a young male from pup, to outcast, to a full and honored member of his tribe. K. M. Hirosaki explores the solitude that is the wizard's lot, and the acts of madness that arcane power can inspire.

Uncle Oakie taks us to the myths of ancient Greece with a charming story of budding love between a young centaur and a human youth, while Mwinzi carries the reader to the far end of the globe, setting his tale of tragic romance in the courts of feudal Japan.

Graveyard Greg, author of webcomics such as "Gaming Guardians" and "Carpe Diem" continues the theme of bittersweet tragedy with a glimpse of the final night shared by two colossal gladiators; while Stephan von Krieger lightens the mood with the foibles of a young tiger who accidentally unleashes mystical beings who knows just what to do with the young lad...

From Karai Crocuta comes the introduction to a young wolf called Kieran, whose destiny and potential outstrip even the expectations of his dragon sensei, and Veritas sets his charming story of college love in a fabulously diverse university for mages, warriors and artisans.

As always, FANG is on the lookout for new talent. If you're interested in trying your luck at getting your prose in the Little Black Book of Furry Fiction, visit www.baddogbooks.com for submission policies and advice.

See you in Volume 3!